THE
MELODY
AND THE MASTER

THE BOOK OF ALL THINGS

USA TODAY BESTSELLING AUTHOR
SARAH M. CRADIT

ISBN: 978-1-958744-15-4

Cover and Interior Design by The Illustrated Author Design Services
Map by The Illustrated Author Design Services
Hardcover Art (Desemir's Offer) by Alexandra Curte
Siofra and Desemir Portraits by Steffani Christensen of Art by Steffani
The Game by Steffani Christensen of Art by Steffani
Editing by Novel Nurse Editing

Publisher Contact:
sarah@sarahmcradit.com
www.sarahmcradit.com

SARAH M CRADIT
WEAVER of WORLDS

For everyone searching for their freedom in unorthodox ways

May you find it

PRAISE FOR
THE MELODY AND THE MASTER

"The Melody and the Master is a masterpiece. Stunning world-building, beautifully flawed characters, and a riveting, engaging plot. You don't want to miss this!"
~*Cameo Renae, USA Today Bestselling Author*

"Sarah M. Cradit has an uncanny ability to weave magic and mayhem into a heartfelt story of love, lust, betrayal and tragedy. With each flip of the page in this enchanting story, I became more and more enthralled with the characters and fantastical world. The final turn of the last page will leave readers high on euphoria and begging for more."
~*Raelynn, @rae.in_wonderland*

"Exquisitely written and so incredibly swoony with characters I don't want to let go of!"
~Candace Robinson, Author of the Faeries of Oz Series

"WOW! Sarah Cradit has done it again and stolen my heart... each book in this incredible world gets better and better."
~Merrit Townsend, @always1morebook

INTRODUCTION

There exists a kingdom set upon an isle, surrounded by a sea no one has ever traveled beyond. The Kingdom of the White Sea it is called, or simply the kingdom, for they have no other name for it.

The individual Reaches—Northerlands, Southerlands, Westerlands, and Easterlands—have their own climates and cultures. Some within these lands are caught in the endless push and pull of kingdom politics, while others have troubles extending no farther than their own borders.

Desemir Trevanion is one such man. Though the Trevanions are no longer the stewards of Darkwood Run, the heir of Shadowfen Hall wields the most power in his tucked-in southeast corner of the Northerlands. His formidable father crafted an agreement, which consolidated control of all imports and exports of the rare and coveted ebony wood of the Great Darkwood under one man: The Master of Forests.

Desemir has a bevy of disgruntled barons knocking down his doors by day, and an equally long line of women vying for their turn in his bed at night. To any looking in on his charmed life, he is brash and unafraid, absent of the weaknesses his rivals are ready to feast upon.

But his brother, Pesha, knows Desemir is far from at peace.

Pesha's magic can only hold these men at bay for so long. The day is coming when their enemies will band together and rise against his brother.

Much farther south, in the upstart Westerland port city of Newcarrow, Siofra Thornheart and her twin brother, Stiofen, suffer under the desperate arrangement they made after becoming orphaned. Stiofen has something the steward of Newcarrow needs. As long as he provides it, Siofra is safe.

But being safe is not the same as being free. Her protection comes in the form of a gilded cage intended to quash Siofra's equally potent—but inescapably deadly—magic.

Uncontained, Siofra is capable of terrible things. What she needs is careful training, but the only people with the requisite skills are their own, the Medvedev, a humanoid druidic race who never leave the tranquil shelter of their Hinterland forests—forests the Thornheart twins cannot return to, for their mother and father were among the Forsaken.

If others discovered the twins are children of the Forsaken, they'd face a fate far worse than the prettily accoutered dungeon the Stanhopes have made their home.

All Siofra wants is for Stiofen to be happy.

All Stiofen wants is for Siofra to be safe.

But Siofra's red wall cannot be subdued forever.

When the inevitable happens, they trade one prison for another. Rotting in a cell, awaiting their fate, they brace for the worst.

Instead, Pesha Trevanion arrives all the way from the Northern Reach, with an offer.

It takes them from a terrible but certain fate to one that is utterly unknown.

But even Pesha does not know the full truth of what he offers the Thornheart twins.

The flame burning in Desemir's dark heart helps him see an opportunity to end his war with the barons for good—and, while he's at it, solve another problem that's been hanging over Shadowfen Hall like a shroud.

Siofra at last has an opportunity to give her brother the life she knows he deserves, a chance to free him from the burden he's carried all these years.

The cost is one she's willing to pay.

But as with all dark dealings, one payment inexorably leads to another.
And another.
And another.

NEWCARROW

Steward & Stewardess
Willem and Marina Stanhope
Gawain Stanhope (son)

The Thornhearts
Rohan Thornheart (deceased) & Moira Thornheart (deceased)
Siofra "Si," 18 (twin)
Stiofen "Fen," 18 (twin)

Others
Chrest
the gaoler

DARKWOOD RUN

Master of Shadowfen Hall
Desemir Trevanion II, 26

Others at Shadowfen Hall
Pesha (Wintersin) Trevanion, 17
Euric (Desemir's Guard)
Wulfhelm (Desemir's Guard)
Cassius (Desemir's Guard)
Gisela (Attendant)
Lieken (Attendant)
Lotte (Head Mistress)

Past Residents of the Hall
Ludwik Trevanion, Deceased (Desemir's Father)
Lidia Trevanion, Deceased (Desemir's Mother)
Arenn Wintersin, Deceased (Pesha's Mother)
Naos Wintersin, Deceased (Arenn's Partner)
Klaus Trevanion (Desemir's Grandfather)
Elaina Trevanion (Desemir's Grandmother)

Other Barons of the Darkwood
Baron Bennett Weaver and wife Elspeth
Baron Edmund Rolfe and wife Pearl
Baron Prentiss Felwood and wife Jocosta

Steward and Stewardess of Darkwood Run
Hughbert and Agnes Arranden

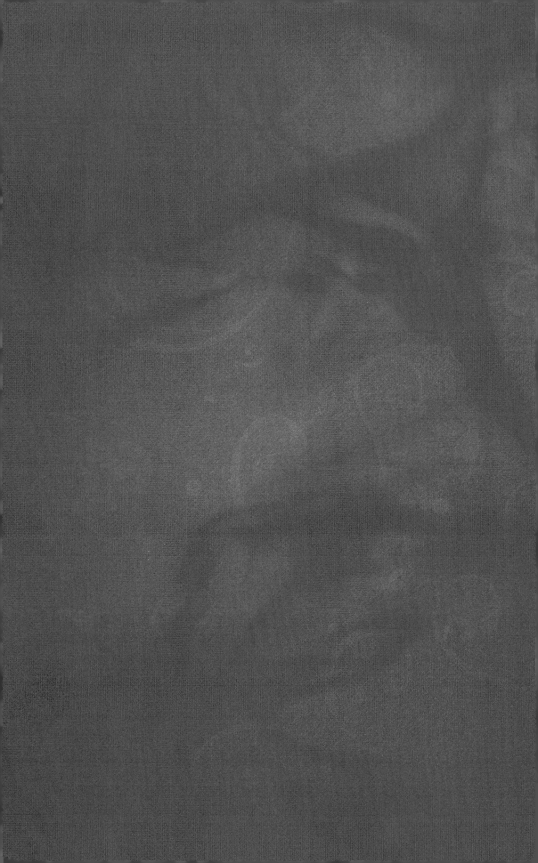

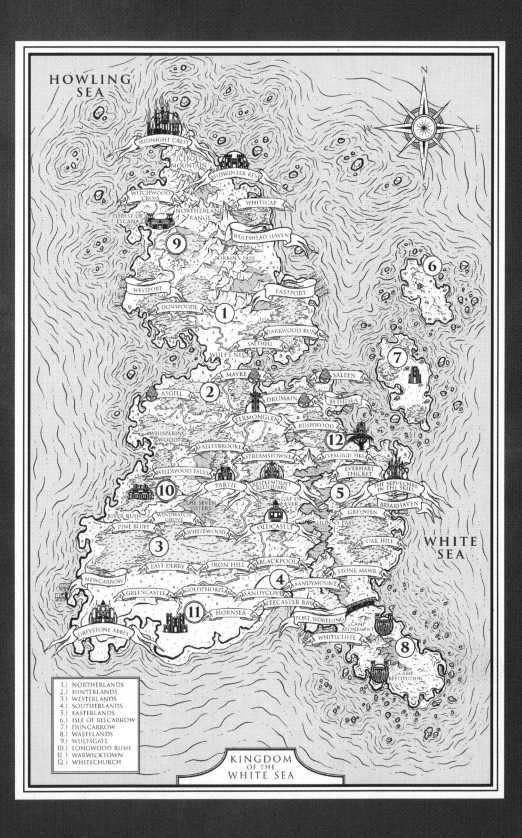

DESCENDANTS OF THE FORSAKEN

ONE

A TERRIBLE TOLL

Siofra's knees were the first to give in to fear's demand. She had no time to recover before Steward Stanhope released a fistful of her hair and sent her flailing toward the stairs that descended into an all-too-familiar darkness. Fen's howling from behind as he joined her wasn't real.

Nothing was.

It could *not* be happening.

Again.

Fen caught her before she sailed to the bottom. She'd done so before, flying from the door all the way to the cold stones below. Siofra had mostly blocked out the agony that followed—and Fen silently sobbing through his panicked healing—but she remembered enough to know she never wanted it to happen again.

"You can't keep doing this. *This* is what happens when you lock her away from the world!" Fen screamed, tripping over her as he clambered to reach the door before it closed—before it was bolted from outside. "Steward!"

1

A violent slide of metal followed. Fen wilted against the wall, one hand atop Siofra's as she lay in a defeated heap across the second and third steps. They waited for what always came next: the purposeful ring of lavish boots on imported marble as the steward returned to a life he'd promised to include them in.

It had been Willem Stanhope's first lie when he had taken in the orphaned twins.

Siofra held her tension with her breath. She felt Fen go stiff beside her. Waiting. For the steward to disappear, so they could relinquish their lingering hope he might change his mind and instead move on to what must come next. What always came next.

But the steward didn't leave. His enduring presence blocked the thin stream of light under the thick metal door, the same door Fen had hurled himself against enough to have broken arms, shoulders, and wrists. Enough for them to know the past two years hadn't made him any more capable of bringing it down.

"Ahh..." The steward breathed out a resigned sigh. The leather from his soles slid with the hint of a shuffle. "This *is* for your own good, girl."

"You know her name," Fen spat. He swelled as if he might go for the door again, breaking more of himself in another wasted attempt, but he seemed to remember he was still holding Siofra's hand and calmed. "She's not a *thing*. I've done enough for you that you can at least address my sister properly."

Siofra strained against the muzzle Willem had fastened over her face after everything had devolved to chaos in the town square. She needed the cloying, scratchy fabric *gone*, but she couldn't will her hands to obey the command. They were frozen with the rest of her, still locked on the screams and blood from not even an hour past.

"*Siofra* made a grave error today." Willem's words were strained, almost regretful. "This is why we have a rule of silence for her, why she cannot speak when we allow her beyond your room. Why she cannot even *breathe* without lowering her eyes.

2

You're her brother, Stiofen. Her keeper. I hold you accountable for what happened today."

"She was *provoked*." Fen's voice shook, his breathing labored. "You expect her to do nothing? To let foul men lay hands on her in the middle of town while no one, *no one*, intervenes?"

"I expect," the steward said evenly, maintaining tight control of his words, "for her to have learned some cursed self-control by now! She's nearly *nineteen*, old enough to be a bride. But how could I ever find her a husband like this?"

"How can she have self-control when she's never been taught? You won't let her train with someone who understands what she is and what she can do. I've told you—"

"And who would train her, Stiofen? Are there more of you mucking about the kingdom that I don't know about?"

"If there were, we wouldn't have needed *you*," Fen hissed. His spittle dotted Siofra's arm.

She yanked on Fen's hand and blinked her eyes when he turned to look down at her. He would know what it meant, the question she needed answering.

Fen rolled his jaw and asked, "She deserves to know how bad it was, Steward. You can't lock her up for a crime and not tell her what it was."

"Well, Stiofen," Willem said with a cold sigh, "when the bodies are counted and the stones cleansed of blood, I'll be sure to inform you both how many men, women, and children your sister is responsible for sending to the Guardians today."

Siofra surrendered to the predictable exhaustion that flattened her when the steward's steps thundered down the hall and turned to distant echoes.

She awoke to Fen fussing over her some time later, muttering curses as he spread his hands over her battered body, pulling the pain away.

He'd removed the horrid swaddling at some point. She spotted it on the floor in a heap when she returned to her senses.

"Was it really so bad?" she whispered, pinching off the deep breath that followed. She didn't want to retreat from the truth. It happened despite her desperate efforts to stay present, to *stop*. But it had always been like someone else had taken over, pushing her crudely aside until the damage was done and a terrible toll paid.

Fen had said it was her mind protecting herself from what she couldn't control. It was a nice thought.

Siofra knew better.

Guilt had bought and paid for her cowardice, indulging her a reprieve her inadvertent victims were denied.

Fen shook his head as he grazed his hands over her, still mumbling. Siofra winced at even the softest swipes across her tender flesh. She might not remember the specifics of how she'd earned the cuts and bruises, but she wasn't spared from feeling them afterward.

"Fen?"

"I don't know. I don't know, Si. It all happened so fast." His words tumbled out in a rush.

"Did it? Or are you protecting me again?"

He rolled back on his heels and wiped his brow. More guilt swelled into her heart at the sight of his dwindling vitality. Magic took so much from them both. The difference was she should be able to control her chaotic outbursts. He paid for *her* sins, as he always had. He'd keep paying for them as he did the steward's bidding, in the man's quest for dominance of Newcarrow and the control of the newest southern port in the Westerlands.

"I..." Fen took a swig from the wineskin. He shook his golden hair. "It *was* fast, all right? That deviant at the fish market grabbed you, thought you were... one of the midnight women, I suppose. And I... I was with the steward across the way, buying skins, and by the time I heard you scream, there was so much..." He swallowed.

4

Siofra's grief and frustration demanded tears, but she had no more to give. She rolled over on the bed, flinching at the sore spots Fen had yet to heal. "Go on."

"That's it, Si—"

"It's not." She closed her eyes again to fend off a tremble of nausea. She spread her mouth into a tight, firm line. "And if you don't tell me, and Willem won't allow me to be trained, then how will I ever, *ever* get this under control?"

Fen shrugged. His violet eyes fluttered to the side, at her bindings.

This is why we have a rule of silence for her.

Except when she was alone with her brother, the only one immune to her terrible chaos.

Anywhere else, she was blindfolded, gagged, or both. Her magic required a combination of sight and voice, and the steward had presented the dungeon as an alternative to being constantly bound.

Neither option afforded her space to breathe.

"What I do know..." Fen nodded to himself, his eyes downward. "What I know, Si, is it wasn't as bad as Willem wants you to believe. No one died."

Siofra rubbed a hand against her mouth as she laughed, clipping the sound into something crude. "*This* time. If that's even true, and you're not lying to me."

"Lying to you?" Fen grimaced without looking up. "You have *every* right to be angry. But not with me."

Siofra said nothing.

"We have to leave."

She laughed at the absurd suggestion. "And go *where*?"

"Anywhere!" Fen cried. He leaped to his feet and flung his arms wide. But he was still unsteady from the fatigue and quickly settled back down on the edge of her bed with an apologetic glance to the side.

Their beds were nice. So were their twin bureaus and the tapestries keeping the icy dungeon warm, except in the bleakest days

5

of midwinter. The steward gave Fen vellum and charcoal to draw, and the stewardess had built Siofra a small library.

The twins had been given many nice things by the steward and his wife. But the gifts came with a lock, which opened only from the outside, and the unfettered use of Fen's gift of flourishment.

If the Stanhopes didn't depend on Fen for their prosperity, they'd have disposed of the Thornhearts a long time ago.

"We're adults, legally capable of caring for ourselves," Siofra said, already weary from what she knew was coming. She didn't want to argue with Fen, ever. He was all she had.

"What does the law mean to men who enslave?"

His words left her hollow. "We're not slaves, Fen."

"Aren't we?"

Siofra pressed her face into the pillow with a discouraged grunt.

"Si, they're never going to let us leave here. You know that, right?"

Siofra recognized their roles had reversed. Now *she* was the one trying to advocate for leaving. But the sinking feeling that followed—that this attempt came on the back of misplaced hope—made her wish she'd said nothing. "They won't have a choice—"

"Who do you think is coming to advocate on our behalf? The *law*?" Fen laughed bitterly. "Mother and Father's people, who don't even know we exist, and if they did, would turn us away as descendants of the Forsaken? Or worse, try *us* for their crimes?"

Siofra's voice already burned from the small bit of use. She tangled her golden curls over her face in a shield. It added a hue to the dim light from the handful of candles Fen had lit at her bedside.

"No, Si," Fen said, shaking his head. "*No.* You're *not* disappearing on me again. We need to talk about this. Forcing you to be silent whenever he lets you out isn't the answer. For all their rules, accidents still happen. Like today, how could you have known a man would tear away your gag?"

Siofra said nothing.

6

"Accidents will continue to happen until we can find someone who will *teach* you how to control your magic."

Siofra sighed, suddenly feeling cross. "My voice hurts. My body hurts."

"Yes, well, I'm trying to heal you, but as you can see—"

"Yes, I *can* see!" Her breathy scream ended with a rasp. "That once again I've tired you and hurt you, and I'm tired too, Fen. Tired of *that*."

Fen's voice lowered. "That's not what I meant."

"I know." Siofra released her curls. "But Steward Stanhope is right. Everyone is safer when I'm locked away." She rolled back to her side to face him. She'd been mulling something over a while but hadn't unearthed the courage to say it. "But you... *You* should go."

Fen recoiled as if struck. "Without you? Not a chance."

"You're not the problem. I am."

"You're not a problem, Si." Fen lay beside her, his eyes looking into hers. They had always done this, since they were young and their mother and father unendingly shouted about all the things they didn't have, in a realm that wasn't theirs and didn't want them. Since before Fen learned how to make things flourish and Siofra was still ignorant to the cost of her rage. "The steward and his wife, for all their gifts, all their supposed kindness, would lock you away until you're old and grey to get to me."

"Which is why you should *leave*," she whispered.

"I wasn't finished," he said gently. He reached for her hands under the blanket. The fatigue in his eyes, from healing her and cleaning up the remains of her mess, was too much for him to hide now. "You should never have been locked away. Mother and Father, for all their faults, would have done anything to prevent this. The only thing keeping the Stanhopes from selling you to the highest bidder is that they *need* me. I'm their flourisher, right? Without me, their wealth would stall. Without me, they'll lose the stewardship they've lied and schemed to achieve because their debts will consume them. Their lenders will come calling, and

7

they'll have nothing to give." He kissed the top of her forehead, at her hairline. "Let me rest a bit, and we'll continue mending you. But no more talk of us separating, Si. It will never happen."

Siofra stirred again when a hard band of light brought the stairs into jarring illumination. Fen leaped up, his arm draped over his eyes, while she narrowed hers to begin adjusting.

Daytime then.

They'd slept the night away.

She'd learned to count the hours in the absence of a sun to watch, but the madness of yesterday had thrown her senses into disorder.

The door at the top of the staircase gently clicked closed. A bolt slid from the outside. Soft, tentative steps trailed downward.

Fen flopped back against her second pillow, but Siofra perked. She crawled over her brother and limped toward the staircase to see the stewardess, Marina, tiptoeing across the stones with a stack of books in her arms.

Siofra grinned in spite of herself. Marina had always been kind—not kind enough to set them free, but she was afraid of her volatile husband too.

Every week or so, she brought more fantastical tales for Siofra to read. *More ways for you to escape reality,* Fen called them, but he always helped organize her stories on the shelves and even read to her when her spirits were low.

Marina gingerly set the books on a desk next to the candelabra. It had burned down so far, there were hardly any wicks left to light. A soft halo framed the stewardess's pale face, her dark locks piled in precise loops atop her head. She only took such care when she was expected in public. Siofra couldn't help but wonder what fresh promise Marina's husband planned to dangle in front of the residents of Newcarrow—and what it meant for Fen.

As always, Marina blew out the candles, shuttering herself into the safety of darkness.

"You poor thing." Marina stretched her bony, bejeweled fingers toward Siofra's face, visible only from the daylight peeking through the thin window. It was enough light to make out small details but not enough to call upon her magic. "Willem said it happened too fast for him to help you."

Siofra flinched at her touch, which was both soothing and repellant. She liked the stewardess, but Marina was a reminder there was no escaping a bad situation, only an effort to make the best of it. If Marina, a proud and highborn stewardess, could not change her own circumstances, how could Siofra, an orphan with a magical secret so dark she had no hope of ever concealing it?

"It happened fast, all right." Fen swung his legs over the bed. His sway was subtle, but Siofra didn't miss it. He was still recovering his strength. "But this is why he shouldn't have pulled me from her side. Your husband said she could handle the transaction from the fishmonger alone because he needed me to double his gold, and this... *This* is what happens."

Marina cast her pensive frown to the side. "He's exceptionally cross this time. It must have been very bad."

"Cross? With us?" Fen shot forward with an incredulous glare. "I *made* him, Marina."

"Stewardess," she stated with a light *tsk*.

Fen crossed his arms. "I could refuse, you know. I could bring all of this to an end."

Marina's eyes narrowed, giving her a feline likeness. "I don't have to tell you, Stiofen, what would happen if you did."

"He doesn't mean it," Siofra said quickly. She tried to regain Marina's attention, to take it off Fen and the mouth he could never regulate, but the stewardess was back on her feet, walking toward the bed.

"I can only do so much for you if you're ill-behaved," she warned. Softness melted off of her like the shedding of an outer layer, revealing fresh menace. "All these things I bring to you, all these—"

9

"Pretty lies," Fen cried. He lifted a pillow and hurled it at a wall, his gaze never leaving Marina. "Lace painted over darkness. Plush pillows to mask the rot of isolation." He thrust his arm toward Siofra, his fingers shaking. "You're killing her down here. Do you know that? Do you care? She almost never sees sunlight, and when she does, she is so poorly prepared for being out in the world that terrible things happen. I agreed to this, for her, and now, *for her*, I'm telling you there needs to be some changes, or—"

Marina hushed him with a slap. The sting rang across the stones, silencing all three of them. She looked as surprised as they were, regarding her own hand as if it were a stranger.

"That wasn't... Forgive me, Fen."

Fen clutched his face, glowering in rage behind his hands. "You think we need you?" His laugh bordered on maniacal. "It's *you* who needs *me*. Which means you need *us*. Your husband puts Siofra in danger again, he'll be the one on the other end of her wrath." He leaned in. "He says yesterday was bad? He left out the part where I stopped Siofra before anyone died. Before *Willem* was caught in the red wall. Next time, I won't be so accommodating."

Siofra shook her head at Fen, to insist she'd never do that, never let it spread so far.

But would she know how to stop if Fen wasn't there to ease her down?

Marina rose back to her feet with a controlled exhale. She smoothed down her dressing robe, darting her eyes around the dark room that had become Fen and Siofra's beautiful prison over the past few years. "If I share your words with Willem, he'll have her mouth stitched closed. Then he'll toss her in a sack and throw her into the White Sea. Is that what you want?"

Fen glared in response. His fingers flexed.

"No," Marina said. "Nor do I. So rather than lamenting your plight, try instead counting your blessings. It might surprise you how framing your thoughts in a more optimistic way can make the intolerable tolerable."

"If he hurts her, I'll never help him again," Fen spat. "He knows this."

"If you were no longer useful to him, then he'd dispose of you too," she said with a soft, fatalistic sigh. "This is the life you were given by the Guardians, Stiofen. You were gifted with a magic that makes more of what men need. Your sister was cursed with magic that takes it all away, in a blink of her ire."

"I don't follow your Guardians," he refuted. "Don't believe in them."

Siofra tried to speak, but she couldn't fight the stifling claw of suffocation.

"No, you wouldn't, would you?" Marina lifted the hem of her dressing gown and glanced toward the stairs. "It makes a sort of sense though, doesn't it? The Guardians provide balance to our realm. They would never create such a creature as your sister, who only needs to open her mouth and sing her beautiful song to devastate an entire village."

Marina made her way back up the stairs without a good-bye. Siofra heard her knock, to signal the guard. The bolt slid back into place.

"Si, you can't listen to her. She's—"

Siofra held up a quavering hand. Her breaths distorted, some clipped, others ragged, like climbing down an uncertain stairway.

Fen ranted and raved about their captors, scraping his imagination for colorful revenge fantasies, all to avoid the truth.

But Siofra knew Marina was right.

And if Siofra loved Stiofen as much as he loved her, she would find a way to set him free.

TWO
MASTER OF FORESTS

Desemir Trevanion held court at the head of the too-long ebony table built for a king, while his half brother, Pesha, blended seamlessly into the shadows.

They were both where they belonged, staged in the roles determined by their talents. And Desemir had his share of talents, Pesha had to admit. Magic was not the only way to snare people.

Desemir sank low in his high velvet chair with a bored look. A strand of his near-black hair arced over one emerald eye. His dark-embroidered cuffs came to a peak over the back of his hand, which he swatted around with a dispassionate air as he pretended to listen to his guest. As usual, his blouse was only buttoned to his chest, leaving his mother's onyx amulet gleaming against his throat like a threat requiring no words.

The princeling was playing his part a little too well, Pesha thought, but glamouring was Desemir's magic, not his. Pesha's would be needed soon enough.

At the other end of the dining hall, cloaked by both distance and the blinding gleam of chandeliers, sat one of the Trevanion

13

rivals, a baron named Bennett Weaver. He'd come to Shadowfen Hall to amiably discuss their troubled trade agreement—or so he'd said. Both brothers knew better.

"As I was saying, your father would not have wanted this enmity." Weaver practically had to scream to be heard on the other side of the room. He was far enough away to undoubtedly miss the wry smile playing at Desemir's mouth as he spun his late father's ring around his middle finger.

"Do you see my father in this room, Sir Weaver? If so, I should like to speak with him," Desemir retorted. "To ask him why he failed to warn me that *his* allies would not be *my* allies."

"Desemir—"

"My friends and family call me Desemir. Since you are yet neither, I am Sir Trevanion to you. Master Trevanion is even better."

Pesha studied the older man across the room as the first flicker of understanding became a fracture in his confidence. Desemir wasn't his father. He might have inherited Ludwik Trevanion's notorious talents, but he'd been given his own set of flaws. Allowing other men to puppeteer him was not one of them.

"At least be open to an amendment," Weaver said. "We once shared these forests, Sir Trevanion. The Great Darkwood belonged to all men."

"Five men, specifically. But continue."

The corners of Weaver's mouth drew it into a tight frown. "Your father increased his borders and coffers at the cost of his alliances."

"Your own coffers swelled when you sold your acreage to him. You had no qualms at the time."

"We had plenty of qualms. It was not a fair trade."

"Seemed a fair trade to me." Desemir stopped spinning his ring. "Tell me, when does a deal become unfair? When the money runs out?"

"He *regretted* it, son. He knew what he'd given up... the alliances he'd left on the table with all our signatures."

"I am not your son. The Guardians favor me too much for that," Desemir said coolly. "But you're right. He knew precisely what he'd given up. My father was a man who understood well that men are fickle, but gold is absolute."

"I don't think you understand—"

"Say what you've come to say." Desemir exhaled. He dropped both of his hands in his lap. Pesha noted that while the old baron was two cups into his wine, Desemir's goblet sat untouched. But Pesha didn't need to note what he already knew. It was the men who found themselves in his brother's company who should pay more mind to the intentional subtleties of Desemir Trevanion.

Weaver grunted something to himself before speaking. "You know what I'm asking. Sell my acreage back to me. I'll pay twenty percent over what your father paid. That is *more* than fair. You'll gain in the deal."

Desemir cocked his head. "Not more than I'd lose."

Pesha inhaled a soft, inoffensive breath through his nose that drew no notice to his corner skulk. The rich, smoky aroma of aging leather, intermingled with the rare ebony wood from the Great Darkwood entirely under Trevanion rule, reminded him who he was. Why he was there.

His time was coming.

Soon.

"Thirty."

"If you intend to continue reciting numbers at me, let me save you the breath," Desemir countered. He rested his head against the velvet pillow that had been raised and restitched to fit his seated height. Ludwik had been a shorter man. "I don't intend to sell any of it back. I'm content with my role as Master of Forests, as will one day be my son."

Weaver was overcome with emotion so strong, it stole his next words. He blubbered out a few failed attempts before emitting a red-faced warning. "You are not equipped to take *all* of us on."

Desemir leaned forward slightly, pretending to strain. "I'm sorry. I didn't quite hear you. Was that a threat?"

"There are four of us, Trevanion. One of you." Weaver's mouth twitched, curled. "One of those men is the Steward of Darkwood Run. You'd go against him, would you?"

Pesha tapped his tongue to the roof of his mouth. It was a wonder men were still so reckless with Desemir, but that was the thing about mining secrets. If men spoke of what happened to them in Shadowfen Hall, they'd reveal the very thing they most needed protected.

Desemir flicked a nod at Pesha, the one he'd been waiting for. Desemir commanded the silence lingering over the long stretch of table as Weaver awaited a response he wasn't going to get.

Pesha stepped forward and caught Desemir's wink as he passed, moving to the other end of the room to fetch the wine carafe. He moved fluidly down the tapestry-covered stones, soundless, as unnoticed as he'd been when standing in his brother's shadow.

Weaver was still locked in his own dumfounded glare when Pesha passed behind him, closing his eyes and listening. He lifted the carafe without looking, without slowing, and as he rounded the corner, heading back to his brother along the stretch of the table meant for kings, he grinned to himself.

"Well?" Weaver demanded.

Pesha set the carafe on the table and leaned in. Lips at Desemir's ear, he whispered what he'd heard. What his brother needed to end this.

Desemir looked back at him with a hard tilt of his eyebrows, as if to say, *Really?*

Pesha lifted one shoulder and fell back.

As far as secrets went, it was a big one.

"Are you trying to frighten me, Sir Trevanion? You think I'm scared of you?" Weaver asked, shaken by his confusion. "I don't have to take this from a *boy*—"

"I'm twenty-six," Desemir said, calm as the lake beyond the manor. "And you'll be taking nothing. Not from me anyway."

Only Pesha could see the quiver in his knuckles. The splotch of red in his cheeks as he moved from playing with his dinner to killing it.

"Not unless you want all the Northerlands to know the reason your wife has been..." Desemir shook his head, exhaling. "The one responsible for the missing women on your land. Tell me, Bennett, when she chops them into bits and feeds them to her hogs, does she save some for herself? Or do her delusions only go as far as murdering the women her husband has had impure relations with?"

Weaver's red face paled. His hands fluttered before plummeting to his lap. He pushed back from the table but didn't stand. "Where did you... Why would you say such a thing?"

"I should think your first words would be a denial."

"Of course I'm denying it! What foul imagination. What... What..." Weaver gripped the arms of his chair, made of ebony like most things in the room—the same wood he'd come to beg and barter for. "You are no man, Desemir. To even suggest... You have no evidence."

"Tell me more about what it is to be a man. I'd love lessons from the one who cannot even subdue his wife's inclinations." Desemir's mouth threatened to break into the same amusement that danced in his eyes. "But... perhaps you're right. Let's not leave such an accusation to the foulness of imagination. I'll send word to Lord Dereham in Wulfsgate that we want to borrow one of his Ravenwood priestesses to come read Mistress Weaver's thoughts and clear this up."

Weaver's flailing ceased. His mouth and eyes joined the stillness.

"No? Then we're finished here." Desemir shoved back from the table. He rapped twice on the double doors, and his personal guards, Euric and Wulfhelm, entered. "See that Sir Weaver finds his way back to his carriage without too much trouble."

Pesha's brother didn't smile until sounds of Weaver leaving could be heard through the front gate. He spun toward Pesha with a twinkle in his eyes, passing his head back and forth in slow disbelief. "I was *not* expecting that."

Pesha couldn't help but laugh. "No, nor was I."

"Weaver's wife has always been an odd one, but there's a fairly impractical leap from odd to murder and dismemberment, don't you think?"

"I think..." Pesha stepped forward and leaned his hip against the table. "I think though this secret serves you, we cannot let more women die."

Desemir tilted his head with a fast nod. "No, of course not. I'll send word to Weaver once he's had a day to cool. Let him know we have eyes on the baroness should she think her behavior worth continuing."

"And will we? Have eyes on her?" Pesha didn't want his brother to get so distracted by winning that he forgot what mattered most.

"Of course. I'm as horrified as you are, Pesh." Desemir's upper lip cocked. "But did you *see* his face? Guardians bless, for once I wish he'd been sitting right in front of me. Do you think she eats them too?"

Pesha lowered his eyes. "I don't know."

"Ahh, come on. What is it?" Desemir leaned forward, eyes aimed up at him. "You should be proud of yourself. It took you, what, half a second to mine this man's darkest secret. And *what* a secret it was! He wouldn't dare come at us again with his nonsense about selling his part of the Darkwood back to him."

"Forgive me if I don't find humor in what his wife is doing. She should be in a cell somewhere, not living a life of luxury."

"Do you want me to have her killed?"

Pesha did a double take. "*What?*"

"The secret will ruin him whether she's alive or dead. We can't exactly send her to trial because then it won't be a secret anymore, but we *can* hold her to account, if it will ease your heart?"

"My heart?" Pesha pressed both of his hands to his chest. "What about yours?"

Desemir sank against his seat, leaning back. "What's really bothering you?"

"That's not enough?"

"Nah. I know you. There's something else eating you."

Of course there was. It wasn't anything he hadn't said already, but Desemir had a maddening habit of only hearing what he liked and discarding the rest.

Perhaps today would be different.

"How long..." Pesha paused. "How long do you really think we'll be able to subdue them with this trick?"

Desemir shrugged. "It's no trick, Pesh. It's a skill, one you have used to protect our family since you were a boy. And secrets are forever. Do you foresee a time when Weaver will accept the disgrace that will come if the realm finds out about his wife? When Cheltam will be just *fine* with everyone knowing his only son and heir is actually a bastard, conceived by his wife's sister? I can't even *wait* for Steward Arranden to make his play so I can knock the shit-eating grin from his pinched little face."

Pesha lowered his head with a troubled sigh. "Sometimes you take my words and twist their meaning."

"I do not." Desemir looked genuinely affronted.

"You're doing it now." Pesha looked up. When he looked at his half brother, he tried to see himself in the man. Even nine years apart, there were enough differences to remind him he wasn't supposed to be a part of Desemir's family at all.

Des loves you. He'd be upset if he knew you were even thinking it.

Desemir held out his palms in defeat. "Apologies. What did you mean then?"

"I fear that while they cannot take you down alone, if they band together, your peers can and will rise against you. Weaver himself said it."

"They aren't my peers. They're hardly barons anymore, having sold their greatest treasure to our father. Shadowfen is the only barony without a village, and yet we *own the Darkwood*, Pesh. No one comes close." Desemir crossed his arms. His head tilted to the side. "Does that really worry you?"

Pesha hesitated. Nodded.

Desemir jumped up and clapped one arm around Pesha, tearing him away from the table. "Let me be the one to worry, Pesh. Tonight, we celebrate."

Pesha felt a groan start in his belly. "You celebrated last night."

"And? Distractions are good for a man. They keep his troubles away until he needs them again."

"What you need is an heir, Des."

"I do. You're right." Desemir didn't wound him by pointing out Pesha could never inherit Shadowfen Hall.

"I know the women are fun for you—"

"Could be fun for *us*. I know, I know you have to focus and be vigilant when they're in my bed, but I don't mind sharing. I could send for some men tonight, just for you." Desemir grinned. "Yeah?"

Pesha quickly shook his head. "That's not for me. I wish it weren't for you."

Desemir gave him a playful shake. "Then help me find a wife, like we talked about."

"Every woman I present to you fails to meet your unreachable standards."

"The women you present are fine. The fact that they're daughters of my adversaries is not."

"There are only so many highborn women in the Darkwood, Des."

Desemir glanced toward the open doors and the towering windows at the arrival of dusk that was settling in among the timberline of the Great Darkwood. "Go on, rest up. After the fire I started today, I expect at least one of these women coming to call will be hiding a dagger with my name on it."

THREE
SHACKLES OF SERVICE

Siofra spooned viscous porridge into her mouth. Sense alone guided her hand. Her eyes were blindfolded, and her chair had been shoved into the corner, facing away from the Stanhopes and Fen. They couldn't gag her mouth when she was eating, so it had to be her eyes. They believed she needed both to unleash her song, and sometimes she did. The magic was unpredictable. But it had evolved over the years and was evolving still. One day she might be just as deadly in the darkness.

A guard hovered beside her, as though Siofra would intentionally hurt anyone.

Fen was allowed at the dining table. It was a meaningless gesture, to keep him content enough to continue performing.

Siofra felt his gaze on her throughout the break of the morning fast. Twinsense, he called it, the way they read each other's hearts. But she didn't need her twinsense to know Fen's temper toward the Stanhopes balanced on a razor's thin edge.

Gawain, their capricious, over-indulged son whom Siofra trusted even less than his parents, was present as well, which was a surprise. He rarely showed himself before noon.

"Has Lady Blackwood sent word?" Gawain asked. He added a ridiculous lilt to soften the question, but it still came out like a demand.

"You'll know when she does." Willem's neat response was decisive, inviting no rebuttal.

Gawain, however, possessed the subtlety of a boar. "Well? Is she going to acknowledge us or not?"

"Patience," Marina urged, her tone soothing, honeyed. Siofra heard the fear between the woman's words though. She heard a lot when her eyes were bound, because her ears took the lead among her senses. "Your father is already a steward, dear. The rest of our honors will come."

"Patience? We've done what the old men in Greystone never could and given our lady a true southern port! We've increased her Reach's wealth by over five percent, and the outlook is even higher." Gawain scoffed. "The least she can do is acknowledge us as a Great Family of the Westerlands. We've *earned* it."

"You're welcome," Fen muttered, hushed.

Siofra suppressed a grin, despite that no one would see or care.

Willem either didn't hear Fen's jab or chose to ignore it. "All good things take time, son. Lady Blackwood knows the bounty we've laid at her feet with Newcarrow. A *true* port city, and not the utter failing Greystone Abbey has been. She will not fail to recognize it."

Gawain made a puckering sound and flopped back in his chair.

Siofra rolled her eyes under the blindfold. Gawain was old enough for his mother and father to be shopping for a suitable bride, and still he acted like an intemperate toddler.

"Is the porridge to your liking, Siofra?" Marina called out sweetly. The woman's spoon pinged against her bowl as she continued her meal without awaiting a response. "Please don't speak.

Nod if it's fair. Shake your head if we can bring you anything to make it more pleasing."

Siofra had nothing to offer. She raised another tense spoonful to her mouth. The tacky oats congealed on her tongue, almost choking her on the way down. She imagined what it might be like, writhing on the floor as the world blinked away, taking her guilt and sorrow into the oblivion.

You mustn't ever speak like that. Think *like that.*

Those were Fen's words. Her thoughts often came to her as Fen's. He could conjure her intended thoughts just as easily, which was how he understood how dark her intentions had become, why he was so worried about her. The last of her fragile hope had been winked away two days ago in the Newcarrow town square.

"Siofra?"

"You'll get nothing from her," Fen snapped. "And why should you, bound as she is? Like a prisoner."

"She's not *bound*," Willem stated. His spoon clanged into his bowl. "It's merely her eyes we have covered, so she cannot fix them on anyone. You, of all people, should know why we must do this."

Siofra had never *fixed* her eyes on anyone. But she was glad the Stanhopes were confused about her magic. If they understood how unpredictable it could be, they'd never let her out of the dungeon at all.

"Then why put her in the corner?" Fen's chair creaked as his voice became more animated. "Why invite us up here at all? Unless you want something big from me again, and you think *this* is enough to make me agreeable?"

"If I want something from you," Willem said, testiness creeping in, "I get something from you. Right?"

"We've come a long way from your speech about adopting us, giving us a family... Haven't we?" Fen accused. Siofra sensed venom creeping into his words. He had never harbored such hatred in himself when their parents had still been alive. It terrified her what would happen when it boiled over, changing him forever, shaping the angry boy into a bitter man.

All because of her.

"Well," Willem said, biting down on his words, "you have always been welcome to join us, Stiofen. It's your sister who cannot be up here unattended, for reasons I should not have to keep explaining."

"So it's Si's fault?" Fen snorted. "Her fault she has no training, no mentor to guide her?"

"And where would I find such a creature?" Willem retorted.

"You better mind your mouth, whelp. Don't forget, we know what you are. We could hand you over to someone far worse," Gawain threatened. Siofra sensed his expression, the glint of power and privilege that was unquestionably his. "We could tell everyone we have one of the forestfolk living in our own town, see how they feel about it."

"Gawain," Willem warned.

"Medvedev aren't criminals in this kingdom. Even the king respects our borders," Fen retorted. "We only live in exile because of men like you, who would exploit our gifts."

"If you weren't in exile, you'd be in the Hinterlands with your people. Ah, but they don't take well to Medvedev who murder their own kind, do they?"

"*Gawain*," Willem said again.

Siofra felt Fen's stunned silence from across the room. He shifted in his chair before clearing his throat.

"Say that again, and I'll respond as you deserve." Fen's tone turned deadly.

"Boys," Marina said, as if they were squabbling over who got the last helping of porridge. "Gawain, your father has some news for you. Fen, this should please you as well, as it involves your sister and giving her more freedom."

Siofra held her spoon in midair as she waited to hear what "freedom" they were offering this time.

"Perhaps now isn't the time," Willem said, a low grunt backing his tenor.

"Would it not bring everyone cheer?"

"Well?" Gawain demanded with a petulant, impatient scoff.

Willem groaned. "I wanted to wait, Mar. To tell them each on their own first."

"Too late for that," Fen said. "Go on then. What freedom are you offering my sister?"

Siofra released her bowl onto the small tray and sat back, listening. Nerves had her hand tapping against her thigh.

Willem's sigh echoed around the room. "Very well. Lady Blackwood has blessed a union between Gawain and Steward Richland's daughter. What's more, Richland has invited you, son, to live in Pine Bluff and sit on his council." Willem's smile was almost audible. "I take it as a promising sign he sees the strategic advantage in allying with Newcarrow. If he does, the other stewards will fall in line, and our lady will have no choice but to officially recognize us in the peerage of Great Families."

Gawain cawed his approval with a hard slap to the table. "I like the sound of that, Father!"

Siofra exhaled. Gawain was leaving. She'd no longer have to endure his lewd innuendos.

But Fen didn't sound relieved. The darkness in his voice was thicker than the gruel. "And what does this have to do with Siofra?"

Siofra absorbed the silence behind her. For several excruciating moments, no one spoke. No one made even a sound.

"Ah, well." Willem coughed. "The place on Richland's council came with a condition. It seems his daughter, the one he is offering in marriage, is barren."

"*Barren?*" Gawain exclaimed.

"Some accident, when she was young. Left her maimed." Willem sighed. "You can imagine the difficulty in brokering a union with a daughter in such a condition."

"I don't *want* to imagine it," Gawain cried. "I won't do it!"

"Will you let me finish? I believe you'll be pleased with the deal I've secured for you," Willem said. Some of his calm had returned, but tension still prevailed at the table. "I've spoken to

Richland personally. He understands it would be unfair for you to take a deformed bride to your bed, and he offered the council seat in concession—"

"Some concession!"

Horror seized Siofra to hear them speak of the poor girl in the same way they'd always spoken of her.

"And..." Willem went on, unruffled. "He also recognizes that, as my only son and heir, you must continue our line. He has agreed to let you bring a mistress who will bear your children, and allow your wife to claim them as her own. As long as the Reach believes these children are both Stanhope and Richland, then it's of no matter to me who bears them."

"A mistress." Gawain mulled it over. "Would I get to choose her?"

"I have already chosen her." Willem's robes ruffled.

Fen gasped. "No!" He knocked his seat back. "Are you mad?"

Siofra swallowed a gasp.

Gawain's mistress.

No.

No, the steward would never do that to her.

Would never go so far.

But he would. He knows one day we'll stop helping him. It's the only way he can ensure he'll have access to our magic indefinitely.

"I thought you would approve of this," Willem said, cool and even. "Siofra could have a life beyond the dungeon of our keep. There would be strict rules, of course, for the safety of Gawain and his new family, but—"

"A *life*?" Fen's palms slapped the wall when he backed into it. "As the plaything and broodmare of this bloated monster you call a son?"

"Mind your words, lest I take your tongue," Willem whipped back. "Gawain, sit back down."

Fen's laugh was a dark, desperate sound that pierced her heart. "Absolutely not. We refuse."

26

"I'm sorry if I didn't make myself clear, Stiofen," Willem said. "This is not an offer. I've already decided."

"Father, ah, you've outdone yourself. If you only *knew* the fantasies I have about this one—"

Marina *tsk*ed her son into silence.

"I don't... I don't *care* if you've decided," Fen said, rambling. "I don't care! You *need* me, and you know the agreement. I help in exchange for Siofra's safety. Without it, I'll never help you again."

"She'll be safe with Gawain."

"She will *never* be safe with *him*."

"Marina, dear, will you call for the guards? Stiofen isn't ready for this conversation."

Siofra listened, horror grabbing hold of her heart, as Fen screamed at the men—as he was then dragged away, still howling, calling her name. She braced herself for the guards to take her too, but she remained untouched long after her brother's cries had faded to echoes.

"Siofra. Darling." Willem was behind her now. His too-smooth fingers swept her hair back over her shoulders, grazing her neck, sending a shiver of disgust down her back. "You understand this is necessary, right? That you are merely a yoke around your brother's neck, keeping him from happiness? He could have a life if you were not such a burden to him."

Siofra nodded. Fat tears ran down from under her blindfold, passing across her lips.

"He will still work for me, but I'll grant him his own land. His own keep. He'll have a wife and a family, things he could never have if he's shackled to being your guardian."

Siofra felt Gawain join his father. She'd know his simpering wheeze anywhere. He licked at his lips with an animalistic grunt he was too ill-mannered to suppress.

Her stomach churned and lurched, realizing she would hear those sounds forever, would *feel* them as this creature took whatever he wanted from her, whenever he wanted it.

"You'll talk to your brother then? Convince him this is what you want?"

Siofra hated herself for nodding. Hated he was right.

"Good girl." Willem clapped his hand atop her shoulders. "You leave in a few days. Marina will pack a trunk for you, with lovely gowns and other things young girls fancy."

"Yes... Yes, of course," Marina sputtered. "Anything you please, Siofra. I want you to be happy in Pine Bluff."

"I'll make her happy enough. Every night," Gawain replied.

Happy.

The word had no meaning to Siofra Thornheart.

But it could mean something to Stiofen.

Siofra buried her sobs as Willem led her back to the darkness of the dungeon.

Pesha slumped in his chair in Desemir's lavish bedchamber, waiting for his brother to tire of the three women who'd arrived from one of the midnight taverns in Darkwood Run. The evening had already stretched into night. Even the women were spent, yawning into their arms between turns, burying their exhaustion in goblets of imported wine.

But *quick* and *pleasure* had no intersection for Desemir. He met neither his conquests nor his challenges halfway, vanquishing both with equal fervor. The only time Desemir had ever snapped at Pesha with real anger was when Pesha had suggested that these gratuitous interludes were a poor replacement for what his brother really desired.

Love, Des. A proper family.

And what would you know about a proper family, eh, Pesh? Your mother whored herself for my father for years. As if that wasn't enough, she had to kill my father, too, and then herself. So do tell me, brother, what a proper family looks like. Be sure to describe it with the vapid, grasping detail of a man who's never seen one.

28

The soft apology later hadn't dulled the sting, but it *had* dulled Pesha's urge to place unwelcome truths in front of his brother.

Desemir slapped his hands against a woman's ass and turned his fingers to claws as she, the redhead of the trio, conjured what must have been the last of her energy. He urged her on, jerking her hips against his in tight, swift thrusts. His bared teeth, set between cheeks splotched with exhaustion, disappeared when his mouth parted with a suspended scream. He hinged the redhead against himself as his spasms ran their course.

Pesha waited. Would Desemir trade the redhead for one of the others in an endless round, or was he actually... could it be...

Desemir rolled over and panted against a pillow.

"All right, ladies," Pesha said, clapping his hands once. "Get dressed, gather your things, and Gisela will send you off with your tea. Be sure to drink the whole flask."

"Yeah, yeah," one of them muttered, her pale ass jiggling as she collected her dress and undergarments. "Wouldn't want a surprise in nine months."

"You find yourself with child from this night, it won't be a surprise. It will be a hostile act," Pesha warned. "Drink the tea, you'll be invited back. Don't drink the tea, well..."

She rolled her eyes. "We get it." She leaned in, close enough to press her breasts, stained with a sheen of sweat, against his forearm. "Next time maybe ask for more of us? He's tireless."

Pesha grunted. Nodded.

When they were gone, he drew the heavy velvet curtains, sheathing the room in darkness, save for a sliver of moonlight cutting across the rug. He went to leave as well, but Desemir's groan stopped him.

"Did you read anything malicious in their intentions tonight?" His voice was muffled by his pillow, but Pesha understood well enough.

"If I had, they'd already be dead."

29

Desemir made a sound that was almost a laugh. "You jest, Pesh, but one day... One day there *will* be an assassin in my bed. Will you be ready for her?"

"No," Pesha admitted. "And neither will you."

It would be pointless to add his own fears to the mix, that one of these men the Trevanions had crossed *would* one day send someone to kill Desemir—would one day succeed. Pesha's reading of whispers was their only defense, but it meant staying as close to his brother as possible, always. As long as Desemir's desires were at odds with his safety, Pesha's fears would never rest.

Desemir rolled over, his head falling to the side as he watched Pesha through bleary eyes. "You think I lack the mettle to defend myself?"

I think you lack something, and you won't find it like this. "I'm retiring for the night. Unless you need anything else?"

"Don't say it like that..." Des inhaled a lungful of air, then released it. "Like you're my servant and not my brother."

Am I not both?

Does it matter that my service is born of love and choice?

"Are you happy here, Pesh?"

Pesha crossed his arms, glad to be covered by the room's shadows. "You're my brother, Des."

"That's not an answer."

"It's the only answer."

And it was.

Any other would lead him down a selfish path, wrought with guilt and terror of the unknown.

Ludwik might have treated Pesha like he were an animal belonging in a cage, but Desemir had only ever given him love. He had never asked for anything that Pesha had not first offered. It was Pesha who insisted on sitting sentry in the shadows of Desemir's celebratory nights, to be certain his brother was safe. Pesha who'd placed himself in charge of his brother's guard, a responsibility that meant he'd forgotten what a full night's rest felt like.

Pesha had thought about what his life might have been like—could still *be* like, as he was not even eighteen yet and had many years ahead of him to find love, find joy of his own.

But there would be no love, no joy, if he could not be certain of Desemir's security.

"Brother," Desemir murmured, followed by more that was lost to the call of sleep.

Pesha left. As he slipped out, he nodded at the four guards who stood sentry just beyond the double doors, confirming the night watch had begun. Euric and Wulfhelm were already retired to their quarters, behind the hidden doors in the bedchamber as to be always at the ready.

"Sir," they all replied. Those weren't the same men who, when Ludwik had been alive, had turned their noses at Pesha in disgust, the bastard son of their beloved master—the curious boy who colored his hair and knew their darkest secrets.

Desemir had unceremoniously turned every last one of those men out when he'd become baron. He'd kept the most loyal and added more like them.

"Good night then," he said in kind and moved farther down the hall toward his own chambers.

Siofra waited until Fen was asleep before she slipped from her bed and crept to the corner of the room. She stepped onto a chair and stretched to the tips of her toes so her eye was pressed against the jagged hole in the stone.

The dark indigo of evening coated the world, but she could smell the sea and hear the gulls cry as they swept over the passing tide. She closed her eyes so her ears would take over, listening for the one sound she most needed to hear.

And then the melody came.

Twin falcons Aio and Atio swooped through the air, sounding their song. They'd saved it for her, a promise that although they'd been forced into separation from their Medvedev, they were never far away. A Medvedev's familiar was never far away for long, and that bond was one of the few things that made their druidic race different from men. The Medvedev were the first occupants of the White Kingdom, but instead of respect, there was fear. Instead of alliances, there were uneasy truces. Where they would have been happy to share the kingdom that was originally theirs, Medvedev were forced to hide in the Hinterland forests the crown had declared "off-limits" for men.

The Stanhopes didn't know who their familiars were, and if they ever found out, it would be one more threat to hold over them.

Sometimes Siofra thought she could hear her mother's and father's familiars, the cat and the crow, nearby. That couldn't be right, for a Medvedev's familiar died with them. And Rohan and Moira Thornheart were very much dead.

Siofra should know.

It was her inability to control her dark magic that had led to their execution.

And if she couldn't find the courage to free her brother, she would surely be the death of him too.

FOUR
THE RED WALL

Gawain shoved a rough hood over Siofra's head, adding protection to the gag she already wore. She sensed Fen nearby but not close enough to take his hand. His tension flowed over her, somehow soothing hers, like the ebb and flow of a tide over sand.

Gawain wasn't going to harm her—not yet anyway. He needed something from her, badly enough to sneak her out before his mother and father awakened. He'd threatened to slit both her and Fen's throats if she made a sound. Bringing Fen along wasn't part of his plan, but the alternative was Fen screaming loud enough to wake everyone in the keep.

"Watch your step," Gawain groused as he shoved her forward and upward. She tripped over the carriage door, tumbling inside. Fen cursed and jumped in after, righting her before Gawain could lay his thick hands on her again.

She heard the comforting caws of Aio and Atio overhead, but neither falcon dipped close. They didn't dare. The relationship between the twins and their familiars was fractured enough from years of separation, without adding imprisonment, or worse.

The carriage spurred to life. Fen secured Siofra against the rutted jostles in the road that was still being built. Everything about Newcarrow was new, built or imported by Willem's father—the man who had founded Newcarrow by running roughshod over nearby Greystone Abbey, the extant port town turned half-abandoned mess. The Stanhopes had even stolen Greystone's citizens, dangling new opportunities and guaranteed prosperity. Whether they could deliver on those promises was yet to be seen.

Siofra lifted her head, sucking in as much air as she could through her bindings and cover. The fresh breeze rolling off the sea was almost refreshing. She'd stopped wishing she were someone else, someone who could stop to enjoy such things, but she'd gotten so much better at retreating, pretending... traveling to a place in her mind where she *was* someone else, at least until reality ripped her back.

"Where are you taking us?" Fen demanded.

"You'll see." Gawain's usually high voice was tight, strained.

"Your mother and father will rise and break fast within the hour. What will they say when they find us gone?"

"Nothing, because we'll be back before it happens. If your sister can perform."

Siofra felt Fen lean forward. "*Perform?*"

"Not like that, you mutant whelp." Gawain grunted.

Fen wound his hand tight through Siofra's. His touch calmed her racing heart but did nothing for the dread creeping up from her belly and spreading through every inch of her. She couldn't tell if Fen had gathered Gawain's meaning, but she'd reached the conclusion quickly enough.

There were only two things a man could ever want from someone like Siofra. If he didn't want her body, it left only her mind.

Her magic.

Fen's hand squeeze was an attempt at assurances he couldn't give. She hadn't yet had the heart to tell him she'd agreed to go along with the steward's plan and was leaving with Gawain for Pine Bluff the next day.

And that, this time, there was nothing he could do to save her.

The carriage stopped. Fen thrust his arm out before Siofra could pitch forward off the seat.

Fen moved to stand. "What is this place?"

"I thought you could read, druid. It's a speculation hall." Gawain brushed past Fen, knocking him into Siofra as he jumped to the ground.

"Don't touch her," Fen warned, swatting the air before taking hold of Siofra's hands again. "Easy. There... Yes, that's the first step. Other foot. Good. Now hop."

Siofra tensed before she leaped forward and crashed into Fen. He caught her in his arms, solid, and kept her close as he led her behind Gawain, into whatever a speculation hall was.

"Closed," Fen remarked drily. "Damn."

"Not for us," Gawain said. He pounded on the door. The booms echoed into the still morning until the roar of the sea buried them again. "Say nothing. Say nothing and you'll be safe in your beds soon enough. Say *anything* and my threat from earlier stands." He returned to his frenzied knocks.

"Eh? Gawain, do you know the hour, friend? I... eh..." The man on the other side answered with a nervous edge to his drowsiness.

Siofra squeezed Fen's hand. She could almost read the situation better blindfolded.

Gawain barged in and slammed the door behind the twins, choking out the fresh sea breeze and replacing it with the nauseating aroma of sweat and smoke piled upon piss.

Siofra was jerked out of Fen's grasp, and she stuttered to find her footing until Gawain gripped her forearms in his fists and settled her in front of himself like a weapon.

Which was exactly what she was.

Fen's stunned silence confirmed it.

"You know why I'm here, Chrest." Gawain grunted. "So let's get this done, so you can go back to your whores, and I can get on with my day."

"What... Who are *they*?" Chrest asked, confused. He sniffed the air. "Why's she have a bag over her head?"

"She's my backup plan, in case you had excuses instead of gold for me."

"Your gold..." Chrest caught up to the moment.

"I'll be leaving tomorrow to become a proper man. A husband." He cleared his throat. "You know how I came by the gold I lent you. I have to replace it before I leave."

Siofra gagged.

"And you need it at this hour?" Chrest scratched at his beard.

Gawain shook Siofra in front of him. "Do you have it or not, Chrest?"

"I... Of course I do. Of course I do. That is, I *will*, once the sale comes through. Been waiting on it ah, a month now?" Another scratching sound followed his weak attempt at deflection.

Gawain shifted. His grip on Siofra's forearms loosened. "You're sure you don't have it now?"

"Well, Gawain, I *do* have it. It's a matter of delivery, friend, of exchanging value for coin. The bankers need to do their thing and then I'll sign the deed, and it will be—"

"All right then. Siofra, kill him."

"*What?*" Chrest shrieked, tottering backward on the wood, a stunted laugh dying in his throat. "Did you just order this girl to kill me?"

"Have you lost your mind, Gawain?" Fen cried. Siofra took his hand to silence him but could feel his astonishment overshadowing his reason. "Your father will have you flogged for this."

"No more or less than he'd flog me for the gold I borrowed from his coffers to lend to this maggot," Gawain answered. "Anyway, he won't be hearing about it from either of you, will he?" He leaned in, his breath heady, moistening her ear through the thin hood. "Come on, Siofra. You do this, and I'll go easy on

36

you later, when it's just you and me. When Fen is no longer here to fight your battles. Yeah?"

"What do you mean?" Fen asked. "When it's just you and her? If you think Siofra will ever agree to go, you're mad."

"What in the Guardians is going on here?" Chrest demanded. "What is she?"

"Look. If you need gold, let me flourish some for you," Fen said reasonably, though he was practically panting. Desperate.

"You'll do that too, whelp," Gawain said. "But Chrest doesn't get to steal from me. And so your sister is going to deal with that for me first."

Siofra shook her head. She breathed the word, *no*, through her gag, where it was safe, where she could harm no one.

He could beat her or starve her or whatever he had planned for her as his mistress, but she would never kill for him. She would never, ever take a life intentionally.

Gawain again shook her in front of himself, rocking her nearly off her feet. When he ripped off the hood, she tried to bury her face, but he wrenched the gag off next. She pressed her hands to her face in wild desperation, and he nearly broke her wrists prying them away from her eyes.

"*No, no, no*," Siofra whispered. "No, Gawain, *please*, you don't know what you're asking. You don't know—"

"You brought this little waif to settle things?" Chrest's fear had been replaced by an emboldened wonder. He snorted.

Gawain reached forward and lodged Siofra's chin into the crook of his elbow, forcing her head upward. "Look at this man. Look at him!"

Chrest had the good sense to duck, though his reaction seemed more from confusion.

"Siofra, look at me. Look at *me*." Fen wrapped his arms around her to pull her away, but Gawain swung and connected his fist to the side of Fen's face. Fen flew to the wall with a sickening thud and went silent.

"Stop!" Siofra screamed. "I *won't* do it. You cannot make me do this!"

"Why isn't he dead?" Gawain demanded. "Your eyes are open."

"It doesn't work that way, you fool," Siofra hissed through her teeth, kicking her legs up and off the floor to no avail. She hung by his elbow, choking through her attempt to speak. "Now let me *go!*"

"Guardians, Gawain. You're hurting the girl," Chrest admonished.

Siofra wanted to laugh. He wasn't afraid of her, but he should be. He should be running for his life.

"I have your gold, all right? I'll call on the banker this afternoon, get a rush on it. I didn't know you were in such a hurry, or I'd have done it sooner."

Gawain's hold on Siofra eased. She coiled her muscles, ready to bolt, but in a move so fast it stole her breath, he had his hands gnarled around her breasts. Siofra cried out in pain.

"Well, if you insist there's no score to settle, why not sample my latest possession?" His hot breath curled around her ear, sending a jolt of sickness straight to her belly. "I don't mind sharing, as long as I get to go first."

"Now that's a visit I'd welcome at all hours!" Chrest exclaimed. He sanded his hands together as he closed in. "We should end all misunderstandings this way."

"Absolutely," Gawain said, but the venom hadn't faded from his voice. "Shall we get on with it then?"

"Si..." Fen murmured, desperately trying to regain his senses. "Si... No, he's doing this to... to bait you... Si..."

Siofra flung her elbows back into Gawain, but he was too strong, too sturdy. He dragged his lips crudely along her neck, absorbing her tears, turning them into his own pleasure. She felt it pressed behind her, a reminder of the others in her life who had used her for their selfish purposes and then locked her away.

"Si..." Fen's pained groans eclipsed what he said next.

"Let me go. Gawain. *Let me go.*" She panted as the red wall came up inside her, like a scorching from within. Like her insides had been set aflame and left to burn without answer.

But there *was* an answer.

There was always an answer when the red wall called to her... and only *one* answer would ever quell its eternal fire.

Siofra spun around and erupted with a blinding flash of white light, silencing the squabbling men as time suspended in the grip of her panicked wrath. Sounds became fluid, melting into the heat as it scorched the room, turning wood to splinters and flesh to fire. She knew there were screams, but it wasn't the same as hearing them, not the same as seeing the carnage born of her heart.

It was over as fast as it had begun, but she wasn't ready to stop. There was still fire smoldering, awaiting address. She ripped the dangling binding away from her face and turned toward the door.

Fen barreled into her from behind, sending them both hurtling to the hard boards.

Darkness returned to the dim room. Wheezing, Siofra scrambled to her knees, but Fen was on top of her again, protecting her from the brutal reality of what she'd done, yet again.

"No, Si, no. No, *come here*, don't look. Don't look."

Siofra used the last of her strength to shrug him away because she *had* to see. She *had* to know because this was who she was, who she was born to be, a murderous monstrosity with no self-control. The least she could do was face her crimes.

But as she surveyed the wreckage of bone and blood, of the mangled mix of both that made no sense—a puzzle she could not solve—Siofra's daze turned to a swoon. Gawain and Chrest were both dead, but they no longer resembled men at all. What should have been horror was more like wonder as her awe-filled gaze swept the remains of her fury, which had painted the room with evidence of her dark gift.

"Si..."

Fen was unscathed. Medvedev magic couldn't be used with ill intent against another Medvedev, but he didn't just avoid her harm. He also had a dampening effect on her darkness. It was the difference between only two men dying and everyone else in the vicinity also being swept in her anger. Had Fen not been knocked senseless, he might have saved Gawain and Chrest too.

"He... I...." What was she going to say, that Gawain had made her do it? Had pushed her over the edge and she'd had no choice but to follow?

Was it even the truth?

Or was it more truthful to say that no matter how she might protest or lament, she *enjoyed* the tingle of power charging her from limb to limb, elevating her to a place no one could follow—to a command no one could match?

"We have to go," Fen was saying over and over, to himself, to her, and to the remains of the two dead men. "We have to go, Si. We have to *go*—"

"Go *where*, Stiofen?"

The use of his full name seemed to pull him out of his daze. "Anywhere but here. We could—"

"Go back to his mother and father, where we get to explain how I *killed* their only son and heir?"

"He made you do it!" Fen screamed as he stumbled back to his feet, ambling to the side to avoid a severed arm.

"Ah, and you think your explanation will be sufficient?" Siofra laughed. She wondered if her brother heard the sound the way she felt when she made it: like a snake, flashing its tongue among prey that had started the day believing themselves predators.

Today wasn't like the other times for those would-be predators, and not only because the morning had ended in death.

Could Fen see it too?

Could he *feel* it?

Stiofen dragged his hands down his face and left them over his eyes as he exhaled into whatever plan he was concocting. She

40

nearly laughed aloud again at the futility of whatever was swirling in his mind. There *was* no going back. No leaving.

"We have to... Well, we just have to do what I said before. Leave Newcarrow."

The current passing along her skin faded to a hum. *No! Come back. Stay with me.* She tapped her palms against her legs, willing the fearlessness to return, to nestle back over her like a protective blanket. Without it, she would be once again lost. She would be the cowering little Medvedev girl with no control over her mind, heart, or body. She would be the liability holding Fen back from a better life, one where he didn't have to worry about his murderous sister.

"Come back," Siofra whispered. Her knees wobbled. She braced herself against a wall, only to cringe when her palm landed in a splatter of blood. "Don't leave me this time."

"Si?"

"Stay with me." She moaned, sucking in a gulp of air before she went down. Fen made it to her side right as she crashed to the splintered floorboards.

Fen liked to say Siofra "escaped" when she closed up after an episode—that delicate stretch of time when he was left alone to deal with the awfulness of what she'd done. It wasn't because he actually believed what he was saying; it was because he desperately wanted to.

Because if she couldn't control any of it, what hope was there?

This time had been different from the others though. She'd lingered in consciousness longer than ever before, and she'd seemed almost... almost...

No, don't think it. Don't even think it. If you believed even a part of her enjoyed killing, you'd love her less. It would make it all impossible.

The bigger problem was the cell they'd been thrown into when Chrest's business partner had arrived. His screams had torn through the early morning, rousing more people than Fen could fend off with a distraction. He'd never been more grateful for Siofra disappearing into herself as he had when over three dozen Newcarrow residents had shown up demanding answers.

These men, they tried to hurt her. They tried...

Fen had abandoned his defense before he even finished the thought. For what could he say to explain the carnage? Siofra hadn't stabbed these men in panicked self-defense. She'd *eviscerated* them, with her mind.

Her heart.

And the cage, the cell, would protect the town from more of the same, but what of him? What of Siofra, who wouldn't remember any of it when she came around? Was it the end for them, as it had once been for their mother and father?

There was nothing Fen could do either way.

Their gaoler had a magus of his own, and that magus had warded their cell against the use of magic. Fen couldn't even heal Siofra's gnarled, bluish ankle or the cuts on her arms and face, which she'd collected sometime along the violent ride between the speculation hall and Newcarrow prison.

They'd lost track of Aio and Atio. Fen hoped they'd escaped, but he knew they hadn't. He and Siofra would feel it if they traveled too far.

The Stanhopes had come twice, trying to free them. *Our property,* they'd screamed to no avail, and when it didn't work, the stewardess wailed that if anyone had a right to the monsters in the cell, it was the mother of the slain.

But the gaoler was a stickler for law and order, it seemed.

Fen and Siofra would remain until their trial.

Or until the Stanhopes figured out a way to use the gold Stiofen had created for them to twist the law to their bidding. Gold that would soon run out.

Siofra cried out in her sleep. In pain. Whether physical or emotional, he couldn't know.

Fen closed his eyes and let his hand travel down her matted hair in mindless strokes.

Pesha stood slightly off center in the long row of ceiling-to-floor windows stretching the main passage of Shadowfen Hall. Beyond the dense panes, the sun was just rising over the lake, lighting a shimmer of brilliance over the unbothered surface. *Pesh's Lake*, Desemir liked to say, for if Pesha hadn't loved it so, hadn't *needed* it so, Desemir would have filled it to be rid of the insects that swarmed along the surface in late springtide.

Darkwood Run was one of the few bastions in the Northerlands that even had a springtide. Winter seasons were characteristically cold, but in springtide, the forest came alive, flourishing with vibrant color and animating with life. The streams ran clear and unbound by ice, and the precious ebony wood at last peeled, to be turned into baskets and pouches and sold all over the kingdom. The peel lasted only a fortnight, but profits from the harvest were so bountiful, the Trevanions could live off that revenue alone.

But they were months away from the bloom season. The cold, frozen forest, veiled with a soft cloud of fog, reminded Pesha there was still time to wait for the top layer of the lake to thaw, so he could venture down and be whole again.

"Still mesmerized by the fog?" Desemir asked, joining him at his side. He passed Pesha a steaming mug of tea, which Pesha accepted with a grateful nod.

Pesha caught a glimpse of his half brother from the side. Desemir's silken robe was ruffled, his dark hair telling a similar story in its tousled spikes. It hadn't been a celebration night, which meant the disturbances in his appearance had been the result of more terrible nightmares.

Desemir had but two effective escapes from them: women and spirits. But their father had been too familiar with the drink, and Desemir was wary of becoming too like him.

He could finally address the guilt that rots him from the inside. That might ease the dreams too.

"Fantasizing about springtide," Pesha confessed, unsure why he bothered to explain. Desemir had understood what was on his brother's mind before he'd asked the question.

"Soon enough." Desemir clapped a hand on Pesha's back. "I can still have a pond built into the earth, underground in the dungeon. It's dark down there—and a bit miserable, I know—but you'd be closer and wouldn't have to endure this pain most of the year."

Pesha shook his head. "It's not so painful anymore, Des. It's just..."

"Just what?"

"Nothing."

Desemir rolled his shoulders with a drawn exhale. "Were you around when the raven came in?"

Pesha tore his gaze away from the lake. "What raven?"

Desemir's grin cut through a shadow of stubble, which would be gone before they convened for supper. "Fancy a trip south?"

Pesha turned all the way around to face him. "How far south?"

"As far south as you can go without hitting the sea, I expect. I looked on a map. Ever heard of Newcarrow?"

Pesha wrinkled his nose. "Upstart port town that destroyed another in its creation? I've heard of it."

Des laughed. "A bit like what happened with the Arrandens and us, wouldn't you say?"

Pesha grunted. The Trevanions had once been the stewards of Darkwood Run, until the Arrandens came in and swept the stewardship from under them with dark dealings. Their grandfather had been the last Trevanion steward. Ludwik had contrived the forest acquisitions as a form of retribution.

Pesha sipped his tea. He winced at the burn and set it on a nearby bench to cool. "What business do you have in Newcarrow? You aren't thinking of *trading* with them, are you?"

"Of course not," Desemir said quickly. He stared into the forest, one hand picking at the seam of his robe, near his chest. "Do you remember the promise I made you, after your mother killed our father?"

Pesha winced at the smooth way Desemir jabbed the knife into him.

"You believed me then. Do you believe me now?"

Pesha nodded and returned his gaze to the lake.

"We have a chance now to make good on it, Pesh. To right the terrible, terrible..." Desemir clenched his mouth shut, trapping the tumultuous emotions Pesha sensed beneath the surface. It was the most he'd said on the subject in years. "There are two of them, two Medvedev. They've been locked away, and—"

"What?" Pesha paled. His breath stuttered as he dug through his thoughts for words.

"*Two* of them," Desemir said again with a knowing nod. "That's the rumor anyway. Steward Stanhope has been hiding them away, according to my contact down there, but now they're in the custody of the town gaoler, awaiting their sentence for killing Stanhope's son. I need you to confirm. If it's true, you'll bring them back here, and we'll see to it that no one ever hurts them again."

It couldn't be true. But Desemir wouldn't lie to him, especially not about Medvedev. And if it *were* true, and Pesha did bring them to Shadowfen Hall, how would it work out?

Would it be like...

No. He's not Ludwik.

"I've already sent word to the gaoler—"

Pesha laughed, running a palm across his forehead. "You just knew I'd go, did you?"

Desemir wrinkled his mouth into a playful frown. "You're from the Consortium of the Sepulchre, there to escort them to their new life under a firm thumb of training and discipline in magic."

Pesha scoffed, rolling his eyes. Even in jest, he bristled at the mention of the Sepulchre. Ordinary magic practitioners might fare well under their tutelage and rules, but someone like *him*? Like the two his brother was sending him to collect?

"The very suggestion is loathsome, I know," Desemir said. "But you must understand, Pesh, the Sepulchre is the only governing body in this kingdom with the power to overthrow the sentence decided by their local lawmaker. As their crimes were of magic, there's no other way to see them released." He sighed. "It won't be long before the Sepulchre *actually* gets wind of this, so time isn't on our side."

"Their sentence," Pesha said, his thoughts catching up. "They really killed the Stanhope heir?"

Desemir's face darkened as he pulled a breath through his teeth. "Let's send for your trunk to be packed, and I'll show you what the raven said."

Siofra yelped a sharp cry when her injured foot brushed the cell wall. She quickly recalled it, but that hurt more, and when she chanced a glance downward, she saw why: her ankle and foot were swollen to twice their size, painted in an array of blues and purples, hued by yellowing at the edges of each bruise. A few days, then, they'd been in the cell if the yellow had come, but while the bruises would heal, her foot, without aid, would not.

She searched for Fen and found him huddled on the other end of the bench. With a start, she saw violet hair at his roots and reached up to touch her own in horror. Magic had always covered their secret, but they had no power in the warded cell.

A jostle of metal sounded atop the steps, followed by the steady descent of boots thudding on the way down. Fen jolted forward, rushing to the bars.

The gaoler huffed, tugging at his waistline as he sidled up to the cell. He snuffed and squinted, adjusting to the dim light of the dungeon.

"Came to tell you, trial is over."

"What?" Fen twisted his hands around the bars, head cocked. "*Our* trial? It's over?"

"Ayuh." The gaoler roughly cleared his throat, swallowing whatever he'd unearthed. "Over and decided. As expected, you were both found guilty."

"Guilty!" Fen cried. "Of what?"

"Murder, of course."

"You had a trial for us, without us, without hearing our side, and it was enough to decide our guilt?"

His utter disbelief was almost funny to Siofra. Had he really expected they'd be free to go after she killed two men? With forbidden magic? And when one of the men had been the son of their steward?

"You sound surprised." The gaoler laughed. It escalated into a phlegmy cough. "Then, most criminals are for some reason. Never understood it."

Fen rattled the bars and screamed. "That's not how trials work, gaoler!"

"No," the gaoler agreed with a twitch of his nose. "Unless the crime was committed with magic, and then the Sepulchre decides these things. As I expect you two would know, being illegal magic do'ers." His lip curled in a sneer.

"The Sepulchre," Fen said with a disgusted snort. He bounced back off the bars, flinging his arms. "Ahh, of course."

"Don't look so relieved, boy. A hanging would be quicker, less painful than whatever fate awaits you at their hands." The gaoler laughed to himself with a slow head shake. "You have three days to ruminate on the possibilities."

"The Sepulchre," Siofra whispered to herself when the man was gone. The Consortium of the Sepulchre in the Skies regulated magic in the kingdom, but Medvedev were not, officially speaking, part of the kingdom. They were anomalies as far as the realm was concerned, despite that their time in what men called the White Kingdom predated such a name, or men at all. Most Medvedev stuck to their Hinterland forests, but Siofra and her brother had been ripped from those lands as infants when their parents had been expelled for leading an uprising against their chieftainess.

To an organization like the Sepulchre, who could only guess at what magic the Medvedev held within them, Siofra and Stiofen would be wonders to study and dissect.

There would be no punishment from the Sepulchre, at least not the traditional kind.

The gaoler was right.

A hanging would be more merciful.

FIVE
ALCOTT UNDERHILL

Pesha's carriage pulled into Newcarrow just as the violet hues of dusk nestled into the horizon, dimming the world.

A tangy, briny gust wafted from the port, set to the shrill caw of gulls overhead. Darkwood Run was also close to the sea, but the Great Darkwood shielded them, creating the illusion they were farther inland.

Though Pesha loved the sea—and had personal, intrinsic reasons for that love—the mawkish effect of just-built Newcarrow and the unbridled call of the harsh Southern tide burrowed into his marrow like an uninvited guest.

He pulled the curtain back a hair as he passed through Newcarrow proper. Gleaming, freshly painted establishments caught the last trickle of sun, the dying light glaring off windows just placed. The road was finely packed and not yet traveled enough for the wear that would add texture to the path.

His attention was drawn to the bustle of residents walking along the boardwalk. Women in lace, men in velvet. Pesha scrunched his nose and flopped back against the bench. It wasn't enough for the Stanhopes to claim land that wasn't theirs and move the southern port from Greystone Abbey to Newcarrow, bankrupting the former town. They had to flaunt their absence of scruples, like painting rouge on a cave troll.

Pesha wrung his hands in his lap as his agitation returned like a slap to the gut. He'd never before been so far away from Eshe. He'd grown accustomed to being separated from her for half the year or more, but he always *felt* her nearby and knew she could feel him in return. Each roll of the carriage's wheels set a new record for distance. There was no sensing her this far away. He'd never know if something happened to her, if she needed him.

As the carriage bounced along, he turned his gaze forward, willing his unwelcome fears to fade to clarity so he could focus on the reason Des had sent him.

There's nothing you can do about it until you return anyway. She'll understand.

Of course she would. That wasn't the point. As long as he was away from Shadowfen Hall, Pesha and his familiar would both suffer.

Des knew it and had sent him anyway.

He's your brother, not just by blood but by choice. He could have cast you out when Ludwik died, but he held you closer, offered you every-thing. He would never hurt you intentionally. He sent you because he trusts no one else with the twins. He knows they're safe with you.

He grunted and closed his eyes.

He loves you. He isn't your father. He will be a better man if fate allows it.

Pesha and his family had a complicated relationship with fate.

As did, he imagined, the brother and sister he'd come to collect.

Siofra had stopped counting the hours. Days had been lost, at first to the fugue of her fear and then to the fever tearing through her frail, twisted limbs, burning her from the inside out. It wasn't as hot as the red wall, but it promised an ending just as final.

Fen was at the bars again, demanding a healer as his voice grew increasingly hoarse. She was surprised he had any screams left. Not one had received an answer, except for the night they had been denied supper as punishment for his disturbance. But sometimes eating was worse, because what passed for food had either been overrun by rats or was half-rotted. She'd thrown up more than she'd digested.

"You're wasting precious energy," she said, her voice barely above a moan. Her eyes traveled toward the cut on her leg, the one Fen said had brought the fever on. It was scorching to the touch, the red spidering outward from the center. She'd once seen a man lose an arm that had looked the same.

"They want to sell you to the Sepulchre? They should probably consider how they're going to keep you alive long enough to do it." Fen huffed. He slammed his palms on the metal, rattling the bars in their housing, then backed into the bench.

Siofra fumbled for the waterskin. The stream water inside had not been passed through a cloth filter but was drinkable at least. After a long sip, she was able to speak again. "Perhaps it won't be so bad."

Fen snorted. "I know you don't believe that." His foot jerked out when a rat squealed past. A whole colony of them lurked in the many shadows. Siofra even had names for some.

"I believe we're still alive for a reason." Siofra pressed the waterskin to her chest and rolled slowly onto her back, grimacing through the pain that was now a constant companion. She'd spent the long hours devising ways to protect Fen from whatever came next, but she would have no power over the men at the Sepulchre. They would bind her magic, as their local enchanter had done with their cell, and she'd be defenseless.

She had no bargaining power without the use of her magic. Nothing to offer in exchange for them releasing her brother.

"If Mother and Father hadn't gotten themselves banished from Clahnn Asgill—"

"Hush! Don't even think it," Siofra hissed. She kicked her good foot at him. "If they have enchanters here, they can read your thoughts and your whispers."

Fen rolled his head against the mossy stone with a bitter laugh. "Ah, you think they've guessed we're Medvedev already? Look at your hair, Si. Well, you can't, I suppose, because you have no mirror, but *look at mine*. I can't cover our violet hair without magic, and in another few days, the color will be more violet than blonde, won't it?"

Siofra's hand fluttered to her scalp, but her eyes were on Fen and the telltale lilac that would betray their truth to the realm: that they were Medvedev. Violet eyes were rare in the kingdom, but not enough to raise suspicion. But violet hair? Only an avian Medvedev had it naturally.

Aio and Atio flew somewhere nearby. She knew they were close because the pain she felt when they ventured too far was worse than what rocked her poor ankle, and the infected wound farther up on her leg.

"There's a *reason* Medvedev don't cross paths with the Sepulchre, Si. We breathe the same as men, bleed the same, and have more in common with them than we do differences. They can't even tell us apart from men at a glance. But we'll always only be specimens to them, nothing more."

Siofra didn't argue. Was it not what they'd been to the Stanhopes too? To the family before them who had taken in the Thornhearts after their mother and father had once again angered the wrong people?

There was no freedom to be found in the White Kingdom, not for the Thornheart twins. And there was no home to go back to.

It would have been torture to be Gawain's mistress, but Fen would have been safe.

They both threw their attention to the sudden light beaming down the steps. Boots clomped and keys jiggled.

"Two people," Siofra whispered.

Fen kneaded his fists against the rotted wood bench.

"There. Pitiful things, aye? Come back when you're ready to sign for them." The gaoler thundered back up to the surface set to the same hard clinks of metal.

Siofra blinked through the haze clouding her vision. She gingerly swung her legs over the side to sit, fighting the swell of nausea from her first movement in hours. No matter how painful, she couldn't let this man, this *mage*, see her so vulnerable.

Soft steps echoed and trapped in the dirt walls. A man far younger than she'd been expecting came into view, his hands folded before him. His dark, wavy hair framed eyes that were the brightest blue, even in the dim light of the dungeon. He lowered his gaze to his feet as he approached.

Fen's hand shot out to the side. Siofra took it.

The man looked up. A soft but apprehensive smile spread across his unlined face. "My name is Alcott Underhill, and I've come to escort you both to the Sepulchre, where you'll be safe."

"Safe?" Fen released her hand and leaped forward, then pressed his face to the bars. The man didn't retreat. "At least speak true to us about your intentions. We may be bound from our magic, but we're not fools."

Alcott pressed his lips tight with a sigh. "I understand your fear, Stiofen."

Fen shook the bars and released them with a dark scoff. "Right."

"You said we'll be safe," Siofra ventured aloud. She couldn't take her eyes off Alcott.

"He's *lying*, Si."

"The Sepulchre doesn't punish the innocent," Alcott said coolly. His gaze traveled from one to the other, rapidly scanning. He seemed to be studying them with the same intensity Siofra realized she'd been examining him with.

"We're not innocent," Fen said. "Never have been."

Alcott tilted his head, aiming his gaze at Fen. "You were abandoned as children and then made to serve highborns, no?"

Fen turned away.

"The Stanhopes would see an example made of you," Alcott said. "After all you've done for them. After you gave them an entire town and a stewardship." He shifted his weight between his feet. "What happened to their son is unfortunate, but Gawain Stanhope was no victim, nor was his associate. I... the Sepulchre... recognizes the situation for what it is."

"Trying to sell us on going, are you? When we have no choice?"

"How do you know all that?" Siofra asked. She badly wanted to stand, to go toward this man to see him more clearly. His kindness both scared her and drew her in; she wanted to understand it... to make sense of the darkly serious mage, who dressed like a man of maturity but couldn't be any older than she was.

The man's mouth twitched into a quick flash of a grin. "I needed less than an hour to read the whispers here and form a read on the situation. The residents of Newcarrow know their steward didn't come by his wealth honestly. They suspect magic is involved, but they don't understand magic. Not your kind anyway."

"Our kind," Stiofen muttered, shaking his head.

"We won't speak of it here." Alcott turned his head back to look at the stairs. "You have been made the instrument of weak men your entire lives. That will not be the fate awaiting you."

"You have no reason to be truthful with us," Fen spat.

"As I have no reason to lie to you," Alcott countered. "But it's also true you have no reason to believe me. Either way, we'll be clear of Newcarrow by morning, which won't be a moment too soon for the two of you. The Stanhopes are spitting mad, but fortunately for you, they have no power over the Sepulchre. If they did, you'd already be dead."

"We leave here with you, you bind our magic. We'll have no defense," Fen replied. He pitched forward. "If you want us to believe you won't harm us, no wards."

Alcott inhaled a long, hard breath through his nose. He exhaled into a nod. "No wards," he said. "But I suspect you'll find your magic doesn't reach its usual potency in my presence."

"What does that mean?" Fen demanded, but Alcott was already heading back to the stairs. "What does that *mean*?"

"Gather yourselves for the long journey ahead. I'll be back when your release is signed," Alcott called over his shoulder as he disappeared from sight.

"I don't trust him. He's a liar, like all the rest." Fen seethed. He jumped up to pace the small cell, muttering to himself as he processed Underhill's claims.

Siofra's fear screamed louder than it ever had, but there was a calm coating it. The feeling was new. Mystifying.

Alcott was a dangerous man.

Fen was right; they couldn't trust him. He'd said what he needed to keep them calm and placated, but he would turn on them when the time was right.

Siofra was ready to follow him just the same.

SIX
HARBORING FUGITIVES

Once free of the town gates at the north end of Newcarrow, Pesha pushed the driver to ride hard and stick to the forest. The two demands were ill-suited for the Thornheart twins, with one so sick she had the tines of death written in her eyes and the other trying—and failing, for all his efforts—to heal any part of her.

Pesha ignored the boy, Stiofen, and his icy, accusing gaze. He read his anger for what it was: a lifetime of honing his defense against a world that would use him and, worse, use his sister. But it was the erratic pattern in Fen's finger twitches and his occasional flash of rage-filled eyes barely concealing his distress that left Pesha wishing he could prompt even a semblance of a smile from him.

Siofra seemed so small and lost, curled up in her brother's lap. He could almost forget the crime she'd been accused of. The *power* she'd used against another living creature. Two creatures. The Medvedev called it forbidden magic. But with no one to teach her, it had grown unabated, unpolished.

This is the real reason Des sent you. You're the only one who can temper her magic without hurting them.

Stiofen's glare cut through the silence as they bounced across the hard terrain of the forest of Pine Bluff. Had the boy realized they were heading north, away from the Sepulchre, and not east? Or had he just spent too much of his life on guard and knew no other way to be around a stranger?

Siofra stared at nothing, one arm dangling so her fingertips bounced off the moving floor. Her matted hair was pasted to her flushed face. The spot on her leg, which would kill her if he didn't address it soon, pulsed like an angry sun.

Pesha glanced out the window. They'd reach the river shortly.

"Is it because of you that I can't heal her?" Fen finally asked.

"Yes." Pesha didn't look at the boy.

"She'll die, Underhill. She *is* dying. Look at her." Fen rolled forward when Pesha didn't reply. "Look at her!"

"She's not going to die."

"I don't know the crest stitched behind your head, but I know it isn't from the Sepulchre," Fen stated. He'd been working up to something, distrust dancing behind his cynical eyes. "If we were still going east, we'd hit the Compass Road soon, wouldn't we? But we're not. So we won't."

Pesha grunted and turned his attention back to the passing forest.

"Another collector." Fen wiped a dirty hand across his face, replacing old grime with new grime. "What wishes can I spin to life for *you* then?"

The tragic bitterness in the boy's biting words almost pulled the truth from Pesha.

"Can't even answer me? After all I'll be doing for you... or is it your master? Your cloak is nice, but you wear no rings. No gold around your neck. Who do you serve?"

Pesha ground his jaw with a tight inhale.

Fen laughed. "At least the Stanhopes looked us in the eyes when they took from us."

"Then why did you kill their son?" Pesha hadn't meant to say it aloud, but it silenced the boy for a few merciful moments.

Fen's tone eased. "It wasn't like that."

"Ahh."

"Do you care about the truth? Or just getting your gold?"

On his way into town, Pesha had absorbed the whispers, the rumors. Most in Newcarrow seemed to accept Steward Stanhope had acquired his wealth by magic, revering him for having such rare gifts at his disposal. They followed his shadow hoping to catch a glint of his shine.

They didn't care how he'd come about the gold that had turned them from poor to rich overnight—nor about the young twins who'd suffered so the town could thrive.

But they *would* turn on Stanhope when they realized his coffers had dried up. The steward would no doubt do anything to get the source of his power back before that happened.

We just need to reach the river. We get there, we're under the dominion of Longwood Rush, and the man would never air his troubles so close to Lady Blackwood's domain.

"There's no gold for me," Pesha said, his words constricted with a light grunt. He knew better than to engage. Of course they had questions, but providing answers had not been part of his charge. If Desemir said he wanted to protect them, he meant it. Pesha had no choice but to believe him when he said it had nothing to do with the past.

Fen pitched forward. He nearly toppled when the carriage ran over a root. "I'll kill you before you touch her."

Pesha glanced past the curtain, spotting a glimpse of River Rush. He sighed with relief and tapped the roof. The carriage came to a slow halt.

He leaned in, meeting Fen's wild eyes. "You're right. I'm not from the Sepulchre. I'm from the Northerlands, and I've come to help the two of you."

"*Right*," Fen replied in challenge. "Help us? No man exists who would help us without wanting for himself."

"Presently, I need you to go down to the riverbank with my guard and wash up. Bring back some dampened rags when you return. We'll need them. Oh, and on your return, please also collect some firewood. We'll make a short camp here before we continue on."

"And leave her here alone, with you?" Fen's head shook in tight shakes.

Pesha exhaled into another grunt. He swung the carriage door open. "Unless you want her to freeze to death, we need a fire."

"It's all right, Fen." Siofra's small voice surprised them both. "A fire sounds nice."

Fen's lip curled, his eyes grazing Pesha with fire of his own. "And you?"

"Me?" Pesha looked down at Siofra. "I'm going to save her life."

Desemir wilted on his chair at the head of the massive table his grandfather had built, it was said, with his own hands. Trevanion history was full of fables. Some were true, most probably not. It had never stopped the family from repeating them.

Almost a week Pesha had been gone, and Des hadn't slept more than two hours a night. There was a simple cure, but he'd promised not to partake until Pesha returned. That was the deal; he'd go to Newcarrow if Des behaved in his absence.

And without an heir, there were risks he couldn't afford.

He rolled his father's ring around his finger, letting it fall past the knuckle, almost into his palm. The piece had been forged from pure gold, then embossed with their standard, the mythical lion. It was a legacy, upon piles of legacies left in his charge, and the unwieldy ask of ensuring the Trevanion name lived up to the legend: that their enemies—a list longer, even, than their legacies—must fear the myths more than they questioned them.

He snaked his hand forward and gripped the carafe of wine by its neck. No one was around to see him drink straight from the bottle except Wulfhelm and Euric, who both waited patiently for him to finish ruminating so they could escort him to his apartments.

Pesha was right about one thing.

Well, he was often right, but telling him so meant enduring his insufferable gloating.

The parlor trick with his whisper reading was only going to work for so long. Men only had so many secrets dark enough that they'd die before revealing them.

What Desemir needed was to make an example, one that would leave the men of the Darkwood trembling in their bespoke leather boots. One to keep their acid tongues from his doorstep and their assassins from his bed.

Des, what you need is an heir.

"You're right, Pesh," Des whispered, slurring as the wine went to his head. He didn't allow his thoughts to slip into the dark place where his own terrible secrets lived. Pesha's calming influence wasn't even required to avoid opening the wrong boxes in his mind. He'd lost the keys long ago. "About both problems. And it's why I've sent you to solve them."

Siofra felt the man draw near before she saw him. She'd fallen asleep again, and he'd moved to be beside her on the bench. The carriage door was closed, the compartment still. The rush of a river's current roared beyond.

Fen wasn't beside her anymore. He must have gone for firewood after all.

"I'm going to touch you now," Underhill whispered. "To heal you. Nod if you understand."

Siofra closed her eyes again, her breaths shallow and less frequent than they should be. She nodded.

Smooth hands slid along her knees and then upward, moving across the inside of her thigh where her flesh throbbed so hard, her heartbeat thumped behind her eyes. She jolted at the charged

61

touch of his healing hand, a shock of pain arcing up into her chest as it left her body and sent her beyond consciousness.

When she woke again, the sharp pain in her leg was gone, replaced by a dull twinge. But she was still acutely aware of her gnarled ankle, which wouldn't bear her weight even temporarily. She remembered how the strange man had carried her from the jail to the carriage against Fen's resounding protests.

"This might put you out again," he said softly as his fingertips caressed the swollen flesh, forming a barrier.

And it did.

When Siofra's eyes fluttered open once more, the rest of her pain had calmed, and Underhill was back on his own bench. Watching her.

"How do you feel?"

"You know how I feel because you're the one responsible for it." Siofra swung her healed legs over the leather and sat up. On a whim, she pulled both up, crossing them over the seat. "You're not from the Sepulchre, but you know magic."

Underhill nodded in confirmation.

"You practice it in hiding."

"Not exactly."

"Not exactly?" Siofra cocked her head. "You trained at the Sepulchre then? You have their permission to practice?"

"No." Underhill folded his hands. "What led you to hurt the boy? Gawain?"

Siofra lowered her eyes.

"I'm not judging. Nor will I punish you for it. I expect he deserved it."

She fought back a laugh. She even believed him. But it didn't make him a safe place for her secrets.

"Your falcons are resting on an overhead branch. Well, yours anyway. Fen's went with him to the river."

"I don't know what you're talking about."

"You're from Clahnn Asgill is my guess. But I'm no authority on the matter."

Siofra's gaze shot back up. "You *really* don't know what you're talking about."

Underhill smiled. "The only time men have said that to me is when I knew precisely what I was talking about."

"I'm no man."

Underhill's lowered his eyes and raised them over her. "No, that much is clear."

"What do you *want* with us? Really want with us? Even if I believed you didn't want Fen to make you wealthy—"

"We're already wealthy, well beyond anything the Stanhopes could imagine."

Siofra sneered. "The men I've known wouldn't let that stop them. They can't help themselves. They know no limit, nor even the meaning of the word."

Underhill raised his brows and sat back against the leather. "My brother wouldn't disagree with you."

Siofra narrowed her eyes. "It's to him you're taking us?"

He watched her with his head rolled to the side against the back of the bench. "My brother is a good man, Siofra. He will care for you. Protect you."

Siofra shook her head. None of it made sense. Nothing so kind ever came free, even if Underhill seemed kind enough. "But *why?*"

"He's protected me. I'm safe with him. And you will be too."

"Protected you from what? Why will you not speak plainly? If I cannot control my fate, then I at least deserve to know what it is!"

The first tickle of the red wall formed in her belly. Her eyes flashed wide in fresh panic, and she scrambled forward, reaching for the door.

Underhill's hand clamped atop hers. He forced her to meet his gaze.

"Siofra," he said, gripping her hand tighter. "You could sing the loudest song you've ever sung, and you'd never hurt me."

Siofra's chest heaved with the helpless wrath coursing up under her breastbone, beating against the back of her chest. Her skin tingled with the first embers of fire.

"Go on. Try it."

"No!"

"You'll be fine. And so will I."

Siofra shook her head and trained her eyes on their joined hands, refusing to look even sideways at him. "No, you don't understand. You don't know what you're asking me. You cannot know."

"I can," Underhill said, cool and even, "and I do."

Siofra whipped her eyes upward, meeting his. He looked as calm as he sounded, ready for anything, but how? Why? Why would he invite death, unless...

Siofra lifted her voice and sang. Her notes pierced the small carriage, startling birds and small animals in the forest beyond. She forced her eyes to stay present, clamping them to Underhill's, daring him to beg for her to stop, to admit he'd let it go too far.

He only smiled.

Siofra's hand recoiled, and she crawled back onto her bench.

"My name isn't Underhill," the man said. "It's Pesha. Pesha Trevanion." He waved a hand over his hair, turning it a pale blue. "Clahnn Asgill as well, though I've never been to our lands, and I suspect I never will."

Siofra gasped and pulled both of her hands to her mouth. Another Medvedev. There. In front of her. Living in the realm. Living... living a normal *life*, one of wealth and prestige.

Pesha changed his hair back. He pointed at her head. "I saw the hint of violet as I was healing you. I've corrected it for you and will do the same for Fen until we're home and he can tend to himself again."

"I don't... I don't understand..."

"Just as you cannot harm Stiofen, you cannot harm me. Only beneficial magic, like healing, works on each other, or what I'm doing now to keep you from inadvertently killing every creature in this forest: dampening."

"But why? How?" Siofra reproached herself for what sounded like childish questions. "Does your brother harbor fugitives?"

"Fugitives? Is that what you are?" Pesha laughed. His dark, glamoured hair tousled as it shook. "He's my *brother*. He knows what I am."

"So, your brother is... He's..."

"He has no magic, nor Medvedev, in his blood," Pesha replied. "We're half siblings. But he knows our plight, Siofra. He respects our history. Unlike most men, he knows he has nothing to fear from Medvedev, that our main differences lie not in the way we were made but where. You can be who you are around him, and because I'm there, you cannot hurt him."

Siofra crossed her arms, trying to absorb his words, what they meant. There was another Medvedev sitting before her, who moved about the kingdom unreservedly and without trouble. And he was offering them the same freedom?

How had she not seen he was one of them?

"And..." Siofra swallowed and lifted her chin. "What will your brother expect in return?"

Pesha watched her, his lips twitching as he readied a response, but the carriage door swung open.

Fen stood, arms full of wood, just as angry as before—but considerably cleaner.

"Right." Pesha clasped his hands together. "Time to get some decent food in you both."

Fen shook Siofra, breaking her from a long-held daze. He added no words, but she only had to follow his saucer-wide eyes to understand.

She straightened against the bench, rubbing the last of the sleep from her eyes. The moonlight cast a pale reflection on a broad lake, set in the middle of a dark, teeming forest filled with the tallest trees she'd ever laid eyes on.

At the far end was a keep so towering and stately, her breath caught. The soft light revealed more with each second of their slow approach. Spires twirled into the sky, twined with black and glimmering gold. Long windows yawned from the field below to the crest of the second story.

Pesha followed their wonder-filled gazes with a knowing smile. "Welcome, Siofra and Stiofen, to your new home: Shadowfen Hall."

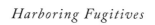

INTO THE
DARKWOOD

70

SEVEN
SHADOWFEN HALL

Desemir rapped the underside of the table, channeling his impatience into the smooth, dark wood. The last of the sun's light had already dipped behind the forest line and was being replaced by stars.

They should have arrived already, even accounting for the unexpected delay at the bridge.

It had been a full tick of the moon earlier when the guards had spotted Pesha's carriage entering Darkwood Run. Euric had ridden out to warn him that the evening's storm had washed out part of the road, so they'd rerouted, taking the longer path through the forest. It was the last anyone had seen them.

The ruts and roots in the Great Darkwood made even daytime travel suspect. Of course it would take longer.

Still.

I met your brother just past the abbey, Des, Euric had said. *Directed him true before he could find out about the road the hard way.*

And his guests?

They were there too.

How did they seem? Eager? Afraid? Uncertain?

You only asked me to steer Pesha to a more certain path.

Didn't see their faces then?

Can't say I did.

Desemir had already strung together his own interpretation of the outlaw sibling duo. He imagined their pale, wan faces and saucerlike eyes, their hair bedraggled from the storms raging both within and without—discarded orphans of the fantastical stories in his library, where he'd rather be, instead of sulking alone in the dark of the Counting Hall, jumping at every clap of thunder.

Though, did they still call one an orphan when he or she reached adulthood?

We're all orphans here at Shadowfen Hall.

Pesha's raven, sent from just beyond Longwood Rush, was light on detail but confirmed what Desemir had heard.

The twins are safe. They have been through quite the ordeal. The brother is protective and distrustful. The sister is guarded but curious. They are both turning nineteen soon, so if your plan for the brother included a grant of land, it will be a simple matter. Expect our arrival by week's end.

Pesha was right to assume Desemir had land bequeathment in his plans, though would he have agreed to travel south if he'd known Desemir's intentions toward the sister?

Would *she* have come?

And was it even what *he* wanted?

Would it change anything?

Probably not. Nothing can.

Wulfhelm creaked the door open just wide enough to stick his head in. "Desi."

"They're here?"

"Approaching the gates. You want us to send them straight here?"

Desemir nodded, returning his gaze back to the dark gleam of the tabletop. He tensed. "No, Wulf... not here. They'll be starved after their trip, especially with how Pesha eats."

Wulfhelm snickered. "Won't be a problem. Lotte has had the kitchens in a frenzy all day."

"Of course she has." Des laughed. "Dining hall then. I'll find them there."

"And later?"

"Later?" Desemir called with a slight look back.

"You know what I'm asking. Are we bringing any women up tonight?"

Desemir twisted his tongue against the back of his lips. He chuckled to himself, wondering not for the first time what the rest of Darkwood Run *really* thought of his ravenous sexual appetite. There was no place for judgment within his walls. Protection of Desemir was not a contingency of employment but an extension of loyalty. And if Lotte realized her sleeping draught did nothing for him—that only exhausting himself to the brink, to the point of near blackout, got him through the long nights—she'd take it to her tomb.

Desemir's distorted reflection matched how he felt inside. "Four tonight," he said finally. "But bring them later than you usually do. Past midnight. Pay them double."

"Four it is."

"Was there something else?" Desemir asked when the door remained open. "Wulf?"

Wulfhelm stepped in and pressed the door shut. Desemir twisted around.

"You should know, Desi. There are whispers among the staff—"

"What have I told you about whispers?" Desemir gripped the smooth arms of his chair as he shoved out of it, standing to face the most trusted among his guard. Wulf wasn't as old or as tenured as grizzled Euric, but he was a fierce, loyal warrior who had never refused an order, never questioned even the most audacious asks. He'd begun his life as Desemir's childhood playmate and had chosen the training required to be his personal guard.

To hear him speak of whispers was beneath him, beneath his training, his iron will. "Did someone send you to ask me what they themselves fear asking?"

"Come on, you know I'm no chinwagger, Desi." Wulfhelm held his shoulders back, prideful. "I have no care for fishwife gossip."

"I would've thought so, but here you are." Des spread his arms. Dropped them again, slapping his palms against his thighs. "Whatever it is, say it. There are no whispers in Shadowfen, Wulfie. None that do not belong to me."

"They're saying..." Wulfhelm cleared his throat. His thick hands were folded over his torso in a tight lock. "That the children your brother was sent to retrieve—"

"They are not children," Desemir replied.

Wulfhelm flexed his sharp jaw, uncertainty flashing in his pale eyes.

"Go on."

Wulfhelm raised both of his brows with a quick toss of his head. "That they're the same as your brother. That they... come from where he does."

Desemir's stomach clenched. Pesha's secret wasn't one, not at Shadowfen Hall. But neither was it spoken openly about. When Ludwik had died, Desemir had cleaned out their ranks, ridding the Hall of those who shared Ludwik's loathing of the Medvedev.

Those remaining were more than staff.

They were Desemir's chosen family.

"And if they are?" His mouth twitched, not quite a smile. "If they are, Wulf? Will it matter to you? Will it be a problem for you?"

Wulfhelm recoiled in mild horror. "Desi, really? No... No, of course not. You know me better than that. I ask because if it's true, we'll need an immediate review of our security. We won't need to close rank, as we did after your father died, but we *will* need to increase the guard, and soon. If anyone discovers you have them..." He shook his head. "The sooner we begin selection, the quicker we can pass prospectives through our rigorous review. It can be a time-consuming process. Only one in twenty ever make it through, as you know."

Desemir met his old friend's eyes. "Pesha is the head of Shadowfen Guard. He's who you should discuss this with."

"I will. But Pesha prefers us not to mention his... well, ancestry."

"He's not the only one." Desemir passed his hand across his mouth. "I'll speak with him myself. For now, assume the answer is yes."

Wulfhelm lowered his head. "As you wish."

"And, Wulf?"

The warrior looked up.

"I'll look to you to quell the whispers. Our guests aren't curiosities, just as my brother is not. Protect what we have. I won't have that rot spread over our home."

The door opened again. Euric looked in. "They're here."

Desemir inhaled a deep breath through his mouth. Exhaled through his nose. With a nod at Wulfhelm, he said, "Ready the guard. I want no trouble as we welcome our new friends."

"Who will escort you?"

"No one. I changed my mind. I won't be coming out to greet them," Desemir said. Quick, hot relief washed over him. Until Wulf had asked, he hadn't grasped how nervous he was. Old fears resurfaced, spiked with a regret so heavy, it was all he could do to not sink through the floor, into the earth.

Would she read it in his eyes, the sister?

Maybe you want her to.

Maybe you want her to know.

"Desi?"

Desemir's cheeks filled with his exhale. "Go on then. I'll be here the rest of the night."

The carriage door flung open, and Siofra's shuttered view was replaced by the immediate sensation of leaving one world for another. She became aware of scents unfamiliar, of the responsiveness of the earth under her tattered boots, which supported an ankle still healing. A breeze carrying a sharp but comforting aroma that she pieced together, through groggy eyes, came from the same forest they'd ridden through.

The opulence coming into view had roots older than the trees, and it was built with stones predating the arrival of the foreign kings, with histories long forgotten. She began to grasp the differences between the wealth of the Stanhopes and the formidable legacy belonging to men like the Trevanions.

With the light fog descending over the darkness, she couldn't see far enough to discern the full spread of the manor. There appeared to be a large wing capping each end, forming a U shape around the front gardens. The spires she'd glimpsed on the ride up, peeking above the tops of the monstrous needled trees, towered high above her, the gold in the swirls catching the moonlight with a reflective gleam. And the windows... There were so many windows, each one with a candle flickering in the center.

"How big *is* this family?" Fen murmured, wearing a dazed look she assumed was a match for her own.

Siofra looked up to see Aio and Atio soaring overhead in elaborate loops. She smiled to herself.

Show-offs.

The two falcons twirled higher in the night sky, disappearing to explore on their own, leaving her and Fen to their breathless inventory of the estate.

Siofra's daydreams were still occupied with the endless maze of gardens when Pesha gently nudged her up the broad stone steps. Her ankle throbbed, but it didn't deny her support. Pesha's healing had been thorough, and it had seemingly taken nothing from him to do it.

She snapped her eyes forward, landing them on two guardsmen with the same crest from the carriage—a lion of all things, which wasn't even a real creature—emblazoned on their armor. The younger one, with sandy-blond hair and ice-blue eyes, worked his mouth into a smile he landed on her. When she smiled back, he nodded once.

The other, the one with the scars etched upon his cheeks like a battle map, raised a hand toward Pesha, who returned the gesture.

"Euric," Pesha greeted. "Is my brother in the Hall of Counting?"

"He'll meet you in the dining hall." Euric looked past him, past Siofra and her brother. "And these two? Trunks? Satchels?"

"Nothing at all," Pesha answered with an almost apologetic glance downward. "Lotte will see to their needs, I assume."

"You assume?" An older woman, her hair greying into tight curls at her temples and framing a deeply lined forehead, brushed past Euric without so much as an excuse. "Ahh." She exhaled with her whole body, shuddering into a crooked smile. "Look at the two of you. You've been through your paces; that's for sure. Couldn't even have them bathed, Pesha?"

Pesha grimaced. Whoever the woman was, he deferred to her like a child to a mother. "They rinsed in the river. I couldn't very well launder their clothing when they had nothing to change into."

"You created more mud than you cleaned, I'm afraid." Lotte shivered, running her hands down her biceps with flair. "Well, no need to catch a chill out here. Come on, come on!" She shepherded them in with a jolt of her chin at Pesha.

Siofra was the first to follow. Fen rushed up beside her. When they were several steps inside, leaving the night behind, Siofra buried a yawn in her elbow. She cut it off midway as the monstrous central hall stretched before them. The doors closed with a weighted thud after Euric and the other guard entered, choosing a position close at their backs.

Shadowfen Hall, Pesha had called his home. She saw where it might have earned such a name. Everything was darkly furnished and upholstered, from the gleam of the near-black floorboards to the velvet divan in the center, to the tall timekeepers stretching toward the open second story. The elaborate chandelier was stuffed with more candles than Siofra had time to count. They blurred together, casting only a soft glow, enough to light the way but not to reveal what lurked in the shadows and corners.

Lotte continued on. She rounded to the right, past the two staircases that twined up into a darkened second floor. Siofra found herself squinting in an effort to see anything at all, but all she saw was the moon peeking through the window at the upper landing.

"My name is Amaralotte," Lotte explained as her skirts brushed the stone in her brusque pace. "But you may call me Lotte. I'm the head mistress of the Hall, which means not a thing happens under this roof that I'm not already aware of or responsible for. All attendants and grooms take my direction, follow my lead, and if they do both, they go on to enjoy very long, satisfying tenures inside the walls of the greatest estate south of Wulfsgate. That is to say, if either of you have needs, you need only to speak of them to anyone on my staff, and they will be met. And there is nothing here you cannot explore or enjoy, except the west wing." Her pace slowed some. "The west wing is off-limits."

Siofra tried to listen but kept tripping over herself as she trained her eyes out the windows lining the long hall. Beyond was the lake she'd seen on their approach. It was dark and haunting, like the manor itself. The moon played off a layer of ice, lighting its splinters and cracks.

"Ah!" Lotte came to a stop in a tall doorway and spun around. "Now then. Your names?"

Siofra and Stiofen exchanged stupefied looks.

Pesha came up from behind and placed a hand on each of their shoulders. "This is Siofra, and this is Stiofen. They've been through the paces, as you said. Perhaps taking them straight to their bedchambers is in order."

Lotte scrunched her mouth. "Have they eaten?"

Pesha squinted, thinking. "We stopped before sunset."

"Then they'll be wanting more, won't they?" She reached out and pinched one of Pesha's cheeks. "All skin and bones, always have been. Just because *you* don't like to eat doesn't mean they're not famished."

Pesha flushed with embarrassment. Siofra was amazed at the casual, easy way Pesha's staff had with him. If a Stanhope servant even made eye contact when not explicitly asked, they were sent away.

"Hmm." Lotte shook her head at him once more and then turned toward Siofra and her brother. "Are you then? Hungry? You must be."

"A little," Fen answered for them both. He'd never sounded so small. Gone was the piss and fire of Newcarrow, of the tense journey north. "But not if it requires you to go to any trouble for us."

"No trouble," she insisted, batting the air. "As it is, we've already prepared a little something for you. So come in, have a seat, and we'll have everything brought out."

"A little something" turned out to be a feast fit for royalty—a spread for ten men, not two underfed nearly nineteen-year-olds who gawped with glazed eyes as they considered where to begin.

As Siofra funneled to her plate everything from candied tubers to meats she didn't have names for, watching Fen gleefully feed himself with both hands, it occurred to her how strange and nice it was to sit at a table. To not fear for what might happen if she opened her mouth or made eye contact.

Throughout the meal, she was aware of being studied by everyone in the room. She and Fen were a curiosity, as much for their heritage as their history. She didn't think she could bear seeing it in their eyes, so she resisted the urge to look up.

But upon reaching for another roll from the basket, she accidentally swept her gaze over the young guard, Wulfhelm. She searched for judgment but saw only kindness. He again offered a crooked smile and lowered his eyes back to his folded hands before she could react.

Lotte barked orders at young men wearing dark satin uniforms dotted with gold buttons and flared ruffles pluming from their wrists. They rushed out new plates, refilled the goblets Siofra and Fen couldn't seem to stop emptying, and added even new delicacies to the already-stuffed trays.

Pesha didn't eat any of it. He sat at the end of the table, his hands laced in his lap. He glanced up occasionally at the twins but kept his eyes on the door as if expecting someone to walk through. He rolled his head against the chair with heavy eyes.

Mostly, he aimed his gaze out the window, in the direction of the lake.

A memory of him revealing his hair flashed into Siofra's thoughts.

Blue hair. His familiar is aquatic.

Pesha caught her watching him and whipped his gaze to a far door, just as someone walked in: a young woman, tall and lithe, wearing a fitted dress that matched the midnight blue and gold of Lotte and the other staff.

"Good evening. I'm Gisela." Her cheeks formed into soft apples when she smiled at Siofra. "I'll be your personal attendant at the Hall, Siofra. I'm here for anything you need."

Siofra dropped the bread she'd been picking apart and passed a look back and forth between the attendant and Fen. "Oh, I... I wouldn't know what to do with an attendant."

Gisela glanced at Pesha and then back at Siofra. "It's Master Trevanion's wish that all your needs are tended, whatever they may be. If you're finished with supper, I'm here to escort you to your bedchamber, where a warm bath, fresh linens, and a new nightgown will be waiting." Gisela turned her eyes toward Fen. "Stiofen, Lieken, your personal groom, will do the same for you. He'll be along shortly."

Siofra searched Fen's face for how to react, but he was just as stunned.

80

"None of this is necessary," he said, winded, his belly protruding from the race to fill it. "We appreciate it but have nothing to offer in return."

Siofra's attention darted to Pesha, to see if he'd noted the lie, but he was eyeing the table with a vacant stare.

Gisela folded her hands and nodded once. "I understand. But Master Trevanion would have it no other way."

"Where is Master Trevanion?" Siofra asked. She craned her neck toward the door Pesha kept checking.

"He's been waiting all week to meet you," Gisela replied, her voice low and buoyant, like a cloud. Siofra read nothing but warmth in the gentle blink of her brown eyes. "To meet you both."

"He's occupied then?" Pesha's question had a bite to it. His mouth pursed as he awaited Gisela to confirm something Siofra didn't understand.

Gisela framed her mouth in a tight line before responding. "Not as I understand it, Sir Pesha."

"Not presently, or not at all?"

Gisela's troubled look passed over the twins, the guard. "Your brother awaits you in the Hall of Counting."

"He called for me?"

"Not exactly." Gisela looked to the younger guard for help. "It was Wulfhelm who—"

"He ordered four," came Wulfhelm's abrupt answer.

Pesha grunted and pushed back from the table. He managed an uneasy grin for Siofra and Stiofen. "Gisela and Lieken will take it from here. Rest up, and you can meet my brother tomorrow."

Siofra's cheeks flushed with panic. "Wait! Pesha, I thought... If you're not here, then..." She choked on her remaining words.

Pesha nodded. "We need to fear only your anger, Siofra. Are you angry right now?"

She shook her head.

"Get some rest."

Pesha left. Wulfhelm followed, but Euric and the attendants remained.

Her earlier panic faded to something she hadn't experienced before, a tingle of restless anticipation. Pesha hadn't just tempered her magic. He'd been their connection to this brand-new world, their bridge from the last one. Although they hardly knew him, they'd had a few days to get used to him. Everyone standing before them, waiting to serve, was a stranger.

Gisela extended a hand from across the room. "Are you ready, Siofra?"

Siofra set her spoon aside. She looked at Stiofen. "What about my brother?"

"Lieken will be here soon."

"Fen's not coming with me?"

"To your bedchamber?"

"I..." How could Siofra explain that she'd never had the luxury of her own space? That she'd never slept more than a few feet away from someone else?

"It's all right," Fen said. It wasn't like him to be so calm in the face of such uncertainty. His gentle mood was as unfamiliar as everything else they'd encountered tonight. "I'll come find you."

We're both too exhausted to even tend our fears.

Siofra yawned into her sleeve and nodded. She pushed out her chair and went to greet whatever remained of her curious evening.

Gisela promised Siofra a full tour when she had a night's rest behind her. She led her back the way they'd come in and ascended the right staircase, which was so long and elaborate, she had to blink to make sure she wasn't imagining it. Though still wearing her filthy, ragged dress, Siofra held her head back and imagined what a princess might feel, all eyes drawn to her as she departed a fete in her honor.

Fen wouldn't approve of such thoughts, but Fen wasn't there. Days ago, he'd never have let her be taken away by a stranger, nor would she have gone, but the magic of the dark palace in the forest had gotten to them both.

"Just this way," Gisela said, leading her down one of several hallways. They passed room after room, and Siofra lost count after a dozen. She was grateful for the thick carpet covering the floorboards as her worn shoes slid over it.

At the end of the hall was a long window that seemed miles away. When they finally reached it, they took yet another turn, into what Siofra guessed was the east wing she'd seen from outside.

"You'll become acquainted in time. It helps that only part of the Hall is available for you to explore."

"Why only part?"

"The south wing is Master Trevanion's, and the west wing is closed." Gisela stopped and slipped a key into the lock of one of about a dozen doors in the wing. She stepped in and held the way open for Siofra as she beckoned her to step forward.

Siofra's hands flew to her mouth from the rich assault to her senses.

All around her, the room was accoutered in the soft spoils of someone of far better birth: white-bristled brushes and velvet chairs that slid up to dressing tables made of polished silver. A sumptuous full tester bed was arrayed with layers of silken veils colored in jewel tones. The mirrors, covering walls and hanging above tables, heightened the spell, which suddenly broke when she fixated on how she looked standing in the midst of the room's wonder.

A grime-covered orphan, dropped into one of the tales of her books, where she didn't belong.

She'd stepped onto a fur rug of some kind and was sinking into its plush escape. In a haste, she shimmied out of her filthy shoes to keep from spoiling something so luxurious, then spun as she kicked them away, trying in vain to take everything in.

Tears welled in her eyes, and as she turned, to be rid of the gloom settling into her belly, Gisela had her folded into her arms.

"Siofra," she said, her lips grazing her unwashed hair. "I don't know much about your life before this, but you wouldn't be here unless it was a life worth leaving behind. Let it go. It has no place here. Master Trevanion... Desemir... He's a good man. He wants you to have these things. Without guilt." Gisela pulled back and held Siofra out. "Understand?"

Siofra nodded. She rolled her lips inward as tears passed over and cascaded along her chin on their way down. "No one has ever..." She couldn't finish.

Gisela patted her cheeks. "No one had ever shown me kindness before either. I hope you'll find happiness here, as I have." She released Siofra and brushed past her, moving to one of the dressing tables. "Your nightgown is here. Linens are there." She gestured past the other table. "There are three dresses hanging in your bureau until we can bring the tailor to size you for more. Just beyond that door, you'll find a privy and a bath. Lotte had hot water sent up while you were eating. It's had enough time to cool, so it should be just right."

Siofra eyed the door with bewildered gratitude. How long had it been since she'd had a proper bath? With warm water, and not the remnants of what the stewardess had left after her own indulgent bathing?

The thought of sleeping in the beautiful bed afterward was unimaginable. No bath could cleanse the crimes staining her soul.

"Thank you," she managed to say. Her voice choked. "I..."

"Your brother will be just down the hall. But don't fuss yourself over that tonight."

Siofra nodded, tugged between Gisela's words and her new reality.

"I'll take my leave then," Gisela said, backing away. "Should you require anything..." She pointed at a taut string to the left of the door. "Tug on this. It rings down in the servants' quarter. Your wire is rigged to make a trill unique to this room. We'll know it's you and come right away."

Gisela might as well be describing foreign magic, Siofra thought. "I won't need anything, Gisela. How could I..." Her eyes wandered again. "Thank you."

"Good night, Siofra. Tomorrow is a new day."

Siofra had fallen asleep in the bath. Her long clean hair dripped onto the stone floor, setting a soft rhythm that kept her gently tethered to her dreams, which were, for once, welcome.

Her dreams were not far from reality, replaying the wonders of the day, marveling at what it had been like to actually *speak* with people without being blindfolded or gagged, to not be a constant source of fear for everyone around her with no consideration for her own. No one had acted the least bit afraid of her, though they must know she had the power to kill every person in Shadowfen Hall.

The water was cold when the door to her outer chamber closed, startling her back to her senses. Her heart leaped, thrumming with a flash of fear as steps sounded beyond the privy door. She drew her knees to her chest in a weak attempt to cover herself.

The steps stopped just outside. The person knocked.

"Siofra?"

She didn't recognize the deep, melodic voice from her earlier introductions.

"Yes?"

"It's Desemir." The man went quiet. "I came to offer an apology for not joining you at supper. If you're indisposed, I can meet you at morning meal instead."

"No," Siofra said in a rush. Water sloshed all over the stone as she scrambled to exit the bath, then tripped over the lip of the basin as she dove for a linen to wrap around herself. "No, I'm coming out."

"Are you all right in there?"

"Perfectly. I only need a moment."

"I don't want to trouble you. You've had a long journey."

Was he serious? The man who had saved her life, had dropped her into one of the stories that only existed in her imagination, didn't want to trouble *her*?

"No, please stay. I'll be right out."

She heard him move away from the door.

Siofra quickly whipped the linen over her clean skin and then shrugged the nightgown down, tugging it over her sticky, damp flesh. It was a perfect fit, though inappropriate for meeting the master of Shadowfen Hall.

A handful of robes hung from a corner rack, so she snagged one and shoved her arms inside in clumsy jabs as her heart raced at the thought of keeping Master Trevanion waiting.

Siofra pulled her tangled wet hair out of the back of the robe. She knew she must look a fright, but there wasn't time to fix it, nor anything nearby up to the task.

With a resigned sigh, Siofra wrapped the robe tight and opened the door.

Master Trevanion stood on the other side of the room, his back toward her, arms linked behind him. He wore dark satin and velvet, like his staff, but the gold woven through his raiment was considerably more pronounced. It traveled around his arms in curlicued patterns and up into his collar, which covered the back of his neck, rising to tickle his ears. His dark hair turned to soft curls at his temples and nape, settling in every direction but smoothed down, evidence of a day long spent.

An empty sword belt hung off his hips.

It's Desemir, he'd said, as if they were already on such familiar terms.

Desemir turned, wearing the start of a grin, his face a series of angular lines on soft, tanned flesh. His mouth formed the deep swoops of a bird in flight as his smile widened. Mossy-green eyes, beset by a hint of lines at the corners, turned upward.

"Siofra." His sigh was weighted with relief. "You're here."

"I'm here," she said. Her hands clung tight to the robe, clasping it at her neck.

Desemir's unassuming but intentional gaze swept over her, lingering just long enough to preserve the appropriateness of their unchaperoned encounter.

86

Siofra forced her eyes toward the fur carpet before he realized she'd been staring.

"You seem afraid," Desemir said. "I understand why you might be, but I want you to feel safe here." His hand traveled to his neck, where an onyx pendant draped between the gaps of his tunic.

"I'm not afraid," Siofra said truthfully. Something in his eyes, in the glossy, fixed way he studied her, made her think he'd know a lie. "I just don't know why I'm here."

"You'll be safe here," he said again. He leaned against one of her dressing tables, his hands curled around the edge. She spotted the same mythical lion on his ring, blazing in gold relief, from the carriage crest. "I understand you like books."

"What?"

"Pesha told me." He flexed his fingers against the edge of the table. "Shadowfen Hall has an impressive library. I'd be happy to walk you there tomorrow."

"I do like to read..." Siofra said, her voice so quiet she almost repeated the words.

Desemir's shoulders lifted and fell. "Consider the library, and everything else at Shadowfen Hall, entirely at your disposal. Nothing inside is off-limits—except the west wing, as I'm certain others have already explained."

Siofra shifted, kneading the fur rug with her bare feet. "No one does this much for someone without expecting something in return."

Desemir nodded. He broke his gaze from her, fixing it off to the side. "I do have an offer for you, Siofra. Your acceptance of it won't preclude me from aiding you and your brother, who both deserve more than this kingdom has given you. But I hope you'll see the opportunity in it, see what it could do for us both."

Siofra wrapped her arms tighter. "What offer?"

"It's late." Desemir pushed himself off the table. His hand scratched across his neck as he approached. "And you need rest. We'll speak more of it after morning meal." He came to a stop several inches from her. She was able to see the hint of dark

87

crescents under his eyes and two white hairs playing at his temples. His mossy eyes turned emerald, then amber, and she nearly lost herself in them... in the heady fog of his breath, tinged with the barest hint of liquor. The aquiline curve of his lips, when he started to speak, made her belly weak.

Desemir Trevanion was the most handsome man she had ever laid eyes on, and *that* terrified her far more than anything else he might offer.

He reached forward and nudged a tangled mat of hair off her face. "Pleasant dreams, Siofra."

As his flesh passed atop hers, Siofra's breath hitched. She held it still, her throat constricting with the force of her violent, erratic heartbeat as he appraised her once more before he nodded and turned to leave.

She waited for the sound of his fading steps before exhaling into both hands.

EIGHT
DESEMIR'S OFFER

Siofra spread her hands along the long table in the Hall of Counting, mesmerized by the depth of color in the endlessness of the wood's swirls. She'd never seen wood so dark, its onyx hue holding the deception of depth. But in the light—the subtle sway of the chandelier as the house shifted with activity, responding to the force of men moving in the hall beyond—she could swear it was violet. And then gold. Violet again. As if crafted from magic.

But if that were true, then most of the furnishings she'd seen in Shadowfen Hall were crafted from the same magic. It seemed unlikely, though no less so than a dashing hero whisking them away to a charmed life.

"Ebony wood," Pesha explained.

Siofra's hand recoiled in shock at his voice. He'd been so quietly holding court in the shadows that she'd forgotten he was there.

"Not a very original name," Fen said. He tried to sound personable, but she read the tension in his shoulders, the way he fought the clench in his jaw.

"As is true of most things named in this kingdom." Humor tickled the corners of Pesha's mouth. "We know they didn't learn it from us." He returned his attention to his hands.

Siofra found them curious, the subtle ways Pesha reminded her and Fen that they were alike, but he never invited further discourse. After his admission in the carriage, he'd called himself a Medvedev only once more, so Fen could hear it directly. When he was in a more talkative mood, Pesha sometimes explained the world beyond their small window. Nothing more about who he was. Why or when his mother and father had left the safety of the Clahnn Asgill lands, nor how they'd ended up in the Northerlands.

Siofra couldn't help marveling once more at how she was allowed to speak without restraints. She didn't know if it made her new benefactors trusting or foolish.

The doors sighed when they cracked open. Desemir entered, Wulfhelm and Euric holding a respectful distance at his back. When their master sank onto the tall, ornate chair at the head of the table, Wulfhelm stayed inside and Euric moved to the hall. They closed the doors in unison.

Desemir leaned against the velvet pillow stitched at the perfect height for his head. He spun the lion's head ring around his finger, switching his gaze between Siofra and Fen. When his juniper-colored eyes landed on her again, she resisted a stinging urge to lower her own.

"Are you both well rested?"

"Yes," Fen said quickly. "Thank you." He leaned forward, tossing a glance at Siofra before returning his gaze to Desemir. Siofra recognized the look in his eyes. He was being polite, but it wasn't the same as being friendly. "No one has ever shown us such kindness. I fear we've done nothing to deserve it though. And you must know we have no means of repaying the favor."

"It's not kindness if a gift demands repayment," Desemir said coolly. His eyes, amber in the sunlight reflecting through the window at the far end of the room, settled on Siofra. "And you, Siofra? Was the bed to your liking?"

"The bed?" Siofra swallowed. Nodded. "Yes..." Her voice failed her. "Yes, thank you. Sir."

Desemir coiled back. "It's bad enough I have to hear it from my staff, who are like family to me. Call me Des or Desemir."

"Desemir," she whispered. She felt Fen judge her from across the table. "Everything has been wonderful. But it's as Fen said. We're confused why you would bring us all the way up here. Why you would help us at all." She chewed the inside of her mouth. "You told me last night you had an offer for us."

"You met him last night? When?" Fen asked. She sensed him strain forward over the table, but she kept her attention on Desemir.

Desemir's neck stretched taut as he tilted his head to the back and then to both sides. A bead of sweat lingered at his temple, threatening to break away. "Would you not like to eat first?"

"We had breakfast sent up for them before they came down," Pesha called from his chair, hidden in the shadowed corner. "But perhaps you and I should speak first? Des?"

Pesha buried his surprise in a casual tone, but Siofra had spent her life listening in lieu of speaking, and she read the situation clearly.

Whatever Desemir was about to say, he hadn't shared it with his brother first.

Desemir raised a hand. His gaze burned into the dark wood. "Siofra, Stiofen." With a hard blink, he looked up. "Would it be fair to say that you have lived in fear your entire lives?"

Siofra didn't know how to answer. Fen, his expression uneasy, didn't either.

"Des?" Pesha asked. "Have you even slept?"

"No," Desemir answered without looking back at him. He twisted the ring around and around. "Everything I know about the Medvedev, I learned from my brother. And within this limited knowledge is a truth bigger than any of it: no one belongs in a cage."

Siofra lowered her eyes to her lap. Her heart thrummed faster, toward whatever terrible place Desemir was leading them. She

91

was unwittingly transported to the past, when the Stanhopes had made their ambitious offer. They'd showered the twins with sumptuous meals and bespoke clothes, promising that it could be their life, always, and all for such a small price as Fen's help. *It will be nothing. A little here and there. You will live as a prince and princess. We'll enjoy what Fen builds, together.*

All lies start like this, or no one would believe them, Siofra thought. There were no laws to protect orphans from ruthless opportunists. No contracts signed to protect their interests. Choices were always simple when she only had one.

"Pesha is no doubt reading my whispers right now, anxious to get ahead of the words I didn't tell him I planned to say." Desemir slumped against his chair. He turned an appraising look on Siofra. "So I'll say what I need to, and you'll decide whether what I offer you is worth your time or not."

Siofra studied Desemir's strange eyes. They were green again, flecked with comets of gold. She sank into them, into the depths where whispers lived, where secrets rotted him from the inside out. She witnessed darkness creeping around his heart like invasive vines, sliding into his throat to choke him.

She lowered her gaze.

"Pesha has told me how bad things were for you in Newcarrow. You've never had anyone looking out for you, and have suffered greatly for this. Fair to say?"

Siofra and Fen both nodded.

"You need protection." Desemir paused when the wooden timekeeper in the corner trilled the arrival of a new tick of the sun. "I have a need that cannot be met by anyone I presently know."

Fen flopped back, shaking his head. "So you *do* need me." He rolled his eyes. "Of course."

"I already have more gold than I could ever spend, Stiofen. Anything you could offer me would rouse my enemies more, not less." Desemir kept his attention on Siofra as he spoke. She absorbed the intensity of his inspection, even with her own gaze focused on her lap. "It's been only Pesha and me here for several years now. We're the only Trevanions left in Darkwood Run. My parents and grandparents are gone. My aunts died when I was a child, and left no heirs of their own. And though I would give every last board and nail of this cursed place to Pesha if I could, everyone knows he's a bastard by birth, and that would call attention to him that would eventually expose him to the monsters roaming this realm. All I can offer him is a generous trust and a lifetime of anything he could ever need or want."

Pesha sighed and shook his head. "It's more than enough. You know that."

"It'll never be as much as you deserve," Desemir countered. He returned his focus to Siofra. "You should know my life is overrun with adversaries, men who would take what they lost in fair trade, who threaten me and my life for having what they want." Desemir folded his hands and bowed over them. "I rarely leave Shadowfen Hall anymore because it requires a full guard to protect me from assassins lying in wait, from arrows sailing in from the Darkwood. *My* Darkwood. I don't expect it will ever change."

Fen tried to catch Siofra's attention over the table. She lifted her shoulders in a light shrug without looking up.

Desemir unlatched his hands, holding out his palms, which she caught from the corner of her eye. "But as long as I remain without an heir, men will continue to think themselves clever and search for ways to pick me off and take the leavings built by my forebears. I need sons, and to have sons, I first need a wife."

Stiffness settled over Siofra's chest. Fen's eyes stung her from across the table with unasked questions.

"My offer, Siofra, is that in exchange for marrying me, for bearing me children, you will be safe here as long as—"

"Marry you!" Fen leaped up, toppling his chair.

Pesha was behind him in an instant. His eyes fluttered closed as he passed a hand across the back of Fen's neck. Fen cooled, reclaiming his seat, the flush in his cheeks already subsiding. The only lingering sign of his brief outburst was the crazed look in his eyes.

"Let him finish," Pesha ordered, though he trained his darkened expression on Desemir.

Siofra, stunned, stared at the three men.

Desemir's chest rose with a deep, stabilizing breath. "In exchange, you will have everything you could ever want. Anything in this house, the grounds. I will import you the finest lace from the Westerlands, spices from the Easterlands. Any food or item you desire, from any place in the kingdom, it's yours. Your familiars will have free roam within our borders, protected from the bows of hunters. You'll have your freedom, and you can even take lovers. What I'm saying, Siofra, is you'll live as free as any man, and with the wealth of a lord. Stiofen too. I'll gift him part of my own land, a title. He'll have a life ahead of him of his own choosing. Free of fear. Never again to be placed in a cage."

Fen started forward again, and Pesha sent another easing palm over his neck. He hovered behind him, hands planted on Fen's shoulders, waiting for the next opportunity.

Siofra gripped the seat of her chair, dragging her nails against the hard wood to quell the anxious rumblings in her chest.

"All I ask is for you to come to my bed with reasonable frequency. I will never hurt you, will never do anything to make you uncomfortable. Fidelity won't be a requirement of our union, though I will ask you to be judicious with your choices when we are actively trying to conceive. I don't ask for love, nor do I offer it in return. We will be merely filling a need. A duty." Desemir lifted his brows with a soft laugh. "Though, no one could fault us for enjoying this duty more than others."

Fen squirmed in his seat, but Pesha was quicker.

Siofra couldn't look at her brother.

Nor the Trevanions.

Nor even the youthful guard, Wulfhelm, who had been watching her the entire time with kindness in his eyes.

It wasn't that Siofra was embarrassed or affronted. She wasn't even scandalized with the easy way this man—this older, beautiful, darkly charming man—so casually spoke of his bedchamber activities and her prospective role in them. When matched against the terrible things that had been said to Siofra Thornheart over the almost nineteen years of her life, *this* was merely surprising.

A bride.

A *wife*.

Siofra had never envisioned herself as a wife; it was never a life available to someone like her. She was either a burden or a tool, and neither role left a place for her needs or wants.

The true reason Siofra couldn't meet the eyes of any man in the room is that, though she would demure—pretend to think it over, show a reasonable amount of consideration—she had already made up her mind.

It wasn't only her chance at happiness, however unconventional.

It was the life Desemir was offering Fen.

He would be free. And he would enjoy his freedom in the knowledge she was safe.

Siofra caught the barely subdued rage in Pesha's eyes as she swung her head upward. His tight mouth trembled, veins throbbing at his temples.

"If you decide this offer is not to your liking," Desemir said. "I will still see that your needs are met. I've already sent word to Newcarrow that the two of you are property of the Sepulchre now, sealing it with a pilfered stamp of their crest, so that puts to bed the matter of the Stanhopes. I'll still offer you a small plot here on the Trevanion acreage, where you can live comfortably for the rest of your lives and, more importantly, protected from others. If you'd rather leave here, I'll send you with enough gold for you to make your own way in the kingdom, and with luck, you'll find a place safe enough to make a different life for yourselves. Then again, perhaps not. Pesha can tell you what happens to displaced Medvedev in this kingdom. We've heard worse stories than the ones you bring with you." Desemir set his jaw. "I don't say it like that to make you feel threatened. I say it because I know the only place in this whole realm Pesha is safe is here, with me. *This* is what I'm offering you, Siofra. Safety. Safety for you and Stiofen. And anything your heart could ever desire. I do not think what I ask for in reciprocation is so terrible, in comparison."

"I see." Siofra said the words to show she'd heard. It wasn't what she wanted to say. She withheld her acceptance for appearances only—mostly for Fen, who would need the most convincing.

Desemir nodded at his hands. "I've said what I came to say." He pushed back from the table. It seemed he was going out of his way to avoid Pesha's eyes. "Take your time, Siofra. Think on it. Speak to your brother, though I can guess his thoughts well enough. I know what it is to want to protect your sibling, Stiofen." He flashed Fen a lopsided grin. "Enjoy the grounds. Both of you. Nothing can harm you here."

Desemir turned and left. Pesha released Fen and marched out after him.

Fen launched himself backward, stumbling across the carpet as he ran around the table to her side. "We need to go. *Now.*"

Siofra shook her head. She adjusted her eyes toward the doors, still open.

"Why are you shaking your head?"

"I need to think." She reached back, grasping for Fen's hand until she found it. She gave it a quick squeeze and release. "Alone."

"Are you going to tell me what *that* was?" Pesha hurled his words from the hall before chasing Des into the library. He tried to slam the doors behind him, but the heft created an awkward resistance, and it was more of an anticlimactic *whoosh.*

"Not now, Pesh." Desemir rubbed his head with one hand. The other flexed in pulses at his side.

"Not now?" Pesha stepped forward. His shoulders clenched as he held back an anger he hadn't felt—at least not about Desemir—since right after their father died. "You *sent* me down to Newcarrow under a false pretense. You *knew* if you had told me the truth—"

"That you wouldn't go?" Des's hand flopped back to his side. He slumped over the back of a nearby chaise. "That's exactly why I didn't tell you."

Pesha's nose flared with his labored breaths. "You *lied* to me."

"I told you I wanted to help them. It wasn't a lie." Desemir spun around and leaned back on his hands. "I know you can't see it now, but this *is* helping them."

"You cannot marry her!"

"Why?" Des shrugged. "Because she's younger than me? She's three years older than my mother was when she married. The same age as yours when she was invited to Father's bed."

"You know it's not about that." Pesha ground his jaw. Was Desemir really going to make him say it?

"I'm not forcing her to do anything, Pesh. People have been taking her choices from her all her life. I'm giving her one she can decline and still come out ahead."

Pesha snorted. He raked a hand down his face, sighing. "How could she ever refuse such an offer?"

"She might," Des said, maddeningly calm. "She still gains if she turns down my proposal."

Pesha wanted to release a scream. One seared the back of his throat, coating his tongue. He exhaled instead. "You planned this."

Desemir's face erupted with shock. "You think I orchestrated the madness in Newcarrow? And then exploited it for my own gain?"

Pesha shook his head, pressing his mouth so tight, his lips disappeared. "Dammit, Des. You *know* that's not what I mean. For months, you've been after me about finding you a wife, and I've been *searching*—"

"In the wrong places," Desemir stated. His head fell to the side as he watched Pesha with a cool look, which only stoked Pesha's fury. "You keep saying I need to settle down. Have a family. You judge me for bringing different women to my bed—"

"No," Pesha replied, shaking his head. "No, I don't *judge* you, Des. I worry for you. It's different."

"You know I cannot marry anyone here. Every bride they would send me would come with a yoke around my neck, courtesy of her father. You think it's hard fighting the other stewards off now? How much harder would it be if they were tied to us through marriage? If we had a spy under our very roof." Desemir threw out his hands, gesturing around. "I'm surrounded on all sides by enemies, and still you think casting a net in our backyard is the right place for this?"

Pesha spun away. Desemir was right, but it didn't justify what he'd done. "You should have asked me to make inquiries beyond Darkwood Run years ago. I can't read your mind."

Des snickered behind him. "Can't you?"

Pesha straightened, crossing his arms as he shook his head. "You know I would never do that. Not without your permission."

"And you know," Des said, "I would never make a choice like this lightly."

Pesha turned back around. He buried his gaze in the floor. "You can't..." He swallowed. "You can't fault me for my concern."

Desemir twisted his lips and pushed off the chaise. "This is not that, Pesh."

"What if it is?"

"It's *not*." Desemir approached Pesha. "We're both older now. We can make things right."

"Make things right?" Pesha paled. "Do you hear yourself?"

"We weren't the ones in control before. We are now."

Pesha groaned. "That changes nothing."

"It changes everything. Father is gone. I'm not him. Neither are you." He reached forward and clasped his hands on Pesha's arms. "I can help Siofra and her brother *and* solve a problem that's been plaguing this house for years. She has no family. No one knows her here. There will be no politics in this marriage bed, no feuds. In your heart, Pesh, you know this is good for her and

98

good for us." He squeezed, lowering his head to try to urge Pesha to look up. "I'm sorry for not telling you. I am."

"Curses, Des," Pesha whispered. His anger had already begun to fade. *He* needed to be mad at Desemir because no one else ever would. There wasn't anyone left to temper his fickle moods and wayward choices.

But it was also clear Desemir believed what he was saying. And Pesha's love for his brother was greater than the sum of his concerns over what, he was certain, would prove to be an ill-fated decision.

"If she says no?" Pesha asked.

Des backed off with a quick shrug. "I'll keep my word. I'll take care of them both."

Pesha whistled as he breathed out. "And if she says *yes?*"

Des cast his eyes to the side, running a corner of his mouth under his teeth. "Well. If the Guardians still smile on our ancestors, I'll soon have a son, and it will not be quite so easy for our enemies to dispose of House Trevanion."

Siofra sat on the edge of her bed, waiting for Fen to finish. She studied his frenetic pacing, his hands raking through his hair, eyes bulging as he emphasized the right words, paused in all the right places. He was so predictable, she could have made his speech for him. She correctly anticipated when he would rise, when he would come back down.

"I appreciate your concerns," Siofra said, forcing a calm to coat the edge in her voice. She smoothed her hands along her dress. "They are noted."

Fen's head jerked as he sputtered, "Noted? My concerns are *noted?*"

"You're cross with me," she said. She counted the tiny, delicate flowers stitched into the satin of her sapphire dress. "And—"

"I'm not cross with you," Fen snapped. He slammed his mouth closed and inhaled through his nose. "Si. If I *sound* cross, you know it's not with you. I'm just... I'm just so tired of men coming into our life with promises we know they have no intention of keeping."

"You say that as if it's happened a dozen times," Siofra replied. "When it was only the Stanhopes who betrayed us so."

"You really don't remember the other patrons who took us in, promising Mother and Father work only to kick them out again, knowing we'd starve?"

"I remember." Siofra picked at one of the flowers, letting the thread push up under her nails. She snagged one of them, creating an unseemly loop. "I also remember their fear when they learned what Mother and Father could do, what it might bring upon their doorstep if others knew we were there. Either way you look at it, they were either knowingly helping magic doers or they were allied with Medvedev, which might be a worse crime in the eyes of a kingdom that has *never* understood we're not all that different from men. Can you blame them?"

Fen laughed. He folded his hand around a bedpost. "Oh yes, I *can*. For what kind of monster would turn out a family with children?"

"A kinder one than the monster who would take them in and exploit them," Siofra said softly.

Fen dropped his hand and turned away, resuming his pacing. "Yeah, well, that's over now, isn't it? Even if we wanted to go back..."

Siofra tugged harder on the dislodged thread, making the damage worse. "Say what you meant. Even if we wanted to go back, I killed their son, right?" She recognized the warning tickle, the first sign the red wall was rising. If she let her mind go where Fen was unintentionally leading—if she acknowledged the horror of what she'd done—she would lose control again, and it would be innocent people caught in the wake. People who had so far only been kind to her.

"Si... That wasn't your fault."

100

She heard caution in his voice, the gentle coaxing that had become second nature to him in order to temper what she couldn't control.

With a strained smile, she raised her head. "I didn't tell you what happened that night in the carriage when you went for wood."

Fen stiffened.

"Pesha asked me... He asked me to hurt him. To give myself over to the red wall and..." Siofra pressed her hand to the mangled embroidery. "He *stopped* it. He stopped it cold, Fen. Not like with you, where you can only ease it." She looked up. "How many times have you said I need someone to train me?"

Fen shook his head with a scoff. "He's an outcast, same as us, Si. He's never even been to our homeland. What makes you think he knows any more than we do?"

"His mother trained him. *Taught* him. She didn't force him to pretend he wasn't who he was, to squash any hint of magic. He may not know our homeland, but he knows himself. He knows his magic." She paused. "He knows mine."

Fen's light twitch revealed his surprise. He glanced her way without looking at her. "That doesn't make this situation safe for you. It doesn't mean... you have to *marry* his brother in exchange for Pesha's help."

"He can't help me if I'm not here. He'll never leave his brother, nor would I ever expect him to."

"You understand Pesha's protectiveness but not mine?"

"When have I ever said I didn't understand yours, Stiofen?"

Fen recoiled at her use of his full name. "You actually don't understand it, Siofra. You never could."

Ahh, but I do, Fen. All those nights I pretended to sleep while you could not, how I watched you retreat into your troubled thoughts when you thought I couldn't see it. You've convinced yourself you need no greater purpose than to keep me safe from the world. That if you can accomplish such a task, you will have lived a full life. We both know one day you'll wake up and realize you've given your entire life away without ever having lived.

But Siofra could say none of it.

Fen would do everything in his power to stop her if he thought she was making the choice because of him.

Then again, if he knew she was also doing it for herself... for the promise of something to look forward to, at the side of a man who offered more than she could ever offer in return?

He'd think she'd lost her mind.

And maybe she had.

A week ago, she'd resolved to surrender herself to a future as the mistress of the repellant Gawain in order to broker a better future for her brother—to shatter herself in order to make Fen whole.

Today, she had received another offer. A decidedly more enticing one that taunted her courage but also lifted her confidence. An offer that was *hers* to refuse or accept.

Even if it was completely mad.

"Is it the dresses? The food?" Fen's voice was searching.

Siofra stifled a laugh. "You think I'm so easily wooed by such things?"

"I don't know!" Fen threw up his hands. "I can't fathom it, how you've so quickly decided this is the best choice for you. If nothing else is kindling a warning in you, then consider the man's own words. Desemir said he needs an heir because he's beset by *enemies.* How does this make you safe, Si?"

"Perhaps you're right," Siofra said. Then she lied to him. "You've given me a lot to think about. I won't decide until I've had time to consider all of it."

Fen wilted with relief. "That's all I ask," he said, and she knew it, too, was a lie.

"Then let me rest a bit. The past days have started to catch up to me, and I need to clear my thoughts."

NINE

THE TERRACE

Siofra successfully escaped into her thoughts for the remainder of the afternoon. She continued through supper, as she half listened to Desemir carry on about some extortionate demand one of his rivals had made. She observed Pesha's patient nods, his responses breaking through practiced smiles at the appropriate times with the appropriate words. It wasn't unlike the way she communicated with Fen when he was on a tear about something.

Desemir's eyes flitted toward Siofra as he spoke. He'd spin his ring with the opposite hand, regarding her with curious peripheral skims, as if he wanted to say something to her but didn't dare.

She understood, because she herself was bursting with things to say.

Silence was safer.

Fen buried his attention in his meal. He hardly looked up. Even when Pesha tried to engage him with questions, Fen returned single-word answers.

When the meal ended, Gisela escorted Siofra back to her chambers. Halfway through the long walk to the east wing, she broached the subject of Desemir's offer.

"I can imagine what you might be thinking," Gisela ventured aloud, her eyes forward. "Wondering why he chose you. Why he sent for you from across the kingdom when he could have had his pick of wives in Darkwood Run."

Siofra was too shocked at Gisela's directness to do more than say, "Yes."

Gisela nodded to herself. "He's a peculiar man, Desemir—a better one than he wants others to believe he is. I can't tell you why he chose you, Siofra, but if I thought he had any intentions beyond what he shared with you, I would say so."

Siofra laughed under her breath. "And go against your master?"

"He isn't like that," Gisela replied. "The only person in Shadowfen Hall who Desemir is hard on is himself."

"You think highly of him."

They rounded the corner into the east wing.

"Are you..."

It took Gisela a moment to catch Siofra's meaning. "A *mistress* of his? Guardians, no! He doesn't... That is, he keeps that part of his life separate from all of us."

"Ahh."

"He..." Gisela seemed to contemplate whether to go on. "He rescued me from an unfortunate situation. I was thirteen when I was orphaned and couldn't support myself. My only living relative, an aunt, sold me instead of helping me... and Desemir bought me. He bought me to free me. Promised me I would be safe here, and I was. I am."

"Wow," Siofra whispered. "And are you free? Could you leave at any time?"

"I could if I wanted, but I don't want to. Des is family now. Pesha is family. Lotte. All of them. They're my people, Siofra, and I wouldn't want it any other way."

"Did he make this same offer to you? Of marriage?"

"No," Gisela said. "Nor did he make it to any of the others here, as far as I know."

"I need to speak with him," Siofra said when they reached her door. Even the thought of being alone with him again made her breaths quicken, but it was the only way to say what she needed to say. "Alone."

Gisela nodded. "Shall I tell him to come to your chambers?"

Siofra considered the question. It was bad enough he'd come to her the night before, but a second time? As Lotte had informed them last night, nothing happened at Shadowfen Hall that she didn't know about, which probably included Desemir's midnight visit. The last thing Siofra wanted was for others to think she was inviting anything untoward.

You're seriously contemplating marrying this man, and you're afraid they'll think you're letting him into your bedchamber?

Siofra cleared her thoughts. "Is there somewhere we could speak privately but not so..."

Gisela lowered her chin with a laugh. "I understand. The terrace, perhaps. It's a fair evening, and the skies are clear. Private enough for a conversation, but not so private it should stir whispers."

"The terrace then," Siofra said, nodding. "An hour?"

Gisela's head twitched into a light bow. "I'll tell him."

Desemir braced against the stone railing, surrendering himself to the endless view of the Great Darkwood. At night the trees blended together, forming a jagged border that went on forever, separating Shadowfen Hall from the rest of the kingdom. The moon lingered overhead, a crescent sliver reflecting off the still lake. Gusts brought the soft, peppery aroma of pine to the terrace. He inhaled, settling the steadying scent into his chest.

All of it was his to protect and keep safe, a legacy hundreds of years deep. He'd inherited it at the height of their prestige, and he would not be the Trevanion who sent the family backward.

But ah, he was exhausted. Always on the offense. Always deflecting a threat before it rose high enough to coil and strike. For every worry he vanquished, two more cropped up.

Earlier that afternoon, Steward Arranden had invited him to a council meeting. Arranden didn't *have* council meetings. It was an invitation to an ambush. Desemir wrote back indicating he was indisposed, but the invite would come again. The problem wasn't going to go away.

Desemir tilted his head back, eyes glazing as he counted the stars. Some said they were the physical manifestation of the Guardians, but there were thousands of lights in the sky and only six Guardians. He didn't believe in deities anyway. Trouble sorted itself according to luck and perseverance, not divine intervention.

"Desemir?"

He returned to himself at the sound of her small voice. Small, but not scared. It would be easy to read Siofra's wide eyes and dulcet tone as meek, but it would be a mistake. Desemir had been reading people his whole life, and the young woman he'd invited into his yesterday held an entire world inside of her.

"Siofra." He watched her step gingerly onto the marbled stone of the terrace. She lifted her skirts in awkward bunches, like a woman who had never been dressed properly. He would change that, if she let him.

"Thank you for meeting me here," she said. She settled against the balcony, leaving a respectable distance between him and herself. Her golden hair fell in long waves down one side of her dress, the snarls sparkling against the pale light of the moon.

But that, like her docility, was a lie. Magic kept her curls golden. Dimmed the violet shine of her eyes, which disguised something even more forbidden.

"I understand why you wouldn't want another meeting like the one last night." Desemir dragged his palm across his mouth. "Looking back, it was a poor choice coming to your chambers alone. Stay here long enough, you'll see me make my share of them."

106

Siofra lowered her eyes with a polite laugh. "Your brother says you have an uncanny sense when it comes to others. A sort of magic that isn't quite magic."

Desemir lifted his brows in surprise. "I wouldn't have guessed Pesha thought very highly of this particular skill of mine."

Her head tilted. "Why's that?"

"I don't know," Desemir said with a light shrug. He followed her gaze to the sky, where two falcons stretched their wings. "I suppose because he spends so much of his time lecturing me on my tactics."

"His opinion matters to you."

Desemir screwed his mouth into a quick frown. "He's my brother."

"Half brother. Right?"

"No difference to me," Desemir countered. "Blood is blood."

Siofra crossed her arms and looked off into the forest, determined. "I came to tell you I accept your offer." She shook her head when the wind pushed her hair into her eyes. "And your conditions. But I have one of my own."

Desemir's chest tingled with the quick rise in his pulse. "All right."

"We do this early in the morning, before my brother wakes. Tomorrow. The next day. However quickly you can make it happen." Siofra turned her eyes on him. "He's completely against this, as I imagine your brother is. I need to do this on my own. Once it's over and behind us, he can rail about it until he's red in the cheeks, but it will be done."

Desemir inhaled the cool night air, nodding slowly as seconds passed. "I didn't have my heart set on a large wedding anyway." With a playful grin, he added, "Too many chances for those whoresons to try to take me out. Not going to make it any easier for them."

Siofra nibbled the corner of her bottom lip as she laughed. "Is it really as bad as you say it is?"

Desemir's smile faded. "Not so bad that I want you to count it among your worries, Siofra." When the last syllable of her name left his tongue, he realized it was a name he would say for the rest of his life. The woman who would stand at his side, bear his children. There'd be no romantic love between them, but friendship, perhaps, if they were fortunate. He'd never needed it from his conquests, but that was not what she was. She would be something he'd not yet defined.

Siofra unlaced her arms with a sigh. "That's all I wanted to say. You'll tell me when?"

Desemir held out his hands. "Why not tomorrow? No reason to drag this out. I'll send for our minister tonight. We have an abbey on the grounds." He frowned when the next thought came to him. "We can do a second ceremony, according to your customs, if you want."

Siofra shook her head and pushed off from the balcony with a light saunter. "I wouldn't know a thing about Medvedev customs. Tomorrow it is then." She tossed a smile over her shoulder as she approached the door. "Good night, Desemir."

TEN
ME AND THEE

A brisk breeze billowed through the gossamer curtains, inviting a light but not unwelcome chill into Siofra's room. If she hadn't already been awake, it might have stirred her to curl up for a bit more rest. But she *was* awake, had been for a while, so instead it stirred her to rise for what she must do.

No. What she *wanted* to do.

She'd slept in irregular pockets of time, each an all-too-brief reprieve from the dark downward spiral her thoughts had traveled. Was she making the right choice? And for the right reasons? Would she come to regret it, which Fen and Pesha both seemed convinced was inevitable? Was she an absolute fool for thinking she could choose *anything* for herself, when she'd relied on the wisdom of others her whole life?

The answers didn't matter. She'd chosen her way forward. There was nothing to do but embrace it.

Someone slipped into her chambers without knocking. In a panic, she crushed the edges of the blanket in her fist and scrambled back against the headboard.

But it was only Gisela.

Siofra eased as Gisela swept in and marched straight to the curtains to draw them, inviting more of the sunrise into the room. Aio made a passing swoop and then disappeared again.

"It's time then," Siofra said. She flexed her legs under the blankets, stirring them to life.

Desemir had made everything come together in a few short hours, just as he'd said he would. Siofra didn't know why it should surprise her. She knew little about the man she was about to marry, but he wore his fierce determination like a veil of pride.

Gisela buzzed with excitement. "I brought you a dress." She stepped into a band of light. "It was Desemir's mother's. She was a touch taller than you, but I expect it will still fit. Unless you want to wear something else?"

Siofra blinked away the remainder of her sleepless night and examined the cream gown, hung on the mirror. Its train swept long, dusting the floor, and it had a lace bodice and a satin skirt. She didn't possess the words or experience to describe what seemed to her a form of magic she'd never be familiar with.

If Desemir's own mother had worn it, then it must be appropriate for the occasion. "I don't have anything else. This will do fine."

"And your hair?" Gisela hooked the dress upon the edge of the cloak rack. "Would you like it up or down?"

"Oh... ah... I don't know." Siofra chewed her bottom lip. "What do you think?"

Gisela screwed her mouth, her eyes in a half squint. "Your golden curls are so beautiful down, but... but I think if we sweep it back off your face, it will allow your violet eyes to shine." Her grin was conspiratorial. "He may fall in love with you on the spot."

Siofra, who had spent her life praying gazes never lingered overlong on things that made her different, frowned. "Love isn't the agreement we made."

Gisela made a soft sound in her throat as she turned toward the dress. "Did your mother prepare you for your wedding night?"

Siofra wrapped the blanket around herself and slipped out of bed. "My mother taught me to fade into the background and remain there. Beyond that, she had little to offer." She pressed her forehead to the window, passing her gaze over the haze of fog shrouding the estate. She could just make out Aio stretching her wings on the breeze. Atio appeared beside her, and they paired their movements. "Why, is there something I should know?"

Gisela whistled through her teeth. "Let's take this day one moment at a time." She glanced back. "We should go. Desemir doesn't like to be kept waiting."

Desemir paced the narrow cobbles of the modest abbey. The path bisected the five dust-covered rows, which had remained empty since Desemir had been a boy... since his mother's death, an occasion he only thought of in detached passing. The past belonged where it was.

The symbols of the Guardians were arranged in a reverent semicircle on the altar. He had no affinity to any of them, not like his mother had. She'd prayed most to the Guardian of the Unpromised Future, who was said to either cause or prevent terrible things—a rather absurd way to claiming responsibility for everything. It was clear to Desemir how the Guardian felt about the late Lidia Trevanion.

Pesha worked to stoke the fire, but nothing would cut the chill. Their breaths swirled out, dissipating at the ends of the next ones. The minister, going beyond the usual duty of a Reliquary servant, swept the leaves and wiped the dust from the pews, occasionally passing a flash of judgment Desemir's way at how evident his lack of faith had become.

In hindsight, Desemir should have sent some staff in the night to prepare the small stone building, which had been in disuse for almost fifteen years. There just hadn't been time. From the moment Siofra had whispered her acceptance, he'd immersed himself in pulling everything together. The quicker the day was behind them, the better for everyone.

Before Siofra could change her mind.

Before *he* could change *his* mind.

Pesha was especially cross this cold morning. But he had *come*. Desemir didn't know what he'd have done if Pesha had refused. They were all each other had in their lonely, isolated world, and he couldn't fathom approaching the day without him.

Pesha lifted from his crouch with a focused gaze on the open doors. "Des."

Desemir turned and saw Siofra flitting through the fog as she cut across the sloping gardens and down the hill. His mother's cream dress caught the wind like a sail, billowing out to the side. Folded into his betrothed's joined hands was a bouquet of flowers Gisela had no doubt assembled.

Pesha's breath caught behind him as the women drew close. "When I met her, I thought to myself, this is a woman who had to grow up too fast," he muttered. "But she's not weaker for it, is she?"

"Some of us were never children," Desemir murmured. He took slow steps toward the door. "As you and I know all too well."

"You're sure, Des? You're sure this is what you want?"

"I'm sure there's never been two people with more to benefit from each other, and more to lose if they turn away from this chance."

"That's not an answer."

"It is for me." Des swayed as he gripped the edge of one of the doors, watching Siofra step across the uneven stones of the path toward the abbey. Her hair was piled at the crown in a garland of gold ringlets, her chin lifted in a touch of bold pride. "I've told you before, Pesh. You want to marry for love? I'll support you. Just as long as you understand why I cannot."

Pesha sucked in a breath through his teeth. "Gisela did well with her."

"Mm." Des bit back a smile.

When Siofra reached the steps, she lifted her skirt, stained at the hem from the damp grounds, and raced up into the abbey.

Desemir opened his mouth to greet her, but his words died when her violet eyes snared his. He hadn't seen the pulse of Medvedev power running just underneath her smooth, pale flesh before. Within her, Siofra held the power to kill him—a power she might yet use.

Because of it, Pesha would never stray far. Even last night, he'd been posted in the shadows when Siofra had come to the terrace.

He can bring his chosen love to Shadowfen Hall when the time comes, Desemir thought, but what if Pesha wanted a life beyond the grounds?

Pesha leaned in from behind and whispered against his ear, "Breathe, Des."

"You look lovely," Desemir managed to say. Transfixed, he held a hand out, and Siofra folded hers against his palm. "Are you ready?"

Siofra nodded. A deep flush swirled in her cheeks, which would've been hidden if she'd worn her hair the way she seemed to prefer: mussed and across her face, like a veil.

"There's still time to change your mind," Desemir said. His pulse rocketed. "I'll provide for you and Fen, as I promised. This needs to be something you want. I won't have your regret on my conscience."

Siofra lowered her eyes with a soft laugh. "What I want... No one has ever asked me that." She swept her gaze upward and locked it on him. "But you're the first person who has ever offered me anything that had my own needs in mind."

Des suppressed a grin. "And what are your needs, Siofra?"

Siofra rolled her bottom lip in, out. "That's why I'm here. To find out."

"And you know..." Desemir cleared his throat, maddened by his perplexing attack of bashfulness. "You know what I'll need... from you? You're amenable to this?" He quirked his mouth to the side. "Agreeable?"

113

Siofra cast a look at Gisela. "I understand I have much to learn. But... But perhaps it will not be such a chore to teach me."

Desemir pivoted to cover the sudden throb her guileless words had produced. "I think we'll manage." He nearly choked, turning all the way around to face the altar. "We shouldn't delay. The rest of the Hall will be waking soon."

The minister was an old man, close to the end of his promise. Gisela had explained, on the chilly walk to the abbey, that Minister Purcell had been the dedicated minister of Shadowfen Hall since Desemir's grandfather had come of age—a boyhood friend of the old baron. Minister Purcell had pleaded to stay on and live out the rest of his usefulness at the Hall rather than face Reliquary reassignment in his twilight years.

The reason Desemir had agreed, Gisela had told Siofra, was because Purcell had proved his loyalty. Though the minister's gnarled hands struggled to hold the dusty tome, and his rheumy eyes strained for the words he should know by heart but had forgotten, he would surrender his life to the Guardians before ever telling anyone what he'd risen early to do that day.

"You are both of sound mind, pure mind?" Purcell asked. He drew his words across a gravelly cough. "You come to me heart open, mind willing?"

Desemir's head bobbed in a series of short, impatient nods.

Siofra cast an uncertain glance his way before turning back toward the minister and saying, "I do, yes."

"And it is both your wishes that you cast aside your old lives for a new one, joined not until the severance of death but for the inexorable span of eternity?"

Siofra caught Pesha's heavy stare. He pointed it at the altar, at some unclear spot. His disapproval hung over him like a woolen cloak for all to see.

At least he's here. At least, in the end, he supported his brother.
He had no choice. He has to protect Desemir.

114

From you.

"Mistress Siofra?"

Siofra dragged her attention back to the minister with a tight, shamed gasp. "Yes. That is my wish."

Was this really happening?

Fen should be here.

He'll never forgive me.

Desemir's eyes shifted toward her from the side. She clenched and forced herself to look forward.

"Master Desemir, you will take your bride's hands in yours while I—" The minister coughed. "While your brother, perhaps, ties the ancestral knot around both of you."

Gisela had to nudge Pesha to return his focus to the ceremony. "The knot," she whispered.

Pesha passed a bewildered look between the minister and Desemir. "The knot... ah, right."

Desemir inhaled a deep breath and held it.

Pesha stepped forward. "You'll have to guide me, Minister."

Desemir's anxious shifting drew even Gisela's notice. Siofra tried to catch her friend's eye, to share her confusion, but Gisela and Desemir were locked in a potent gaze that heightened Siofra's unrecognized fears.

Desemir turned toward Siofra but was still focused behind her, on Gisela, as Pesha fumbled with the rope. When the minister reached in to guide Siofra's hands atop Desemir's, at last the thick spell was broken.

Desemir snapped his focus back to Siofra with a dazed blink.

"Is everything all right?" she whispered as the men bound their hands and wrists in the thick, scratchy rope.

Desemir nodded. "Just remembering the last time I was here. It wasn't a happy occasion."

"I'm sorry."

"Don't be." Desemir looked at Pesha, who retreated as the minister nodded in approval of his work.

"Very good, Sir Pesha. With that, we can begin." The Minister launched into more hacking as he turned a dusty page, sending a plume into the cold air. "The Sacred Vows of the Northerlands are simple. Mistress Siofra, I understand you are new to us, from the Westerlands. Their vow recitations are more involved, wordier. I do have them here, if you prefer—"

"No," Siofra said with a swift shake of her head. "This is my home now. These will be the traditions of my children. I want to know and respect them."

Desemir's mouth turned with the start of a smile.

"Then we'll begin," Minister Purcell said, with an agreeable nod at her and then at Desemir. "No one is more familiar with the precarious line between life and death than a man or woman of the Northerlands. Winter is what we know. It is in us, around us, a part of us. And in the direst, bleakest days and nights of midwinter, where the promise of springtide is but a myth beyond our reach, we are never closer to our beloved Guardians."

Purcell turned the page. "Our bones are ice. Our flesh is snow. But our hearts are fire, the fire that kindles the spirit of the Northerlands, that coarsens us to any hardship, any suffering. That fire sets us apart. That fire is what gives life."

A moist sheen of sweat built between the press of Desemir's and Siofra's palms. Siofra flexed her hands, but the rope was too tight. In response to her nervous shift, Desemir wound his fingers through hers.

"Please read these vows to your bride, Sir Desemir," Minister Purcell said. He spun the book toward Desemir, nearly dropping it to the abbey floor.

Desemir cleared his throat and leaned down to read. "My... My flame is unique. There is only one of its kind. There is nothing I possess worth more. It is my light in the darkest months, my heat when the ice has forsaken us." He swallowed a breath. "I share it now with you, Siofra. I join my flame to yours, creating a unified blaze. Though we have ahead of us the darkest of nights, the coldest of days, as long as we are me and thee, our fire will illuminate the stars in our immortal sky."

Desemir pulled his head back with a shivery breath. He tried to smile at her but instead pressed his lips inward, fighting something Siofra didn't understand. But the others did. It was written in Pesha's doubting eyes and Gisela's warm caution.

"And Mistress Siofra," the minister said, turning the book her way. "Will you read yours now?"

Siofra nodded. She shrugged away the strangeness of the others but was achingly aware that every eye in the abbey was trained on *her*.

"My flame is unique," Siofra read. She had Marina to thank for teaching her the letters of the kingdom. Not everything had been so terrible.

Stop trying to convince yourself to go back.
There is nothing there for you.
There is only forward.

Siofra braced herself and continued. "There is only one of its kind." She looked up to catch Desemir's eyes, but his were focused on their hands. "There is nothing I possess worth more. It is my light in the darkest months, my heat when the ice has forsaken us."

Did it really get so terrible in midwinter?

She realized how little she knew about her new home. Of the people who would become her family.

All of it.

Desemir pulsed his hand against hers in gentle encouragement.

She found her voice again. "I... I share it now with you, Desemir. I join my flame to yours, creating a unified blaze. Though we have ahead of us the darkest of nights, the coldest of days, as long as we are me and thee, our fire will illuminate the stars in our immortal sky."

The minister clapped the book closed, sending another whorl of dust into their faces. He hobbled to the side and set it on his altar. "Who will make the cut?"

Pesha stepped forward. His tight expression was unreadable as he accepted the dagger from Purcell with a curt nod. He looked at neither Desemir nor Siofra as he sawed the blade through the thick rope. Before it could fall to the stones, he passed it to the minister.

Minister Purcell dropped the knot into Desemir's palms. "This belongs on your hearth, a constant reminder that you are now so much more than you ever were before. More than you could ever be alone."

Desemir's nod was low and reverent. When his gaze came up, it landed on Siofra. She trapped a sob from the shock of relief it produced. She needed this, to *see* him. For him to see *her*. She wasn't afraid of what she'd done, only of how little she knew of the man she'd chosen.

Desemir transferred the rope to one hand and cupped the other against her cheek. His touch set a gentle shiver through her, one she was still recovering from when he brought his mouth to hers in a quick but firm kiss.

"Your fires are now a blaze," Purcell said. The man's eyes watered as he watched Desemir. "A blaze that must be protected at any cost."

"At any cost." Desemir exhaled. "That's it then?"

Purcell nodded. "I'll wait two days before registering your union with the Reliquary. Will that be enough time for you to manage your affairs here?"

Desemir gestured his agreement. "Yes. Thank you, Horace."

The old man balked. His eyes shot toward Siofra.

"She's my wife now, Harry," Desemir said with a tight smile. "No need for pretense around her anymore. You know how I hate it."

Purcell's face flooded with relief. "Very well, Des. I wish you both all the happiness in the realm." He nodded at Siofra. "Siofra, welcome to Shadowfen Hall."

The flaps of his robe fluttered as he ushered himself down the narrow aisle and exited into the foggy morning.

Desemir turned back toward Siofra. "Are you all right?"

Siofra nodded in place of speaking. Her heart lodged in her chest.

"You're ready for this?"

Siofra found her words. "For what?"

"Breakfast," Pesha answered for his brother. Acerbity cut through his words. "Where you both get to explain to the rest of the Hall, including Stiofen, how you spent your morning."

Desemir stared at the sumptuous spread, paralyzed by choice.

He hoped it was how the others interpreted his present state of overwhelm as he sat at the head of the table in the dining hall, waiting for the right words to come.

Pesha sat at the opposite end, radiating with even more anxiety than Desemir. He pulled a tart to his plate with a hasty flick of his wrist, though everyone knew he didn't eat tarts, and he regarded it with a progressively appraising look as he nodded to himself.

Stiofen absorbed the tension, his own food untouched as he seemingly tried to make sense of the intentional silence. Siofra's behavior only compounded his confusion, as he watched her tear into her morning meal with admirable fervor.

Gisela and the guards hovered, shifting from one side of the room to the other in anticipation. Lotte's unusual turn with quietude was a sign, if nothing else was, that something was deeply amiss at the Trevanion breakfast table.

The timekeeper struck quarter noon, an even nine ticks of the sun, filling the room with its low, ominous intonation. Desemir's mother had been the one so fascinated with the strange inventions. They were still novel in the marketplace, prone to mechanical problems that required the handiwork of trained men—of which there were presently only a handful in the kingdom—but while Desemir had removed most reminders of his father, those were the few treasures still left of his mother.

Stiofen snapped his hands away from his plate. The clang of his spoon drew everyone's attention. "I don't need to be an empath to know something isn't right here."

Siofra's head whipped upward, her mouth overstuffed with fruit. She managed a helpless shrug before turning her eyes on Desemir.

Desemir couldn't help but enjoy Siofra's artless absence of modesty. He couldn't recall the last time he'd dined with a woman who hadn't pretended to be disgusted by the idea of food.

His quick smile faded at Stiofen's silent demand for an answer.

"Nothing is wrong." Desemir dropped his hands to his lap but then rebuked himself for indulging his nerves. He could hold his own against men twice his age and higher ranked, but a young man in his charge unnerved him so?

Stiofen again turned his eyes on Siofra, who was back to avoiding him.

Desemir strained his spine in an unsatisfying stretch. "Quite the opposite," he said. He returned his hands to the table, laying them out to show everyone—guest to staff to, yes, even Pesha— he had nothing to hide. "We have some wonderful news to share with everyone in the Hall."

Pesha knitted his brows, his tart frozen in examination. The edges of his jaw twitched.

"We?" Stiofen asked, still trying to snare Siofra's attention away from her food.

Desemir stretched one hand toward Siofra, nodding at her to take it. She stopped chewing, darting her panicked gaze from his hand to his face.

Desemir flicked his eyes downward, assuring her it was all right.

Siofra swallowed her food slowly and then lowered her face to dab it with a cloth napkin. Without looking at her brother, she slid her hand away from her lap and placed it in Desemir's.

"Si?" Stiofen asked.

Desemir caught his brother's eyes again. Pesha resembled an elk-kind caught in a bowman's sights.

"*Siofra?*" Stiofen asked more urgently.

"It's fine," Siofra said, shaking her head. She folded her hand into a ball in Desemir's palm, and he closed his fingers over it, offering her what he hoped was strength. "It's fine, Fen. I've just... I've come to a point in my life—"

"A point in your life?" Stiofen shoved his plate aside and dropped onto his elbows, leaning in.

"When it's time for me to make decisions for myself," she stated. She glanced at Desemir, and he gave her a tight, encouraging nod. He tried to add a smile, but she'd already looked away.

"Make decisions for yourself..." Stiofen cocked his head. "What does that mean? That you think..." He passed his eyes from left to right, seemingly aware of how many were watching, listening. "You think I've made *bad* choices on your behalf? That I've held you back from living your life?"

Siofra's hand pulled loose from Desemir's when she pitched forward over the table. "No, Fen, that's not what I mean at all. You know that isn't how I feel."

Stiofen reeled back. His chair bounced when his back connected. "Do I?" He dragged a palm down his face. "Just tell me. Tell me the *truth*, that you've already made up your mind... that you only *pretended* to consider this man's offer when you knew *all along* what your answer would be."

Pesha turned his scrutiny to the underside of his tart.

Siofra crossed her arms and rolled back in her seat. "I wouldn't have to *pretend*, Fen, if you trusted me at all."

"You think I don't *trust* you?" Fen's mouth gaped.

Siofra lifted both her shoulders with a clipped inhale. "I know you don't. You love me, but that isn't the same."

Fen's stare was incredulous. "How could you say that? To *me?*"

Desemir cut in. "Maybe... Perhaps this isn't the time. Why don't we—"

121

"It's already done," Siofra blurted. She unlaced her arms and held them out, her chin high. "Desemir and I were wed this morning in the abbey."

Stiofen's angry smirk froze on his face. "No..."

"Yes." Siofra lowered her arms, settled them on the table. "*Yes*, Fen. And you can ask me why I did it or why I chose to do it behind your back, but the more important truth is that our bodies may be free from that dungeon, but your mind is still there."

"My mind? What does *that* mean?" Fen demanded.

"It's time to accept we may actually have a chance at something resembling normalcy."

"We just got here!" Fen slapped his hands onto the table. "We don't even *know* these people!"

"I've had a contract drawn up." Desemir braced for Stiofen's anger. "It details everything I offered you before, Stiofen. The land. The title. The gold. I signed it last night."

Stiofen spun in his chair. "What about me suggests I would accept any price to sell my sister?"

"Siofra wasn't yours to sell. She chose for herself," Desemir replied. "And for you."

"*What*? No." Stiofen turned again toward Siofra. "Tell me it's not true... that you sold yourself to his man for *me*?"

"It's not..." Siofra sighed, closing her eyes. "Not entirely true."

"Not entirely true?"

"Desemir was the first man to offer us both a life, without the cost of servitude. A *life*, Fen." Siofra shook her head. "Imagine it. Living. Not just surviving."

"He's gotten in your head. He's twisted your thoughts—"

"No," Siofra asserted. Her eyes glazed with tears, but they didn't spill. "For once, my thoughts are my own."

Stiofen shook his head from side to side in slow horror. His words stuck in his throat, mouth waving as he vacillated between trying to speak and willing himself not to. He shoved back from the table, eyes cast to the side.

Then he twisted out of his chair and fled the dining hall. Lieken set off after him.

"That went well," Pesha quipped with a lift of his brows.

But Desemir's focus was on Siofra alone. Her head, still held high in defiance, shook out of time with the tremble in her chin. A hard, slow blink released the tears she'd been holding, sending them in rivers down her flushed cheeks.

"Are you all right?" He reached toward her but withdrew at her light but clear recoil.

"It's done," Siofra said. Hands shaking, she moved back from the table and stood. "I'd like to rest now. I hardly slept last night."

"Of course. I'll escort you—"

"I can find my own way back," Siofra said. "I'll see you again... tonight."

Desemir nodded, helpless, and watched her depart, Gisela in tow.

"As for the rest of you, I have something to say," Desemir said when she was gone. "Siofra is my wife now, and Stiofen is family. If I never hear another cursed 'sir' from any of you, it will be too soon."

"Are you going to let me in?"

Lieken guarded the door to Stiofen's chambers with impressive commitment. Siofra burned her gaze into him, but the young man only scowled and chucked his chin higher.

She tossed a confounded glance back at Gisela.

"Open the door, Liek." Gisela's soft command rolled off her like silk shifting across skin.

Lieken twitched with a disheveled blink.

"Des needs us in the Hall of Counting." Gisela's next attempt was a smooth lie. "Siofra is Fen's sister, not an enemy from which he needs protection. Come on. Let's leave them to speak."

"He said no one. In or out," Lieken barked. "Mistress" he added with a guilty mumble Siofra's direction.

"No formalities, please," Siofra said with a somber sigh. The surface of her flesh felt numb, her nerves still locked on the tense dining room exchange. "But I really need to get in that room, Lieken, and it will be far easier on both of us if you simply step aside."

Gisela raised both her brows in a knowing nod, which Lieken studied.

"Des really needs us?" Lieken asked. He brought a hand to his neck and half squinted.

"Mhmm," Gisela purred. "Best not to involve ourselves in sibling squabbles anyway. When the emotions die down, and they will, you'll be glad you remained neutral in the matter. Siofra and Stiofen are both part of this family now. They're not going anywhere, either of them."

Lieken swallowed a deep groan. When his gaze swung back up to Gisela, he forced a smile. "All right then."

He fancies her, Siofra noted, amused. *And she knows it.*

She waited for them to disappear around the corner before letting herself in.

"No. *No,*" Fen cried, barreling toward the door. "I don't want to talk to you. I can't even *look* at you."

Siofra closed the door behind herself and leaned against it. "Well, you should try, Fen. I'm the same person I've always been."

Fen slammed his palm against a bedpost with a snort. "You can't fool me. I know you better than anyone. And it's why..." His face screwed inward, pained. "*Dammit,* Siofra! What the curses were you thinking?"

"What you're really saying," Siofra said, using all her self-restraint to mask the quaver in her voice, "is you liked me better when I was meek and compliant."

Fen recoiled. "*What?* That's... no. No. Do *not* put words in my mouth."

"Use yours then, and explain this to me."

"I thought I explained quite well the dangers in this offer." Fen thrust an arm toward the door. "And I thought... I *thought* you heard them, but you clearly were only humoring me. You told me what I wanted to hear, knowing I'd believe you."

"You're right," Siofra confessed. She rolled her shoulders back. "I knew as Desemir was making the offer that I would take it."

Fen's eyes widened in their sockets. "So easily the lie came to you, did it?"

"I didn't want to lie to you," she replied. "I wanted... I wanted to speak to you as equals and have your faith in me that I was capable of choosing my own way."

Fen tossed his head back. "That's not fair, Si. You're acting like I look down on you, *talk* down to you, when our lives have never been as simple as that. We've been in survival mode since the *day of our birth*. We don't get the luxury of the same choices most get. Everything we do either contributes to our survival or threatens it."

Siofra pressed her palms to the door. She stretched her fingers, channeling her anger there so it wouldn't slip into her words. "That's your problem, Fen. You have only ever seen our future in those terms. Never... never considered there might be a path for us with happiness sprinkled along the way."

He threw his head back again, with a disdainful laugh. "Oh, Si, you read far too many fantastical tales. You want happiness? Well, I'm more concerned with keeping us both *alive*."

"This marriage does precisely that."

"You've signed up to become his plaything! His broodmare."

Siofra lowered her eyes. "I..." Her head shook, freeing fresh tears. "Will I now go to his bed, bear his children? Yes, and what of it, Fen?" She looked up again. "I never... never in all my life thought there might be a future for me with a husband, with children of my own. And *you*. You'll be a landed baron! You'll—"

"You didn't do this for me," he spat. "And if you did, you're admitting you've never listened to a word I've said, because I never *wanted* a life away from my sister. I know who *I* am. Do you?"

"My choice is made." Siofra held her head high, but she trained her gaze on the bureau, past her brother. "And it was *my* choice to make. No matter what you might think, there was no one but me who could have made it."

"How nice for you, Si." A dark shift transformed his face. "How nice for you after almost nineteen years of my protecting you, *choosing* to protect you, that when faced with your first real choice, you think with desire and not reason."

Siofra felt a flush ignite in her head and spread across her flesh, plummeting to her feet.

"You're not denying it?"

"If this is really what you think..." Her voice choked. She'd been wrong to follow him so fresh off the hurt. She wasn't as strong as he was. She'd come to convince him otherwise, and all she'd done was prove him right.

"It is." Fen wrapped his hand around the bedpost. His grip turned his hands white. "So, go on then. Collect your prize—"

"*Fen—*"

"But as for me, Siofra? I'll take *nothing* from the man, because unlike you, I see through to the heart of him. I knew his offer for what it was before he'd finished speaking." He ground his jaw. Tears swam in his eyes. "If my sister wants to be his whore, well... I cannot stop her. But I won't contribute to the indignity by selling myself too."

Siofra rolled against the door, flailing for the knob. She turned it and slipped out before he could see how deeply his words had cut her.

ELEVEN
MISTRESS TREVANION

Siofra's eyes glazed with her thoughts as Gisela brushed her thick curls. They sprung back in defiance, creating a fluffed golden mane that trailed down her back.

"I'll just wear it up, like I did this morning," Siofra said to Gisela in the mirror.

A grin cracked through Gisela's determined expression. "Tonight is a night for wearing it down."

Siofra angled forward to snag the goblet of wine off the dressing table. She fingered the base as the brush was raked through her snarled ends, then released it without taking a sip.

"Am I..." Siofra sighed, pressing her lips together. The question was safer unformed, but she'd been withholding her words her whole life. It was time she learned to start using them.

To use them so unreservedly, and with so many, was a freedom it would take time to embrace.

"Are you what?" Gisela asked.

Siofra's heart skipped at even the idea of saying it aloud. "Nothing."

"I don't know much, Siofra," Gisela said. Her head tilted in the mirror, eyes meeting Siofra's. "But I know when a woman says, 'It's nothing,' it's very much something."

Siofra pulled her gaze back to the untouched goblet of wine. Years of silence had been oppressive, but speaking her insecurities was almost as bad as living them. Accepting Desemir's surreal offer wasn't only a change in her and Fen's circumstances; it was a chance to think better thoughts. To dream better dreams.

"You may find you feel better not keeping it in," Gisela gently urged.

"It's nothing, only..." Siofra fumbled the attempt, changing her words several times before continuing. "I don't know what he expects, Gisela. What... he likes. That is..." She winced, reproaching herself for her inexperience—how her naivete held her back from even simple conversation. If she could only put her thoughts on display, others would see there was so much more to her.

Gisela paused her brushing. Her shoulders rose and fell in a sigh. "You want to know about Desemir's women."

Siofra tilted her head toward Gisela. "His women?"

Gisela's smile skipped. She laughed to cover it. "You're asking if you're what he usually enjoys and asks for. Whether you're to his liking, according to his tastes."

Siofra relaxed again. "I know he didn't marry me for anything so frivolous, but I don't want him to regret the offer if I'm not... well, *pleasing*."

Gisela shook her head and resumed brushing. "Siofra, you are one of the most pleasing creatures I've ever laid eyes upon. I can't pretend I know what Desemir Trevanion is thinking, or *was* thinking when he made you his offer. But I can say, with reasonable confidence, that he gained in his arrangement, well beyond the business agreement." She winked at Siofra in the mirror, her mouth turning up at the corners. "And he knows it too."

"How..." Siofra's laugh ended before it began. "How could he have gained anything with *me*? Any woman could bear his children. I understand why it cannot be someone here, in Darkwood Run, but he didn't have to go all the way to Newcarrow for a bride either, especially not one with my troubles. He says he doesn't want..."

"To use you?" Gisela reached past Siofra to set the brush on the dressing table. "It's not my place to speak on the complicated nature of Des's dealings with Medvedev. There's guilt there, from what his father..." Her eyes widened to clear her thoughts. "If Des wanted to use you for your especial gifts, he would've been upfront in those intentions. To do otherwise would create a rift between him and his brother, and there's no one he loves more than Pesha."

Siofra cast her eyes to the side in frustration. "Pity, then?"

"Pity? No." Gisela knelt at her side. "He saw an opportunity to help you *and* help himself. Where's the harm in it, if everyone benefits?"

Why was Siofra doing this to herself? Driving a wedge between her own thoughts to convince herself that a bid for happiness was an invitation for more pain, more failure? She'd accepted his offer because a part of herself still believed in hope, but what if Fen was right?

Even if he is, it's done. It's done, and now I make the best of it.

Gisela rose again and took her place behind Siofra. She slipped her hands onto Siofra's shoulders, over the delicate lace straps of the gown she'd given her for the night ahead.

Siofra allowed herself one indulgent assessment in the reflection. She saw herself as she always had, as the girl who must blend into the world, never be seen. The buoyant waves, spots of rouge on her cheeks and lips, and provocative nightgown changed nothing.

"I could tell you what happens next, but it would deny you the delight of discovering it for yourself. But I will give you this advice." Gisela's voice dropped to a conspiratorial whisper. Her cobalt eyes twinkled in the mirror. "If he offers you pleasure, Siofra, *take* it."

Pesha escorted Siofra down the long hall with the tall windows. He seemed angry, harnessing words better left unsaid. His only communication was when he'd nodded once, to indicate her robe had slid down, revealing her bare shoulder.

He wasn't happy with his brother's choice, but at least he'd stood by Desemir. Fen refused to see her at all, even skipping supper to avoid her.

He just needs time. He'll see what this can be for us.

Pesha took a left at the top of the stairs, toward the west wing, which Siofra recalled as being off-limits to her. But he only moved halfway down the first long hall before he turned down another, presumably the south wing, and came to a halt outside ornate double doors as imposing as the ones leading into the Hall of Counting. Wulfhelm and Euric stood sentry on either side. When Siofra and Pesha approached, each guard leaned in to open a door.

Siofra charged forward, determined to leave her fear in the hall. She turned to thank Pesha for the escort, but he'd come in behind her and was already closing the doors behind them.

"You're not... staying, are you?"

Pesha nodded, offering no explanation. He flashed a wave at the other side of the room before he disappeared into a corner.

And what a room it was. Siofra had been enchanted by her sumptuous apartments, but Desemir's defied imagination.

The walls on three sides were carved into an intricate series of tableaus that seemed to tell a story, wrapping around and down. Like all things in Shadowfen Hall, they were crafted of the precious ebony wood Desemir held so dear. She tried to follow the story, illuminated by four hanging candelabras, but her eyes were instead drawn to the room's centerpiece.

A bed, twice the width of hers, commanded attention from anyone who entered. It lorded over the entire chamber, with its satin netting and woven posts. The covers, turned down at the sides, provided a hint of the evening's potential.

A broad balcony bisected the fourth wall. The delicate curtains caught the breeze, revealing the night sky beyond.

Siofra's eyes were still inspecting the display when she spotted Desemir. He sat in a wide chair softened with crimson velvet, his shirt buttoned down to the middle of his chest, legs parted and to the sides.

An uncomfortable flutter traveled downward from her chest. Heat flooded her cheeks.

She waited for him to stand, to do something, but his eyes, glazed and dazzling emerald against the candles burning around him, were fixed on her, drinking her in and watching her take his measure. The urge to cover herself was as strong as her desire was foreign. When he at last pushed himself out of the chair and rose to his full height, she saw the bottle in his hand.

"You are..." Desemir set the bottle aside. His dark, mussed hair turned her already-untoward thoughts down an even more indecent path. "You're here."

"I'm here," she answered. The cool night forced a chill through her, reminding her how thin her dress was, and why.

"Can I get you anything? A drink?"

Siofra shook her head. She didn't dare meet his eyes. He couldn't see her inconvenient desire, which was not part of their agreement.

We will be filling a need.

A duty.

"You've never done this before, have you?"

Siofra shook her head at the ground.

"Siofra..." Desemir's face was hidden by a break in the light when he stepped ahead of the candles. "What can I do to ease your fear?"

"I'm not afraid of *that*," Siofra assured him. "Or you."

"Is it Pesha? You'll forget he's even here," Desemir said. He seemed like he might come closer, but he stopped at the end of his bed. "It's for both our safety."

Siofra spun away, swallowing her shame. Not only had she brought inexperience to her husband on their wedding night but also mortal danger. She might dream of a different life, but there was nowhere she could go, no one she could be, to hide from who she was.

"Are you all right?"

"I don't know," she admitted. She wrapped her arms tight around herself, a shield not for her but for everyone else.

She jumped at the sudden flourish of warmth at her back signaling Desemir's arrival. He passed his smooth palms down her bare arms. "Come with me."

Desemir untangled one of her hands and gently tugged. He led her across the plush fur rug toward the open balcony. She couldn't help but search for Pesha, trying to locate his chosen shadow, but he was practiced at disappearing.

Desemir stepped out into the night. He removed his slippers, nodding for her to do the same. The icy stab of cold from the exposed stone sent her flesh on alert and reignited the ache in her ankle. The surface of her skin pebbled as he nudged her forward until she had both of her hands spread atop the thick ledge.

Desemir brushed his arms around the side of her, an embrace from behind, and rested them just outside hers on the carved stone.

"Look," he whispered against her temple.

Siofra gazed into the dark sprawl of forest, trying to discern his meaning without making him explain it. Her pulse rushed at the shape of him, the commanding press of his hips against the middle of her back, buckling her knees. His muscled arms, passing again along hers as he reached to point, pushed her heart into her throat.

"Everything." Desemir answered the question she couldn't bring herself to ask. The raw sentiment in his voice disarmed her.

"Everything you see in front of you, Siofra, is now yours as well. It will all belong to your son one day."

Siofra lost her battle with the sway, which sent her head falling back against his chest.

"As far as your eyes can take you, there is nothing but what is ours. Nothing, and no one." He took a step back. Before she could turn, he'd released the ties at the back of her nightgown, and it fell to the stones in an unceremonious heap. "No one can see you out here. No one but me. Not Pesha. Not the greedy, grasping men of Darkwood Run. Out here, you are truly free."

Siofra rushed to cover herself, her nudity, but Desemir peeled her hands back in gentle strokes and settled them back at her sides.

"This is freedom, Siofra." Desemir's hot breath teased her scalp. He brushed his palms along her hips, traveling across the arcs of them, bowing inward as his hands met on her belly. "Freedom to live. Freedom to *feel*. There is no past or future out here. There is only right now. You've been making choices for yourself, for what *you* want, since you arrived on my doorstep. So choose."

Desemir's fingers danced a path farther down. Reflex drove Siofra to rise to the tips of her toes as his hand plunged lower, slipping between her legs. Her head arced upward in breathless surrender, hair wedged between her back and his chest. He brought his mouth down to hers, causing her to radiate a song of her desire against the crush of his tongue.

Desemir stroked the length of her, driving her higher up on her toes in thrall to ecstasy. He pressed just the tips of his fingers inside her, enough for her to know that if he stopped, if he didn't go *deeper*, she would lose her mind.

"Let go. Whatever haunts you, it can't find you here." His warm breath tickled her ear.

He slipped his fingers out, returning his focus to the sensitized bundle of flesh that separated her from her old life. Her toes curled, legs turning to jelly. Desemir caught her, gathering one firm arm around her torso to bring her up off the stones and hold her aloft. The other plunged back between her legs.

"You said no one has ever asked you what you wanted." He moaned against her ear. He rolled his hips against her, the thick throb trapped by his trousers an agonizing tease. It wasn't enough. It wasn't *nearly* enough. "I'm asking you now, Siofra."

Siofra didn't know how to articulate her needs, to describe the relentless crests of pleasure lifting her higher and higher up off the stones, out of her skin. "I want..." She drew in her lip.

Desemir pinched his fingers, and desire swelled through her like waves cresting and crashing on the shore. He held her suspended, while she thrashed in yearning, her aches becoming needs, becoming desires.

She knew what had happened because she'd made herself come before, late at night when she was the last one awake. Hand under her blanket as she whimpered in silence.

Nothing had prepared her for how it would feel guided by skilled hands.

When Siofra's quakes softened to shudders, Desemir eased her back to the ground. Her skin on fire, she clung to the ledge for purchase, inviting the cool surge of stone that had only moments ago been unwelcome.

"More?" he whispered, leaning in to nip at her earlobe.

"More, yes." She panted. "But I'm ready for something else now."

Desemir fumbled with his belt behind her. She heard his trousers fall, felt him step out of them. His bare flesh covered hers from behind. His bulge, once painfully restrained, had been freed and pulsed against her ass.

Who am I? she wondered as she lifted herself once more, to receive him a different way. It was an act born of instinct, not experience, but his fractured groan told her it was right. His hands, cupped underneath her, jerked upward, parting her, and they both cried out as he slid into her.

Desemir buried himself to the hilt and stilled. His organ jerked inside her, and she melted in anticipation she was wholly unprepared for. There was pain, but Siofra was no stranger to pain, and if that was the punishment for surrendering her innocence, she welcomed it, for she knew what real pain was.

"Does it hurt?" Desire scorched his voice. "I can go as slow as you need."

"It doesn't hurt." Siofra moaned, shaking her head. She rocked back against him. "And I don't want you to go slow."

Siofra clung to the balcony as Desemir thrust forward. She lost herself to the force of his gentle but brutal intimacy and wondered again who she was, who she'd become... whether she was meant to be there, or if this was merely a taste of what could be if she were someone else.

He hastened, their flesh slapping as he entangled his hand in her soft curls and screamed into the night, filling her with a torrent of warmth. His cries echoed against the nothingness, fading as the warmth did.

Desemir released her and stumbled back. She held tight to the balcony, struggling to find solid footing as she strained to recover her senses.

But then he scooped an arm under her ass and lifted her. He carried her across the stones to the other end of the balcony before easing them both onto a long, soft chaise.

Desemir spun her in his arms and landed her so she was astride him. Siofra looked down at the gleam of sweat sheening his muscled chest. His green eyes turned amber when his head rolled back and caught the moonlight.

Siofra ran her hands along the lower edge of his belly... the rough patch of hair beneath... and just below that...

She looked up. Desemir raked his tongue along his bottom lip and nodded with a drawn-out blink.

I like this. I want this.

I may not know the words to tell him, but I can show him.

Siofra rolled her hips upward, and when they came back down, sliding over the length of him, there was no longer even a whisper of pain. This time, *she* was in control.

Desemir slipped his middle finger between her legs, detonating a bright spasm in her.

He wasn't the only one who had yearnings left to sate.

Siofra shed the last of her insecurities and arched her back, dropping her palms onto his thighs as she ushered in her life as Mistress Trevanion with welcome abandon.

"Siofra. Siofra. Wake up."

Siofra rolled at the intrusion, nearly toppling off the chaise. Her first thought was how wretched *cold* she was. She looked down and realized Desemir's blouse, draped over her, was her only cover.

"Hmm?" She coiled her legs up to preserve warmth. If she kept her eyes closed, she might return to her amazing dream.

"We have to go."

"Go..." Siofra opened one eye. "Pesha?"

He gripped the wooden arm of the chaise with both hands, but he'd directed his gaze away, avoiding her. "Get dressed. Quickly. Come on."

She pulled the shirt tight against herself and tried to sit without exposing half her body to him. "Why are you acting like this? Where's Desemir?"

"Get dressed. *Now*. Please."

"All *right*." She attempted to keep the shirt in place while she searched for her dress, but she needn't have bothered. Pesha seemed as if he'd rather gouge his eyes out than look at her.

As soon as she had the dress shrugged on, he tugged her arm, urging her back into the bedchamber. She tripped on the frame of the door on the way in, but he didn't stop.

"Has something happened?" She struggled to match Pesha's frenetic pace. "Are we in danger?"

Pesha didn't answer.

Siofra whipped her gaze across the room as he dragged her out of it. There was no sign of Desemir.

When they reached the hall, he drew her closer, folding her elbow through his as he fell into a more normal pace. "I'm sorry about that. It was necessary."

In a confused daze, Siofra looked back the way they'd come. "Necessary for what? What's going on, Pesha?"

Pesha waited until they'd rounded the corner before he spoke. He released her and folded his hands, dipping his chin against the tips of his fingers. "You weren't supposed to fall asleep."

"And why would that be?"

"I don't suppose my brother told you about his *nocturnal* activities?"

"His... what?" Siofra stepped away from Pesha and crossed her arms in lieu of the robe she'd regrettably left behind in the race to extricate her from the bedchamber. "Nocturnal..."

Pesha forced his hands back to his side. "Dammit, Des."

"What aren't you telling me?"

"Look, Siofra." Pesha stepped closer. He reached out and cupped her shoulders. "Desemir is... He has trouble sleeping. He's tried everything... draughts, meditation, leeches. They don't work. Nothing does, except..." His head bowed. "He calls for women, to be sent to his bed. Most nights. Or the ones he wants to sleep anyway."

Siofra backed away. "What?"

"He should have told you. He was wrong to not... to leave it to me." Pesha closed his eyes. "You weren't supposed to fall asleep in there."

"He never said a thing!" Siofra cried. She shuffled backward until she hit the wall. "Why would he... He doesn't need other women anymore. He has me."

"I'm sorry," Pesha said. "I am. But this is the man you married, and it won't be the last of the uncomfortable realizations you make about him."

137

"Maybe you're wrong. Maybe he won't need them tonight." Flashes of the evening streamed through her thoughts. How she'd bent and bowed to his pleasure, taking something for herself, for once. The ache forming in her chest spread down and outward, blistering, until there was no part of her that could escape it. "Ask him."

Pesha lowered his eyes back toward his feet. "He's the one who told me to see you back to your chambers so Wulf could bring them up, Siofra."

She pressed herself further against the wall, rolling her cheek against the stone with a wince to stay her tears. "I see."

"Let's get you back. I have to return."

Siofra recoiled when he reached for her. She wiped her eyes on her arm.

Fidelity won't be a requirement of our union. Desemir had explained what he was offering. She'd chosen to not hear it.

Suddenly she understood what Gisela meant about "Desemir's women."

"He makes you sit in there and watch, doesn't he? Like he did with us?"

Pesha flushed. "I didn't see anything tonight. And he doesn't *make* me do anything. It's a choice."

"Ahh. Well, so is inviting women who are not his wife up to his bed on his wedding night."

Pesha nodded with a resigned sigh. "Desemir told you who he was when he made you the offer. If you want to be happy here, you'll need to learn to make your peace with it."

TWELVE
LABYRINTH

Siofra waited for Pesha to disappear around the corner before she darted back out of her chambers. Tears layered over her sweat, clinging to matted hair she couldn't be bothered to address. She'd lingered only long enough to change into something more practical than her thin chemise and pile a thick cloak atop it.

With a snap, she pulled the hood taut, disguising her face to anyone who might catch her on her way out. Who might have *questions.*

As she reached for the door, she fought a tender swell of emotion threatening to turn her into a mess of angst and sadness. But it wasn't the residents of Shadowfen Hall at risk tonight. Only self-inflicted pain awaited Siofra. Her red wall was tucked safely away, because it wasn't anger she felt just then, but something far, far worse.

Stupid girl. Foolish girl. This isn't one of your stories.

Once confident she was alone in the central upstairs hall, she raced down the series of endless halls until she reached the central staircase, where she paused again to catch her breath.

139

Even if there was someone, what would they think of you? That poor naive Siofra got her feelings hurt by the business of men? That their beloved Desemir must already be regretting their arrangement?

There was no one above or below, but as she descended, she caught the echo of lusty giggles coming from Desemir's apartments farther down the hall.

Siofra wrapped her cloak tighter and scurried down the steps. She expended the force of her weight on the handle of one of the double doors, and when she'd opened them enough to wedge herself through, she slipped into the night. She didn't look back as the entrance hummed with closure behind her.

Siofra wound through the endless garden she realized was a maze, as she had become lost in the midst of it. She could see no more than a few feet ahead as she wove to the left and right, around corners and zigzagging back to address her second-guessing, wondering if she was even still heading in the right direction... if she was not making it *so much worse* by stubbornly trudging farther and farther into the labyrinth and away from the known world she'd left behind.

Above her, it was still that world. The night sky held court, a celestial show of light against dark. She paused to regard the stars, the same ones she'd beheld—with hope, with peace—barely an hour before, when Desemir had whispered to her about freedom.

Hot tears coursed down her cheeks, obscuring her already uncertain path. And what did she care about seeing? What did it matter when she'd been wrong, wrong, *wrong*. Wrong to lead with hope, to mistake happiness for safety, to assume she understood Desemir's claim that fidelity wasn't part of their arrangement. Wrong to not listen to Fen when he'd insisted he knew what was best.

Siofra's small, choked cries turned to sobs as the maze stretched on, whipping her to and fro but not out. She turned one corner and then another, but every hedge and flower and

vine looked the same. She swore she was right back where she'd
started, eyes fixed and blurring on the same winter blooms.

She collapsed to her knees. Her head lolled upward, tears running backward over her forehead and into her hair, which was still
mussed from what had been the best and worst night of her life.

"Why did you make me like this?" she asked the flowers,
the shrubs, the weeds, and the thorns as her body rocked with
incomprehensible misery. "*Why would you make something like
me at all?*"

A shrill caw tore through her heartache. Her eyes flashed
open and saw Aio, alone, gliding in smooth passes overhead. Atio
wasn't with her, but the reason was simple: Atio was with Fen,
and Siofra was not.

He might never speak to her again.

Siofra clasped both of her hands over her heart as she cried,
feeling the soft breeze that carried Aio down from the sky, where
she hovered just above the maze.

Siofra closed her eyes and listened, not to her anguish, still
wailing within, but to the wordless song of her familiar, a kinship
as old and even more sacred than the one she shared with Fen.

She climbed back to her feet and brushed the fallen leaves and
dirt from the front of her dress. She nodded to herself as her feet
again found the garden path, and she directed her gaze upward,
focused on Aio alone as the falcon led her out of the labyrinth
and into the field beyond.

Relieved laughter clogged her throat when she broke free.
Before her was a long downward slope and then the lake. Beyond,
past the cool surface and into the darkness, the forest slept.

Siofra nearly slid down the hill as her boots caught the soft
mud from the recent rainstorm. She was practically sprinting by
the time the incline leveled off, and she raced the rest of the way
to the water, her curls and cloak snapping behind her.

Siofra bowed over the frozen lake, catching her breath. She
was grateful for the ice fracturing her reflection, protecting her
from more hard truths.

Aio swooped lower, until she landed on a fallen log at the bank.

"Thank you, Aio. Though I know I didn't deserve it, for all I've neglected you these years."

Aio elongated her brown-and-gold wings, flapping them in disagreement.

"I've been ashamed. For not being strong enough to control who I am and too weak to fight those who preferred me in a cage." Siofra dropped down to sit. She stretched her legs, digging her heel onto the layer of ice coating the lake's surface. "And you've been very patient. For many years."

Aio's response was one only she could hear.

Siofra laughed. "Really? You would have preferred being in the *cage*, with me, and not free to fly, to soar?" She stilled, listening. "No. That's not the life I want for you, Aio. You deserve so much better. You deserve a Medvedev who isn't an abomination—who can coexist with you in the way we were born to do, free and unfettered. If only you were bonded to someone who could give it to you."

Eyes on the sky, she counted down the stars until her pounding pulse receded. Her tears dried, leaving her face tight and raw. The exhaustion taking hold was almost peaceful.

"I thought this could be the place where we might enjoy freedom," she said, after a comfortable pause. "But I also thought I was stronger. Desemir was clear about what this was. It's why I accepted his offer, because I know nothing of love, and to have an offer that didn't require it was a relief. And I know I only just met him, and yet..." Siofra's chest rose and held. She drew out her exhale, imagined it skipping across the ice. "And yet, tonight was the first time someone other than Fen ever made me feel like I mattered. Now I don't know what to believe."

Aio hopped off the log and waddled over, angling her long, lean body from side to side as she traversed the muddy bank. She settled behind Siofra's head and stretched her wings, wrapping them around Siofra's shoulders.

Siofra closed her eyes and allowed the feathery warmth of Aio's cere upon her forehead to lull her away from the hard lessons of the evening.

"You were wrong not to tell her. Not to warn her."

Desemir stretched his aching legs under his blanket, pointing his toes to push the blood back through his limbs, to keep himself alert enough to have the conversation Pesha was so determined to have. "I told Siofra she could live her life however she pleased, an offer few people ever get in their lifetime, man or woman. I was clear this wasn't a closed marriage."

"But your wedding night, Des?" Pesha gripped the end of the footboard, regarding his brother with an appalled look. "You couldn't have taken one evening away from your amusements?"

"Amusements?" Desemir's eyes were already closing. He flexed his hands, attempting to return life to them. "You know that's not what this is."

"Oh, does this mean that, for once, we'll be speaking of what this *actually* is?" Pesha's fluttery blinks evoked images of a petulant child.

"Don't be cruel," Desemir shot back. Exhaustion settled upon his chest. "Was she really upset? You're not just using her to convey your own displeasure with me?"

Pesha flung himself back, hands out at his sides. "I don't even know if I should answer you, seeing as you had *no* care for how she felt when you left me to kick her out."

"That isn't..." Desemir groaned. He had no defense unless he intended to lie, and his relationship with Pesha was still healing from the last untruth. "She seemed so peaceful lying there. I thought if I were to rouse her, she might ask questions I didn't feel like answering after we'd had such a lovely evening."

Pesha snorted. "So you left me to answer them."

Desemir tried to prop himself up on his elbows, but he was fading, and fast. "What..." He sighed. "What did you tell her?"

Pesha crossed his arms and angled away.

"Pesh."

"What do you think I told her? The truth?"

Desemir rolled his bottom jaw. "I don't have the wits for this tonight. Tell me or don't, but I'll be fast asleep before your anger runs its course."

Pesha's dark scowl came back into view when he turned toward Desemir. "I told her she married a man who brings a score of women to his bed every night for pleasure and that she should learn to get used to it."

"Well," Desemir replied, through an all-consuming yawn. "There's no lie to be found in that."

Pesha tossed his head in disgust one last time and stormed out. The door skittered when he tried to slam it, caught by Wulfhelm's quick hand.

"Everything all right?" the guard called.

Desemir, too worn to respond, nodded, knowing Wulfhelm couldn't see it.

But as was always true of his final, waning moments of wakefulness, he no longer had the energy to care.

Pesha found her by the lake. His fear spiked at the sight of her, her arms flung wide, head slumped to the side. But then he spotted Aio, and his unease dissolved to relief.

He approached and dropped into a crouch, his thoughts wandering to Eshe, trapped under the ice until the first thaw of springtide. He wondered what it must be like for a Medvedev whose familiar was always with them. If their hearts were less restless.

But then, that hadn't been Siofra and Aio's experience either. A different kind of separation was still separation.

Pesha crossed his arms over his knees and examined the falcon. She was a sizable bird, large not only for her breed but for any avian creature. A hunter sighting her would turn her story into legend, like that of the snowbeasts purportedly wandering the far north. But Aio would be too clever to be caught by a mere hunter's arrow.

In comparison, Eshe was half the size of the seals that lived off the northern coast near the Howling Sea. But unlike a typical seal, she could transition herself into a form of stasis, as she was in for the remainder of the winter seasons, where she required neither breath nor sustenance for the months she was stuck under the ice.

Pesha mused at the likelihood that Aio could pluck Eshe from the water without much trouble.

"Your familiar. She's in the lake, isn't she?" Siofra asked.

Pesha leaped in surprise. His palms landed on the muddy bank. "I thought you were asleep."

"Aio woke me." Her voice had a distance to it, like she was calling to him through his subconscious. "She knew there was no danger. Not from you."

"Do you speak with your familiar? As you speak with me?"

"No, it's not like that. It's more of a sense. I can understand her meaning." Siofra pushed herself up. Her curls were caked in mud, and her dress would be a loss. She didn't seem concerned about either problem. "Isn't it the same for you?"

Pesha shrugged, eyes transfixed on the lake. While he could still *feel* Eshe in the winter seasons, he had no deeper connection to her while she rested. He could wake her if he wanted to, but it was easier on her to let her remain in her hibernation. "My mother could speak to her familiar. Ren was a weasel, who traveled in her many pockets and whispered terrible things in her ear."

Siofra's jaw dropped. "A familiar who could *talk?*"

"I could never hear anything from Ren but high-pitched squeaks, but my mother would have conversations with him, sometimes long into the night." He glanced over at her. "My bond with Eshe is more like your bond with Aio."

Aio flapped to life and took off into the sky.

Siofra sighed and set her gaze on the lake. "She's shy. Like me, I guess."

Pesha chuckled. It was refreshing to speak so openly with another Medvedev.

"You didn't have to come out here," she said. "I know my way back."

"No trouble in the garden then?"

Siofra fought a grin. "Aio led me out."

"I used to get lost there for hours as a boy," Pesha said. He folded his arms tighter around his knees, resting his chin on top. "My mother would scold me so. She'd send Ren in after me, and I swear he cursed me all the way back, even though I couldn't understand a word."

Siofra laughed. "Still. Must have been a nice place to grow up."

"Mm." Pesha bounced his chin on his knees. "We all know what we know. I had Des, and that was enough."

"Were you always close?"

"In different ways over the years," Pesha answered. "He's almost a decade older than me. When I was little, he looked after me when my mother... when my mother was unable to. As I aged, our bond shifted, and friendship came from that." He rotated to look at her. "I was against the two of you marrying."

Siofra stared into the forest. Her voice shifted, darkening. "I should've taken heed to both your and Fen's warnings."

"Des should have told you." Pesha took a deep breath and released it. "But it doesn't make him a bad man, Siofra. If you can learn to live with the terms of your arrangement, you can live well here."

Siofra recoiled with a scoff. "You're defending him."

"I *understand* him," he amended. "He deserves happiness he'll never allow himself to have. But that has naught to do with you."

Siofra dabbed at her eyes with her sleeve. "So I'm the fool then, for feeling as I do?"

"I didn't say that." Pesha uncoiled himself. "He'll be good to you, as he is to everyone here. But if you're expecting more from him than he can give, you'll be unendingly disappointed."

146

"What about you then? Do you also enjoy a horde of young women in your bed every night?" Siofra's tone was cutting.

Pesha didn't flinch. She wasn't the first to try to compare him to his brother to hurt him. "I've never had a woman in my bed." He rolled his lips together, contemplating whether to share this part of himself with someone who was still, in many ways, a stranger. "Only a couple of men."

Siofra turned all the way around to face him. "And where are these men now?"

"Doesn't matter," Pesha said. "I have no room in my life for a relationship. Seems trivial to even think of something so frivolous when I have a greater charge here at Shadowfen Hall."

Siofra nodded to herself with a short, bitter laugh. "You and Fen have much in common. Your words would be better used on him."

"Mm." Pesha leaped to his feet. He reached a hand out toward her. "Let's get you back."

"So your advice is I should learn to not feel, like you?" she asked as she let him help her to her feet.

Pesha pressed his mouth tight before saying what he needed to say—what she needed to hear. "My advice, Siofra, is to pick your happiness where you can." He pushed a tangle of curls back off her face. "And to artfully elude agonizing about what you cannot."

THIRTEEN
THE ANCIENT ART OF ALCHEMY

Siofra fought Gisela at every turn, grumbling as she was dragged out of bed. The curtains had been snatched wide to allow light to bathe the room. She abjectly refused to meet Gisela's eyes in the mirror as the attendant dressed her and brushed out her curls.

"I can do this myself. I don't need your help," she muttered, wrinkling her face into an unflattering frown. "I'm not a highborn. Nor have I ever wished to be."

"You can be cross for as long as it pleases you," Gisela said pleasantly, unmoved by Siofra's foul mood spreading over their morning ritual. "I can take it."

Siofra squirmed on the bench to dispel the ache taking hold of her body. Her head throbbed in tune with her heavy, sensitive limbs, as if she'd evoked terrible magic in the night. "I should hope so, Gisela, seeing as you're the one who *lied* to me."

"Did I lie?" Gisela set the brush aside and went to work on the stays of Siofra's pale-blue gown, one of the dresses that had appeared after the wedding. She wrenched them tight, eliciting affronted grunts from Siofra, who went green at the thought of the spread of food awaiting them downstairs.

"You could have told me what he does. If I had known, I might not have..." *Been so unreasonably hurt by it.* "Looked so foolish."

"I don't speak for your husband, Siofra. I am not obliged nor permitted to share his secrets with you."

Siofra snorted. She blew a curl off her face. "No, you can only hint at them, right? Like it's a game to you, watching. You're enjoying my discomfort, my..." Siofra scrunched her nose, searching for the right word, one that would not make her look even more ridiculous than she must already. "My *distaste*."

"I should say not," Gisela countered. It was her turn to look wounded. "I've taken for granted, perhaps, that you are not from here and so cannot know Desemir's reputation as the most prolific debaucher in our corner of the Northerlands. I never considered this might not be common knowledge across the realm."

"Most prolific..." Siofra gaped, aghast, but diverted her eyes again when she caught Gisela's. "What a curious thing that a man like him would wish to marry at all."

"Ahh," Gisela answered, grinning. "Well, that's easier to understand. As far as men are concerned, there are two kinds of women in this world: those they'd only fuck and those they would marry and start a family with. The former list is seemingly endless. The latter..."

Siofra winced at Gisela's choice of crude word. It prompted a painful reminder of the way men would speak to her in the market.

But was that not what she and Desemir had done last night? He may have spun the evening with his charm, snaring her in a web of his especial magic, but then he'd left her, discarded, her purpose served.

"He would've found less trouble marrying one of his conquests," Siofra said. She pinched her shoulders back together. "He treats me no different."

Gisela finished tying the ribbon at the gap between Siofra's shoulder blades and backed away. "I realize how it must seem to you, but I can assure you, his conquests do not have free rein of Shadowfen Hall. They do not dine at his table. Sleep under his roof." Gisela cocked her head. "Would the night have been easier for you if I'd told you?"

"*Yes!*" Siofra exclaimed, glaring at Gisela in the reflection. But the heat in her cheeks quickly subsided. She wilted with the heaviness of her confusing defeat. "No." Her head shook. "I don't know. The night was... It was not... That is... It was actually very *nice* before..."

"Before he kicked you out."

Siofra nodded.

Gisela's face erupted in a smile. It softened Siofra in spite of herself. "So you enjoyed it?"

Siofra's face reddened again, for a diametrically different reason. "To tell you the truth, it wasn't what I expected. I've always only ever heard of marriage described as duty, and that wasn't duty, not as I have known duty to mean. It was..."

"Amazing?" Gisela teased. "Pleasurable?"

"Stop," Siofra whispered, fighting her own smile.

"Seems to me your way forward is simple," Gisela said, leaning down over Siofra to drop her chin on her shoulder. She met her eyes in the reflection. "Take what pleasure he gives you, without guilt. Live the life of freedom and choice you earned yourself in this unbelievable agreement. I've never known *any* woman to be granted such a golden gift. See it for what it is. *Embrace* your good fortune." She lengthened again, standing over Siofra with a deep breath. "For *all* the women of the Darkwood have been vying for Desemir's hand, and he's given it to you."

Desemir trained his eyes on the forest as he rolled his head in broad circles, stretching out the knot that had infiltrated his neck for the past two days. The satisfying cracks and pops set his mind at ease. Grounded him, which he needed. He'd never, ever prepared for a meeting with one of his adversaries, but he'd agonized over his late-morning encounter from the moment he'd sent the last of his women home.

You should have told her.

Pesha's words angered Desemir even more in recollection. And why should he have told Siofra? What they had wasn't a marriage between two people in love—or even a more traditional arranged marriage, where there were certain expectations of a man. He needed children, and she needed protection. There was nothing more to it. But he should have to explain himself, should he?

You're the one who brought her here.

She has no right to be offended.

And you have no right to her feelings. You don't get to throw your hands up, Des. This was your idea. Your responsibility to make it work.

He flicked his eyes up and to the side at the groan of the library doors parting.

"What is this? Gisela?" Siofra's soft voice had a dubious edge.

"You can accept my apology later. You're to have breakfast here in the library, with your husband."

"No, Gisela, no, *no, no.*" Siofra floundered as the door closed, flapping her arms against it as the latch clicked.

A heavy silence followed. Siofra seemed suspended in animation, her hands still raised at the door. But then she spun around, lowering them to her sides. She watched him, saying nothing.

"I asked Gisela to bring you here," Desemir said. He threw a parting glance at the fog cutting off the tops of his trees. "I understand you have questions. I'm prepared to answer them."

Siofra's nose flared, eyes narrowing. She seemed determined to present a different impression, though, when she spread an unconvincing smile between her flushed cheeks.

"Where's Pesha?" she asked.

"I don't know."

"You don't *know?*"

152

"He's my brother, not my shadow."

"Aren't you afraid of being alone with me?"

"Should I be?"

"Well, I have no questions. So we can go join the others in the dining hall."

"I arranged for our morning meal to be brought here." Desemir gestured toward the modest spread on the table built for two.

Siofra's gaze didn't follow his hand though. Her eyes instead passed in disbelief over the rows and rows of books spanning the massive room, stretching to the second story. Thousands there were, with more joining his collection all the time. Books were a rare commodity in the kingdom, worth more than their weight in gold, and it was part of the allure, an assumption he proudly maintained when allowing others in his library. His adversaries didn't need to know he'd devoured many of the books himself when his mind was not so consumed with troubles.

"I thought you might feel more comfortable here," he explained. A sweat broke out on his palms, followed by a perplexing rush of nerves. "Seeing as you enjoy reading."

"There are so many," she whispered in awe. "I doubt even the Reliquary is in possession of such a number."

"Then my work here is done," Desemir quipped. "Feel free to share your observation liberally with any guests we bring here."

An awkward pause bloated the air between them. But then she flashed her gaze on him from the side and laughed. "What others think of you is important to you."

"I don't care what others *think* of me," he answered. "Only what they do with the information."

Siofra cocked a brow. Her initial tension had melted some. "You're speaking of your enemies?"

Desemir smirked. "I prefer 'adversaries.'"

"Are they not the same thing?"

Desemir stepped closer, brushing his hand across the back of the lounger as he made a path to her. "An adversary has the motivation to harm you but lacks the means. An enemy will procure both the motivation and the means, no matter the cost to them."

"And your... adversaries... lack the means to harm you?"

"Something like that."

Siofra returned her attention to the books. She seemed more relaxed. "You used the word enemy before. When you made your proposal to me."

He shrugged with an easy laugh. "Sometimes it just slips out. Then again, there's also a third consideration, which is opportunity. An adversary may lack the means and still find the opportunity, thus finding another avenue to claiming their status as enemy."

Siofra crossed her arms and watched him from the side. "You spend a lot of time thinking about this, don't you?"

"More than I'll admit to you, looking at me the way you are."

Siofra seemed to have more to ask, but she didn't. She returned to perusing the shelves, but the glazed look in her eyes told him she wasn't really seeing anything.

"Look. Siofra—"

She spun on her heels toward him. "I really need to speak with my brother. Whatever it is you believe we need to discuss here, we don't. You are who you are. I accept it. I've moved on from it. *Now* can we join the others in the dining hall?"

Desemir pondered how much of what she'd just said was truthful and not. No doubt she was eager to speak with Fen, and it would be pointless to tell her that her brother needed time.

But there were things she needed to hear, and if Desemir said them right, she would.

"Let's compromise," Desemir said. "Candor is more my style than coyness. I *know* you have questions, Siofra. Pesha told me."

Siofra turned her cool look back toward the books with an annoyed roll of her eyes.

"So let's agree to get them out of the way now. This morning. Then we can move on, as you say. Move forward, understanding each other better. I'll have them take our breakfast back to the dining hall, where we can enjoy it with the others." Desemir folded his hands in front of him. "I have something I'd like to say to you as well, and as it's time sensitive, I prefer we not delay this conversation any longer than we have to."

Siofra chewed the inside of her lip, still eyeing the books. What followed was a slight gap in her emotional armor, the briefest of moments where he could read her, as he had always been able to read others. It seemed more important to her that he *think* she had moved on. She feared disappointing him, when he'd been the one to disappoint her.

She shrugged as she tilted a book off the shelf, dropping it into her hands. "Fine."

Desemir sighed, startled by the relief he felt. Dealing with adversaries was a simple, tidy affair because he had no need for them to like him. He could say what he wanted without dressing. He could even have *fun* with it, much to Pesha's dismay.

But Siofra was going to bear his children, Guardians willing. It would not do to have her embittered throughout the process.

"Lovely," he said, with a flick of a smile. "I'll send for tea."

Siofra held tight to the book she'd pulled from the shelf. She'd selected it randomly, knowing nothing about its contents. The embossing had been long since wiped away by time and neglect. There was nothing in particular about its spine that had swayed her to choose it, and once she had the unknown dark-blue book in hand, she felt silly, and she couldn't help but wonder if Desemir was thinking the same.

She addressed her nerves with a drum of her hands on the underside of the tome as she watched Desemir transfer the large tray of tea and biscuits to a table next to the chaise. His shoulder muscles flexed under the dark fabric of his waistcoat as he fumbled with balancing the steaming contents, a skill he'd clearly never needed to learn. The light frown teasing the corners of his mouth, an unexpected sign of vulnerability, left her stomach in knots.

It was astonishing how she could go from being annoyed to enamored with Desemir in the span of the same thought. She couldn't reconcile her feelings—for good or ill—with what little she knew of the man she'd frivolously married.

Desemir recovered himself and poured her tea. She accepted it but set it aside, trying to read him in absence of knowing him. He didn't seem nervous, but he'd had years of experience in mastering difficult conversations.

"I should have been forthcoming about my evening activities," he stated. He'd poured himself tea as well but had left it beyond his arm's reach.

The steam simmered in the air, and Siofra chose that to focus on.

"I'm not... That is, I never considered you might care, which is a reflection upon me, not you."

Siofra pressed her tongue to the roof of her mouth, her eyes on his untouched tea. She wondered if he even liked tea and, if not, what he preferred. Yet another thing she didn't know about him.

"Siofra?"

She shook her head and shifted her attention back to him. "It was just unexpected. That's all."

He leaned back into his corner of the chaise, opening his arms. His mossy eyes gleamed as he studied her. "'Unexpected' is the way my adversaries describe me. You are not that. So. Ask me anything."

Siofra pulled the book closer, clutching it against herself as her arms crossed. He expected her to ask *something*, but she didn't know where to begin. She'd had plenty of questions last night, but with the clarity of morning, she was no longer convinced the answers would make her feel better. "Do you... Do you do that every night?"

Desemir's arms dropped to his lap. "Most nights."

"Why?"

His jaw hardened, throat bobbing when he swallowed. "I haven't been able to sleep for years. Lotte's tried a number of draughts, but—"

"Pesha told me that part already," Siofra said, cutting in. "I'm asking *why* you can't sleep. Why you need to exhaust yourself to get through the night."

Desemir cast his eyes to the side in thought. The question unnerved him. She saw it in the light flex of his left hand, the other gripping his mother's pendant. He clearly didn't want to answer, but he would, because talking had been his idea.

"I stopped sleeping after my father died," he finally said. "When everything fell to me."

Siofra didn't think he was lying, but she sensed it wasn't the whole truth either. "How many years ago was that?"

"Seven. Eight." He waved a hand. "I've lost count."

Siofra suspected the opposite was true; Desemir could no doubt recite, to the day, how long his father had been gone. "And..." She guided the book against her torso with her breaths. "My being here isn't..." She twisted her tongue in her mouth. *Just say it.* "Enough?"

Desemir slung his arms over the back and side of the chaise. He dragged his gaze over her before answering. "It wouldn't be fair to put that on you. My vigor is more than what one woman could bear."

Siofra met his eyes, matched his intensity. "You don't know what I could bear."

His head tilted to the side. "If this upsets you—"

"It doesn't," Siofra lied.

Desemir's mouth parted, his tongue swiping the edges as he formed his words. "Did I hurt you last night? Was I too... ardent?"

Siofra laughed. It felt somehow easier than existing in the seriousness of their conversation. "No, you didn't hurt me."

Desemir twerked his brows and mouth. "Well then. Was it enjoyable?"

Her nervous laughter turned into a hitched breath and warmed cheeks. "I have nothing to compare it to, but yes. It was…"

It was what?

Nice?

No. It was more than nice.

Nice was for the warm baths and delicious tarts she'd enjoyed at Shadowfen Hall.

Incredible?

Perhaps.

But incredible wasn't an option. Incredible was for passionate lovers who could not bear the thought of separation. It was perhaps, even, for the women who decorated Desemir's bed long into the night with their ardor, confident in knowing their place in his world, unburdened by the confusion of emotions.

There was no room for incredible when her charge was duty.

"It was fine," she said.

Desemir seemed disappointed, like she'd slighted him. "I see. I had aimed for the night to be pleasing for you."

"For me?" Siofra asked, skeptical that *her* pleasure was front of mind for him.

"For us both. But yes, for you. As it fell to me to deliver your first experience, I tried to make it memorable. And, in doing so, have perhaps created confusion."

Siofra tried to smile. "There's no confusion. I know what this is."

"Just the same, I'll be encouraging you to take lovers as well, when there's no risk of them fathering your children. Your happiness will bring joy not only to me but to the others here at the Hall. And, one day soon, to our children." He cleared his throat. "And I can change our evening sessions into something more traditional, if you prefer."

"You don't need to change anything for me," Siofra said. She reeled from how much he'd said with so few words. "I wouldn't know the difference either way."

"Mm." Desemir's eyes never left her. "Back in Newcarrow, was there never someone special? Someone you fancied?"

"I thought you understood what my life was like before I came here."

"No," he said, "but I'm beginning to." He leaned in toward her. "Is there anything else you wanted to know? Any other questions that will put your mind at ease to have answered?"

I want more than your half-truths. But you'll never give them to me. Nor do I have any right to demand them.

Siofra shook her head.

"Good." Desemir sat back. He looked relieved. It was then she understood that despite his dogged insistence on having this conversation, he wasn't at all happy to be having it. Her reaction last night had made it necessary. "Then I'll say what I came to say, and you can go find your brother."

Siofra released the book, suddenly anxious to be touching it at all. It wasn't his words that unnerved her but the way the cords in his neck pulled at his jaw. How he'd straightened into an almost formal pose.

"Harry hasn't taken the paperwork to the secretary in Darkwood Run yet. He's due there tomorrow. Until he's filed our license of marriage, nothing is official."

Siofra burrowed against the pillow behind her. So she was right to be nervous. He *was* having second thoughts after how she'd acted last night.

"I'm giving you the choice now to undo what we have done." He clasped his hands in his lap. "If you're having regrets, it isn't too late."

Siofra stuffed back the emotion welling in her throat. "Is that what you want? To undo it?"

Desemir spun his father's ring. "No, Siofra. It isn't what I want." He again looked at her. He'd somehow succeeded in eradicating any former emotion from his expression. He was unreadable. Aloof. "I want our arrangement to work. We will both prosper if it does. But I'll not have your unhappiness on my conscience along with everything else."

And what is everything else, Desemir?

"Then you needn't worry," she replied, steeling herself so he wouldn't see her relief and mistake it for more of the girlish emotion that had driven her running to the lake. "Now that I know about this side of you, you'll brook no further trouble from me."

Desemir practically leaped to his feet. She caught a soft whiff of his sweat. It whisked her back to the night before, their deeds on the balcony. "Good. Then we understand each other."

"We do."

Siofra didn't move from the chaise when he stood. She watched him walk away, his words a jumble in her mind as she struggled to catch up to all he'd said, linking it with all he'd meant.

He turned back just before the door. "I brought you to the library for a reason. I suspect you don't believe me, but your happiness *is* important to me. I want only accord and amity in our halls, and if your needs are met, then I'll have upheld my part of things."

"My needs?" Siofra's heart leaped in her chest.

He passed his hand around the room. "I only ask for an hour of your time each night. The rest of your hours are yours, and... Ah, well, let's just say that as a boy I would get lost in here, and it was almost as good as disappearing into one of these stories." He pressed a smile into his face and met her gaze. "It's yours now. Consider it a gift, a token of my friendship—and my intention."

"You're..." Siofra shook her head. "You're *giving* me an entire library?"

Desemir's careful expression wavered. "Do you not want it?"

"No, I..." She drew a shuddering breath. It was happening again, the conflict inside her that she couldn't define. "Thank you."

"Enjoy the volume you selected. *The Ancient Art of Alchemy, Part Seven.* One of my favorites, as a boy, though most of what J. Howard claims has been disproven, with time." He bowed his head and started to back away. "I'm an open book, Siofra. Next time, come to me."

"Of course," she whispered, holding her breath as she watched him leave.

Pesha found Stiofen on the east wing veranda tearing off hunks of his bread and feeding them to his giant falcon, Atio. Atio's enthusiastic wing flaps seemed to indicate his approval, of food that surely wasn't part of his natural diet.

Stiofen's easy, unguarded smile, a rough contradiction to the hostility he'd offered in his time at the Hall, sent a curious flutter across Pesha's chest.

And then Stiofen *laughed*. The sound rang with delight and reached Pesha as he hovered at the door, deciding whether to stay or leave.

"No, you *cannot* crack open the ice and eat the fish, you brigand," Stiofen chided Atio, who was still flapping himself into an excited fit. "There's plenty on the grounds to suit you."

Atio lifted his beak toward the sky and cawed his displeasure. As the falcon lowered his head back down, his dark, beady eyes locked on Pesha. His flapping subsided.

Stiofen followed Atio's shift in attention, his smile not just fading but dying altogether. His violet eyes pulsed with accusation, but also something less clear, akin to the intense glares he'd leveled on Pesha in the carriage.

"Here to scold me for not joining the rest of you for breakfast?" His playfulness was gone. *This* was the boy Pesha recognized, while the other was the one he wished he were better acquainted with.

Pesha took a tentative step onto the decorated stones of the veranda, hands looped at his back. "I am not. Your sister didn't join us either. Nor did Desemir."

Stiofen snorted, rolling his eyes as he turned his head toward the forest. "Too busy playing happy families."

"No, certainly not." Pesha inched forward. "Something happened last night, and it upset Siofra very much. Desemir wanted to speak with her alone this morning, to clear things up between them."

Stiofen's face twitched, still stubbornly holding onto the derision he'd summoned with Pesha's arrival. "He upset her? Why am I not surprised?"

"You haven't asked if she's all right." Pesha paused his advance in the middle of the veranda, at the center of the floor's swirling patterns radiating outward toward the edges.

"I'm sure you would have led with that." Stiofen tucked his hand under Atio's beak with a loving stroke.

"She wasn't all right last night," Pesha replied. "I'm sure she could use her brother right now."

Stiofen shook his head, eyes on Atio. "Unlike you, I don't enable the dangerous whims of my sibling." He dropped his hands away from the falcon. "You're wrong anyway. She doesn't need me. She made it *painfully* clear."

Pesha chanced a closer approach. When Stiofen didn't bark at him to keep his distance, he moved to the half wall of the veranda and took a seat several feet away.

Atio took off but hovered nearby.

"Is that the requirement for your love, Fen? Her unquestioned obedience?"

Fire flashed in Stiofen's eyes. "You think you understand, but you don't. You may be Medvedev, and you might be displaced from Asgill lands as we are, but you'll *never* know what our life has been like. What we had to do to survive. What I did for *her* so the men who used me wouldn't discard her."

Pesha offered Stiofen the stunned silence he'd been after. "That's true. I don't know. I've never lived anywhere but here, and I've never endured the struggle you describe."

Stiofen's lips curled as he seemed to wage a battle with himself. He swung his gaze along Pesha, lingering beyond what the examination required. "Then *what*, Pesha?"

Pesha was struck with the strange urge to reach forward and take both of Stiofen's hands in his—to crush them to his chest as he discovered the words Stiofen needed to let go of the anger that had kept him going for so long.

He fought the urge. Buried it, alongside his others.

"None of that makes me wrong," Pesha replied. "That life is behind you. I would never have brought the two of you here if more of the same awaited you."

Stiofen pursed his mouth. "No, you just sold my sister in marriage to a man who has more enemies than friends, which is supposed to be somehow *better*."

Pesha decided to not tell Stiofen that he hadn't known Desemir's intentions ahead of time. "You give Siofra little credit for having her own mind."

"And *you* don't even know her."

"I know she needs her brother no less than she did before she married."

Stiofen scoffed. "What, you're her champion now?"

"That's your role. I'd never try to take it from you," Pesha answered softly. If only he had the magic adequate to mend Stiofen's wounded heart. His suffering was as clear as Siofra's, but while he wore his like pride, she wanted nothing more than to shed hers. "I just thought you should know."

"Know what? That she regrets making such a rash, ludicrous choice?" Stiofen laughed bitterly, shaking his head. "Of course she does. Don't need the gift of divining to have predicted it."

Pesha nodded to himself. Despite the explanation he'd given Stiofen, he couldn't say why he'd come outside. Where there was a hint of a truth there, waiting for him, he left it unaddressed. "Desemir has asked to see you later this morning."

"Has he now?" Stiofen's look indicated exactly what he thought of the request.

"It's about your land and title."

"Which I *told* your brother, I don't want."

"Just the same. You'll go? Even if it's only to remind him of your refusal?"

Stiofen waved a hand at him. "Why not? I've nothing else to do here."

"Is this all you've eaten? Some bread?" Pesha asked, pointing at the crumbs lining the wall.

Stiofen twitched at the unexpected shift in the conversation. "I..." He sighed, lowering his eyes to his hands. "Yeah."

"Still hungry?" Pesha asked. He gestured toward the door. "I can bring something out for us, and we could..." He fought a laugh. "Enjoy it together, in silence, while you practice your glare on me some more."

Stiofen hesitated before nodding. His quick glance up revealed something almost impish, but it was gone before it could build to a grin.

Pesha ignored the skip in his heart. "I'll be back before you can decide your loathing is greater than your hunger."

Desemir caught his brother squirreling away an armful of food from the dining hall. His mouth curled in amusement. "You *have* heard of a tray?"

Pesha grunted and shifted his balance. "I can manage." He cast an anxious glance down the hall. "Did you need something?"

"I can call for Lotte—"

"I said I was *fine*," Pesha grumbled. He sagged to catch an orange before it rolled from the crook of his elbow. "I talked to Stiofen, as you asked. He'll be along to see you later."

"You're testy this morning." Desemir reached for the grapes and cheese to help him, ignoring Pesha's vexed glare. "You'll be pleased to know I've spoken with Siofra and all is well."

Pesha's rigid expression softened but just as quickly turned skeptical. "That sounds far too easy to be true."

Desemir popped a grape into his mouth, enjoying the crisp snap. He'd toyed with growing his own, starting a vineyard, but their proximity to the sea meant the soil was too sandy to produce anything worth drinking. "You were right. I should have told her before. She was perfectly fine about it once I explained things."

Pesha's brows knit together. "Was she?"

"Your surprise wounds me."

"I am dubious," Pesha agreed. "Where is she now?"

Desemir shrugged. "More than likely enjoying the library I just gave her."

Pesha twitched his head. "You *gave* her the library?"

"That's what I said."

"How does that work, exactly, when the library is part of the manor, which belongs to you and only you?"

Desemir frowned. It was a fair question, requiring a firmer resolution. "You're suggesting I draw up paperwork. Make it official."

"I'm suggesting... what?" Pesha's look was incredulous. "What goes through your mind sometimes?"

Desemir lifted his shoulders into a heavy, satisfied sigh. Pesha might be skeptical, but Siofra *had* seemed much better after their talk. Desemir had accepted his own role in her upset last night and had affirmed, both to her and himself, to be mindful of it going forward. What more could there be?

"Can you..." Pesha nodded at the grapes and cheese. Desemir carefully transferred them back. "Thank you."

"Where are you off to with all this pilfered food anyway?"

"I..." Pesha's cheeks bloomed in a way Desemir hadn't seen for years. "Taking it to Stiofen. He hasn't eaten."

The corners of Desemir's mouth drew up in a smile. "Are you now?"

"Is that all?"

"Go on then. It can wait."

"Is there something else I should know?"

"I said it can wait."

"Des. You know I'll just stew on it until you tell me."

"Ah, well. I've decided..." Desemir had begun to have second thoughts about the idea, but if he *didn't* do this, if he didn't show off his bride to the whole of Darkwood, there would be doubt, and from doubt could spring mutiny. There could be no question of the legitimacy of his future heir. "In the absence of a proper wedding, I'd like to have a ball in Siofra's honor."

Pesha's head tilted to the side. "A ball. The kind where you invite a lot of people? People who want you dead?"

Desemir tapped a finger in the air. "The very same."

"Ah. Well then, no. It's a terrible idea and the last thing you need right now."

"Brilliant," Desemir said, feeling decidedly better about it, having spoken the words aloud. "I'll put Lotte on it right away. She'll be thrilled to finally have something to celebrate again."

FOURTEEN
A PIECE OF THE SUN ITSELF

With Desemir being mostly too busy to show her around, Siofra spent her time learning the grounds of Shadowfen Hall on her own. She mapped the Hall in her head—all but the west wing—and practiced getting lost so she could find her away again. She even dipped into rooms Gisela said weren't in use anymore, like the solarium, and explored as much of the grounds as she could on foot. Once, she even went into the forest to lay her hands on the ebony wood that consumed her husband's life.

When he'd ask her how her day was, she always had a story to tell him, and he at least *seemed* eager to hear every one of them.

Sometimes he even told her a story of his own. Her favorite so far was the way he described his late mother and her obsession with timepieces. He spoke of her in a mix of love and awe, and between the words, Siofra could see the young man he'd been before his flesh had toughened and his heart had hardened.

In the evenings, after supper, she read until Desemir summoned her to his chambers. The library alone was enough to give her peace, providing a means to weather her increasingly confusing emotions, letting them disappear into the pages of other people's stories.

It was there Desemir found her. She'd retired to the library earlier than usual, and his presence in the middle of the day made her jump straight out of her chair.

"I didn't mean to startle you. Sit," he said, and took the tall chair across from the one she was curled up in. "What are you reading?"

Heart still thumping, Siofra held up the book.

"Ahh. *Enid and the Forty-Seven Horses.*" He rested his boot atop the opposite knee, nodding. "When I was a boy, I thought the story was for children. Now that I'm older, I know better."

"I'm almost finished," Siofra said as she marked her place and set the book aside. She immediately regretted it, because it left nothing for her to do with her hands. She laughed. "I'm wondering how you ever thought a tale about a girl cursed to murder every horse she comes across was a story for children."

"I suppose it was the element of adventure. Everything she experienced as she sought to break the curse. The friends she made along the way." Desemir shrugged his hands out. "But then she doesn't break the curse at all."

Siofra crinkled her nose. "Well, thanks. I hadn't gotten that far."

"I've spared you the pain." He flashed her a grin before pushing off from the chair. Her gaze followed him as he moved to the center of the row of shelves and searched them, hands linked behind his back. "Do you prefer happy endings?"

"Only if they're realistic," Siofra said carefully.

Desemir threw her a quick glance over his shoulder. "Why do you say that?"

She regretted saying anything. "No reason."

"Tell me," he said. He turned all the way around and watched her. "Please."

Siofra turned her gaze on her hands, wrung together in her lap. Natural, gentle inquisitiveness always disarmed her. It had from the moment she'd met him, when he'd come to her room after her bath looking as nervous as she'd felt. "All my life I've watched others go through theirs knowing they had control over their fate. Even the sick or destitute can make choices, however limited. They can find their joys, however muted. Those were not experiences available to me."

"And now?" Desemir inhaled a thoughtful breath. "Now that you've made choices for yourself? Are your joys still out of reach?"

A rush of warmth spread across her chest. "Not anymore," Siofra said. "Thanks to you."

Desemir didn't respond to that. He cast an awkward look to the side and then returned to perusing the books. Siofra tried not to watch, instead focused on stilling her inexplicably erratic pulse. Was it the conversation? His gentle way with her? His rare appearance before supper?

She didn't have time to ponder the answer. His shadow fell over her, and a moment later, he'd set three books in her lap.

Desemir's breath tickled her scalp from behind. "Start with these. Our heroes and heroines find their joys, in the end, but they work for every last one." His mouth brushed the crown of her head in what felt like a kiss, though she knew she'd misread it. "I have to go meet your brother. I'll see you at supper, Siofra."

Siofra waited for the heavy doors to close before bowling over in a dizzying exhale.

Fen had managed to avoid Siofra all week. They each lived their separate lives, passing each other in the halls like specters. He'd evaded the trap of group conversation by taking his meals on the veranda, where Pesha often joined him.

Pesha was a curious creature. Fen was bewildered by the Medvedev who made excuses for men, in particular the lecherous brother who could do no wrong in his eyes. Still, there was something in Pesha's careful words and searching gazes that calmed Fen. He couldn't reconcile the Medvedev who served men willingly with the quiet, thoughtful Medvedev who existed in the comfortable silences between them as they ate their meals on the veranda.

When it was just him and Pesha, Fen could almost relax.

But Pesha wasn't with him in the carriage ride Desemir had swayed him into taking. It was the first good look Fen had allowed himself to take. Desemir was unquestionably handsome, Fen conceded, but arrogant. He flashed his gaze around like merely looking at something gave him authority over it. Which Fen supposed was true. According to Pesha, Desemir had inherited far more than he had any right to.

Desemir leaned back against the crimson velvet, head rolled to the side, assessing him.

Fen refused to dignify the assault by asking about it. He pointed his attention out the curtained window and left it there.

"Has Pesha told you much about the Great Darkwood?" Desemir asked. Fen stole a glance from his peripheral and saw the man had unbuttoned the top of his shirt in order to play with his amulet. It was a woman's necklace, but he didn't seem to care. "In all the time you seem to be spending together?"

Fen shook his head.

"Ah. I don't suppose you ever heard of it before you came here?"

"No."

"Your old keeper had. Stanhope. He purchased the entirety of his yearly limit in one haul. Tried to pay me double for more, but I refused."

Fen rolled his eyes toward the window.

"It doesn't surprise you."

"Stanhope, greedy? When you've said something novel, perhaps I'll be surprised."

Desemir snaked an arm past Fen and slid the window open. Then he flopped back and spread his arms across the seat, inhaling with flourish. "Smell that, Stiofen. The earthy pine of the needled trees that keep us fed, keep us safe."

"Smells like trees."

"Not just any trees." Desemir rolled forward, dropping his elbows onto his knees. "This is the only place in the entire kingdom where ebony wood grows. The bark is dense, dark, and serves many purposes. It can support the sturdiest home, make tables and chairs that last centuries. But its bark, which peels for only a fortnight in the springtide, is as thick as leather but resistant to the dampness that rots the soft hides. The profits we make in one season from the bark alone could support Shadowfen Hall for a decade. Every last one of these trees peels, and rather than surrendering the gold to the earth, we turn it into something useful. The barony of Shadowfen may not have a village, but what we do have is worth far more."

"You don't need to sell me on your forest. I don't particularly care."

"You should care. Because I'm cutting you in on a portion of the profit." Desemir angled his head to snare Fen's attention, but Fen stubbornly pointed it at the field and lake as they passed. "Two percent of all bark earnings. Two percent of all timber sold. I'll make it a condition of my will for my heir to honor this arrangement, just as he would honor the one I made with my own brother."

"As I told Siofra, Pesha, and then you, when you summoned me to your office, I don't want anything from you."

"Your pride," Desemir said, "won't serve you when it matters most. It's a gift, Stiofen. For Siofra more than you, I'll admit that. If she sees you settled, she'll settle as well. And she has been... decidedly unsettled these past days."

Fen shook his head. The man was unbelievable. "Being bribed into a marriage you can't refuse will do that to someone."

Desemir retreated. He settled back against the bench. "Tell me something. Are you both so much worse off now than you were in Newcarrow?"

Fen denied him the pleasure of an answer, but Desemir's question had taken root long before Desemir had asked. Fen's belly had

171

never been fuller, his bed never softer. The simplest freedoms, like the authority to walk from one room to another without escort, provided enough contrast that he had to admit things *were* better.

But things had been good in the early days with the Stanhopes too. And the steward hadn't been sleeping with his sister.

"Once, the Darkwood belonged to no one." Desemir returned to his reverie about the damnable forest. "But then men came along, and the predictable happened. Two wars were fought over these woods, and the five men who emerged victors divided the spoils. And, for almost two hundred years, that's how it was, until my father conceived of a way to take it all."

"Why would you think I want to know about your forest?"

"Because you now have a vested interest in protecting it with me."

"I told you—"

"You certainly did," Desemir agreed. "But I also heard the words you didn't say. The ones your pride would keep you from."

"Why Siofra?" Fen blurted. His chest heaved with the expulsion of words. "Why my sister?"

Desemir seemed taken aback, but his hesitation was brief. "The answer isn't as complicated or nefarious as you appear to want to make it, Stiofen. I needed a wife. I couldn't choose one within my own society, and even my peers across the kingdom, in other Reaches, have potential ties with my adversaries. Siofra is... unique in that she came with none of that. No family. No name anyone would recognize. As it happened, she also needed something I could give."

Fen squeezed his hands into fists to keep the tremors away. "So this has *nothing* to do with her magic? With mine?"

"Have I asked you to use your magic?"

"Not yet." Fen hadn't used it either, not once. He'd be happy to never use it again.

"I have no need of a flourisher. I have more than I'll ever need," Desemir said. His eyes narrowed slightly. "You've spent enough time with Pesha—"

"I hardly know Pesha," Fen stated, a hot flush coursing into his cheeks.

"To understand I have a soft spot in my heart for displaced Medvedev," Desemir said, continuing. "When I learned of what Siofra had inadvertently done, I knew it could mean only one thing. I would have helped the two of you no matter what. But Siofra could see the wisdom in joining our fates in a more permanent way. Unfair as it is, Medvedev can't live normal lives in this kingdom. We're all stronger as allies, and you are safer here than you are anywhere else but your homeland."

Fen shook his head through his incredulous laughter. "*You're* not even safe! How can *we* be?"

"Look around you." Desemir thrust his hand out the window, weaving it through the rain-laced fog. "We are completely surrounded by a forest no one can enter without my authority. The only paths through are heavily guarded and gated. Anyone attempting to circumvent it would be slowed by the unforgiving undergrowth that has overtaken the rough loam that plagues this region. They would be stopped altogether by the uncommon root systems of our ebony wood, which protrude in deadly spikes from the ground like the cypress of the Westerlands, making the forest utterly unhospitable for horses. And if that wasn't enough, there are the few who did slip through and died for their efforts."

Fen caught Euric, the grizzled guard of few words, leveling his pale, intense eyes on him. The man was so quiet, Fen had forgotten he was even there. He shook it off and returned his attention to Desemir. "If all that is true, then your reasons for choosing my sister make even less sense. If those who would take from you— hurt you—cannot even *get* to you, then your choice in a bride is nearly endless, isn't it?"

Euric tapped the roof of the carriage. It came to a stop, and the guard jumped out, drawing his sword.

"What is it?" Fen asked. He felt like a fool when his pulse hastened, but the talk of enemies had gotten to him.

"Nothing," Desemir said. He slid the window closed and sat back. "Euric is only standing guard."

"Against what?" Fen struggled to see, as the fog obscured all but hints of the landscape.

"Anything." Desemir rested one foot atop the opposite knee. "There's another reason I asked you to ride with me today."

Fen's distrust returned. He ran his tongue along the back of his teeth with a stoic glare. "Here it comes. At last."

"There will be a ball in three days' time. Here at Shadowfen Hall."

"A... *what*?" Fen leaned forward in disbelief. "A ball, as in..."

"Our wedding was private, and a public showing will be needed to establish legitimacy. And... it might help lift Siofra's spirits if she's welcomed in a more formal way."

"You're going to... invite these same people you work so hard to keep out of your forest and your land *here*?"

Desemir's cool expression was maddening. "It must be done. We could host it elsewhere, but it would leave us even more exposed. It has to be here, at the Hall." He tapped his thumb against the hard leather of his boot. "I need you to make amends with your sister before that night comes."

Fen shook his head. "You are an unbelievable man, Trevanion."

"Desemir. Or Des. Please."

"I have nothing to say to Siofra I have not already said."

"It's not your words I ask for. But your presence. Your..."

"Magic," Fen said with a hard sneer. "And there it is."

"Your *calming* effect on her. There will be many people here, most of whom will be imagining their own furnishings decorating our halls, and Pesha will be consumed with that. He won't have time to soothe her as well."

"Or..." Fen leaned back, crossing his arms. "We can just let her do as she pleases and let the results—or the remains, as it were—fall where they may."

Desemir folded his hands under his chin. His eyes closed, as if he were drawing the strength needed to deal with his unruly brother-in-law. "I'm not asking for myself. I'm asking for her." His eyes opened. "Don't let your pride and anger put her in danger."

"*Me*? *I'm* putting her in danger? You're the one—"

"Ensuring she is *seen*, that others know she is, in fact, real, and so the legitimacy of her children will not be in question." Desemir lowered his hands. "Her firstborn son will inherit *all* of this, Stiofen. Every acre. Every splinter of wood. Blade of grass. And you, her brother, and Pesha, will be the only other men in this entire realm who have a stake in it." He tapped the roof. "But not if you can't get over yourself."

Desemir tossed his cloak at the rack without slowing. What a stubborn fool Siofra's brother was. The other men of the Darkwood would salivate to gain back even an acre. He'd offered Stiofen a permanent two-percent stake and *still* he had only glares?

"Shall I escort you to the Hall of Counting?" Euric asked.

"I'll escort myself. Tell Lotte I'll sup in my quarters tonight." Desemir raised a hand. "If you see Pesha, send him my way."

Euric nodded and headed down the hall.

Desemir held an exasperated breath and released it.

Stiofen had jumped out of the carriage and made straight for the gardens, and his falcon. That was another thing on Desemir's mind these days. He wasn't used to making room for a Medvedev's familiar. Pesha's was largely out of sight. But the twins' falcons could not be ignored. The birds must be protected, at any cost. That meant no flying beyond where the Trevanion guards could protect them.

He would speak with Siofra on it.

But first, he needed a drink. Just one. Never more, for that had been his father's way, and Desemir sought to be as unlike Ludwik as night was to day.

He made his way down the hall, past the rows of portraits of his lesser ancestors: cousins, daughters, and distant aunts and uncles. The Trevanions who mattered—he thought with a disdainful laugh—hung in the Hall of Counting itself, the center of business and politics of Shadowfen Hall. Now that he was married, he would need to summon the portrait artist to add another. He hoped one more would soon follow.

As he neared the vestibule that would take him into the Hall of Counting, the jarring sound of giggles slowed his pace. A few steps closer and he identified both the one laughing and the one prompting the melodious sound.

"It's all in the wrist," Wulfhelm explained. Desemir recognized his tone. He'd used it enough on the young girls of the Darkwood when they had been younger and life was simpler. "If they're looking at your left hand, which is the one that *appears* to be doing the trick, then your right hand will go unnoticed as the card slides from under your sleeve. Like... so."

"It's like magic," Siofra mused.

Wulfhelm's tone grew serious. "It's a trifle compared to yours, Mistress Trevanion."

Siofra's soft laughter rang along the stone walls. "Siofra. Or Si."

"Si." Wulfhelm made a considering sound. "I like it. It rhymes with sea, and I've always loved the ocean."

Desemir clenched.

"Go on. You try it now," Wulfhelm said.

Desemir stepped around the corner into the vestibule.

Both of their smiles died. Wulfhelm was the first to recover, looking guilty enough to vindicate Desemir's annoyance. "Desi. Have a nice ride?"

"Can we talk?"

Wulfhelm tossed a glance back at Siofra.

"Alone."

"Sure." Wulfhelm's mouth tightened in a nervous smile as he nodded at Siofra. "I'll see you..."

"Yeah," Siofra said, aiming a confused look at Desemir as she left them. "I'll see you."

Wulfhelm reached to open one of the doors, but Desemir clamped his hand down on the frame, blocking it.

"What was that?"

"What was..." Wulfhelm scratched the back of his head. "She came looking for you. I said you were out."

"And?" Desemir demanded.

"And... She saw me playing with my cards. Asked me about it. I showed her the trick. You know the one."

Desemir crushed a laugh through his hardened jaw. "I've known you your whole life, Wulf. There's how you speak to your friends, and there's how you speak to the women you want in your bed."

Wulfhelm's eyes flashed with panic. "No, *no*, Desi. That's not—"

"It better not be," Desemir snapped. He slid his hand to the doorknob. "Just know that when I said she could take lovers, I didn't mean *you*."

Wulfhelm balked. "Right."

"You know what? Tell Lotte I'll still be dining in my chambers tonight, but I won't be alone. My wife will be joining me."

"Sure, of course—"

Desemir ripped the door open and moved inside before slamming it in Wulfhelm's face.

Desemir was upset about something. Siofra could tell, in spite of his ineffective efforts to seem in a cheerful mood. The calm, easy way he'd spoken to her in the library was gone.

He'd hardly touched his supper. His hands were too occupied with a story he was telling her, about Steward Arranden. Except the story wasn't for her. She was just the person who happened to be sitting in front of him when the words came out.

But that wasn't what was bothering him.

"Are you going to go? To this meeting?"

"No." Desemir looked affronted at the suggestion, scrunching his nose. "And anyway, it's not a meeting. They just want to lure me in alone to confront me."

"You're too smart for that," Siofra replied. It seemed to be what he wanted to hear.

"Mm." Desemir balled his napkin and tossed it onto his plate. His expression darkened further. "Wulfhelm said he showed you his card trick."

Siofra was happy to have something to offer the conversation, but she saw Desemir wasn't smiling. "Ah. Yes. I'd never seen anyone do that before."

"Mm."

"And you? Do you know card tricks?"

"Me?" Desemir's laugh was strained. "I wouldn't know where to find the time. Managing the business of the Barony of Shadowfen takes more time than I have."

"Can I..." Siofra almost didn't finish. "Is there something I could help you with?"

Desemir finally met her gaze directly. "You really mean that, don't you?"

She balked. "Of course I do. I wouldn't have asked if I didn't."

He almost smiled. "Your candor is refreshing. Most men don't say what they mean at all, only what suits them in the moment. And your offer is appreciated... When the time is right, I'll teach you the ledgers. If you want."

"I want to learn everything you're willing to teach me," she said with a hard swallow. He was speaking evenly enough, but something was amiss; she *felt* it.

"Mm." He returned his attention to his plate.

"Is something wrong?" Siofra reached for her wineglass but thought better of it. "Have I done something to displease you?"

"You?" Desemir cast his eyes to the side. His tongue passed across his lips. "Come here."

Siofra swallowed. "What?"

178

Desemir pushed back from the table. He held up his hands and gestured toward himself. "Come over here, Siofra."

Siofra darted her eyes over the remnants of her meal. The half-drank wine. Her napkin, bunched in her hands, an outlet for her nerves. Over a week she'd been his wife and she'd had not a single night off from his bedchamber. But inviting her to eat with him alone? That had been a first.

She moved tentatively to the other side of the small table. When she was close, he looped an arm around her waist and tugged her forward. She fell onto his lap, her legs falling over either side of his thighs. A knot lodged in her throat when she felt the hard bulge that was ready for her without any of the kissing or touching he usually started with to warm her up.

Desemir ran his hand up her back in one continuous, possessive stroke. When he reached her scalp, he wound his fingers through the back of her hair, making a fist. He jerked her backward, but her gasp died when his tongue traced the length of her neck in a slow, arduous path, traveling downward to her breasts.

Siofra's heart raced with confused delight. Her earlier uneasiness began to melt away.

With his other hand still wound around her hips, Desemir bounced her over him, matching the movements with quick, hard thrusts upward.

He released her hair and pulled his hand around to the front, shoving it up under the skirt of her dress in one fluid effort. Her scream of stunned pleasure, when he sank his fingers into her, undulated against his mouth, still pressed against her throat.

He pulled back to look at her, his eyes wide in revelation. "You were ready for me."

Siofra's panting kept her from speaking.

"Are you satisfied here?" He moaned into the hollow of her neck. A chorus of stilted whispers were all she could offer in response as his fingers plunged deeper, the knuckles of his other hand slamming against the inside of her hips. Too much of this would bruise her, but she didn't care. She never wanted him to stop.

179

"I asked you a question, Siofra," Desemir said again, low and forceful. He slid upward, rolling her sensitive spot between the pads of his fingers. His hand moved to the small of her back, a silent command matching his tone.

Siofra cried out as a sharp bolt of pleasure rocked her. Desemir removed his hand from inside her and used it to free himself from his trousers. He slid his dry hand under her ass and lifted her up and back down again, guiding her onto his cock.

Siofra's mouth gaped, head falling back in complete surrender as he buried himself inside her. The hand on her ass curled inward, and he dug his fingertips into her flesh as he guided her to ride him.

"Yes," Siofra whispered between breaths. She wrapped her arms around his neck and rode him faster, losing herself to the synchronicity of their combined thrusts, the perfection of his driving, insistent pleasure.

"Louder," Desemir commanded.

"Yes." She tried again, but the word cracked as he thrust so sharply upward, she almost fell off his lap.

"*Louder.*" He pushed the word through clenched teeth, bouncing her faster, driving upward to meet her with every stroke.

"*Yes,*" Siofra cried. "*Yes!*"

Desemir gripped her chin between his thumb and forefinger and forced her to meet his amber eyes, half-closed to match his mouth, parting, closing, parting, as he rode the same delectable wave.

Holding her at the back, he lifted as he stood and laid her on the table, settling her between his empty glass of wine and untouched plate of food. She rolled her head to the side, panting to catch her breath.

With his palms on the inside of her thighs, thumbs dug into her soft flesh, he plunged in, pulled out, and plunged in again in long strokes. Once he found his rhythm, he broke it, lashing into her with such force, her ass came up off the table.

"Guardians," he hissed, teeth clamped down on his lip. He quickened some more, driving her back with every staggering blow.

His eyes still locked on hers, he moved one hand from her inner thigh to the part of her crying out for him—*begging* for him to finish what he'd started, to relieve her of her unbearable agony.

Desemir pinched her flesh between his fingers. Stars exploded behind her eyes, and a rapturous dizziness followed close behind when he released and pinched again. Released. Pinched. Released. Pinched. It was too much. She could hardly breathe, and she thought she might die right on the spot if relief didn't come fast.

Siofra's legs flexed, twitching as she rose higher and higher. Desemir's thrusts turned to pounds, bruising her in a way she'd welcome a thousand times over.

The thunderclap of pleasure was so sudden, her scream turned to a soundless gasp. She arched up off the table, angling away from the assault that was too much. Desemir clamped his hand onto her back.

"Don't run from it, Siofra," Desemir whispered. "Claim it."

Siofra climbed even higher before she finally crashed, writhing and whimpering beneath him. She met his eyes just in time for him to seize up and cry out. He spasmed against her, the force of his own release as destructive and unspoiled as hers. The warmth flooding inside her calmed the last of her shudders until she was nothing but a shadow of her former self. Her cheek landed on the table, forehead nudging the wineglass as her breathing slowed to normal.

Desemir released her and stumbled back. He turned away and shimmied back into his pants, ambling toward the drink cart.

Siofra struggled to sit, but her arms and legs hadn't regained strength. Instead, she rolled off the table and landed in a crouch.

She wanted to ask him what had happened, but she didn't know how, nor how to tell him she wanted more.

181

She didn't get the chance to do either. As he poured a drink, he said, without turning back, "That'll be all for tonight, Siofra. You can go."

Siofra flushed with embarrassment. She was frozen in place, half of her still buzzing from whatever he'd done to her, the other facing the understanding that he didn't want her there. The moment had passed, and he wanted to put it behind him.

Her knees wobbled as she rose to her feet, gripping the table on her way up. She waited for him to take it back, to ask her to stay.

But he didn't turn.

You should say something.

Good night.

Thank you.

Anything.

But pride clamped her mouth closed.

Siofra adjusted her skirts and forced herself to keep her composure until she reached the hall.

As she struggled with the door, it flung inward, knocking her back. Wulfhelm stood on the other side with a sheepish grin.

"I didn't see you there, Si. Did I hurt you?"

Siofra shook her head. She tried to speak but found she still couldn't.

"Good night then," Wulfhelm said as she brushed past and stumbled into the hall. She heard him ask Desemir what time he wanted the women sent up, but then the door closed and, with it, Desemir's response.

She pressed her palms to her face and breathed in, sucking air through the tight gaps of her fingers. Out, pushing hard along the same path. She turned, splitting her fingers and expecting to see Euric, but he wasn't there. No one guarded Desemir's door, at least from the outside.

Her hands fell away, swinging at her side. The red wall tickled her lungs but swelled no higher.

But anger wasn't the prevailing emotion slinking up from her toes and into her belly. She'd been his fool once again. How desirable he'd made her feel... Her knees bowed at the remembrance of his command, the way he looked at her, his eyes tinged with flames. That same fire became her shame, for he'd discarded her, the same as he did with the other women when their purpose was served.

Maybe she was wrong about them too. What if he was gentle with his hired women? What if he talked with them, *knew* them? What if he loved—

Siofra's head whipped toward a ghastly sound coming from farther into the west wing. Like a braying wolf.

It stopped just as quickly.

She held her breath and waited, listening. Seconds passed, and she'd accepted it must have been her imagination when it happened again.

Instinct shifted her steps toward the strange sound, a caterwauling of sorts that sounded completely out of place inside Shadowfen Hall. But as she continued following the forlorn cries, she wondered how she'd mistaken it for an animal at all.

Siofra drew closer to the wailing, heightened enough that it must be close. The corner that would take her all the way into the west wing—and beyond where she was allowed to go—was only a few feet ahead. If she took too many more steps, she'd be breaking the only rule Desemir and Pesha had set for her.

Siofra screamed when she was swallowed from behind. She flailed against the assault, but in the next second, her arms and legs went to jelly, her mind clearing. She slumped back into the arms of the one who had caused it...

And looked up into the eyes of Pesha.

He righted her and took a step back. "What do you think you're doing?"

"Where did you come from?" Siofra asked. She turned toward the corner, but the sound had stopped. "I—"

"I was in the room with you and Des," Pesha explained, as indifferent about it as he might be about the laces of his boots.

"You're so quiet, I forget you're there most of the time now," Siofra said, her voice trailing as she shifted her head again to listen for the sound.

"You shouldn't be here. Let me get you back."

"I don't need an escort, and..." Siofra waved a hand at the corner. "Who lives back there?"

Pesha's blink lasted a half second too long. "No one lives back there."

Siofra's head fell to the side as she shook it. "But I heard someone, someone *crying*—"

"You didn't hear anything," Pesha insisted. "There's no one there. The wing is closed off because it's dangerous and has fallen into disrepair."

Siofra's expression widened with a new fear. "Then we have to go in there because someone has clearly gotten themselves hurt!"

"You heard nothing," Pesha said again. "But I'll send Euric in to look. You'll go back to your room?"

"Uh, I..." Siofra swung her gaze again to the corner. Silence, since Pesha had arrived. Had she imagined it after all?

"Pesha. You're needed," Euric called from down the hall. "It's time."

Pesha seemed to brace himself. His eyes closed briefly before he responded. "I'm coming." To Siofra, he said, "I'll have Wulfhelm take you back."

"I don't need an escort, and I'm starting to take offense at the offer," Siofra shot back. Had he witnessed her little breakdown in Desemir's chambers, the one she'd tried so hard to hide from Desemir?

"Euric, send Wulf out," Pesha yelled just as Euric disappeared back inside. His eyes flicked toward the west wing again—only briefly, but Siofra caught it.

"You treat me like a child sometimes," Siofra said. "You were supposed to teach me. You promised me you would help me learn

184

how to understand my magic better, and you... You're always with Fen."

"He's alone here." Pesha practically grunted the words. It was clear that speaking them brought him discomfort.

"*He's* alone?" Siofra shook her head slowly. "You know, he's only alone because he's choosing to be. Because he's stubborn. And *you're* only feeding it, encouraging him to eat on the veranda, to avoid everyone."

"You're fortunate he loves you enough to be as hurt as he is, Siofra. He's—"

"Euric said you had need of me?"

They both turned toward Wulfhelm making a brisk path toward them. He had one hand on his sword, the other resting deep in a pocket, as if going for an easy, afternoon stroll that might result in a duel.

Pesha's face filled with relief. "See that Siofra gets back to her room safely."

Siofra glowered at Pesha, but he'd already turned and left. She left her glare on his back until he entered Desemir's room.

The corner of Wulfhelm's mouth cocked into a wry grin. "I'd ask what I missed, but not sure I want to know."

"I don't need an escort." With Pesha gone, Siofra glanced back at the corner leading into the west wing.

"Ah, well, let's humor him anyway." Wulfhelm held out a broad arm, covered in thick layers of cloth armor. She wondered how often he had real need of it. Not as often as the scarred Euric, surely, for Wulfhelm's cheeks were still soft and unmarred.

She took his arm with one last reluctant look back. Maybe she *had* imagined it, but she had definitely not imagined Pesha's anxiety.

They moved in silence past Desemir's chambers, where her husband readied himself for the next round. She held her head high and back, swallowing to clear the lump in her throat.

Wulfhelm's gaze lingered on her a moment after they passed. "How are you liking the Hall so far, Siofra?"

"It's hard to judge it against past experiences. But it's lovely, and everyone here has been so kind."

"That's the way Desi likes things."

"I still can't believe you call him Desi." She stopped herself from laughing.

Wulfhelm's heavy shoulders lifted. "Boyhood mates. And he doesn't like anyone here using formalities unless we have guests." He grinned again. "You're not a guest anymore, are you?"

Was I ever? she wondered. Desemir's intentions for her began before he'd even sent Pesha to Newcarrow. But Shadowfen Hall was still a long way from feeling like home.

"You'll get used to it," he said. It seemed he walked slower for her sake. He was much taller than she was, but she hadn't been lagging behind either.

"So they tell me," Siofra answered. "How long have you been here?"

"Desi's guard?" Wulfhelm twitched his jaw. "I started my training when we both came of age. I've been his personal guard ever since." He thumbed behind them. "Euric, though, he served Desi's granddad. Older than he looks, that one."

"How old is he?"

Wulfhelm's eyes widened with a very serious look. "*Old.*"

Siofra giggled in spite of her foul mood. "What made you want to be a guard, of all things?"

"Is there any greater honor than the one you earn when speaking the vows of the Soldier's Creed?" Wulfhelm responded. "I could've joined the Rhiagain Guard and served the king. I passed my trials easily enough, but..." He paused with a heavy exhale. "This is home. Always has been. And I couldn't leave such an important job to someone who didn't love Desi as much as I do. He's my brother, blood or no."

"And Pesha?"

Wulfhelm shook his head. "Doesn't like me much."

"Why?" Siofra asked. They were close to turning into the east wing, but she couldn't help hoping he'd go slower still.

"I guess because I'm the one who usually brings the women," he said. With a screw of his mouth, he turned to look at her. "I shouldn't speak of that in front of you. Apologies, Siofra."

"I'm not delicate," Siofra replied. "Not the way Des and Pesha seem to think."

His gaze swept her once more before he pointed it forward. "Not sure why they would think that. Nothing about you seems delicate to me."

Siofra jerked her elbow against his in a move so uncharacteristically playful, she wondered why she'd done it at all. "How do I seem to you then? Like a bull crashing through a dinner party?"

Wulfhelm took a moment to consider it. "When I first saw you, I thought I was looking at a piece of the sun itself." His face scrunched as he made a chiding sound. "Forget I said that."

Siofra stopped at the corner and made him face her. "No. Tell me what you meant."

"It was stupid, and I've gone and put my foot in it, as I'm known to do. Words are not... my thing."

"Please?" Siofra pleaded.

His breath shuddered his whole chest. "You looked so small coming out of the carriage, but I saw strength in you. Anyone here would be a fool to underestimate you."

Siofra's pulse throbbed. Did he know what she could do? Had Desemir told them? "I..."

"It was a compliment. Forgive me, Siofra."

"Si," she replied. With a friendly pat on the arm, she looked up at him. "I can take it from here. Good night, Wulfhelm."

"Wulf," he called, after she'd already begun walking toward her chambers. "Or Wulfie, if you like."

"Wulfie," she whispered to herself with an under-the-breath laugh.

When she reached her door, she turned to wave, but he was already gone.

Desemir had no awareness of how tightly he'd been gripping the balcony until Pesha came out and started ranting. Desemir had learned when to listen and when to let his brother run his thoughts down.

Desemir released the balcony and waited for Pesha to finish.

"You're losing it, Des. It's only gotten worse since the twins arrived."

"You have an annoying habit of underestimating me." His eyes fluttered closed. "You always have."

"You think you're fine? Then take the night off."

When Desemir held his response, Pesha kept rolling on, more of the same, for several more minutes.

Desemir capitalized on a short pause. "That all?"

"It's not *enough* anymore. We need to wall it off, add a door only you and I can open."

"You want me to wall off a whole wing?" Desemir massaged his fingers against the tense spot between his brows. "Has Wulf returned?"

"What? Why?" Pesha fidgeted with clear annoyance.

"I need to speak with him."

"Did you hear anything I just said to you?"

"I heard all of it," Desemir replied. Pesha gawped at him, as he always did when Desemir portrayed a calmer demeanor than his brother deemed necessary. But Desemir's skill at calming himself was the only reason he was still alive. If he rose to every incident with the level of excitement Pesha did, Shadowfen Hall and everyone in it would have been razed to the ground.

"But you're not going to do anything about it. Are you?" Pesha asked, issuing a challenge with his tone.

"Not tonight." Desemir lowered his hand. "Wulf?"

Pesha threw up both of his hands and stormed into the bedchamber.

Desemir inhaled the moment of peace that followed.

He closed his eyes, shutting out the day.

He cleared his troubles as the pine traveling on rain filled his head, his lungs.

There was no room in his mind for conflict.

He thought this very thought only a few more times before it was gone, the remainder of his composure restored.

"Desi?"

Desemir opened his eyes and gestured for his old friend to come forward. He couldn't blame Wulf for the suspicion he wore, but Desemir intended to allay it.

"Forgive me for how I acted in the hall earlier this afternoon," Desemir said. His words came easily now. They always did once his peace returned. "I know you were not being untoward with Siofra."

Wulfhelm exhaled in relief. He gripped the doorframe with one hand and nodded. "I was only being kind, as I thought you would want. That's all."

"I know," Desemir assured him. He came toward Wulfhelm and planted an arm around his shoulders. "And it makes you the perfect person for the job I need to fill."

Wulfhelm cocked his head. "What job?"

Desemir set his glance on the forest. "Siofra will need her own guard now. It cannot be just anyone—only someone I would trust with her life, as I have trusted him with my own."

"*Me?*"

"She likes you." Desemir's eye twitched only slightly when he said it. "She seems comfortable with you. Which will serve the dual purpose of knowing she'll accept you in the role, and also not be so lonely. I have far too much to do to keep her occupied, and it will set my mind at ease to know I don't have to. You understand?"

Wulfhelm nodded with a dazed look. "What about you? Euric is great, but he's... well, old."

189

"Cassius is ready, don't you think?"

"Cassius is an excellent soldier, but—"

"It's decided." A weight transferred from Desemir's chest, passing across his flesh before it caught the wind and left him altogether. "You'll start tomorrow."

FIFTEEN
EXQUISITE CREATURE

The Trevanions hadn't opened the ballroom since before
Desemir's mother had died. It was an addition to Shadowfen
Hall by Desemir's grandfather, Klaus, built to please his young
bride, who was eager to entertain highborns of the Darkwood.

The Great Hall was more than sufficient and had served the
Trevanions for many generations of fetes and celebrations. But
when newlywed Elaina Trevanion had gotten wind of a new style
of room—sweeping the bigger keeps and manors of the kingdom—and mentioned it to her husband, she'd also happened to
reveal that the Arrandens were having one built. Klaus would not
find himself on the back of a trend. Worse, behind an Arranden.

Ludwik had avoided the room because he'd claimed it was
haunted by his mother's ghost. Desemir didn't know if that was
true, but he'd calculated the risk and decided there was little to
be gained.

You know you have to open the ballroom, don't you? Pesha had
needled him. *If you're so determined to go through with this, you
better do it right.*

191

"Done right" was the precise result. Lotte had outdone herself, Desemir thought, as he surveyed the vibrantly decorated room from the comfort of his stately chair on the dais. There were few colorful blooms in midwinter, but she'd collected enough to make it seem like the cavernous room was bursting with florals. They dangled from rafters and were woven across the tables lining the sides of the room. Gisela directed the kitchen staff where to place the exorbitant preparation of food and drink, while Lieken swatted curious onlookers from the sculpture he'd made from a block of ice, which Euric and Cassius had helped him excavate from the lake. He'd fashioned it into a lion, matching the Trevanion sigil. Even Desemir was impressed at his artisanship.

Every last worker at Shadowfen Hall had a role to play. While Desemir preferred for them to enjoy the evening as guests, hiring outside help to fill the need for such a grand celebration would have only heightened their risk on a night already brimming with it. The only men he'd brought in from outside were the musicians, staged in the center of the room.

Pesha was positioned at Desemir's side, Euric and Cassius behind him. Pesha refused to sit. He needed every last one of his senses tonight, he'd said. There was nothing Desemir could say to cool him. Pesha was too frustrated to understand the necessity of the celebration, only seeing the threat.

How they all judged his choices, not knowing what it was to wear the burden of all their fates. None of them, not even Desemir's beloved brother, could ever grasp that their idyllic seclusion was bought by playing the game, not avoiding it.

The last-minute invites hadn't discouraged any of the invitees. Every highborn family of Darkwood Run had come, and even some from nearby Eastport and Salthill, but most importantly, all four of his adversaries were in attendance: Bennett Weaver and his wife, Elspeth; Edmund Rolfe and his wife, Pearl; Prentiss Felwood and his wife, Jocosta; and, of course, the steward himself, Hughbert Arranden, with his wife, Agnes.

Most had brought their children and children's families. Rolfe had brought two of his six daughters—the same daughters he'd tried, one by one, to offer to Desemir—who were dressed as if tonight was their coming out... hedging their chances in case the new Baroness Trevanion was not up to standard.

"Where's Stiofen?" Desemir asked after he'd performed a mental check of everyone in the ballroom. "And more to the point, where is my wife?"

"Fen is just there," Pesha said, with a nod toward the long table of wine carafes.

Desemir leaned forward a touch and squinted. He made out a glimpse of the boy's light hair between the pitchers.

"As for Siofra... Gisela told her it would be improper for her to arrive on time. That she would be expected to make a grand entrance, like a lady." Pesha snorted. "As if anything about this event is expected."

Desemir glanced at his brother. "Gisela is *here*, helping serve. We didn't leave my wife alone with all these spiders crawling about, did we?"

"Wulf is with her."

"Mm." Desemir turned forward again, shifting in his chair. "Did she get the ring?"

"Yes."

"Is she wearing it?"

"You'll have to ask her."

Desemir locked eyes with Rolfe and afforded him a curt nod. "She only needs to wear it tonight."

"Which I told her," Pesha said testily. "If you wanted the message emphasized, you should have delivered it yourself."

Desemir had no defense. Since the evening he'd abruptly excused her, they'd not spoken. He hadn't sent for her, and they'd taken their meals separately.

He shifted in discomfort as he recalled the hurt in her voice.

That it had created such conflict in him was vexing. He'd behaved according to his side of the offer. It wasn't a crime to enjoy his time with her. To desire her. They were both quite fortunate to possess such an intense attraction to one another, because duty could have just as easily become a chore.

Letting her linger after would only confuse matters.

For both of them.

Desemir clenched at the sight of Arranden approaching the dais. Pesha tensed, their reactions timed in perfect unison.

"Hugh," Desemir said with a joyless smile. "Thank you for coming." He flashed a slightly less hostile one at Hugh's wife. "Agnes, you look lovely, as always."

Agnes did not look lovely. She was not a comely woman, something she must have been aware of already. But she accepted the compliment with a gracious smile.

"It was an invitation I couldn't refuse," Hugh answered. He flashed his teeth, a spectacle of cracked and rotting tines that made it difficult for the man to hide his addiction to poppies. "To see the young woman who finally snared our Baron Trevanion? She must be a gift from the Guardians themselves, to be a more favorable choice than a woman of the Darkwood." He made an overdone show of looking around. "And where is she, your new wife?"

Desemir grimaced, uncomfortably aware of the sweat beading at his temples and brow from the sweltering assault of the fully lit candelabras. The trilling music swelled in crescendo. "She'll be arriving soon."

"Wants to make a grand appearance, does she?" Agnes asked with a waggish look. "Already acting like she's been highborn her whole life. Her training must be going well."

Desemir started to challenge the assumption, but it would only prove him to be at a disadvantage. Of course Arranden had looked into Siofra's past and found nothing. But finding nothing was far better than finding *something*.

"Indeed," Desemir retorted with a tight smile. "And she makes a finer show of it than some who have."

"You'll allow me a dance, of course," Hugh stated.

194

"Siofra may dance with whomever she pleases."

"Siofra..." Agnes said it slowly. "Such an unusual name. Where did you say her people are from?"

"I didn't," Desemir answered. He noticed Rolfe and Weaver had paused their respective conversations to observe the interaction. "Enjoy yourselves. It may be some time before we have another fete at Shadowfen Hall."

Hugh nodded as he looked around. "Agnes, dear. Will you give us a moment?" When his wife was gone, he said, "Does it really take a wedding celebration for you to meet with me?"

Pesha shifted at Desemir's side, alert.

"Seeing as all your invitations have been dressed-up threats, you'll understand my hesitation in accepting any of them," Desemir countered. His hand twitched as he fought the urge to brush away the sweat beading around his temples. "And my answer hasn't changed. I won't be selling back even an acre of the Darkwood."

"You'll remember how your father stole it from us in the first place. The *means* he used."

Desemir had always suspected there was more to his father's acquisition than he'd been told, but he preferred not knowing. The choice to steal the Darkwood had been his father's, and it had become Desemir's fight to keep it. "The work of your generation, not mine."

Hugh took another step closer. "That's precisely my point, Desemir. *You* have the power to undo the machinations of Mad Baron Ludwik. His legacy does not have to be yours. There can be amity between us all once more. Nothing has been done that cannot be undone."

"Mad Baron Ludwik?" Desemir scoffed with an eye roll. "Is that really what you're all calling him?"

Hugh recoiled. "You seem surprised. I can't fathom why. Everyone knows your own relationship with the man was strained."

"Is that not true of all father-and-son relationships?"

"Your father was an unreasonable man. You are not."

Desemir snorted. "You have all presumed to know me, Steward. And you have all been wrong in your presumptions."

Hugh adjusted, standing straighter. The steward was a short man, and he seemed to remember that in the moment. "It doesn't have to be this way."

"Doesn't it?"

"You know what you're saying? You know your refusal to compromise, with *any* of us, can only be taken as an act of aggression?"

Euric and Cassius stirred into position.

Hugh noticed. "Easy, lads. There'll be no fighting tonight. We don't muddy business with pleasure."

"Take it as you will," Desemir said with a dismissive flick. "I—"

His throat choked his words. An awed hush fell over the crowd. Even the musicians skipped a few notes as everyone turned to watch Siofra enter the Shadowfen ballroom.

Pesha drew in a sharp breath. Euric made a brief sound of approval.

Desemir rose to his feet as he took her in. She seemed so small next to smartly dressed Wulf, who had her wrist tucked into the crook of his elbow. She wore her golden hair down, curled over one bare shoulder like a gilt waterfall.

And the dress... It was as if the sunrise had become something tangible. A radiant burst of light and sparkle was dusted across the flared tulle skirt of the ornate yellow gown.

It should be me at her side, Desemir thought, but he just as quickly dismissed it.

"Where..." Hugh cleared his throat. "Where *did* you find this exquisite creature, Desemir?"

Mine was Desemir's next thought, an assertion equally true and not.

Siofra swept her wide, uncertain gaze over the people watching her. She nibbled at the bottom edge of her mouth, then abruptly stopped. In her eyes, he saw her calculating, adjusting to the situation.

Desemir caught Stiofen approaching the dais from the left. The music resumed, whispers replacing silence.

But all he could *hear* was the fitful thrum of his own heart.

Pesha leaned in close. "Go dance with your wife, Des."

Desemir shook his head in tight passes. "I..." He swallowed. "I can't. I have to stay here and receive my guests."

"I have the situation under control." Pesha's tone was gentle, more agreeable than it had been since before the twins arrived. "Go on."

Siofra caught his eyes when her head turned. Her shoulders dropped in relief, though she didn't quite offer a smile. She seemed to be waiting for his first.

Desemir's throat felt stuffed with an entire bale of wool.

Smile, you fool. Show her you approve. That you're proud of her.

No. She's playing a role, as are you.

It can never be more.

You must never allow it to be more.

"No," Desemir at last said to Pesha. "Let the others dance with her. It's what they're here to do."

Desemir returned to his seat. He rolled his hands over the arms of his chair, willing his control to return.

Siofra's heart plummeted when Desemir returned to his conversation. She waited for him to look up again, to change his mind and show her *something*.

When he didn't, she was thrown into the reality of the evening, as hard as if she'd been shoved from behind. The assault of sound and color sent a screech through her ears, a blinding light into her eyes. Wulfhelm was asking her something, but she couldn't hear anything except the stunning baritone of her biggest fears come to life.

There were *so many* people. Each of them so easily wore the gowns and suits they were born to wear, all undoubtedly noticing she was not.

She adjusted the low bosom of her dress and blinked through her daze. Wulfhelm tightened his hold on her and caught her before she tripped over her long hem.

"Hey," Wulf said, edging closer. "What's wrong? You don't seem like yourself."

"Will you dance with me?"

"What was that?" His grip on her eased. "Apologies, Si, I thought you just said you wanted me to *dance* with you."

"That's because it is what I said." Siofra swallowed and glanced up at him. "I just need a moment to gather myself, and if we're dancing, then..."

Wulf threw his glance in Desemir's direction. "I'm supposed to be looking out for you. I don't know what Desi would think."

Siofra reached for his face and turned it toward herself. "I don't care what he thinks. He's up there, and we're down here, aren't we?"

Wulf was still looking at Desemir. "It's not that I don't want to, Siofra—"

"Then what's stopping you? Did he tell you that you couldn't touch me?"

His face flooded with color as he stammered his response. "He... Eh, he might have, yes."

Siofra stepped in front of him and held out her arms. "I don't know how to dance. You'll have to teach me."

Wulf shot another wary look over her head. He turned toward her and whistled in a hard breath. "Give me your right hand."

Siofra folded it into his. "All right."

"And then..." He flushed darker. "Stand closer. I need to..." He gestured his free arm in an arc.

"Hold me?" Siofra asked with a laugh. "Are you afraid to?"

"Maybe," Wulf admitted in a mumble. His eyes flashed wide when Siofra pressed herself against him. He fumbled his hand around her and struggled to decide exactly where to land it.

Siofra reached back to guide him into place against her lower back.

"All right then."

"All right then," she said back. "Are you going to tell me what he said to you?"

She yelped when he snapped her into place instead of responding. Before she could ask again, he whisked her across the floor and turned her in time to the music, matching the choreography of the other couples around them.

His hand at the small of her back twitched. The one holding hers was clammy.

"This isn't so hard," Siofra said. She tried to catch his eyes, but he had his attention trained on something behind her.

"This is nothing," Wulf answered. "Pray they do not call for a quadrille."

"What's a quadrille?"

Wulf didn't answer. He spent all his focus on avoiding her.

"Why did Des assign you to be my guard?" Siofra asked. She kept her gaze on his chest. She didn't need to look around to know everyone was watching them.

"I've been asking myself the same thing."

"You're upset to not be guarding him anymore."

Wulf pulled back, lifted her arm, and twirled her before he brought her back.

"You were more talkative the night you walked me to my room," she stated.

"You ask a lot of questions."

Siofra looked up at him. "Does it bother you?"

"A lot of *leading* questions," Wulf said. "No matter my answer, I walk into a trap."

Siofra recoiled. "Is that what you think I'm trying to do? Trap you?"

Wulf sighed. His fingers pulsed at her back. "No, I don't. But you have to understand; Desi is my oldest friend, and you're his wife."

"Does that not also make you *my* friend?" Siofra asked. This was Desemir's doing. He'd chosen his most loyal guard to look after her, knowing Wulf's reticence would leave her even more isolated.

Wulf flexed the hand holding hers. He exhaled a long breath and created some distance between them. "You look beautiful tonight, Siofra. Can we leave it at that?"

Siofra's heart fluttered when she at last understood his reserve. "Oh. I'm sorry. I didn't intend to make you uncomfortable."

He chuckled quietly. "It's not your fault. I'm the one who needs to find my composure, or our tenure together will be awkward and short-lived."

Siofra discarded the rest of her questions. There was no point to them. His easy way with her in the hall, showing her the card trick, and his playfulness on the walk back to her apartments were only possible when he wasn't on display, expected to perform.

She glanced up toward the dais. Her stomach seized at the burning scowl twisted on Desemir's face.

Aimed at her.

"Now I'm the one who's upset you," Wulf said. He flattened his hand at her back and breathed into her hair. "Forgive me, Siofra. I did tell you words were not my strength."

"I don't need your words," she said, meeting Desemir's steely glare. "But I'll happily stay in your arms tonight if you'll let me, for I fear it's the only safe place in this entire room."

"Wulf is going to be in for a world of hurt if he goes for a third dance with her," Pesha remarked as he poured a mug of stream water to cool himself from the glaring heat of the candles, made worse by his festering anxiety. "Des won't like the implication."

"Siofra isn't like that," Fen replied in her defense. His permanent glower was part of his attire, arms crossed as he watched the guests—as he listened, the way Pesha had taught him.

"Oh? I thought you weren't speaking to each other."

"We're not."

"I know she isn't like that. But tonight is all about appearances for Des." Pesha tossed back a mouthful of water. The relief was instant.

"Then *he* should be dancing with her." Fen nodded at the dais. "He knows this is all new for her. She's afraid. How could she know she's making him look bad?"

Pesha followed his nod and had to stifle a laugh. Desemir had never looked so miserable, watching Wulf dance with Siofra. "He's stubborn."

"Hadn't noticed," Fen groused.

Pesha was famished but had to limit himself to preserve his clarity. He picked one of the grapes from his bowl and popped it into his mouth. "I'm most worried about that one." He flicked a subtle gaze toward Edmund Rolfe. "Weaver and Arranden are pushovers, and Felwood lets the others speak for him. But Rolfe? He's a sadist. He isn't only in it for the money. He enjoys the thrill of taking others down."

Fen's frown deepened. "Have you heard anything alarming from him tonight?"

"Nothing unexpected," Pesha answered. He watched Rolfe speak with someone Pesha didn't recognize, but the man's eyes followed Siofra's movements. "He'll want to dance with her. They all will. We'll have to be on even higher alert then."

"Is this all really necessary? Did your brother really have to bring danger to his doorstep?"

"Danger never leaves his doorstep, Fen. We've had a few incidents over the years to remind us of that," Pesha said. Desemir would be surprised to hear him speak of it, because Pesha had torn apart those same arguments time and time again. But Desemir could be both right and reckless.

"What kind of incidents?"

"They can't take our roads without alerting the guards, so there have been a few rogue mercenaries sent *through* the woods. We always catch them. We always adjust our security accordingly. So far it's been nothing we can't handle here at the Hall, but this is why Des never ventures into Darkwood Run anymore."

Fen shook his head. "How could he be so careless, then? With the women he brings?"

"The women are all chosen carefully. We know who their families are. Their mothers, fathers. Children. If that isn't enough to keep them from doing something foolish, we bring them here under heavy guard, and they leave under the same. And they're paid twenty times what patrons pay them for their time in town. They live well. Better than most. Gold has a way of dulling everything else." Pesha's eyes narrowed. "Ah, and there we are. Baron Weaver, saving Wulf from himself."

Fen stiffened. "If he even tries—"

"He won't. They won't," Pesha insisted. "But they would be wise to not overstay their turn with her. Desemir is looking for a fight tonight, and he'd love a reason to start one."

Siofra's dance with the man who had introduced himself as Bennett Weaver was mercifully quick, giving him just enough time to ask about her family, before another man called Prentiss Felwood came to take his place. He stole two dances from her, seemingly oblivious to Desemir's scorching glare, but walked away with most of his questions unanswered.

She was proud of herself. Pesha had told her the barons would try to trick her into revealing things she shouldn't. But there was no need to explain it to her, because she'd spent most of her life reading people. Weaver and Felwood were as transparent as the glass of the tall windows, and she'd maneuvered both conversations with surprising ease, even if they had left her drained.

Between men, she searched for Wulf, and he was never far away.

Desemir's increasingly intense looks became another stalwart predictability of the evening. They left her breathless and flustered, as he often did. He made no attempt at discretion. It was almost like he wanted her to see his disquiet, like they were playing a game only he knew the rules to.

"Baroness?"

Siofra had only just been released from her commitment to Felwood when another man snared her attention. She spun in a flurry, wondering how many adversaries Desemir would let occupy her before deciding it was enough.

"Edmund Rolfe," he said, introducing himself. "Though you would do a blessing to my ears by simply calling me Ned." He whipped to the right. "Wulfhelm, Pesha has called for your aid at the refreshment table."

Wulfhelm shot a dubious look toward where Rolfe pointed, but he nodded and asked Siofra, "You'll be all right for a moment?"

"Yes... of course," she answered. It was not what she'd wanted to say. Not what she felt.

Siofra had to tilt her neck back to see Rolfe's face. He was the tallest man she'd ever laid eyes on. Her head barely reached his chest.

"Ned," she said with a forced smile. Her eyes caught Desemir's again, but she quickly swept them back toward the steward. "You have undoubtedly heard this many times, but your height is alarming."

An aurora of lines appeared at the corner of both of his eyes when he laughed. "Enough to keep you from accepting a dance with me?"

"No, though I fear I may need to shout to be heard."

"I can hear you perfectly well," Rolfe replied. His next grin peeled his top lip back, stretching it unnaturally.

Craning her neck made her dizzy. She looked back down and away. "Then it would be uncouth of me to refuse."

"To say the least." Rolfe bundled her into his arms before she could change her mind. The effect of being so close to him, her eyes level with his thick belly, was no longer simply disquieting but distressing. The forceful way he held her, his hand clamped possessively to the back of her head to pin her in place, turned the dance indecent.

But if anyone else was observing his treatment of her, they said nothing. No one intervened, not even when he pressed her face so tight to his torso, it cut off her breath.

Wulf hadn't returned, or the dance would already be over.

"Siofra, it must be such a hardship for you, being so far from home." Rolfe's fingers tightened to her scalp.

Siofra nodded. She attempted to pull back her head, to create some distance, but he pinned her back into place, a response that removed all doubt the authority was intentional.

He channeled her in steps far too long for her gait, lifting her off her floundering feet. "And yet," he said, "no one seems to know where your home *is*."

"I—" was all she got out before he smashed her face to himself again.

"But we will." He again lifted her off her feet, swinging her around with such force, her head swam with disorientation. "We will, Siofra. And when we do, we'll at last have found the means to get Desemir to deal with us. Any scandal surrounding his heir would be a blow impossible to recover from."

"I can't br—" She moaned into the rough fabric of his vest.

"I could take you out of here right now. Your husband's guard would be on me before too long, but not before I instilled a seed of doubt in the minds of the others gathered at this farce. Desemir's new bride, running off to a closet with Ned Rolfe. What a scandal it would be. It would take so very little."

Siofra squirmed downward, her head passing between his legs as she twisted away. Chest heaving, she stumbled back several steps and straight into the arms of Desemir.

He encircled her from behind in a protective hold. His warm breath at the crown of her head was a reminder that regardless of what did or did not lie between them, he would never let anyone treat her as Rolfe had.

"That's enough, Ned. You've made your point, and now you're done. And I've waited long enough to dance with my wife."

206

SIXTEEN
THE GAME

Time stopped.

At least that was how it seemed to Siofra, who had forgotten herself in the gleam reflecting from Desemir's amber eyes. They pooled with demand, with supplication. He held not her hand but her wrist, clasping the delicate flesh in his fist with such unreserved possessiveness, she forgot how to breathe.

His gaze scorched her, melting her arms, her legs... a sway she fought but was beginning to lose. The fervent, violent way he inhaled and exhaled, glistening lips parted, held her in such thrall that she ached to look away, to return to herself and the carefully spun shadows of her heart. But she could do nothing but surrender to his illicit call.

The game had shifted. The odds were still weighted in his favor, but at least she'd begun to understand the rules.

Desemir's pulse throbbed at her wrist as he held it high, for all to see. For all to know he had at last come to claim her, lest any man be confused about his intention.

"I saw the way you danced with those men." His tongue passed along his bottom lip as he wielded his indictment.

"I thought it's what you wanted from me." Siofra held her chin high, head back. Let him see her. Let them all see him seeing her.

Desemir's lips knit together. The veins at his temple appeared. "I saw how they looked at you."

"And how's that?" Siofra asked. She splayed her hand against the side of his neck and enjoyed his wince in response, but she demurred and slid it back down to his shoulder, where it belonged.

That was not playing by the rules. *That* was his role.

"Like they would eat you alive if you let them." Desemir spun her in tight, severe movements. They jarred her heart at every turn.

"Does that bother you?" Siofra swallowed the lump of fear waiting in the back of her throat.

Desemir jerked her against himself with the hand at her back. A whiff of his heady breath filled her head. "You could dance with every last man in Darkwood Run, Siofra, but you're still *mine*. Mine and mine alone."

Siofra fluttered her eyelids as her head fell back. "Claiming me then, are you?"

Desemir growled. "I don't need to claim what I already possess."

"Does what I want have no place here?"

He leaned down and whispered, "If I were to slide my hand under your dress and up your leg, I think I'd have a pretty clear idea of your wants."

Siofra's heart beat wildly out of control. It left her flesh tingling. It confused her senses, which were both heightened and dulled. He was changing the narrative, and she was letting him. *Encouraging* him. "Well, then it's too bad you lack the courage."

Desemir scowled. His hand pulsed on her wrist. "You're challenging me."

"Perhaps I liked watching you watch me with them. I *liked* how it vexed you. It's why I kept letting them come make their own claims on me, one by one." She licked her lips to make room for more exciting lies. "I enjoyed your displeasure immensely."

His laugh was quick, forbidding. "You're admitting your transgressions."

"Consider this my full confession," Siofra replied, breathless and already utterly lost.

Desemir's mouth coiled into a grin. "Do you *want* to be punished, Siofra?"

Siofra stretched up to the tips of her toes to deliver her answer. "Slide your hand up my dress and find out."

Desemir's groan started deep in his throat. "I could fuck you right here, in front of everyone."

Boldness flashed in Siofra's eyes. "What's stopping you?"

"You think I won't?"

"If you were the man you claim to be, you'd already be fucking me."

Desemir dropped his hand away from her back. He didn't release her wrist. "The things I'm going to do to you would stun the nobility." He then turned and marched away, dragging her behind him, his willing property, his eager claim.

Siofra ran behind him with a smirk she couldn't hide and the eyes of all of Darkwood Run on her.

Desemir held a fistful of her hair as he curved her over the edge of his bed. Siofra clawed at the blanket, desperate for grip, but he gave her no slack. She'd provoked him, so she would get exactly what she'd asked for.

He ripped at the tulle of her dress, grunting at the unforgiving fabric. He jammed it upward, over the back of her, and ripped her undergarments down the center. When she bowed her ass up, he slapped it, then slapped it again.

"You want it too much." He released her hair and dropped to his knees behind her. Before him were folds of glistening perfection. Palpable, visceral evidence of her desire—desire for him.

Desire he'd drawn her into with subconscious intention. None of her coy, confident assertions in the ballroom had prepared him for seeing it with his own eyes.

It shattered what was left of his resistance.

Desemir indulged his urge and flicked his tongue down the center of her with hungry passes. Her cries for more made him go slower, ease off. Mindlessly, he reached a hand down to stroke his cock, to take the edge off before he exploded all over the carpet.

Siofra slid a hand down to touch herself, but he shoved it back up the bed.

"You get pleasure when I give you pleasure," he said.

"Not much of a punishment," she challenged. The soft rhythm of her voice had been replaced by a low, raspy demand. "I'm beginning to think you're all roar, no bite."

"You want a lion? I'll give you a lion." Desemir clenched his teeth as he returned to his feet. He spread her and speared into her wet folds with enough force to knock himself back a step. Snagging the bodice of her dress, he pulled her up off the bed and fucked her, stunting her strangled cries with the force of his castigation.

"Tell me what you did, Siofra." He grunted as he slammed into her. He'd gone easy on her before, fearful of breaking her, but he saw what she'd wanted from him all along.

"I... let those... those men think... whatever they wished." She received his thrusts like she was made for them. "So you would... stop denying yourself what you want."

"And what do I want?"

Siofra whimpered. "To dominate me."

Desemir grunted through the thrill her words had produced. "And what about you? Did you want to be dominated by my enemies? To be fucked by them?"

"Only if you were there to watch."

Desemir exploded inside her. He stumbled back from the force of his spend and bowled over, gasping for breath.

He looked up to see her ass still spread for him, his seed dripping out of her. "I hope you weren't thinking of resting, Baroness Trevanion."

She moaned, turning up her voice to bait him. "This isn't much of a punishment."

Desemir charged forth and entered her again, driving her forward on the bed. Mouth gaped wide, Siofra turned to look back at him just as he said, "Oh, I'm just getting started."

Siofra stirred, passing her cheek against the smooth satin pillow. Her legs shuddered into a long, satisfying stretch, followed by a delicious ache that reminded her of the night's events.

The sun had already cleared the morning, and the day was underway. She'd slept far longer than she had intended, though it had been the most satisfying night of rest she'd had in years.

She rolled to the side with a happy moan. Her eyes fluttered open.

Then panic set in.

She'd slept in Desemir's chambers.

Siofra slithered upward and sat against the headboard with the sheet pressed to her chest. She rubbed the sleep from her eyes and passed them around the room, but Desemir wasn't there.

"You're awake."

Desemir's deep voice startled her. Her mind clambered for the right words, which were somewhere between an apology and an acknowledgment that she'd broken one of his rules.

"It's all right, Siofra."

She followed his voice and saw him emerge from the balcony. He wore only his white shirt from the night before, but he hadn't bothered to fasten any of the buttons. He stood nearly nude before her, offering her a clear view of his hard cuts and lines that she'd only felt—with her hands, her lips, her flesh—hours before.

Desemir propped one hand on the door, watching her.

"I don't even remember falling asleep," she mumbled.

Desemir's incisive gaze issued a gentle command, so she let the sheet fall away. His mouth curled in approval. *Mine,* it seemed to say.

Yours was her instinctive response, which she could have corrected for herself but did not.

"I watched you sleep for a while. You looked so peaceful." Desemir dropped his arm from the door and moved into the room. "I'd like to think I had something to do with it."

"I would thank you, if you hadn't left me to fend for myself at the ball," Siofra quipped, emboldened by his easy demeanor.

Desemir's shrug was infuriating. "You seemed fine to me. And let's not forget you already confessed your enjoyment of tormenting me."

Siofra reddened. It was one thing to say those things in the heat of their passion, but to hear them in normal conversation was startling. "You ignored me."

"I was aware of your every move last night," Desemir said. He approached the bed, and she focused on the decisive grid of his abdominal muscles... the light trace of scars just above them. "But I had business."

Siofra was conscious of her own exposure. She should have covered her breasts with her hair, but it was too late. Her nipples stood erect in the chill of the morning air, and his downward gaze proved they hadn't escaped his notice. "Business more important than the reason for the event itself? You did bring everyone here to celebrate our wedding, no? What do you suppose they all thought of you abandoning your new wife to the whims of your adversaries?"

Desemir dropped onto the edge of the bed. He trailed a finger along the blanket still covering her legs, and when he reached the edge, he pulled it back to reveal the rest of her. "I'm with you now."

Her heart skipped. "Because you *have* to be."

Desemir swept his eyes up toward hers. "Because I want to be."

Siofra's throat constricted. She lacked the words or the experience to define what was happening to her—what had *already* happened to her—at Shadowfen Hall with this man, in this life. She couldn't discern the exact moment she'd shed her expectations of a more traditional love and understood her own desire: to submit to him. To grant him permission to take charge. To trust that he would keep her safe under the warm command of his strong hands so she could explore her needs without the fear of falling.

Desemir jumped back to his feet. "I have nothing in my diary today, and there's something I'd like to show you."

"Oh?"

"Don't look at me like I'm taking you to a hanging. You'll enjoy this. I promise."

Siofra wrapped the sheet around herself once more. "Where are we going?"

"Into the forest," Desemir said. "I'll see if Pesha has time to join us."

With a start, Siofra realized Pesha hadn't been there last night.

She could have killed Desemir. All it would have taken was one wrong word from him... one sign that he had careless intentions...

"You didn't hurt me," Desemir assured her. A mischievous grin appeared on his face. "At least not in ways I didn't ask for."

214

SEVENTEEN
THE TREE

Desemir directed his thoughts toward the forest as the carriage rumbled along the rough road.

It had been reckless to give in to impulse. No matter how potent his desire had been when he'd pulled her out of the ballroom, Siofra was dangerous, and it had been a gamble to assume he could control the matter without Pesha's protective magic.

Pesha hadn't withheld sharing his own concerns. *You were thinking with something other than your head last night. You could've gotten yourself killed, and for what?*

It was a mistake. But it wasn't a miscalculation, Pesh. I read her needs and delivered upon them with—at the risk of arrogance—finesse.

I don't want to hear about your or her needs. I have to listen to them often enough.

What if you didn't? What if she's not a danger to me anymore?

Don't be a fool, Des.

Pesha tapped the roof. "We're here."

Wulf and Euric livened up. Siofra passed a guarded look across all of them. Desemir couldn't wait to see her face when she realized she could trust him.

Desemir led the way into the forest. He still knew the path by heart, though it had been many years. The last time he had been with Pesha, after Arenn had stopped looking after her son altogether. Desemir hadn't known the right way to fill that void for Pesha, but sharing a piece of his own rare boyhood joy had seemed a good start.

When the path opened to the clearing, Pesha and the guards hung back on Desemir's command. They were close enough to intervene, but Desemir wanted to go on alone with Siofra, as a show of faith. The terrified look she'd worn, upon realizing she hadn't had Pesha to temper her, weighed heavy on him.

Desemir held his hand toward her. She glanced down in surprise but took it, and she seemed more sure of her step as they continued.

They rounded a corner, and the tree came into view. Desemir's chest tightened at the sight of it, as majestic and magical as it had always been. Its roots stretched and circled the nearby trees, its branches gnarled and perfect for climbing—for resting and plotting and dreaming. Though the protective veil of childhood had slipped away from everything else, the rest remained the same.

Siofra exhaled with an awed sigh. "How incredible."

"This is where Wulf and I played as boys," Desemir said. Memories of them chasing each other, wielding pretend swords, forced a sentimental laugh out of him. "And Pesha, years later." He turned toward her. "Where our sons will play, when they're old enough."

Siofra's attention remained fixed on the tree. She squinted and traced a finger along old sets of carvings. "D. T. That's you."

He nodded.

"P. T. Well, that's obvious, and W. K. That's Wulf. Who's this? F. W."

Fear flashed inside of Desemir. He'd forgotten those initials were there. Like most things, it had faded into the background scenery of his mind, present but hidden.

Remember why you're here.

He took her other hand and gently spun her. "I haven't been fair to you, Siofra."

"Oh." Siofra's eyes widened in astonishment. Her finger fell away from the tree. "I wasn't expecting that."

"I'm not a good man." He pressed his mouth tight. The words didn't come easy; speaking his vulnerability never had. "And I should have been more forthright about it when I made my offer to you."

Siofra scoffed. She dropped his hands and approached the tree again. "I may not have understood the specifics, but I knew what I was agreeing to. No perfectly honorable man would pluck an unknown girl from the other end of the kingdom if his intentions were entirely pure."

Desemir raised his brows with a chuckle. "I see. And you accepted because..."

"I know very little about life or the world," Siofra said, her eyes still on the tree and the carvings he hoped she'd move on from. "But it doesn't mean I don't have desires of my own. You're handsome." She stretched out one hand and laid it across the dense bark. It looked so small against the broad trunk. "And you were the first person to speak of my needs as if they mattered. I decided the risk was worth taking."

"And..." Desemir twined his hands behind him and stepped closer. "Has this assessment held up for you?"

Siofra turned. Her tongue pinned her bottom lip. She lifted her shoulders.

Desemir's belly twisted with a hard surge of desire. She no doubt read it in his eyes. He considered it might have been her intention, just another sign she was more than he'd presumed her to be.

"It isn't that I don't want to give you more," Desemir said. "I find myself... wildly, irrationally drawn to you. Beyond what I was prepared for."

Siofra grinned at her feet. She tapped her heel against a root.

Desemir scowled. "You're enjoying watching me struggle with my words."

"I won't deny it." She laughed. "You didn't bring me out here to show me a tree, surely."

"I thought it was as good a place as any to speak of our future."

"And I thought our future was clearly defined for us already," Siofra answered. The edge in her voice climbed. "You've offered me no more or less than what you promised."

"No." Desemir inhaled through his nose. Again, the right words evaded him. "What I offered you was duty. After last night, I expect we can both appreciate there's more than that between us."

Siofra met his eyes. "Then hearing you define it will provide clarity to me as well."

Desemir shook his head with a shrug. "I *can't* define it. I only know you've become a... welcome refreshment in my life. And yet the fear I'm creating further confusion between us has caused me some anxiety."

Siofra's chin quivered as she lifted it high. "I already know you could never love me."

"For your sake." Desemir took another step forward. "Not for mine."

"You realize how little sense you make?"

"Yes," he answered, breathless. "I wish I could explain this to you. Just know that your heart would be crushed if offered to me—not intentionally, but intention is hardly responsible for most outcomes."

"You think so little of yourself," Siofra replied. "And yet want others to hold you in such high regard."

"I know who I am," Desemir said. "Who I am not."

"What a limiting way to view yourself." Siofra chewed the inside of her mouth, watching him. "You might be more than

218

you see yourself to be, but you'll never know if you're closed to the possibility."

Desemir sighed. "If you only knew."

But she never would.

He could hardly acknowledge the truth himself.

"Hmm." Siofra stepped toward him and slid her arms around his waist. She leaned up to kiss him. He received it willingly, then went in for another and drew it out. His cock stirred in his trousers, but he hadn't brought her to the woods to seduce her.

Her taste was still on his tongue when he said, "I don't want to hurt you, Siofra. I meant it when I made you the offer, but I mean it in a different way now. Now that I... now that we've had some time together."

"Your terms are still more than fair," Siofra said. She dusted a kiss across his chin. "You offered me life. Who else can say they have?"

Desemir chuckled. "A rather confusing one."

"But a good one," Siofra replied. She was so warm in his arms. Her breath smelled faintly of honey. "One that has fixed me."

Desemir blanched. "Fixed you?"

"My red wall. It hasn't..." Siofra again chewed the inner corner of her lip. "I've felt it only once since coming here."

"Only once? You've been furious with me a good deal more than once."

"Not angry," Siofra said, her voice low, melodic. "Hurt."

Desemir wilted. "Siofra—"

"It's all right," she assured him. Her face broke out in a smile. "I think we understand each other now."

"Do we?"

She nodded. "I'm content with our arrangement. And I would like... well, more nights like the one we just had."

Desemir pulled her tighter. "Would you now?"

"Mhmm."

Desemir braced her and backed her against the tree. She squealed upon impact. "You're in luck, Siofra. That's one commitment I'm more than capable of rising to."

Siofra rolled her face against Desemir's chest. She fell in and out of a languid doze, set to the soft tickle of his hand along the outside of her arm. Despite the chill in the air, from the breeze whipping through the overhead leaves, she wasn't cold.

"Tell me something about you," she murmured. Her breaths came soft and easy. Her heart had finally stilled.

"Such as?"

"Anything, as long as it means something to you."

"Anything?" Desemir rested his cheek atop her head, nuzzling her. "Ah, well... I told you about my mother, Lidia, and her timekeepers. I kept them after she died, despite their quite fussy upkeep."

"You did. I'd never seen them before I came here," Siofra said. "They're most unusual."

"They're still quite novel. So much so that I have trouble finding anyone with the knowledge to repair them. But... I can't bear to part with them either. They remind me of her, when little else does."

"How long has she been gone?" Last time Desemir talked about her, it had felt like recitation. This time he seemed more at ease.

"I've lived more of my life without her than with her." Desemir's chest rose and fell. "If not for her portraits, I'd have forgotten what she even looked like."

"I've seen her portrait in the Hall of Counting. She was beautiful."

"She was." Desemir swept a band of hair from Siofra's forehead and kissed her. "What about your mother? How long has she been gone?"

Siofra didn't seize with panic like she usually did when asked about her family. Curiously, she *wanted* to speak of them. "Both my parents died ten years ago. Something terrible happened." She swallowed. It was the truth she wanted him to have, not some diluted version of events that exonerated her. "They were hung for doing magic. I could have saved them, but instead I ran."

Desemir tensed. She waited for him to toss her away in disgust, but once he settled, he held her closer. "That must have been terrible for you. I'm sorry."

"For me?"

"You were just a child. You did the only thing you could."

"It doesn't make them any less dead."

Desemir leaned forward to look at her. "If you're still holding on to guilt, you have to let it go. They wouldn't want you to carry this."

Siofra pushed him back and reclaimed her place on his chest. "You sound like Fen."

"Well, he's irritable, but he does make good points."

She laughed, but it faded to sadness. "I wonder if he'll ever speak to me again."

"Of course he will. It's not anger keeping him from you, you know. It's pride." Desemir sighed. "I see it for what it is because I'm well acquainted with that battle."

"You? *No.*" Siofra feigned shock.

Des jostled her in response. "Hard to believe, I know."

"Your business last night..." Siofra ventured. "Did it work out as you wanted it to?"

Desemir shook his head. "They're all leeches. Every last one of them. They were happy enough to accept huge buyouts for their parts of the Darkwood, but now the deal is unsatisfactory to them? But it doesn't matter what I think. They'll never stop."

"And you won't sell it back to them."

"Never." Desemir's jaw hardened against her head. "But I have to step carefully. Their fear of me won't last forever."

"Why do they fear you at all?"

221

He laughed. "Pesha reads their whispers. And now I know *all* their darkest secrets."

"How scandalous!"

"Very." His laughter subsided. "Rolfe will be here in a fortnight. I tried to put him off, but it's his turn to sit at my table and make threats."

Siofra shivered. "He's an awful man. It took me seconds to read the rot within him."

"He's vile," Desemir agreed. "But I could see you got under his skin."

Siofra leaned forward. "Did I?"

He nodded.

"Well, I'm glad of it," she said. "I hate that I let him get to me. I saw his intention before I felt it, but by then, he'd already won. He enjoyed my discomfort. Like it sustained him."

"It would surprise me none to learn that man feasts on blood and tears alone," Desemir said. "But take some comfort in knowing he had to watch you walk away with his worst enemy."

"Back to calling them enemies, I see."

"In my heart, I never stopped."

They laughed together. Siofra cuddled tighter against him, wishing it could always be that way.

"You know..." she said after a pause. "I could join you. In this meeting of yours."

"What?"

"If I unsettle him so much, then..." Siofra grinned against him. "Allow me to unsettle him."

Desemir didn't respond right away. "I don't want him anywhere near you, Siofra. I shouldn't even have let him touch you on the dance floor. It was a mistake, one I won't allow a second time."

"I can handle myself."

"I know you can, but—"

"Let me do it." She pitched forward, imploring him. "I *want* to do it. If I can help you, even in some small way, it would bring me happiness."

"No."

"*Please,* Des. I'm telling you I can handle this."

"Siofra."

"Desemir."

Desemir lowered his eyes and shook his head. "You'd sit by me. He'd be forbidden from touching you."

Siofra hummed with excitement. "Of course. Fine."

"If I sense he's upsetting you, even a little..."

"There's nothing to worry about." Siofra craned up to kiss him. "You'll see."

"Where were you? Where did he take her?" Fen was flushed and breathless as he hastened to keep up with Pesha. He ran two paces behind him in the central hall, past the tall windows.

"Into the woods," Pesha answered, brisk and detached. It wasn't the same man Fen had dined with, laughed with.

"For what?"

Pesha rounded into the next hall and stopped just before the library. With a hard sigh, he turned back. "You *really* need to make amends with your sister."

Fen's anxiousness coiled tighter. "I thought you, of everyone, understood—"

"He's being *reckless* with her." Pesha pushed out a stilted breath. He raked his hands through his hair, exhaling again. "You saw him leave the ballroom last night."

"The whole of Darkwood Run saw. It was dis—"

"Reckless," Pesha said for him. His cheeks twitched with agitation. "He locked me out. I couldn't..." He shook his head. "He was in there with her, alone, all night. And then today... *Today,* he wanted to take her into the woods, *alone,* and I refused to let it happen."

Maybe she'll kill the man, and we can be done with this farce, Fen thought, but he said, "If he wants to be reckless, then the consequences are his to accept. It's not your job to make his choices for him."

"I wish it was!" Pesha thundered. "You don't know what it's like, Fen. You..." He trailed off, shaking his head at the ground. "I suppose you do know. And now, we have to watch them both be reckless together."

"Why..." Fen lowered his voice when two of the house staff walked by. "Why did he take her into the woods?"

"To mix up their bedchamber activities? I don't know." Pesha pressed his hand to the library door. "He showed her the tree we both played at as boys. And then he defiled it." He snorted. "He didn't call for more women last night, and he told Wulf he'd take tonight off too."

Fen drew back. "Isn't that a good thing, Pesh? Hasn't this been atop your list of concerns for years now?"

"Not if it means..." Pesha swung his hand back down and crossed his arms. "There's just... *things* you and your sister don't know, and never will. Des may be enamored with Siofra now, and perhaps it's even healing something in them both, but wounds don't heal by laying a satin sheet over them, do they?"

Fen held his hands out in confusion. Pesha was often mysterious, but this was the most he'd ever hinted at something terrible in their past without actually saying it. "I don't understand either of you Trevanions, truth be told. Your brother claims he wants a broodmare without the trappings of love and is now sequestering himself away with Siofra like a man possessed. And you mumble and whine about his evening proclivities, but when he tries to solve his problems another way, that, too, is anathema to you."

Pesha narrowed his eyes. "Whose side are you on here, Stiofen? You're either estranged from your sister or you're defending her honor once more. The two positions have no intersect."

"You whisper about secrets and pasts and yet say nothing!" Fen was hot now. He'd said the words he'd feared saying aloud because of how nice, how unusual, his time with Pesha the past weeks had been. But Siofra wasn't the only one incapable of bringing herself down from a peak once she'd climbed it. "You say so much without saying *anything*, and I'm supposed to understand?"

"No," Pesha said with tight, frantic head shakes. "No, Fen, you're not supposed to understand anything. You're not even supposed to *be* here, but my brother's complicated relationship with his own failings has driven us right to the edge of this cliff! And if you only *knew*. If you—"

"So tell me," Fen stated, interjecting. "Tell me, and I can help you!"

Pesha lowered his eyes with a sad chuckle. "You can't help me or anyone else at Shadowfen Hall, Fen. We're all living in the suspended thrall of a past we cannot change and a future we cannot control." He looked back up at Fen. "But if you really want to help, you'll make sure your sister doesn't bring this entire house down around us and take everything with her."

"You *just* left his side." Gisela spoke her words with reproach, but she was smiling. "You're sure you don't want a break? No one would blame you for needing one. He can be rather intense."

"Mm." Siofra said it as Desemir would, and the familiarity of it wrapped around her like a comforting blanket. She closed her eyes and allowed a part of herself to return to the memories of the past night, of the morning. "We're having the rest of our meals for the day sent to his apartments, and I'll be staying the night again."

"Just you?" Gisela cocked a brow. "None of the... others?"

"Not last night," Siofra said with a stab of pride. "And not tonight."

Gisela grinned. "I don't know whether to congratulate you, be proud of you, or be in awe of you." She swept Siofra's hair to the back. "What changed? Before, his behavior had been so upsetting to you, and now..."

"It was because I wasn't ready to know my place in it," Siofra said. "He and I are... compatible in certain regards."

"Say what you mean," Gisela teased. "And speak plainly."

Siofra turned with a grin that must have lit up her whole face. "I've learned I enjoy sex, Gisela. And... in particular, sex with Desemir, who doesn't treat me as if I'm a porcelain doll moments from shattering. He wants to be in control, and I want to *be* controlled. He breaks me and then rebuilds me, over and over and over, and he does so with my *full* consent and encouragement. I come undone so utterly, it's incomprehensible to me that there could be anything left, then he raises me higher, fills me with an even greater desire than he'd just pulled from me. And once more I am his, and he is mine, and it's all... Well, I lack the proper words."

Gisela fanned herself with a slow, long exhale. "I suppose I did ask you to speak plainly, but I wasn't expecting such candor. I'd say you explained it more than well enough."

"Before I came here, I couldn't even speak of sex without shame. I dared not even think of it, though sometimes, late in the night, I'd wonder what it was like, for women who led normal lives. I never thought I'd know it for myself, being... well, what I am."

"For someone so new to the activity, you certainly speak of it with an unusual clarity." Gisela paused before saying what she said next. "But you mustn't take it as a personal slight if he invites the others back tomorrow, or the next day. You understand?"

"I understand that no one else understands." Siofra laughed at her choice of strange words. It wouldn't have been funny at all to her before, but while the world around her remained much the same, she had changed. Colors were brighter, sounds sharper and more melodic.

"He's certainly mesmerized you," Gisela muttered. "I hope it lasts for you both."

"And why wouldn't it? I know Des and I had a rough start, but we've come to an understanding. We accept each other for who we are and for what we bring to this unusual marriage."

"What happened last night, Si? I saw the way he watched you with those men. Guardians, *everyone* saw him stewing with

226

anger over it. When he came to dance with you and then take you away, I was... Well, I was worried. Pesha and I both followed you to his apartments, but he'd locked us out. And then we heard..." Gisela exhaled with a laugh. "Well, let's just say I knew you were fine. But it *was* curious. And those of us who have known Des for years are perplexed at the recent changes in him. Some are even concerned."

"Des would be greatly displeased to know you're all whispering about him behind his back." Siofra was struck with a wave of defensiveness—possessiveness. "You know he'd rather hear what you have to say directly."

"He says that," Gisela answered. "But everyone knows it isn't true. He hears what he wants to, nothing more. And while every last one of us would die to protect Desemir, without knowing the threat, all we can do is sit and wait and hope that when the time comes, we're armed with the proper knowledge to be of use."

Siofra's pulse fluttered as Gisela spoke. To hear her speak of Desemir as if he were a volcano, unable to quell an explosion, was jarring, but it didn't ring false. He *was* impulsive and volatile, but she was soothing that in him, wasn't she? By offering him a safe place to explore his dark fantasies, he could forego the risks he took every night by bringing strange women to the Hall. And was the safety of his home and people not his top concern?

"I don't understand, Gisela. Is there something you want from me?"

"Nothing but your caution," Gisela answered with a soft, sad smile. "Desemir is dear to me, of course, but so have you become. I hope all of our fears are unwarranted."

"What precisely do you think is going to happen?" Siofra demanded. "Everyone here speaks in such vague morsels, and says nothing!"

"Forgive me, Siofra. I didn't mean to upset you." Gisela turned away, but not before Siofra noticed her wiping her eye. "Have a lovely evening with your husband."

228

EIGHTEEN
THE COST OF BETRAYAL

W hy would you ever think this is a good idea?" Pesha asked. He assisted Lotte in placing candles in a series of neat lines down the long table. Once lit, they would further obfuscate Baron Rolfe's already tenuous view from his distant end of the table. They would dull the echo of conversation, leaving him isolated and disarmed.

The arrangement had been Pesha's idea when Desemir had first begun having such meetings. He'd modified it over the years, making it even more confounding for the men who came to Shadowfen Hall with nefarious intentions toward his brother.

For the meeting with Rolfe, Pesha had doubled his efforts on the candles. Desemir was firm; he didn't want the bastard to have any access to Siofra. To even look at her should be near impossible.

"It wasn't my idea at all," Desemir said. He stood at the drink cart, one hand folded around to his lower back, the other dancing along the wine carafes. "I seem to remember Rolfe likes a deep, bold red. Isn't that right, Lotte?"

"It is," Lotte answered as she bustled down one completed line of candles, taking the flame to them. "And I remember this because it's quite fitting that a man of his dark tastes would indulge himself with a drink resembling blood."

Desemir laughed and shot an amused glance back at Pesha. "Imagine having a reputation so strong, even Lotte has you pegged with such accuracy."

"You insult me, Des. I know everything. Remember?"

"Apologies." He tipped a reverent nod her way. "I've been rightly scolded and accept my wrongness."

Pesha laughed and shook his head as he placed the last of the candles.

Lotte flicked a doubting look back. "If you don't want others to think you're up to no good, perhaps consider that the rougher, more grizzled side of you will light fewer suspicions."

"I'm always up to no good, Lotte."

"She's saying *love* has *softened* you," Pesha teased him in a loud whisper.

"And who in the Hall could even define such a word?" Desemir asked smoothly, avoiding addressing the accusation. "My wife *has* softened me, Lotte. But you've misread the situation. It's more that..." Desemir angled his head in thought. "Shadowfen Hall has been without a mistress far too long, and her presence is a welcome reminder of why there should always be one."

"You've kept her locked away in your bedchamber, so I wouldn't know," Pesha said, deadpan. "She doesn't understand this man as you do. What if she thinks this is a game?"

"He had his hands on her like a predator at the ball," Desemir said. His tone darkened with his demeanor. "He left her feeling... vulnerable. Violated. I won't deny her an opportunity to wield power against him."

"But won't Rolfe think she's there on his request?"

Desemir sighed. He palmed the drink cart and hunched over it. "It *vexes* me that he had the nerve to ask."

"And it will no doubt vex you further to see the slimy, satisfied grin he'll wear, knowing you obliged him." Pesha set the candle box down and went to his brother. "There are other ways for Siofra to reclaim her power. Other times."

"You're not the one he wronged," Desemir said. "And I don't particularly care *what* Rolfe thinks, because once you read his whispers—and we both know a man like Rolfe must possess the most delicious of secrets—he'll forget she's even in the room."

"Prepare to be scandalized," Lotte said in a singsong voice. "I expect what you find will explain all foul doings in the Darkwood far too neatly."

Desemir laughed. "I'm counting on it."

Euric popped his head in. "He's here."

Desemir rubbed his hands together with a grin. "Let's vanquish another enemy today, Pesh, shall we?"

Desemir was already seated when Rolfe arrived. He didn't rise to greet him. Euric and Cassius guided the man to his chair at the far end of the room, without affording him any of the ceremony he was accustomed to.

"I'd nearly forgotten your penchant for flair," Rolfe called when he took his seat. "Even if all the lights of the Darkwood went out, you'd never know, would you?"

Desemir cupped a hand to the back of his ear to signal Rolfe to speak up, though he'd heard him fine. The need to yell across the table was an enjoyable falsehood he continued to perpetuate.

He chuckled to himself at the annoyance in Rolfe's response, twice as loud and half as poised. But though it was an early victory, Des would be a fool to count the meeting won.

Seated in the chair to his right, Siofra directed a cool, haughty glare at Rolfe, which she hadn't broken once since the man had entered the Hall of Counting. The pale-blue dress she wore only added to her iciness. Something inappropriate and ill-timed stirred in his trousers.

231

Pesha shifted in the shadows to Desemir's left.

"You've put me off for months. And that's being generous, Desemir, for it's been years since Ludwik died."

"Baron Trevanion," Desemir stated. "Or Master Trevanion, which I've come to prefer, as it's such a singular designation. There can only be *one* Master of Forests."

Siofra's rouged mouth twitched in approval.

"I care not for your titles or your posturing. And I didn't come here to spar or match witty barbs." Rolfe practically yelled. In the glow of several hundred candles, he looked ready to explode. "You know why I'm here. All of my peers have now had their chance with you, and it's my turn. But unlike the others, I will leave here having gotten what I wanted."

"A rather confident assumption for one who comes with nothing I desire."

Rolfe's tongue flicked across his bottom lip. "I come with an inconvenient truth, Desemir."

"Baron or—"

"You had to put her on display, your little bird? I hardly think we'd have cared enough if we hadn't first laid eyes on your little nymph. I knew the moment I put my hands on her—"

"Careful," Siofra whispered to Desemir, without turning her head. "I'm fine."

Desemir eased off what he was going to say, but he held the knot in his belly to keep himself alert, ready.

"That she wasn't any ordinary woman. That isn't to say it was *easy* to figure out who she is. *What* she is."

Siofra's breathing halted. She held her chin high, but it dimpled in the center with her uncertainty.

Desemir jerked a hard gaze at Pesha, gesturing for him to make his pass. It was early, too early, but Rolfe had no love for pleasantries. He'd come to his point, and if Desemir let it go on any longer without sharpening his own sword, it could take a turn that would put him squarely on the wrong side of the conversation.

"You're a bit long in the tooth for fishwife gossip, Edmund," Desemir charged, his eyes on Pesha as he made his way to the other end of the room. "It's true my wife has no family nor gold of her own, but I should think you could appreciate the expediency of picking a nobody, when picking a *somebody* leaves me with far too much to lose."

Desemir swallowed with an apologetic glance at Siofra. He would make it up to her later.

"Gossip is a tool of opportunity. If it were not, no one would engage in it, except, as you said, fishwives with nothing better to do." Rolfe leaned in on his elbows. "But gossip becomes troublesome when it's seen as truth. It would be easy for you to dismiss my words, but I've come with proof."

Rolfe dug into his pocket as Pesha made a pass at his back.

He held the crumpled vellum high in his outstretched hand. "A letter signed by a gaoler in Newcarrow."

Siofra's pained gasp sent rage shooting across Desemir's chest.

No matter what came next, Rolfe would pay for that.

"A gaoler." Desemir wrenched his father's ring hard enough to send it spinning to his knuckle. "Who can be bought and paid to say anything you please." He snorted to cover the awareness that he was approaching a familiar dark spiral. Emerging from it with his control intact would be impossible. "If that's your *proof* of... whatever it is you're accusing my wife of, you'll be laughed out of even the dodgiest taverns in Darkwood Run."

Unfazed, Rolfe lowered his arm, but his smile remained. "She's an abomination, Desemir, a cruel mistake perpetrated by the Guardians to remind us why we cannot and should not ever coexist with the vile, unnatural Medvedev."

"Si," Des whispered without moving his mouth. "Don't listen to a *single* word."

Siofra started to shake. At first it was her feet, heels tapping her chair, but then a tremble overtook the rest of her.

"If insulting my wife was your strategy, you've already lost." Des ground his knuckles to the underside of the hard table, burying a groan. He kept one eye on Siofra, who was unraveling before his eyes. Pesha's return to him was slow, too slow. "I was never going to sell even an acre back to you, but now I can't even promise you'll be free to leave with your head."

"If I don't return by nightfall, copies of this letter will be released to all our peers. As will the one I received from the dreadfully wronged Steward Stanhope, who was distressed to learn that the young woman who murdered his son was living a life of luxury, never paying for her crime."

Siofra whimpered, whispering what sounded like *no, no, no.*

Desemir's breath caught in understanding.

Her red wall.

After weeks of peace, it was back.

Rolfe couldn't release those letters. They would take Siofra, punish her, and *torture* her, and there'd be nothing, *nothing,* Desemir could do about it. Laws would supersede his rights as her husband to keep her safe. They would strip her to nothing and leave her a husk of her former self.

I will never let them take you, Siofra.

Desemir jumped when Pesha knelt in the spot between him and Siofra. He whispered the secret Desemir had been hanging the entire conversation on.

His heart plunged to the floor, taking all his blood with it. "No. There has to be more."

"It's not nothing, Des."

"It's not *enough,* Pesha." Desemir ground his jaw and set his gaze on the smooth, dark wood of the table. "He can't be allowed to leave here."

"If he doesn't return, they'll send—"

"We can buy off his men!" Desemir hissed from the side of his mouth. "He *cannot* be allowed to leave."

"Desemir? Have I struck a nerve, perhaps?" Rolfe called from the other end of the table.

Siofra's hands, wrapped tightly to the arms of her chair, had gone stark white. Her chair legs started to rattle. Pesha glanced at her in alarm and went to soothe what was building within her, but Desemir gripped his arm. He shook his head, ignoring Pesha's incredulity.

Desemir looked at his wife. He read her dark, dangerous fear and was utterly helpless against what had caused it. He had never felt anything like this before; the *rage* was familiar, but the pain of seeing her absorb a future he couldn't protect her from was unbearable.

"Siofra," Desemir whispered. "Look at me."

Her head swiveled, revealing only her profile.

"Do I sense what I think I do?"

She sobbed. "I can't... Pesha, help me. *Please.*"

"Pesh, no," Desemir said. "This man has threatened Siofra. She has a right to defend herself."

Pesha shook his head in furious disbelief. "Des, this is madness."

"You don't have to hold it back anymore, love. I'll be right here with you."

"Des, let him soothe me, please. *Please,* if the wall rises any higher, it won't just be that man. It will take *everything.* You don't understand. You don't *know* what this is, what *you're asking.*"

"Is everything quite all right down there with your heathen wife?" Rolfe asked, cajoling.

"This is part of who you are. You can be yourself with me," Desemir urged gently. "Pesha, give me a moment with my wife."

"Desemir!" Pesha cried. "Listen to yourself. This has gone way too far!"

"If you want your vengeance, Siofra, no one here will stop you." With the words out, Desemir felt a tremendous sense of relief. "No one will judge you."

"You don't know what you're saying, Des. You don't." She whimpered.

"It's all right. I'll protect you from any fallout. I will keep you safe, as I've promised you."

Siofra bucked forward in her chair and, just as quickly, whipped her head back. She sounded a primal scream but then

235

clipped it and rolled sideways out of her chair, into a sprint as she raced toward the doors. She flailed against them, clawing and still screaming, as Euric and Cassius scrambled to open them. Her screams carried down the hall, eventually fading to echoes.

"Euric, Cassius! After her, *now*," Desemir cried, thrusting his whole arm at the door. "I'll be right behind you."

Rolfe rose, wearing a smile that birthed a new wave of wrath in Desemir. "I believe my point has been aptly made. I'll expect your answer within a day."

Siofra ran so fast, her legs came up off the grass, missing strides. Her tears were like ice on her face against the hard, cold wind whipping her, as she was using all her strength to keep her red wall at bay for a few more moments.

She stumbled and fell to her knees when she reached the lake. She pitched forward, sucking in desperate gasps and choking on the exhales. Her screams had ceased to be sound but were still within her, trapped in her belly, her chest, and her fingers and toes. She rocked forward, backward, forward, backward... begging the wall to recede, to leave, but the light behind her eyes was *blinding*, and the rage—

A sharp pain ripped through her center and spread outward, reaching into the forest, into the field. She clapped both of her hands to her mouth, but the song was stronger, forcing her arms away so it could sound the impeccable, deadly melody into the blood and bone and cell and blade of everything—everything around her.

Darkness beckoned. *Come here, Siofra, where it's safe. Where you can forget any of this happened. Where your pain is trapped and cannot surface.*

"No." Siofra pushed to her feet, swaying several steps through the scorched earth. Her blurry gaze locked incredulously on the ripples passing across the freshly melted lake. "No..." She twined her legs in a half spin, flailing her arms out as she fought for balance. Her hands hit the ashes of what used to be grass, and the horror of it pushed her into the forward, steady movement she'd been after.

Siofra sprinted across the ash, her eyes locked on the forest. Her thoughts couldn't form anything cogent, but something Desemir had once said, about the Darkwood being a perfect place to get lost, filled her with inexplicable hope.

Lost. If she was lost, she could hurt no one.

Siofra heard Aio sound a mournful cry into the night, but she didn't spare a glance upward. She'd failed her familiar too. She deserved no comfort.

When she reached the forest line, she slowed only enough to navigate the dense underbrush. It all looked the same to her, but she didn't need a clear path. She didn't need to remember the way back out. She would go as far as her legs would take her.

She dodged roots and branches, nearly kicking a poor rabbit as she swung into a bramble of briars that clawed and tore at her flesh. When she broke free, several thorny vines were still wrapped around her ankles, but she felt no pain. She'd given it all to death.

The ground started to clear, forming what seemed to be a path. Siofra was considering where it might lead when she was hurled to the ground. The force shoved a breath from her lungs.

"Is it her?" someone asked from several feet away.

Siofra writhed under the substantial weight pinning her. She screamed when a rough sack was pulled crudely over her head and cinched at the neck.

"Has to be," the man sitting on her said. "Rolfe said this would be a challenge. Perhaps the poppies have addled his brain."

They both laughed.

Siofra screamed into the scratchy fabric, but it only made the man shift more weight onto her. Her throat was on fire.

"Think he'll believe she ran straight into our arms?"

"Don't care what he believes." The man ripped at her wrists, binding them with a thick rope that burned her sensitive flesh. "Only that he rewards us handsomely."

Siofra was hoisted up and thrown over the man's shoulder. She saw the forest bob up and down through the cross-stitches of the sack, which cinched tighter with every harsh movement, choking the last of her consciousness.

She was thrown inside what seemed to be a carriage. The door slammed.

"Untouched," the man who'd pinned her said with a growl. "Take your lustfulness to the tavern and spend it there, Ficke."

"Why does he care if we touch her?" Ficke droned. "He's going to kill her anyway."

"Shh." The first man hissed. "I wouldn't want to be the man who spoiled Edmund Rolfe's fun."

239

SONG
OF DEATH

242

NINETEEN
THE BARN

Siofra's introduction to her environment was a blinding stab of pain as it rippled through her shoulders and down to her hands.

Except... No, that wasn't quite right. The pain didn't travel *down* at all. The agony moved upward. She lolled her head back, eyes still fluttering into consciousness, and found she was bound at the wrists, dangling from a large, rusted hook.

Instinctively, she kicked her feet in a scissor motion, but they only caught air, swinging her forward and back, deepening the burn between her shoulders.

She stopped struggling and let her feet still so she could think.

Those men, in the woods.

After you failed to control your gift of death...

No, I can't think about that.

Yes, Siofra. You must face what you did.

For once, I did the right thing! This time I made *myself run, fighting the red wall at every step. Because of it, no one was hurt this time.*

Are you certain?

243

Yes!

Can you be?

Siofra abandoned her train of thought for more practical matters. There was no light to give hints of her surroundings, but the pungency of moldy hay narrowed things down.

Animal excrement was her next recognition.

Wet, damp wood.

Siofra was confident her prison was a barn of sorts.

But whose barn?

They mentioned the vile monster Rolfe. He's going to kill you.

Desemir won't let him. He won't let it get so far.

Even if he responds to Rolfe's demands, you think a man like Rolfe is good on his word?

He knows who I am. He's going to tell everyone.

Yes. But it won't matter anymore, because you'll be dead, and Desemir, ruined.

"No." Siofra grunted and clenched her jaw so tight, her face ached. She was done listening to herself, to her doubts. She knew who she was. She'd been terribly wrong to assume her red wall could be so easily tamed.

Perhaps there *was* an acceptable use for it though.

Whoever walked through the door would wish they hadn't.

But if you kill them before they can unhook you, what good will it do?

I said I wasn't listening to you anymore.

More alert, Siofra became aware of other pains. Her once-healed ankle had seemingly broken again. Her eyes swept downward enough to catch purple bloating around the tops of her feet. Her arms and legs burned with the sting of dozens of untended cuts. Her head was thick with pressure, and she remembered smacking her head on something when she had been tossed into the carriage.

She'd blacked out sometime after, depleted.

Healing wasn't high on her aptitudes, and it would take all her strength if she tried.

No, Siofra decided. She could mend her wounds later. She needed what little strength had returned to her to take down her captors.

Another pain came into focus, though it took her a moment to understand it. Aio. Her falcon wasn't gone, but she wasn't close either. She was far enough away that the dull ache of detachment clawed around the edges of Siofra's heart.

Stay away, please, Siofra tried to tell her, knowing it would go nowhere. *Stay where you're safe, Aio.*

Her thoughts abruptly shifted to Desemir. If Rolfe had sent men to subdue her, had he brought others for her husband? Could it be that he was a prisoner too?

Or dead?

No. I would know.

How? He's no Medvedev.

I can't sense Fen either, but it's because he's not here. Just like Aio isn't.

Or they're all dead.

I can't even bear to think it.

Alive. Dead. Neither matters right now. Getting out of this barn is the only thing that does.

Most of the time, Siofra heard the voice as her own. But it was someone else speaking to her, a person whose tone she'd regretfully forgotten with the relentless passage of time.

In another circumstance, she might have even found it soothing.

What do you suggest then, Mother?

What have I always told you, Siofra? Be still. Gather your energy, and wait. For it's not a matter of if, but when someone walks into this barn, and you'll need a plan before they do.

I know.

You do know. But you're still coming around to things. Your surroundings don't matter, just as the fate of your loved ones doesn't.

I'm listening.

You're getting out of this barn, Siofra Thornheart. But it will be up to you and your wits whether you're alive or dead when it happens.

It took both Euric and Cassius to conquer Desemir's hysteria. They'd cornered him in the Hall of Counting before he could take off for Oakhelm like a man possessed.

"She'll hurt herself. She'll hurt herself, and it's *my* fault. I asked her to do this, and I need to fix this *now*, before it's too late. She *needs* me, you fucking bastards. Let me go. Let me *go...*"

Pesha watched his brother thrash against the grip of his men, waiting for him to tire himself out. He'd soothed him once already, after Rolfe had departed and Wulf went to gather guards for a search party.

But when the soothing had worn off, Desemir stung him with a look that froze his heart.

You ever do that to me again when I have not asked for it, and you'll find we are no longer brothers.

He hadn't meant it. Pesha knew it, and yet the hurt, that even in such dire circumstances Desemir could say something so horrible, was no less.

Pesha's panic tottered over the same precarious edge. He might be the essence of calm on the outside, but on the inside? His fears *screamed* to be allowed to run wild and behave according to their dangerous command, consequences be damned.

But Pesha would never remind his brother how he had pushed Siofra over the edge. Desemir's sanity hung upon an even sharper one.

Desemir howled and screamed at his loyal guards, calling them terrible names and demanding they let him go or he'd send them back to their families. Cassius looked appropriately alarmed, but Euric was a stone wall. He'd been more of a father to Desemir and Pesha than Ludwik had. He knew what his surrogate son needed.

Pesha knelt before his brother and gathered his strength. He bowed his hands over his face and sighed before speaking. "Des. I won't touch you again. You made yourself... clear on the matter."

"I didn't think I *needed* to be clear, Pesh, that it wasn't all right to use your magic on me! You *know* I trust you not to do it, and now that trust—"

"Listen to me," Pesha stated. His hand twitched, eager to reach forward and ease Desemir of the dangerous current running through him. "Wulf and his men are out looking for her now. He cares for her—"

"Wants to *fuck* her," Desemir said. He sniffed and choked out a vitriolic laugh on an exhale. "It should be me out there looking for her." He spat the words and Pesha winced, wiping his face. "Her husband. It's *my* job to look after her, is it not? Is it not my job, Pesh? Not the job of a husband? Not what I am *meant* to do, what—"

"Desemir," Pesha said firmly. "You don't want me to touch you? Fine. But I won't sit here and listen to your ramblings. You want to help Siofra, let Wulf do his job. She can't have gone far. The forest is only so large. He'll bring her back and then you can make this right."

"She was *on fire* when she left this room!"

Pesha had at first thought he'd imagined it, adding color to an already-confounding situation. But she *had* been aflame. Her flesh and hair had been fire, though she hadn't burned herself.

Pesha didn't tell his brother about the field and the lake. There were lies and then there were kindnesses.

Eshe, mercifully, had been untouched by the horror, protected by her stasis.

He couldn't say the same about anything else in the vicinity of Siofra's rage.

"She left to calm herself," Pesha said. He glanced again at Euric, who was still wholly focused on restraining Desemir to his chair. The old man looked almost calm, if not for the cords on his neck bulging unnaturally. "Which is actually a *good* sign, as

Siofra hadn't been capable of making choices like that before, in the heat of the moment."

"Are you making *jests* right now?"

"What?" Pesha replayed his words and realized the error. "No. I'm sorry. If it would make you feel better, I'll go join the search on your behalf."

Desemir's face stretched with a cruel grin. "You want to know what would make me feel *better*, Pesh? If you bastards *let me go find my wife!*"

Flashing a raised brow at Euric, Pesha rose to his feet and turned around. His eyes caught the drink cart. A drink would calm his brother, but there was a fair chance he'd spit it back in his face. Lottie could make a draught, but they already knew how useless those were on Desemir.

"And so where is her falcon then? Aio?" Desemir demanded. "I presume *that's* who Wulf is following, to find my wife?"

"Her falcon," Pesha mused aloud. He spun back around, ashamed it had not occurred to him before. His relationship with his own familiar was complicated. "Yes. Yes! I'll go send word—"

"You mean to tell me *no one* but me thought of this?" Desemir ripped at the two sets of arms pinning him to the chair.

"Pesha!" Fen cried from the door. His steps thundered as he rushed in. For a moment, it seemed he intended to throw himself into Pesha's arms. His face was stained with tears. His chest heaved. "Tell me you've found her. Please. Tell me she's all right."

"They haven't," Desemir spat. "They'd rather stand in here and *talk* about it."

"That's not fair," Pesha replied. To Fen, he said, "Where's Aio? Can you find her?"

Fen swiped at his face, his mouth open. "No, but I can sense Atio. I'll send him to find Aio, and Aio will find Siofra, and..." When Fen looked back up, the hope on his face crushed Pesha's heart. "I'll go right now."

248

Pesha only had time enough to watch him leave before Wulfhelm rushed back in. His face was caked in filth. His wide eyes said what his words hadn't.

"Just tell us," Pesha blurted, unable to meet Desemir's unhinged gaze.

"We followed her path." Wulf clutched his chest as he struggled for air. "She went first to the lake and then into the forest, near the first bend of the road. We fanned out to cover all possibilities, but I stayed on her tracks. I followed them until..." He inhaled a series of steadying breaths. "They came to an end."

"An end? Are you suggesting, Wulf, that she sprouted wings and flew out of the forest?"

"No, Desi." Wulf lowered his eyes to the floor with a hard sigh. "Hers were not the only tracks. There were two other sets, and I followed them to the east road, where they ended. It isn't the road most men take to come to the Hall, so it was..." He swallowed. "A simple matter to identify the hooves and wheel marks."

"Where were our own guards? How was anyone able to take the east road without our notice at all?"

"I don't know. We'll need to do a full investigation, of course, but—"

"So what are you saying?" Des's head shook wildly. "What are you *saying*?"

Wulfhelm looked to Pesha for help, but Pesha's carefully crafted calm was slowly being pulled from under him. The guard turned back toward Desemir. "I'm saying, Desi, all evidence points to someone having taken Siofra... taken your wife... captive."

Desemir sucked in as if stealing the entirety of the air from the room.

Pesha closed his eyes.

The floor wavered.

His heart beat like a drum in his ear.

The world stilled.

And then Desemir sounded a feral howl that swelled to a crescendo over the deafening silence. It drove a hard sob from

Wulf, and even Euric—stoic, smooth Euric—wavered in his hold on Des, shaking his head at the floor.

Pesha rushed to his brother's side and flung his arms around him. "Forgive me, Des," he whispered, his voice cracked and shaking, as he tried to take away even an ounce of his brother's agony.

TWENTY
LITTLE BIRD, BIG BIRD

Siofra screamed when another weight was attached to her broken foot. She squeezed her eyes shut to fight the pain, to drive it inward where whoever hurt her would never know how badly, though she couldn't see anyway with the layers of blindfolds they'd added when they had brought the weights.

The men in Newcarrow told us this trick, witch. Scream all you want. No one is coming.

"Does it hurt, little bird?" her torturer asked. The torrential rain beating the earth mercifully drowned some of the cruelty in his thick voice.

Siofra coiled her head back and spat at him. She couldn't see but hoped it landed square in his face.

"Perhaps not so little." The man guffawed. "But I haven't seen your bird go by, the one with the wings longer than most homes, and those beady eyes they say can rain fire upon the earth."

Aio could not, in fact, shoot fire from her eyes, but it served Siofra better to leave as much of her and Aio's magic a mystery

251

as she could. It would keep their fear alive, which was the only weapon she had.

"Or... Maybe one of our hunters shot it out of the sky. A right feast the beast will make." He proceeded to make disgusting slurping sounds. "Nothing, eh? You'd be all right with that, would you?"

Siofra stabbed her tongue to the roof of her mouth. Oh, she had something to say, but not to him. Every word she used would demystify herself, be used to understand her better.

Her mouth flew open with a piercing scream when he dropped another weight onto her ankle.

"Your shoulder sockets are strong. I'll give you that." He laughed to himself, rifling through something. Moments later, the smell of pipe smoke permeated the air. "Most would have been stretched out by now, lost to the pain. Then, I hear a rumor your kind *likes* pain, so maybe I'm just doing you a favor."

Siofra heard him retreat and settle against some hay. He pulled on his pipe with noises as gross as his feigned eating. "I'm gonna give you some advice, little bird. Advice that could save your life."

Siofra strained against the weight pulling her downward. It was a cruel balance between not moving at all and moving enough to shift her pain around.

"You give the baron something of use, he'll probably let you go. He's a brutal man but a fair one. His problem isn't with you; it's with your husband. A husband you hardly know, I might add. You'd be a fool to die for him, especially when he hasn't even come looking for you."

Siofra forced herself not to react. If Desemir was dead, the man would have said as much. And if he wasn't dead, then he'd be planning her rescue. He'd come for her when the plan was sound.

Her flesh tingled, the first sensation in hours that wasn't pain.

And then, an idea emerged.

"Now about this bird of yours..."

"Rolfe," Siofra choked out. Even speaking was agony. "You want me to talk? Get him."

252

The man hummed a little tune through his laugh. "You'd much rather deal with me, little bird. Trust me."

"And yet." Siofra winced. She was grateful for the blindfold, for he'd surely see the truth in her eyes. "He's the only one to whom I'll speak."

"Now look here—"

"You answer to him. What do you suppose he'll do to you if he learns he had the opportunity to get what he wanted, but you kept him from it?"

"Don't spin this to be something it isn't, you filthy witch. Baron Rolfe doesn't deal with prisoners. *I* do. It's *my* job. It's been my job going on nigh twenty years."

"I'm a baroness, the Mistress of the Forest and of Shadowfen Hall, and I am owed the audience of someone my equal or greater."

Siofra braced for another weight, but the man grunted, seeming to comprehend the conundrum she'd walked him into.

"You'll regret it soon enough."

"A problem that is squarely mine. And my blindfold—"

"Not a chance." He chortled. "For that, he *would* kill me."

Desemir jumped to his feet when the doors opened. Stiofen rose immediately after.

Pesha and Wulfhelm walked into the Hall of Counting with determined strides. Desemir looked from one to the other, attempting to get an early read of whatever news they were about to drop on him. But both men were looking at the table, where Wulf slapped a roll of vellum, which had clearly already been read.

Desemir glared in annoyance. "Is this what I think it is?" He felt Stiofen shuffle closer for a better look. "And you wasted time reading it before bringing it straight to me?"

Pesha was unfazed. He rolled his shoulders with an exasperated breath. "We had to read it, to be sure it wasn't laced with something, some poison."

Desemir flared his hands outward. "And? Was it?"

Pesha set his mouth tight. "No."

Desemir turned his attention to Wulf, who had apparently not looked in a mirror in the past few hours. His hair was a frightful mess. Dirt caked his cheeks in fingered paths. "I want you to tell me."

Wulf whipped his head up, startled. He turned toward Pesha in alarm.

"Don't look at him. Look at *me*."

"She's all right, isn't she, Pesha?" Stiofen asked behind him. He sounded small, like a boy—like Pesha once had, when he'd become Desemir's charge.

"According to Rolfe, she's fine," Pesha answered, flicking his eyes at Wulfhelm. "Go on then. Tell them."

Desemir crossed his arms in impatience. He hoped it might also suppress his fitful heartbeat, which had not normalized since he'd learned Siofra had been taken.

"She's alive," Wulfhelm said with another wary look Pesha's way. "We're assured... that any... *alternative methods* used on the baroness have been minimal."

Desemir's jaw strained with the cords in his neck. He blinked hard once and turned away from the men to pace, where he could spend the unwelcome agitation on something other than over-thinking. "Rolfe is a dead man. But go on."

"He is prepared to send her back to you. For it to happen, he has listed his conditions."

"Well, whatever it is, we'll do it, right?" Stiofen asked. "You said yourself, Desemir, you have more than you'll ever need."

Desemir flicked a hand up. "What are the conditions?"

"There are three options he's outlined here," Wulf answered. His words slowed.

Desemir wanted to go back and rip the vellum from the table, read it himself, but the conflict stirring in him was for himself alone.

Pesha cleared his throat and took over. "The first option is we do nothing, and he kills her."

"That isn't an option at all!" Stiofen shrieked. "Even saying it aloud is a betrayal of Siofra!"

"It's all right, Fen," Pesha said.

Desemir fingered the silver drink tray. He imagined pouring himself a double, perhaps even a full mug of liquor. The burn, as it slid down, would scorch his other confusing emotions until they were naught but ash. "As for the other two options, they undoubtedly involve his desire for the Darkwood, no?"

"If you sell him back his acreage, and just his acreage, he will return Siofra to us, though he does not..." Pesha grunted, again clearing his throat. "He does not make promises as to the condition of her return."

"You *know* what that means!" Stiofen stormed toward Desemir. "You know what it means, do you not?"

"I know my brother hasn't yet read the third option," Desemir answered icily. "And if you don't return to your seat, Euric will return you."

"I knew coming here was a mistake. I *knew* you were a—"

"Finish the thought later. Or don't. Pesh?"

"The third option," Pesha said with a sharp inhale, "is we sell him *all* of the Darkwood, and he returns her unharmed, and the legitimacy of any heirs forthcoming will not be in question. Actually, I believe the word he used here was..." Pesha paused. "Ah, yes. Untouched."

Stiofen moaned in horror.

"Mm." Desemir rolled his anxiety through his shoulders, letting it carve its way through the center of his back.

For all the men of the Darkwood who had tried to take down Desemir, it seemed strange to him that the only one capable had been a young woman who'd spread herself across his life and changed everything in it.

"As far as I'm concerned," he said, controlling the waver threatening the edges of his tone. "There's only one option here."

"Give me a company of men, and let *me* go save her then," Stiofen hissed. "You selfish, cowardly, degenerate—"

255

"We sell him the Darkwood. All of it." The words left Desemir with the last of his unsteady breaths. "Pesha, you'll see to the paperwork?"

"*What?*" Pesha and Stiofen asked in perfect concert.

"We give him what he wants, and we can have Siofra back this very evening. Yes?" When nothing greeted his answer but silence, Desemir looked back to ensure they'd heard him.

Stiofen bowed over in stunned relief.

But Pesha looked almost angry.

"You cannot do it," Pesha said, shaking his head. "You cannot."

Desemir scoffed. "You've developed a soft spot for the trees, have you?"

"Des, that's not..." Pesha pursed his mouth, narrowed his eyes in a wince. "If I thought it would bring her back to you, I wouldn't dissuade you. This forest has been nothing but a yoke around your neck since our father died, and I would... I would *rip* it from you if I could, but you've never let me."

Desemir shrugged. "I'm letting you now. So do it."

Pesha shuffled closer, his agitation visibly mounting with every step. "You and I *know* this man. We grew up with his repulsive sons and simpering daughters. He isn't like Arranden. Nor even Weaver. He is no gentleman. He has no honor. He's doing this as much for the damnable wood as he is to hurt you."

"Desi, we have enough men," Wulfhelm said, stepping forward. He had a hand on his sword already. "We don't have to deal with this rogue. We can save her ourselves."

"A choice that might lose us some of those men, and Siofra besides." Desemir shook his head. "No. No, we meet his demand."

Pesha groaned. "Des—"

"Have I not made myself *clear*, brother?" Desemir spat.

"No matter *what* you give this man, he'll kill Siofra anyway." Pesha's cheeks flamed, his nose flaring. "He'll do it because he *can*. Because he *wants* to. And because once you sign the land over to him, he has no reason to call upon an honor which he *does not possess*."

256

"Fuck." Desemir flinched at the passion rolling off Pesha. It was new, like so many things about their lives these days.

And he was right.

"I'm willing to discuss doing this your way," he conceded. "But I won't sentence her to another night spent under his cruelty. If we can't get her tonight, I don't have another choice but to give him what he wants."

"We will." Pesha grimaced. His eyes welled with tears. "We will, Des. Tonight."

Desemir nodded. "We'll send a messenger to Oakhelm that promises a formal response to his demands by noon tomorrow. We can ask for proof of life, something that doesn't rouse his suspicions about our reticence. Let him go to his bed tonight satisfied, thinking he has us. By the time he knows better, it will be too late for him. We'll have Siofra, and his head will be stuck to the end of my sword." He turned toward Wulfhelm. "You have a strategy here, a way for us to raze Rolfe and everything he's ever touched to the ground? Or are you just fantasizing about getting to put your father's sword to proper use?"

There was no humor in Wulfhelm's fractured grin. "A little of both, Desi. Little of both."

When they released the weights from Siofra's ankles, another pain hit her, somehow worse than the last. She'd adjusted to the stretch, the burn, and all of it was undone as her muscles screamed at her in fresh ways.

She tried to not kick her feet, but they twitched on their own, responding to the freedom. But she wouldn't cry out. It would only take once for Rolfe and his men to decide she was weak and nothing to fear.

Instead, she swallowed the moan, her efforts traveling down her tight, dry throat, which hadn't received a drop of water since she'd been taken. It stoked the realization she was dreadfully thirsty. A hollow pang of hunger followed.

Siofra sensed only one presence in the barn with her, but she couldn't trust her instincts.

"I would ask you for another dance, but it seems you're indisposed." Rolfe's low tenor ripped through the silence, piercing her chest. His boots crunched in the dry hay as he neared. "I sensed something preternatural in you that night. Something that has no place in the Darkwood, nor the kingdom. But only one of those things concerns me."

Siofra set her mouth in what she hoped was an expressionless line. The urge to kick was so powerful, it brought her to tears.

"Did you know, Siofra, you could have already been free, had your husband borne any love for you?" Rolfe stopped drawing nearer and began a circle around her. "Before Cartwright put even a single weight on you, Baron Trevanion had already received and sent back refusal of all my conditions. He wouldn't sell even a *single* acre of his precious ebony wood to save you." He pitched forward behind her with a flash of heat at her neck. "How does it feel to know you are worth so little to him?"

He wants to break you. He knows just the words to do it.

I know, Mother.

"Of course it hurts," Rolfe answered, as if she'd spoken. "While love has little place in a marriage, a man understands the responsibility he bears his wife. Your husband does not even have *that*." Rolfe resumed his circling. "He said I'm free to do with you as I please. What do you suppose he meant by it?"

Des wouldn't say that. It doesn't even sound like him.

Doesn't it, Siofra? You've heard him say such things about others.

As you said. Others. Not me.

No. Of course. We mustn't listen to Rolfe.

"A man like Desemir Trevanion will always act on impulse and then regret it. He gets to deny me and..." Rolfe made a soft sound, almost a laugh. "Be rid of his mistake in the same breath. Even I can appreciate the strategy. Maybe he and I are not so different after all."

He wants to poison me against my husband. He thinks me a fool, that I'm so easily sculpted.

Of course that's what he's doing. He's a monster. But Desemir should have been here by now.

He'll come when he finds a way.

Or when the terms are more favorable to his coffers.

Rolfe stopped in front of her. He inched closer, enough that she could feel his foul breath against her flesh, heating her blindfold. "You called for me. You told my man you would speak if I came. Unless you want me to put those weights back on and add more besides, I suggest you *speak*."

Siofra's voice croaked. No words emerged. It gave her another second to consider whether her plan was as good as it had sounded in her head. "You say..." She swallowed against the dry bed coating her mouth. "You say you know my husband. Well, as I am new to the Darkwood, and I wasn't there for your past together, I cannot say one way or another if that is true. But I—"

Rolfe's hand wrapped around her throat, cinching her words. "Do you or do you not have something to tell me about your husband that will be of use to me?" He tightened his grip, his thumb digging so hard into her flesh, she saw stars. "This same man who has abandoned you to *my* whims, I might remind you. Whims he is already well aware of."

He released her and took a step back. Siofra wheezed and gasped.

"Let's try this again," he said.

You are in no position to play games with this man, Siofra. Tell him you have nothing.

I don't think... I don't know if what he says about Desemir is true, but he's not here now, and the only defense I have against this vile man is that, on some level, he still fears what I'm capable of.

A mere mind trick will not stoke his fear, only his ire.

It's all I have, Mother.

259

The air changed when Rolfe snaked his hand forward again. In her recoil, her head fell into his hand. He tightened it and shoved something against her mouth. "Drink."

Siofra sputtered against the assault of wine. It ran down her chin and slopped onto the floor. When his hold on her firmed, the warm liquid coursed down her throat, coating it with something more welcome than the desert it replaced.

Rolfe removed the wineskin. "That's all you get. Try again."

"What I have for you," Siofra said. Her hands flexed in their bindings. "Is a question."

"I didn't come here to play games—"

"Indulge me, will you? I'm at your mercy. What can I do?"

Rolfe grunted. "You get one. Don't squander it."

"I just want to know..." Siofra gathered her courage. She pointed her toes, bracing through the pain and turning it to strength. He would likely strike her once her words were out.

But uncertainty would replace his anger. *How* could she know such a thing? Desemir had never gotten the chance to use Pesha's whisper-reading of Edmund Rolfe before Siofra had succumbed to her red wall, but as far as Rolfe was concerned, Siofra was pulling it from his mind while he circled her like a predator.

"What?" he barked, impatient.

"How long have you been bedding your daughter's husband?"

A heavy pause followed, then he asked, "*Excuse* me?"

"I asked—"

"Your question is beyond the pale, girl. Spinning tales is more your husband's style."

"I pulled it from *your* mind. You're in love with him." Siofra's tongue trembled against the roof of her mouth. *Breathe.* "You've both talked about sending your daughter away, so you can be together more freely."

Rolfe's fury simmered between them. "That was *not* in my head," he said staunchly. But the doubt was set. It *had* been in his mind, only it had been Pesha to read it, not her. "And what a foul thing for you to say. I expect no less from a creature of your ilk though."

"Baron, I lack the imagination to come up with something on my own. I pulled this from your thoughts, and if we spend more time together, I'll pull more."

Rolfe backed up several steps. "Your magic requires sight, which you do not have."

Siofra licked her lips. "But what do you *really* know about Medvedev magic?"

"Ah! So you admit it!"

"Why would I deny what you already know? What a waste of words it would be."

"Then you will choose your next ones carefully, girl, for they will determine whether I let you starve to death, or find a more unpleasant way to end you."

Siofra gathered the remainder of her courage and spat as hard and as far as she could. Rolfe stumbled in the hay.

"Bitch." His hiss was followed by the sound of hands swiping fabric. "You could have helped me and saved yourself. Guardians know, your husband isn't coming for you. *No one* is coming for you. But now? Now you'll know the depravity Desemir has no doubt told you I'm capable of."

"Then go gather your wits, Baron, and come back when you've successfully managed your fear."

Siofra held her sob until the barn door slammed closed.

Fen was on the veranda, soothing Aio, when Desemir came looking for him.

"I came to see if you wanted Euric to fit you for armor," Desemir said. He wandered across the stones and joined Fen. "Though if you prefer to stay, no one will think unkindly of it."

"No." Fen's voice warbled. He couldn't look at Desemir. "I want to go." He squinted. "Do you really think we'll need armor?"

"I don't know what we'll need. We prepare for what we know and what we don't."

"I've never worn armor before. Will I be able to move?"

Desemir shrugged. "Depends on your definition of the word. I advise you to empty your bowels *before* we leave though."

Fen winced as he imagined trying to relieve himself in full plate.

"This flourishment of yours…"

Fen went stiff.

"I don't suppose you could use it to summon a larger army?"

Fen cocked his head, catching a glimpse of Desemir from the side. The man was grinning. Fen laughed in spite of himself. "No, it doesn't work quite that way. It doesn't work on anything with a heartbeat."

"A shame," Desemir said as he leaned against the short stone wall. He looked at the sky with a squint. "No matter. What we have is enough."

Fen allowed himself a read of the man. Desemir proudly wore his arrogance, as usual, but there was a newly formed crack in it—a place where the fire of his pride had died to embers. He was not a man accustomed to losing. He didn't know how to.

But he won't lose. He can't. If he loses, Siofra loses, and that's not an outcome I could ever bear.

"Thank you." Fen forced the words. "For being willing to fight for her."

"I would've relinquished all of it." Desemir spun and swept his gaze over the forest line. "I never wanted it anyway."

"Then why haven't you sold it back to those men?"

Desemir shrugged. "I don't know, Stiofen. Perhaps I'm more like my father than I care to admit." He nodded at Aio. "And you can't communicate with her, you said?"

Fen shook his head. "Atio can."

"And? What do they say?"

"It's not language as you or I know it. It's more a feeling. A sense." Fen lowered his eyes and ran his hand down Aio's underbelly, in a way he hoped soothed her. "They're hurting." He winced. "As I am."

"It will be over soon," Desemir said, nodding to himself with a hard inhaled sigh.

"I haven't spoken to her in weeks. *Weeks* and now—"

Desemir leaned in and clamped a hand onto Fen's forearm. "It won't serve you to allow your imagination to run. Siofra will be back to us by morning and then you can tell her what you were about to tell me. Yes?"

Fen choked back tears. He nodded.

"Good." Desemir released him and pushed off the wall. "We leave at midnight. We'll use the forest as cover. In the meantime, go see Euric in the armory. I suspect you're just the right size to fit into my old armor."

TWENTY-ONE
MIDNIGHT

Pesha nodded at Euric as he passed on his way into the armory. He liked Euric the best of all the guards. People always spoke of the man's loyalty first, but Euric's greatest strength was his unflappable nature. Even with the entire Hall buzzing with fear and apprehension, Euric's stoic gaze was unchanged. If he shared their fear, none would ever know.

It was what Desemir needed, not Pesha's inconsistent grip on reality.

"Where's Des?" Pesha asked. Ah, how his head hurt. It matched his heart, heavy and unfocused. *You brought them here. You did nothing to stop the wedding.* "I thought he'd be in here."

"With Wulfhelm," Euric answered. He inhaled a tick longer than was necessary, the only sign of his unease. "Readying the horses."

"Do we have enough men? For what we're planning to do?"

"Ask Wulfhelm. It's his plan."

His derision was subtle. Desemir's choice to give the lead to Wulfhelm was a slight to the grizzled veteran. Euric had actually been in battle, not just sparred for the potential of one. He'd fought alongside Klaus Trevanion III. His scars told the story better than any words could.

"And you? What do you think of it?" Pesha asked. If the plan was imprudent, now was the time to step in, not when they were descending upon Oakhelm Keep with the eyes of a village on them.

Euric shifted from one foot to the other, a heavy transfer of weight that clanged with his armor. And was it even necessary? Must they all look as though they were going to war and not a rescue mission?

"Doesn't matter what I think," Euric replied after a grim pause. "And if experience has taught me anything, it's that success is not limited to one path."

"That's a diplomatic way of saying you don't approve of his plan."

Euric's face shifted into a flicker of a scowl. "If it's Desemir's desire to put himself at such grave risk, it's not my job to argue with him. It's my job to protect him through whatever he walks into."

Pesha crossed his arms, watching him. "And how would you have done it?"

"Pesha..." Euric grunted and passed his eyes toward the ceiling with a groan.

"I want to know." Pesha nodded. "I want to know what the great Euric Staghelm would have done differently."

"When two men under stealth can achieve the same outcome as fifty men riding in like a band of marauders..." Euric shook his head. "The baroness will be home by morning. It's all that matters."

"Yes," Pesha agreed, mulling over the guard's words. "And why are you here and not out there, readying with Des and Wulf and the others?"

Euric flicked a nod into the armory. "Waiting for *him*."

"Who?" Pesha turned and saw Fen hunched over a bench, only half-outfitted. "Ahh. Go on, I'll take this from here."

"You certain?"

Pesha clapped Euric's armored shoulder. "Midnight approaches. You can tell Des we'll be right behind you."

"As you wish."

Euric's heavy steps disappeared down the hall.

Pesha stepped into the disheveled armory. The room was rarely used anymore, but it was still lovingly maintained by Euric. It was a wonder the disused armor and abandoned swords weren't rusted, but they'd been in near pristine condition when Desemir's men had raided the room. That, Pesha thought, was the difference between a man like Euric and a man like Wulf. Wulf practiced for war as if skill was all that was needed. Euric prepared for war knowing skill would only take one halfway there.

Pesha was comforted knowing Euric would be riding at Desemir's side, adjusting Wulf's plan with the prudence of a tactician.

The room looked like it had been ransacked, and it had. Scraps of metal, a few discarded swords too dull or old to be wielded, littered the floor. Doors of racks had been flung open, no one having bothered to close them in their bloodlusted excitement. The ripe cologne of adrenaline still clung to the thick, heady air.

In the center, Fen sat alone and half-armored. He'd gotten as far as his breastplate and shoulders and given up, the rest discarded in a heap at his feet.

"Fen?" Pesha approached with hesitation. He couldn't see his face, but the distress coming off Fen was potent in its clarity.

Fen swiped his hand across his face before raising it. "I'm coming. I'm sorry."

Pesha dropped to a crouch before him. His hand traveled toward Fen's flushed cheeks but fell instead upon his shoulder. From there he could see what he'd felt in his approach: grief etched in the eyes of a young man, who had spent his life trying to do right by others and had never done right by himself.

"We'll bring her home, Fen. We will. Des is..." Pesha shook his head. "I've never seen him so determined, about anything."

"Protecting his investment, I suppose." Fen sniffled. He tried for deep breaths but produced only shallow, shuddering ones.

"It's more than that now," Pesha said. "I don't know what 'more' means, because he's stopped talking to me—about this at least."

"You can pull it from his mind. Why haven't you?"

"It would be a grave violation of trust."

"You're too loyal," Fen replied.

Pesha suppressed a laugh. "You realize the irony in *you* making this charge?"

"I had no problem standing up to her when her behavior demanded it." The sting in his words came and went in a flash, swerving into regret. "*Abandoning* her. The last thing I ever said to her was to call her... to call her a whore." Fen sucked in his bottom lip. His shoulders shook with a powerful sob, and he buried his face in his hands, rolling over his knees.

Pesha moved up to the bench and wound an arm around Fen's plated shoulders. Fen stiffened at the touch, the invasion of what he'd surely intended to be a private moment, but then he gave up the pretense, sagging into Pesha in surrender.

"There's no place for regret here, Fen. None." Pesha squeezed him closer, fighting his own tears. He'd been so focused on the changes in everyone else that he hadn't considered, until holding a young man he'd come to care about, how much he himself had also changed. How his life had shifted, been ripped open, exposed. "We're bringing her home. We are. *You* are, because you'll be there with us when we drive that bastard Rolfe to the ground and take back our Siofra. Yeah?"

Fen nodded against him, shaking as his sobs intensified.

"But the first step is getting you into the rest of this armor." Pesha released him and considered the pile with a befuddled chuckle. "I guess I shouldn't have dismissed Euric so hastily."

Siofra had no sense of how long she'd slept. To even call it sleep was optimistic, for most did so intentionally. *This* was whatever followed the consuming pain that had thrashed through her as Rolfe had replaced every last weight.

She swayed above the ground to the harsh lull of the rope creaking against the hook. Her blindfold was still fastened but had slipped sometime in the minutes—hours? Days?—she'd been unconscious. It bisected her vision, bringing the upper half of the barn into dim view.

You remember the day your father and I died, Siofra?

Siofra jerked into a fresh wave of pain. It shot up her leg and into her chest and shoulders like a bolt of lightning.

Are you really asking me if I remember the worst day of my life, Mother?

Well, it was the last day of mine. And as I recall, you and I had just come down from a major row with each other.

No. Not here. It was all she could do to push the memories to the back of her mind on a fair day, but on *this* one? When she needed all of her wits and more?

I don't know why you're in my head. Siofra steeled her jaw. *I miss you horribly. But I need to be strong in here.*

Your father told me the same thing that day. Be strong, Moira. It will only hurt for a little while.

Why are you saying this to me?

He lied, Rohan did. I don't think it was an intentional lie, and I'll never get to tell him so either way. My neck didn't snap upon impact like his did. I got to watch him take a painless exit while I waited for someone, anyone, to come put me out of my misery. Alas, no one did. Except you.

Mother, why... Siofra moaned through the blending of physical and emotional wounds. Hot tears burned her eyes, but they couldn't fall. If they fell, they'd mark her weaknesses for her enemies. *I would do anything, anything to go back and do that day over. I would give my life.*

Your life? The one you handed over to the first pretty man who looked at you?

I didn't know what else to do!

No, Siofra. You could have followed that boy Gawain, and he'd still be alive. And you would not be a fugitive, on the edge of death.

How... Siofra drew blood when she clamped her teeth onto her lip. *How was that a better outcome for me? For Fen?*

You wouldn't be swinging from a hook in a barn, now would you?

No, I'd just be carrying the child of a monster!

Ah, well, it's an outcome that turned out the same, isn't it?

What?

You're carrying the child of a monster now.

No, I'm not... What... No, you have it wrong.

It's early. No one would know if they looked at you.

I would know.

But you do know, Siofra. Because it's not me in your head at all, is it? I've been dead for years. You watched me swinging with my neck broken, frozen in place by your fear. Fen could have healed me. He could have saved me. You could have created a diversion to sneak my broken body out. Anything. Anything but what you did, which was run.

Siofra's sobs shook the weights at her ankles, drawing a scream up through her belly that she fought back into her throat. Tears spilled and streamed down her cheeks, falling off her chin in fat droplets. *I didn't know what to do. I didn't know... Fen grabbed my hand and we ran, and we didn't look back.*

So... what's happening to you right now is a sort of ironic penance, is it not? Your husband having abandoned you to whatever fate... because to come find you would be a risk to him. A risk he isn't willing to take. Just as you weren't willing to take the risk for me, all those years ago.

I would take your place now if I could. She meant the words with her whole heart.

If you want to get out of here, do whatever that man tells you. Tell him everything you know about Desemir Trevanion, and perhaps, just maybe, he'll let your child live. Let you live.

I can't. Siofra sobbed harder. *I won't have that betrayal on my heart.*

270

Then you won't have a heart to consider for much longer.

The door flung open. Through her misplaced blindfold, she saw half of the man who had been her torturer. Cartwright, Rolfe had called him, but he could have been named Death and it would have been just as apt. His black teeth split his pocked face as he sized her up with empty eyes.

"Let's fix this blindfold, eh," he murmured and spat before charging forward.

She squinted to protect her eyes when he yanked on the rough fabric. Though he'd disappeared from her vision, she *felt* his hollow stare.

"Time for something more fun. Fun for me, that is. Rolfe wouldn't want you thinking we go easy on traitors."

Desemir cinched the saddle for the fifth time. He loosened it again with a frown. It had been right the first time, when the stable boy had brought the mare out, but details were important. Desemir was an enthusiast of details. They made or stole victories. Historians liked to speak of broad strokes, but tacticians knew it was the small things that determined outcomes.

"Pesha and Fen are coming out now," Wulf said, pulling up beside him. He tilted his face toward the night sky. "I'll always know it's midnight. Don't need the timekeepers to tell me."

On cue, a low chime sounded from the central hall.

"Mm." Desemir closed his eyes and pointed his face at the moon. "Remember when we used to make our own timekeepers, Wulfie? Out in the woods?"

Wulf chuckled quietly. He shuffled in the packed dirt. "I reckon some of them are still out there, if we had the mind to look for them."

"Sturdy enough," Desemir agreed. He inhaled a lungful of cool air. The promise of a storm burned in his chest. He welcomed it. The men of Oakhelm would be suitably distracted with the business of securing their homes and businesses for the night.

Desemir hoped they'd miss a couple hundred Trevanion men barreling down the hill at them.

"I must beg your forgiveness before we depart." Wulf passed a tentative look to the forest. "I wear Siofra's abduction heavy on my heart. I should have been quicker when we realized she'd gone—"

"But you weren't there." Desemir shook his head. "It was my own fault... for many reasons... but it was my choice to leave her personal guard out of the meeting. Mine alone. And for not seeing Rolfe's plan for what it was until it was too late."

Desemir was grateful when Wulf dropped the matter. There was nothing more to be said. Agonizing over failures only drove them deeper. Desemir already knew his desire to empower Siofra had been the very thing that had led to her capture, but allowing it to be the dominant thought in his mind was to silence the ones that could lead to her rescue.

They needed *all* their wits for what awaited them at Oakhelm Keep.

"She'll be fine, Desi," Wulf said, as though responding to a question. "There are some valleys no man can cross and return from. Rolfe wouldn't risk Arranden's ire for harming the wife of a baron."

"Rolfe and Arranden are lovers," Desemir said, bringing himself back to the moment, to the need pulling him away from the safety of his manor and into a den of wolves. "Rolfe doesn't care if others know. His own men fear him so much, it would change nothing. But Arranden cares. Arranden will do whatever Rolfe asks of him to keep the secret."

Wulf snickered. "Oy. Pesha read that one?"

"Pesha saw another one of his conquests. The husband of one of Rolfe's daughters." Desemir kicked a boot into the stirrup. He swung onto the saddle to the hard clang of plate. His chest piece had been too small, so they'd taken two larger plates and tied them with leather at the sides. He made a mental note to be fitted for a new piece when the danger was behind them. "As for Arranden, I saw it myself, back in our tutoring days."

272

"Boys do things men would not."

"I see the way they still regard each other across a room. Others might not note it, but knowing what I do, it takes no skill to read the meaning. They never stopped." He turned back to see Pesha and Stiofen coming down the steps. "No, Wulf. We're on our own with this one."

"We don't want Arranden's support anyhow," Wulf declared with a prideful huff.

"I don't need what we've never had." Desemir tapped a fist on his chest. Wulf took it as a war cry and mimicked, but if their blood weren't burning so hot, his old friend would have seen it for what it really was: a means of trapping impractical emotion. He couldn't think of Siofra being touched... *punished*... by these men without losing himself, and if he lost himself, he'd be securing her fate.

Turning thought into action was the way.

The only way.

"Fuck him," Wulf decided aloud.

"Fuck him," Desemir agreed. "But let's hope Hugh Arranden stays out of our way tonight, because one of his best men is going to die, and it would be a shame to die with him." He faced forward but turned his eyes toward Wulf at his side. "It will be me who kills Rolfe."

Wulf gulped in air. "No need to filthy your hands, Desi. That's what I'm here for."

Desemir spurred his mare into action. "I want to be painted in his blood before the night ends, so everyone can see what happens when you threaten a Trevanion."

TWENTY-TWO
OAKHELM

The valley ahead was lit by the nearly full moon. The gates of Oakhelm Village were still open, despite the hour. A straggling traveler passed the languid guards without receiving so much as an acknowledging nod.

Desemir and Wulf, with Pesha taking up the rear, scouted the way forward, while the bulk of the men hung back out of sight.

"Impressive defense," Wulf said. "And here I thought we'd at least break a sweat."

"Don't fall into the trap of deception. Even after the famine, Oakhelm is still one of the largest villages in the Darkwood," Desemir replied. His mare shifted under him, snuffling when a cool breeze swept the hilltop. Desemir warmed his hands against his mouth. "The keep, which you can see flagging above the rest, is just off-center, atop the largest hill in the village." He pointed. "Rolfe may not give a toss about his lieges, but he won't be so careless about his own neck. Expect a fight when we reach the keep."

"We should do what Euric suggested, Des," Pesha said. His borrowed armor was ungainly. He'd outgrown the armor of his youth and never been fitted for one as a man. It looked almost as bad as Desemir's cobbled-together piece. "We get Siofra. We get out. No blood is shed that doesn't have to be. We know she's being kept in a barn about a hundred yards from the keep. Unless Rolfe has transferred the bulk of his own guard to watch her, it cannot be so hard to get to her."

"If you can trust a report from a bird," Wulf quipped with an eyebrow wag at Desemir.

"Aio is a *falcon*. She is a *familiar* of a Medvedev, and she deserves both our protection and our respect," Pesha said hotly.

"Aio risked her life to find Siofra," Desemir said, in a tone he hoped put the matter to rest. He also hoped that Aio stayed behind with Atio as Fen had asked them to. The last thing they needed was a tragedy of another kind.

As his eyes shifted toward the thatched roofs and stone towers of the village, he felt more connected to their plan.

Euric rode up beside Wulf. "Pesha is right. There doesn't need to be a war tonight, Des."

"If there is a war tonight..." Desemir let the words hang on the chilled wind. He reached into his saddlebag for a flask and drew a quick sip, enough to take the edge off and warm his bones. "Then it's Rolfe who's invited it. Perhaps he sees me as he does his other peers, weak and ineffectual. But what that man has done will be met with the exact bloodshed, the *exact* response, his actions demand."

"There are women and children in this village," Pesha reminded him.

"And as long as they aren't blocking my path to Edmund Rolfe, then they'll still be in this village when the night is over. Same goes for the men. Let them choose whether Ned Rolfe is a man worthy of dying for."

"You and Pesha stay here with Stiofen," Euric stated. "I'll lead a band of men toward the keep, on foot, where we'll rely on the subtlety of shadows while Wulf goes straight to Siofra."

"Pesha and Stiofen may remain if they choose." Des dropped a hand on his hilt. He'd last swung a sword... when? It must have been at the Darkwood jousts on Torrin's Day, four years past. He'd taken first in several events, to the fury of men feeling themselves more deserving of the honors.

But four years...

It's not a skill one forgets.

"As for me, before sunrise I'll be standing over the body of Edmund Rolfe," Desemir spat. "Who dies by *my* hand. Are we understood?"

Muttered affirmations and nods passed through the handful of men, who no doubt thought he was becoming as mad as his father.

Maybe I am.

Maybe I deserve that.

But tonight isn't about me.

"Wulf, take three or four men of your choosing with you to the barn," Desemir ordered. "You have the map?"

"The one dictated to Stiofen by a b—" Wulf pursed his mouth. "By his familiar?"

"Yes, the one Aio shared with Atio so Atio could share with Stiofen," Desemir said, exasperated.

"Yes. I have it."

"Use it. When you've freed her, you bring her straight back. Don't wait for us. Don't stop until you have her safely delivered to the Hall. Stiofen—"

"I'm going with him." Stiofen spoke from behind them, several paces downhill. "With Wulf. If she's in need of healing..."

"As long as you understand there won't be enough men to protect you *and* save your sister," Desemir said.

"I don't care."

"If we want to keep the advantage of darkness, we need to go now," Euric said. He pointed at the gates. "I'll ride down and take care of the two sleeping guards. Send another in behind me in case there are others not visible from here. We'll signal for everyone to come down when we've cleared the gates, and they'll ride east to leave their horses in the forest with one or two men to mind them. Once that's done, they'll stay to the wall and enter one by one."

"No horses?" Pesha asked with a worried scowl.

"Not unless we want to draw more eyes on us than we can fend away."

"The rescue party will ride in," Wulf said, "for Siofra, so we can make a quick break once we have her. We'll go in one by one. I'll meet my men just inside."

Euric nodded. "And we'll keep two for us, so Des and Pesha can do the same."

"I wouldn't leave my men behind," Desemir retorted. "Everyone going to the keep will enter on foot and leave on foot." He turned toward Wulf with a heavy sigh. His chest felt thick, overstuffed. "For Siofra though? Whatever you need to get her out of there quickly."

"How will we know if you've run into trouble at the keep?" Wulf asked.

"You won't," Desemir said. "Nor would I want you distracted. You and Stiofen have *one* objective tonight, and one alone. Clear your mind of anything else. Understood?"

Wulf pointed his eyes ahead with a slow nod. "I won't leave without her, Desi."

The night sky burst with stars. The moon shined brighter than it did most nights, even for its fullness, and if Pesha believed in the Guardians of men, he'd say it was an omen they were on the wrong path.

But Desemir was determined. That wasn't anything new, but the degree of recklessness—the personal risk he was willing to take—was. He'd ruled in isolation for almost a decade, but he'd ruled in comfort, by staying where he was safe and letting others stand on his behalf.

Poor Euric desperately held onto the notion Desemir would change his mind when they reached Rolfe, but Pesha knew before they had left the Hall that his brother's mind was made. Never mind that Desemir had never killed anyone before. He was prepared to kill whoever stood between himself and the man who'd abducted his wife from his woods.

Pesha watched the men slip past him one by one, following Euric's silent command and filing into separate lines. At his side, Desemir was uncomfortably still. Pesha sensed no fear in him, but it only meant his brother was in more danger than he realized.

When the last of them were inside, Euric snapped his hands in the air to guide the men into place. After the men had surrendered their horses—and voices—Pesha took a moment to go over Euric's instructions once more in his head.

There are six paths to the keep from here. A dozen men will take each one, meeting at the top of the hill. Bands two and three will remain outside to keep watch, sequestered into alleyways and behind foliage. The rest will enter the keep and quietly—quietly!—dispose of whoever lacks the good sense to have run away. If even one of them calls for help or sounds a vocal alert, we'll be surrounded in minutes. Subtlety is our greatest weapon here.

Their group stayed to the wall until they reached the village plaza. It was empty at the late hour, except a few lingering shopkeepers closing up after a long day. Pesha tensed, thinking of the innocent men who may accidentally step into the wrong path, but Desemir was already making gestures at Euric to avoid them.

"We have to cross that," Euric whispered. He wedged his head between the brothers so they could both hear. "Now, we stay to the edges, but unless we want to wind ourselves into our own downfall, the best way is straight through."

"What do we do about them, then?" Desemir tossed a nod at the two shopkeepers left. His hand opened and closed on his sword hilt. He'd been doing it all night.

"I'll send one of the men to ply them with questions. Pull them out of the plaza until the rest of us can cross."

Euric slunk back to coordinate. Desemir's eyes were no longer on the plaza but on the spindly towers of Oakhelm Keep. A hard, dark look stole over him.

Pesha watched in a daze as one of their men distracted the shopkeepers. Despite their confusion, they both followed him into an alleyway.

"Move!" Euric whisper-shouted.

Desemir leaped out of their shadowed cover and led the way as they streamed across the flagstones and into the last stretch of road before beginning to ascend the hill. Pesha raced to keep pace. He heard the others shuffle in close behind him, but he didn't dare look back and damage what little courage he'd brought to this affair.

They slowed when the hill steepened. Euric resumed lead with an exasperated glance at Des as he passed by. By the time they reached the summit, the lean dark pillars of the keep stretching up to touch the stars, the others were already waiting.

Euric stepped out and beckoned the men on the west side of the keep to go in. He turned back toward Desemir and Pesha. "Des, I know you're eager to get in there, but we need them to clear a path. All right?"

Desemir grunted and crossed his arms over his chest. His opposite hand picked up the task of caressing his sword.

A chilled wind swept across the exposed courtyard. Pesha wanted to comment on something as banal as wishing he'd added another layer under his armor, but speaking at all proved difficult. He had nothing to say that his brother would want to hear.

Several pulses of bright light startled him. He squinted to make out the source: a sword, intentionally reflecting the moonlight.

Euric spun around to explain. "They've cleared the entrance, but the farther in we go, the more there'll be. I'm sending another two dozen men into the main floor of the keep to guard stairs and exits. One of our men, Amund, used to work for Rolfe and knows the way to his bedchamber. He'll be with us as we ascend to the living quarters. Behind us will be the last contingent of men, there to watch our backs and to join us should we be met with more resistance than we're expecting."

"You already explained this." Desemir looked at the keep as he spoke.

"The others benefit from hearing it once more," Pesha said, bracing against the chill. It didn't sound soothing coming from his agitated mouth.

They waited for the ground-floor men to enter and begin their swarm. Minutes passed. Des shuffled in restless anticipation.

Finally, Euric nodded. "We go now. But I lead. There's no negotiation on this one. You can stay right behind me, but you will not go before me."

Des groaned and shrugged in response.

Euric stepped out first. Desemir stayed close behind, Pesha right at his brother's back as they strafed across the dark courtyard and into the keep.

Euric pointed and nodded as they moved. They moved stealth-ily, bent low to draw shadows to the floor. As they passed into the central hall and then down another, Pesha saw the faces of men who had served the Trevanions for years. They'd all come to help Desemir exact his revenge, wearing looks matching his.

Woe betide the man who fucks with Shadowfen Hall.

Lying in bloody heaps across the stones were the slain remains of the men who'd been caught in the clearing. Most wore Oakhelm colors, but a few were of Shadowfen.

Pesha jumped at the cry of a pained whelp, followed by the unmistakable sound of steel leaving flesh.

"They found one hiding under a table," Euric whispered over his shoulder. He turned another corner and aimed for the stair-well. Pesha moved forward from the force of the men behind him.

They took each stair one at a time, leaving each fall of their boots to linger before gently connecting. It was an anxious ascent, one made worse by looking down into a sea of Trevanion men, not knowing if one of Rolfe's had gotten away and signaled for help. Pesha stepped over more bodies, too nervous to look to see whether he recognized any of the faces.

No one had gone ahead to clear upstairs. Euric said it was the biggest risk they'd take all evening, but they couldn't chance alerting Rolfe and allowing him time to escape or signal for more men.

Euric had just rounded the top when a sword flashed from the left. Euric met it with an impressive reflex and, without slowing, arced his downward and slid it into the man's belly. When he withdrew it, he held the guard at the shoulders and eased him to the floor to avoid the rattle of armor.

Pesha had started to draw a deep breath when three more guards jumped out. Euric deftly handled the first, but the other two were on Desemir so fast, Pesha didn't have time to realize he needed to unclasp the safety on his own sheath. He ripped it with a scream trapped in his throat. *Come on, come on, come on!*

Desemir blocked both of their blows and jumped back. They came at him in tandem, and he ducked another swing, drawing his sword across the midsection of one. Pesha was flattened against the stairwell when the men behind them swarmed to his aid, but both of the assailants were dead.

Desemir sidestepped to the railing. He grinned and dropped to his knees, clutching the side of his belly that was exposed outside his breastplate. Cut leather straps dangled from each side.

Blood spilled from his mouth, painting his smile red.

Pesha found his footing just in time to catch his brother from crashing to the floor.

The door opened. The sound came from far away—or deep in her imagination. *Elsewhere* to where Siofra was, where she couldn't leave. Her mind was still pulled tight to the sting of the whip that had lashed her flesh, splitting it. She had felt each one, with no dark place to fade into anymore. Cartwright sighed from the other corner as if *she'd* put *him* through the paces.

But if the door was opening, it meant it wasn't just Cartwright anymore.

Rolfe had returned.

She required no guesswork to discern the meaning.

"I said I'd call for help if I—" Cartwright's sharp words were cut by a gurgle at his throat. The sound escalated in urgency and then the thick air of his presence went down with him in a soft thud.

"Now you can come in. But... Steel yourself, Stiofen." A voice she recognized... one she knew, one she *welcomed,* spoke to the one most dear to her heart, and if that was so, then it must mean...

"Siofra... Oh, *no.* Wulf, get her down. We have to *get her down.* We have to—"

Siofra passed out before she heard her brother finish.

"How long..." *Was I out,* she tried to ask, but she was overcome with the realization she was no longer dangling from the hook but lying sideways across hay that scratched at her flesh. On her belly, she realized, because her back was destroyed.

A warm hand braced one of her shoulders, keeping her still.

"I need the blanket in your pack." Wulf. *Wulfie.* "Quickly!"

"It's stuck... It's..." Stiofen sobbed amid the sound of tearing fabric. "There. There."

Siofra blinked through a consuming haze, opening her eyes in time to see a dark-grey quilt flying toward her. Wulf snaked a hand up and caught it.

She blinked again and saw Cartwright, bled out, on the barn floor at eye level to her.

"I need to heal her, Wulf. There's so much blood... Look at her *back.* Look at what these bastards did to her... and her hair is purple, which means she really was defenseless..."

"I can see, Fen," Wulf said. Calm. Collected. Only a hint of vibration laced his words. "But if you heal her now, you'll need aid yourself, won't you?"

"It doesn't matter," Fen argued. "It doesn't matter what it will do to me!"

"It matters," Wulf said, ending the debate. "But I *am* going to ask you to stop the bleeding, so I can wrap her in this. Can you do only that, and not spend the entirety of your energy?"

"I..." Fen's voice broke into another moaning sob. "Oh, Si. Yes. Yes, I can. I can do that."

"No more," Wulf insisted. "No more until we're safe. And we *will* be safe, soon, you understand? But first..."

"Yes." Fen sniffled and pulled himself up from the hay. "Right."

He clambered over and dropped down beside her. The whole of him shook as he tore his gaze across her, looking only once at her face as if he might speak—as if he *wanted* to speak.

"Do it now," Wulf ordered. "If there were three outside, there will be a fourth and a fifth. We don't have time for you to think. Do it *now*."

Stiofen spread his palms over her back, and the mountain of pain that followed thrust her into darkness.

Desemir gripped the wall, his palms flattened, bloody fingers digging into the mortar between the stones. He pulled himself up, swatting away Pesha's attempt to heal him.

The commotion in the hall was already drawing attention.

There was no time.

Euric was already down the hall with Amund, the one who knew the keep. Desemir had to growl to keep Pesha away. The moment would never come again. He either finished or died trying.

Spots flickered behind his eyes as he stumbled along, gripping his wound with one hand. The other was on his sword, so no one would forget *he* would deal the mortal blow.

How many men have you killed tonight?

And do you care?

There was a brief skirmish ahead, as Euric, Cassius, and others slew the guards manning Rolfe's bedchamber. It occurred to Desemir that Pearl Rolfe might be inside, but he immediately dismissed it as improbable. He would stake a great deal of money on Rolfe not having fucked his wife in years.

Euric looked through the gathered men, to meet Desemir's eyes, and tugged his sword from a man's neck. He nodded sideways at the door beside him.

Desemir charged forward, breaking through the group. He didn't stop to acknowledge Euric as he grabbed the doors and threw them wide.

"Edmund Rolfe!" Desemir howled. "You took something of mine, and now I'm here for something of yours."

A man shot up out of the bed, but it wasn't Rolfe. Whoever was under the covers tried to pull him back down.

The hidden man ultimately groaned and rolled forward, propping himself on one arm. "What is the meaning of this? Enzel? Fairchild?"

"If those were your guards, then they only respond to the Guardians now," Desemir said with a strained laugh. He waved a hand, and the doors closed. He felt several of his men swarm in behind him. "I'm here to end the line of Rolfe. There are men searching for your sons as we speak. Or as *I* speak, and *you* listen."

"Desemir?" Rolfe strained in the darkness. It was a pointless question, an attempt for a man to come to terms with what he already knew. "How did you get in here?"

"Your arrogance is impressive to assume I wouldn't. Fifty guards was all you had for us? I brought twice as many," Des replied.

"You sent word. I was expecting your response tomorrow."

"You took my wife. What other response could there be?"

"So you didn't appreciate my offers then." Rolfe shot an indecipherable look at the terrified man still sitting next to him. "I read you all wrong, boy. I assumed the druid to be a trifle, a possession. I didn't suspect you to be capable of *love*."

"As I told Arranden," Desemir hissed, moving closer to the bed as he glared at the husband of one of Rolfe's daughters. Pain was close to overtaking him. He had more to say, so he needed to be quick. "You have all misread me. Have all presumed to know me, and have all, all of you, been wrong. In your case, fatally wrong."

"She's unnatural," Rolfe said with a nervous laugh. His bed-sheet fell away, revealing a pale chest full of hair. "Do you even know what she is? Do you even know what you bought?"

Desemir winced away a wave of pain. "The better question, Edmund, is do you know what you stole from me?"

"You speak of her as a possession, but your actions imply love. Unless you really are your father's son."

"I came to take your head," Des said evenly. He cooled his tone to cover the agony pulsing from his belly. He prayed the darkness covered the blood still running down his legs. "You can make it easy for yourself, or you can make me work for it."

The man at Rolfe's side whimpered.

"Another sound out of you, and I'll take *yours* myself," Euric barked at the paramour.

"Des," Pesha whispered behind him. He didn't finish the thought. He didn't need to. They were already well beyond the point that words could change anything.

"Out," Desemir ordered Rolfe's lover. There was no need to repeat the word. The man scrambled without cover, stumbling and rolling against a lounge chair several feet away.

"You didn't come to kill me." Rolfe held his head high; the waddle at his neck looked like chicken skin in the moonlight. "You wouldn't make such an enemy of Arranden. Of the others."

"*I'm* the man no one wants as an enemy, Edmund," Desemir stated. "Your peers had the wisdom to understand that." He wid-ened his eyes to stave off a wince as he brandished his sword once more. "Have you any last words?"

"You..." Rolfe's unflustered facade crumbled. "I'll tell you where she is."

"We already have her," Desemir said with a shrug as he inched closer. He desperately hoped it was true. He refused to consider the alternative.

"Then what do you *want?*" Rolfe backed against his headboard and practically crawled backward up it. "Desemir!"

"It's Baron or Master. The time for bargaining ended when you kidnapped my baroness." Desemir pointed his sword at Rolfe and swept it in a sideways gesture. "Out of the bed, unless you want this to be a hack job your wife will remember in her nightmares."

Rolfe slid out of the bed, his hands up and shielding his nude body. To see him removed of his confidence, his bespoke threads, was a reminder that men were just flesh over bone.

"Please don't hurt my sons," he pleaded.

"What choice do I have, Ned?" Des tightened his fist around the hilt, making light circles with the blade. "They'll want vengeance for their father, and I came here to end this, not turn it into a lifelong affair."

"I'll order them not to!"

Des approached the broken, huddled man.

Edmund was already vanquished.

He didn't have to kill him.

You touched Siofra.

You scared Siofra.

You hurt Siofra.

You don't deserve the breath you still draw.

Rolfe lowered his hands, confused by Desemir's hesitation.

Desemir inhaled and swung his sword at Rolfe's neck, slitting him ear to ear. A geyser of blood sputtered from the gaping gash.

The only sound aside from the man's final spurting chokes were the sobs of his scared lover in the corner.

"It's over." Desemir tried to look back, to meet Euric's eyes, but dizziness sent him into a light swoon. "I didn't mean what I said about his sons, Euric. I want no harm to come to either of them."

"No, Des. You were right, what you said to Rolfe. They'll seek their vengeance for the rest of their lives. They'll never give you peace."

"Nonetheless." Desemir turned and wiped both sides of his blade on the mussed bed. He flicked a glance at the trembling man in the corner. "You. If you want to live, you'll tell everyone what a merciful man I am. I suffered Baron Rolfe's sons to live, exonerating them from the crimes of their father. I allowed him to keep his head, not take it and display it upon my own ramparts, so he may be buried whole and join his ancestors in the afterlife."

"I'll tell them," the man whispered fervently.

"Do that," Desemir said. As soon as the words were out, he swayed, watching the room spin upward as he met the floor.

Siofra was weightless. Flying. The warm light of the lanterns made the barn welcoming.

Her head lolled, changing her perspective. She wasn't flying; she was bouncing, hurdling forward at a fast clip. She looked up at the underside of a man's chin. Wulf. It was Wulf's chin, and it was covered in blood, which ran along the edge of his sharp jaw, down his neck, and ended beyond where her vision could travel.

Wulf caught her eye. "We're getting you out of here." His breaths were harried, his pulse beating against her arm, soaring.

"You came for me," she whispered. Her head rolled against his arm, her eyes closing.

"I swore to protect you," he answered. She felt his throat twitch with a swallow.

"Am I dead?"

Wulf's neck flexed. He shuddered an inward breath. "No. That was *never* an option, Siofra. You understand?" The bouncing stopped. Wulf's hawk eyes surveyed their surroundings. "Where's the horse, Fen?"

"Over there," Fen said. He seemed so far away. So—

"Behind you!" Wulf cried.

Siofra winced through the jarring melee. When it stopped, she opened her eyes, rolling her head upside down, and saw Fen holding a bloodied sword, his chest heaving in shock.

"No," she whispered. "That's what I do. It's not what he does. I promised him..."

"What's that?" Wulf asked, jostling her back into action. His boots rustled against the ground, and soon she heard other men too, not just Fen.

Where's Des? Why isn't he here?

You know why, darling.

Des, she tried to whisper, but the word was trapped in her mind, warped with all the other dark thoughts and realizations about the life she'd so irrationally chosen.

He must have sent Wulf to save me.

Then where is he? What kind of man lets another man tend to his most personal business?

I don't know. I don't know anything anymore.

You never did. Isn't that the problem?

They hurt me, and I probably deserved it, but now they've made Fen kill. Wulf is covered in blood, some of it his.

Your fault. Your fault! Your fault, your fault, your fault!

"Let me down," she tried to say, but it came out like a string of unintelligible vowels. "Let me down," she said again.

"We're almost there," Wulf assured her. The hand cradling her head gripped her scalp tighter. He propped her higher on his other arm.

"Let me down." Siofra moaned. "Let me down!"

"Just a few more steps—"

"LET ME DOWN!"

Wulf's step faltered at the boom of her words. She pushed off his chest and dropped to the ground, landing in a crouch.

"Siofra!"

"Go! Get out of here!" She screamed as she scrambled forward, half running, half tripping. Her red wall had already risen. There was no tickle. No warning. It surged into her neck, swelling into her throat with hot demand. "Get away from me!"

"What are you doing? We have to—We have to get out of here," Wulf cried, coming after her.

"Fen, get him out of here! *Get them all out of here now!*"

"Oh, no. Oh no," Fen said. "All right, Wulf, come on. Come on, *come on.*"

"We're not leaving her here!"

"Come with me or you'll die. All of you. Everyone who can hear me needs to run north, *now!*" Fen shouted.

The panic in his voice rooted her, just enough to sense they were backing away, doing as she asked, as she *needed,* for she would never, ever forgive herself if she hurt anyone who had not first hurt her.

Siofra sank to her knees. Her chin lifted, exposing her neck as the vibrato rolled forward and exploded into a song. It burst past her lips, becoming a melody that filled the air and consumed competing sounds.

It was a song of death.

And this time...

She sang the song with her whole heart.

Pesha ran after Desemir. He watched his brother pitch forward into the courtyard a dozen paces ahead of the others.

"You stubborn ass, *stop!*"

Desemir didn't stop. He raced harder, approaching the center. The Trevanion men waiting in hiding started to emerge from the shadows in panicked confusion.

Desemir never reached them. He suddenly seized and straightened, as if struck by a bolt of lightning. His body rose in the air—one foot, two feet, three—and then his arms flung to his sides as convulsions racked him from head to toe.

The loudest, shrillest, most terrifying song Pesha had ever heard coated the village like a shroud.

Pesha screamed.

Desemir plummeted to the stones in a heap.

TWENTY-THREE
LOATHING, RESENTMENT

Pesha crushed Siofra in his arms as he barreled through the halls of Shadowfen, blocking out the incessant screeching of Aio and Atio outside. He screamed at Wulf to find Gisela, to bring hot water and fresh linens to Siofra's bedchamber.

And something to sedate her, for the love of those cursed Guardians you all love so much.

Wulf must have complied, because Pesha no longer heard him pacing at his heels.

Pesha raced up the stairs, pressing Siofra's face to his chest to dull her song. That damnable song. She couldn't stop singing it. He'd heard it ringing in his ears since he scooped her out of the alley in Oakhelm and stopped her from killing everyone and everything in the village...

Before she could kill Desemir... but he couldn't think about that if he was to help her. If he remembered, even for a moment, the way his brother had risen in the throes of death, there would be nothing left in his heart for Siofra but hatred.

More loathing, more resentment, bubbled forth at knowing he couldn't be helping his brother, because he had to save his brother's wife. Because Pesha was the *only* one strong enough to subdue her magic for a length of time.

Like a broken spigot, it couldn't seem to turn itself off.

Fen is with Des. Fen will make this right.

Fen is young. Untrained.

He's older than you. And he's trusting you with the one dearest to him as well.

Siofra howled her melody into his bloodstained blouse. He'd discarded his armor in Oakhelm when it had kept him from pacifying her properly. But he couldn't suppress her with this tactic forever. Soon, the force he used to mollify her would steal the last of his vitality, and she'd take every last man, woman, and child in Shadowfen Hall down with her and her immutable rage.

This isn't her fault.

Des might be dead. And you're here, with her, *not with him.*

Pesha grunted and rounded the corner to the east wing. The candles had long been extinguished, but the light radiating—*pulsing*—off Siofra turned the hall to daylight. Her song cracked from her throat in erratic notes, out of tune, her sobs trapped in between.

"We're almost there." He huffed, more to himself, a reminder to focus on why he was with her and not where he wanted to be, with his brother.

Siofra suddenly jerked wildly in his arms. Her violet hair thrashed Pesha's sides. His muscles screamed as he held her tighter still, but her convulsions knocked him off course. He slammed into a wall and paused to collect himself just as Gisela and Lotte appeared like angels.

"Well, what're you just standing there for, Pesha? Get her inside!" Lotte cried, swatting her hands toward him, saying nothing at all about the jilted song pouring out of Siofra nor the light blistering off her like rays from the sun.

Wulf sprinted ahead and slammed her apartment door wide. He rolled his hands, beckoning them in.

Pesha wanted to be grateful. He would be if his rage weren't the predominant emotion driving his every step.

When he had Siofra inside, he made for her bed, but Lotte shrieked at him to bring her into the privy. More workers, their eyes heavy from being ripped from their beds, streamed past with buckets of hot water, which they poured into the tub in procession. Lotte cupped her hand and impatiently gestured forward, but Pesha shook his head.

"I'm afraid if I let go of her..." He couldn't finish.

Lotte's eyes widened with a nod. "Ahh." She reached into her apron and withdrew a dark bottle. "She'll need all of it, thrashing as she is."

"Me?" Pesha shifted Siofra in his arms. "You want me to give it to her?"

"Well, there's nothing to it. You just pour it down her throat, simple as that."

"All right. Fine." When Pesha accepted the draught, his arm slipped, and Siofra's legs dropped. The shift in weight nearly took him down. He ripped the cork cap off with his teeth and spat it aside. "How long will this last?"

"Long enough," Lotte said. At once he saw the horror in her eyes, the fear as she flicked her gaze at Siofra like a protective mother who also feared her child might kill her.

Pesha looked down at Siofra, still twitching and still singing. Her face was again visible to him, fear flashing in her enlarged eyes. Helplessness, like she were trapped inside of a carriage barreling off a cliff.

Guilt pricked his heart.

"What are you waiting for?" Gisela cried. "Give it to her."

Pesha's apology went unsaid as he used the same hand to both pry open her mouth and empty the bottle down Siofra's throat. Her jaw gnashed, some of the liquid gurgling up from her throat before he snapped her mouth closed to trap the draught and her song. She shook in violent spurts, so he held her tighter, letting her thrash out the last of her angst.

They waited.

Wulf paced the doorway.

The women huddled in the corner like frightened animals.

Siofra's melody finally died to whimpers. Her feet lost purchase on the floor, and Pesha caught her before she slipped from his arm entirely.

"Now what?" Gisela asked.

"Now..." Pesha's heartbeat throbbed behind his eyes. "We need to clean her... We need..." He wiped a hand across his eyes and blinked hard. "Once she's clean, I can heal her, but not before. We can't risk trapping all this filth in her blood and infecting it."

Both women stepped forward and held out their arms. Wulf exhaled a pained sigh and turned to give them privacy.

"Watch her back," Pesha said as he lowered Siofra into the bath. He turned when her dress was lifted over her head. "The bleeding has stopped, but her wounds are fresh."

"Guardians deliver us," Lotte whispered in horror.

Gisela gasped at her side.

"Well, the sooner we get her clean, the sooner you can make this right."

Pesha nodded, but he wondered if there was anything that would ever make what had happened right.

He braced himself at the door, waiting for them to finish. Wulf was propped against a wall, a hand over his eyes.

"Arranden is going to kill Desemir," Wulf said. He didn't seem to realize Pesha was listening. "He's going to kill him."

"Desemir knows Arranden's darkest secrets. I don't think..." Pesha was too exhausted to complete the thought.

"Pray those secrets are enough to overshadow everything that happened tonight in Oakhelm."

"Does anyone else in Shadowfen Hall know magic?" Fen whipped his head around. The formidable Euric, the champion sword-fighter Cassius, and so many others—whose names he didn't know—looked so stupidly *helpless* when the need didn't involve a call to violence. "*Anyone?*"

"Just Pesha," Euric said. "What do you need? How can we help?"

Fen tore at his hair, passing his eyes wildly over Desemir's bedchamber. An odd thought occurred to him, that he'd never been in the room before. Never wanted to.

You could let him die.

Siofra would be free.

But she would hate me forever. And so would Pesha.

Fen greedily sucked at the air, forcing some into his lungs where he held it. "You cannot," he said as he exhaled.

Look at him. Lay hands on him. Do something!

"Is he..." Cassius swallowed a moan. "Is he going to..."

"I don't know," Fen confessed.

Look at him!

I can't. She did this... She did this to him, and if she ever learns of it, she'll never recover.

And if he dies, what will she think then?

She doesn't love him. She can't love him.

She doesn't not love him either.

"Stiofen? Are you... healing him now? From across the room?" Euric inquired, interrupting his thoughts.

If it had been another man, in another circumstance, Fen would have taken it for a joke. "I need... everyone out."

"I'm not leaving," Euric stated.

"Then *you* stay." Fen waved at the door. "Everyone else..."

Euric rushed to clear the bedchamber. With the others distracted, Fen allowed himself a look at Desemir.

The man lay diagonally across his bed. Blood covered him hair to boots, masking the true nature of his injuries. He'd been stabbed through the side of his gut and had lost a fair amount of blood from it, but Pesha had closed that wound, buying him time.

And then... Siofra...

Fen approached the bed. He froze, watching for the rise of Desemir's chest. It was faint but there. He ran his gaze over his bloodied, disheveled brother-in-law, at a loss for where to begin.

"I *could* use your help, Euric." Fen looked up. "I need his clothes cut off of him."

"I can do that." Euric rushed forward, relieved to be of use. He started at Desemir's legs, which were still armored. His breastplate had been removed at some point between dismounting and the bedchamber, as well as one of his bracers. Fen worked on the other one, unstrapping the leather from his arm. He tossed the plate to the corner with a clang.

Euric was faster. He'd removed everything below the waist and was running a dagger up through the buttons on Desemir's blouse before Fen could center himself.

"Guardians deliver us," Euric whispered as the extent of Desemir's injuries lay before them. The wound at the edge of his belly had re-opened but seemed inconsequential against the scorched flesh barely clinging to bone.

Euric closed his eyes and began a prayer Fen recognized: a beseeching to the Guardian of the Unpromised Future to pass over their home and return another day.

It was sad that Fen knew prayers of man but knew nothing of a Medvedev's faith.

"Pesha." Desemir croaked. His mangled face rolled to the side.

"He's—" Euric stopped when Desemir gurgled up blood and started to choke on it.

Desemir heaved forward, neck bowed over his chest as he gasped for breath. "I want... my... wife."

Fen caught Euric's eyes across the bed. Euric nodded in understanding.

"This is going to hurt, Des," Euric said ruefully and leaped onto the bed, climbing over Desemir to pin him on both sides. Desemir wailed in pain and passed out.

You could put on a good enough show, make them think you tried your best but it wasn't enough.

And what kind of man would it make me?
The kind that would do anything to protect his sister.
"That's what I'm doing," Fen muttered and wrapped himself around Desemir.

TWENTY-FOUR
WHAT WE MUST FOCUS ON

Gisela wore an exhausted but determined look. "I'm sorry, but she still doesn't want to see you."

Desemir crossed his arms with a wince. Even that was painful. "It's been days since she came home. I've respected her space."

Gisela screwed her mouth and tossed a tenuous glance into the room behind her. "You may have to respect it a while longer."

"What does that mean?" Desemir thrust an arm into the door-frame to bury the rush of pain. Pesha still healed him daily, and he *appeared* perfectly well, but inside he still felt like death was an option. "What aren't you all telling me? I came for her. I didn't leave her there to suffer." He rolled a hard breath inward. "And I'm not upset with her for what happened after. I know it was not... intentional."

Gisela again looked back. "She's physically well, Des, but her mind..." She turned her gaze back on him with a sad smile. "Siofra thinks Wulf saved her on his own. Well, Wulf and her brother. She thinks you... Ah, well, she thinks you left her there because

299

the Darkwood meant more to you. Rolfe told her you wouldn't sell back even an acre to get her back."

"She thinks *what*?" Blood rushed to his face.

"Calm yourself before your wounds pop open. Guardians," Gisela chided. "Everyone knows it isn't true, but Fen and Pesha are insistent that we ease her into the truth slowly. She doesn't remember almost killing you when she sang her song in the plaza. Fen thinks that's all it would take to send her back over the edge. He's comparing it to how she was after their parents died, and he's afraid of losing her. And Pesha still thinks she might slip back into her 'red wall' from the lingering trauma."

"Pesha is in on this lie?"

"He's helping her," Gisela said softly. She lowered her eyes, shaking her head. "Siofra is not herself at all. She wouldn't even see me until today. She was convinced I was spying on her, reporting to you. *Spying* on her." She wiped her eyes. "I love this girl, Des. You know that."

Desemir spun away and fastened his gaze on the end of the hall. "You're telling me *no one* has bothered to tell my wife the truth?"

"Pesha thinks—"

"I don't care what Pesha thinks!" Desemir turned back toward her. "I want to see her, Gisela. Don't make me force my way in."

Gisela recoiled. "I wouldn't... You misunderstand me. You can do as you please, but unless you want her to look upon you with hurt and hatred, you'll wait until Pesha says her mind has improved."

"And what if..." Des crushed his tongue against the back of his teeth. "What if it's *me* she needs, to improve?"

Gisela shuddered with a sigh. "You don't know what happened to her in the barn, Des. What she endured those long hours."

"I imagine those *very things* in my nightmares!" He flinched through the pain his outburst caused. "I *killed* men to get to her. It would have been me carrying her out of that barn, but I took the most dangerous job for myself!"

"She doesn't know that," Gisela said, making a shushing sound with her hands. "And it's best, for now, that she continues not knowing. You understand? This isn't about what you did or didn't do. It's about what Siofra has spun together in her mind to make sense of the horrors. To survive them."

Desemir ran his hand along his face with a groan. "Who all is in there?"

"Well—"

"You, Fen, Pesh. Who else?" He rolled his hand in a circle to urge her on.

"And Wulf," she said quietly.

"Wulf, you said?" Des cocked his head to the side. "Wulf is in there with her?"

Gisela gave him a pained nod. "Well, he *is* her personal guard."

"And she thinks... what... he's..."

"Best to not complete that thought for now." With a tentative frown, she reached forward and patted his arm. "Come back later, Des. She'll recover and then it will be time for truths. For now, let it be enough that she survived Rolfe's terrors."

"Of course it's enough," he muttered. But was it? Was Gisela giving him credit he didn't deserve, assuming he could overlook Siofra's belief he'd abandoned her when he'd risked *everything* to save her? When he existed perpetually on edge, awaiting the law to come to hold him to account for what he'd done?

"I can almost *see* your mind spinning—"

"I want to see her," Desemir asserted.

"Perhaps I'm not making myself—"

"You've made yourself perfectly clear, Gisela. I won't shatter her fragile mind, but I want to hear it *from her* that she has no desire to see me. And then I'll go."

Gisela raised a dubious brow. "You will?"

"I will." He meant it as a promise, but it sounded like a threat.

Gisela shrugged. "You know I can't stop you."

"Were you planning to?"

Her laugh was strained. "For your sake, keep your expectations grounded in what I've told you."

Pesha had been preparing to leave Siofra's apartments when Desemir burst in.

His stomach seized with apprehension. Had he really expected Gisela—or anyone—could convince him to stay away? When Desemir had his mind set, no one had the power to change it.

Pesha directed a series of tight head shakes his brother's way, fearful of what Desemir might intentionally, or unintentionally, say. Pesha had only been able to soothe Siofra for so long before he had to replenish his own vigor. There was no way to know if her current calm was real, an act, or a side effect of the prolonged "escaping" Fen said she was known to do after a bad episode. Now that she was lucid, all they could do was wait and see what happened next—and do everything in their power to keep things from getting worse.

Fen held his breath. Wulf shifted with a nervous throat clearing and moved away from Siofra's bed.

Siofra pulled herself up with what seemed like great pain. Pesha had done the best he could for her, but her wincing and flushed cheeks seemed to come not from a physical ailment but somewhere deeper and unreachable by his magic.

"Siofra," Des whispered. He shuffled like a nervous boy, staying near the door.

Pesha relaxed.

"Husband," she answered amenably. She drew in a weary breath. "And how is your morning? Pleasing, I hope?"

"Siofra—" Desemir twisted his mouth, cutting off his own words. "My morning is pleasing enough."

"Good." Siofra brushed her hands along her nightgown. "With that out of the way, there should be no other duty required of me today, no?"

"No other... What?"

Fen passed Pesha a wary look.

"Only confirming I won't be expected in your bedchamber anytime soon, since I'm with child now, and it was your promise that during such periods I am to be left alone."

"*Bloody hell,*" Pesha whispered, squeezing his eyes.

Des tripped back into the wall. His palms flattened against it, then crumpled inward, like claws. "Did you just say you're with child?"

"Pesha hasn't told you?" Siofra asked through slow blinks.

Desemir scorched Pesha with his incredulous gaze. "*Pesh?*"

"I was coming to tell you," Pesha said. "I'll have Lotte send for a proper physician, and it's still very early... but there's no mistaking the new life I sense growing within her."

"A child?" Desemir's voice cracked. He seemed to fold back into himself. "*My* child?"

"You're the only man I've been with," Siofra replied. "At least up until now."

Desemir shook his head, mouthing, *Up until now.* Color had drained from his face.

"I should go," Pesha said. He tossed a nod at Fen. "*We* should go."

"Not on my account," Desemir stated. He started to recover, his cool confidence returning. "An heir... This is joyous news. Joyous news indeed."

Siofra caressed her belly over the covers. "A blessing," she agreed. "But it also means I get to take a lover now."

Desemir shot Pesha a dumbfounded look. He dragged his gaze back to Siofra. "A *lover?* Right now, after..."

"You promised."

"My concern is—"

"I've been tortured and am fortunate to be alive?" Siofra said for him. "Such an experience causes a person to evaluate their life through different eyes. I see now that I'm but a vessel to you..."

Desemir absorbed her words like a physical blow, but he didn't interrupt.

"And that's fine. Truly. I prefer to know where I stand with people. Most of my life has been a game of guesswork, of never truly knowing. So thank you, Desemir, for making things exceptionally clear to me."

All the color that had previously left Desemir's stunned expression came swirling back, staining his cheeks with the words he seemed agonized holding back.

Pesha glanced at Fen, who wore matching apprehension. They'd spent the past few days nursing her delusions, doling out small bits of truth to keep her from spiraling back into her darkness. It might be weeks or more before she was ready for the full story of what had happened in Oakhelm.

Until then, they had to keep her safe from herself. From the unknown of what Fen said had been her worse episode yet.

Don't say it, Siofra, Pesha silently pleaded. *Let this be enough for today.*

"Seeing as I *do* have an understanding of the dangers facing us after the events in Oakhelm, I've taken a pragmatic view to this choice, which I hope you'll appreciate as well, Husband."

Desemir dragged both hands down his face and dropped them back to his sides. "Go on."

"I cannot very well take the same risks you do, bringing in outside lovers."

"I haven't had women since—"

"I'm tired, and I'd like to finish so you can leave," Siofra stated. The first sign that her cool demeanor was for show flashed into her eyes. "Appreciating how outside lovers would increase our risk, the only suitable solution is to turn my prospects internal. To someone here, at Shadowfen Hall."

Pesha chanced a look at Wulfhelm. The poor guard's face wrung with horror. He eyed the window as though leaping out of it would be preferable to staying to hear Siofra finish.

"Someone here," Desemir said back to her. "Here in the Hall?" He gesticulated in an arbitrary direction.

"Someone we already trust," Siofra replied smoothly. She leaned her head against the headboard with a dreamy look. "Someone who loves you and would never betray you. Someone who... cares for me and looks after me."

The emotion burning in Desemir's eyes seemed to hinge somewhere between fury and devastation. "Well, don't leave me in suspense, Siofra."

Siofra stretched her hand toward Wulf, who pretended to not notice.

"*Wulf?*" Desemir spat. He dropped his shoulders and turned as if he could not possibly have understood correctly. "You want to bed your guard?"

"Des," Pesha warned. He pressed his mouth into a tight line.

"Yes," Siofra answered with a quick, pleasant sigh. "When I'm feeling more myself, that is. I'm still recovering."

"And what does your guard have to say for himself?" Desemir demanded. He thrust his hands out to his sides.

"Wulf," Fen urged.

"Ah... Can we speak outside, Desi?" Wulf asked. He had yet to meet Desemir's gaze.

"He's one of us," Siofra said more forcefully. "He's a *safe* option."

"He's your guard!" Desemir cried.

"And *he* saved my life," Siofra snapped. "Don't forget the promise you made me before we wed. That when I was with child, I could take—"

"I haven't forgotten!" Desemir smacked a fist into the wall. "Guardians deliver me."

"Outside?" Wulf urged. "Please?"

Desemir ripped the door open and slammed it behind him.

"Probably not the right time to remind him to thank Fen for saving his life?" Siofra asked sweetly.

Desemir paced the hall, one hand kneading his neck. "Ah!" he cried when Wulf came out of the room.

Gisela thrust her hand toward the door before it closed, and she slipped back in.

"I *knew* you wanted to fuck her." Desemir wagged a finger in the air and pulled a grunt from deep within, releasing it into the quiet hall. "You are *un*believable."

"Desi, that was not—"

"You're not only my guard, Wulf. You're my oldest friend!"

Wulf looped his hands over his torso, his gaze downward. "I am, and though I had my reservations about guarding her, I agreed, for you."

"So this is my fault? That you want to fuck my wife?"

"*I'm not going to do it.*" It came out as a whispered scream.

"But you want to." Desemir's nose flared. His cheeks were on fire, as was the rest of him.

"No," Wulf replied. He swallowed. "It doesn't matter. I *won't* do it. Si will pull through this strange daze she's in, and she'll return to normal and will regret even suggesting it."

"Ahh," Desemir replied bitterly. His left eye twitched. "So she's Si to you now?"

Wulf glanced back at the door before he moved closer. "You're making this into something it isn't."

"So you're *not* attracted to my wife?"

"I..." Wulf ground his jaw. "Do you want me to lie?"

Desemir burst into laughter. "Oh, I get a choice?"

Wulf shook his head at the wall.

Desemir rolled his eyes so hard, he nearly strained them. He needed to punch something. *Someone.*

"It doesn't matter. She's off-limits," Wulf said quickly. "I won't speak for other men, but as for me? I'll not betray my best mate— the man I've sworn to give my *own* life for and would, in a heart-beat, without a second thought."

"Right." Desemir spun away from him and slapped his palms against the far wall. "So you'll turn her down and she'll run to who? Pesh?"

"Pesha doesn't like women—"

"You don't think I know that?"

"She won't turn to *anyone*, Desi. That's my point. She's not in her right mind." Wulf took a step closer. "When she's *recovered*, when she learns what you did for her..."

"She's not wrong though." Desemir tore his hands away from the wall and looped them over his head. He paced away from Wulf, from the room, from all of it. "It does have to be someone here."

"Your lovers don't come from the Hall," Wulf replied.

"I won't be as cavalier with her safety as I've been with mine." Desemir dug deep for the grit required to say his next words. "If she wants you in her bed, and the feeling is reciprocal..." He enjoyed the squirming discomfort on Wulf's face. It wasn't as satisfying as knocking the audacity right out of him, but it was something. "Then I must accept this is how I make good on my promise to her."

"She feels safe with me." Wulf's attempt to explain away his obvious lust for Siofra almost brought Desemir's rage to the surface again. "She deserves to feel safe. That's all this is."

"I gave my permission," Desemir stated. His neck flexed with his anger, which he fought once more to subdue. "The least you can do is stop patronizing me with your weak justifications."

"I'm only saying I don't intend to—"

"Tell Pesha I need him in my bedchamber." Desemir braced through a new shock of agony. He so rarely wanted to be in his bed, but there was nowhere he needed to be more. On top of the nightmares, there was pain. On top of the guilt, even more guilt. There was no assuaging any of it. No atonement powerful enough.

"Of course." Wulf couldn't hide the relief in his voice.

"*After* he's asked Lotte to send a physician for my wife and her unborn child," Desemir said with a grunt. "I'm going to be a father soon. That's what's important now. Yes. It's..." His eyes swam, and he fell to his knees.

"Desi!"

"What we must focus on," Desemir muttered and planted his face against the floor.

TWENTY-FIVE
THE LONG ROAD HOME
AND OTHER SONNETS

Siofra brushed the back of her hand along Aio's belly. A flicker of joy traveled down her spine. Whenever she touched her familiar, it was like experiencing new magic. It shouldn't be like that, but she'd been denied closeness with Aio for the majority of her life.

The horrors of Oakhelm were a full month behind them. The end of wintertide was approaching, and the first whisper of spring spread a warming hand over the region, so Siofra took a book to the garden. She felt no guilt taking from the library, but she'd take nothing else from the man who'd tricked her into believing he'd protect her.

The title of the book, *The Long Road Home and Other Sonnets by Artemia*, caught her interest when she saw it sitting on one of the long tables that stretched in front of the rows of bookshelves. She hadn't noticed it before; it was as if someone had taken it out, left it for her. But as Gisela had said when Siofra had asked her, no one went into the library anymore except Siofra and the housekeeping staff.

309

"Can I sit with you?" Fen asked.

Siofra let the soft, warm breeze into her lungs and nodded. Atio's shadow covered them as he swooped down to land.

Fen lowered onto the stone bench opposite the one she sat upon. He half smiled and said something about how nice the weather was, then shoved both hands between his knees.

"What are you reading?" he asked, with a nod at her book.

"Oh," Siofra said. She bookmarked her place with her thumb and held the cover up.

He squinted to read it.

"It's very old, like all the books in the library. But it's a series of sonnets written by a young woman who was banished from her home for some unspecified act of treason. It's about how she must find a new way home."

"How, if she was banished?" Fen asked.

"Well, the lesson here, I suppose, is that home is not a fixed place, is it? It shifts as you shift, and changes as you change. I don't think Artemia will end up where she started. I think she'll learn to love a new place, a new home."

"An apt lesson for the Thornheart twins," Fen said with a smile. "It seemed that you, at least, were learning to love your life here."

"Who said I don't love it still?" Siofra replied. "There may not be any in my marriage, but there's love all around me. And as long as I carry the Trevanion heir, there's safety as well."

"Siofra..." Fen folded his hands and twisted his mouth into a tentative frown. "You know I'm not a champion of Desemir, and I still have a lot of... anger toward him for what he did, bringing you here—"

"But not for abandoning me to that monster, Rolfe?"

Fen finally looked up. His eyes were strained with conflict. "There's still a lot you don't know about that night."

Siofra bristled. She rolled her shoulders back. "I know all I need to know." She set the book aside and rested her hand on her belly, which was still small but rounded enough in her gowns to draw gazes downward when others passed her in the halls. According to Lotte, she looked further along than she was, despite the longer gestation, one of the many traits that made a Medvedev pregnancy different from a regular woman's.

Fen shook his head to himself with a controlled exhale. "To hear you say you're only safe when you're with child isn't true."

Siofra's face darkened with a rush of heat. "That what you came out here to say then? Tell me how wrong I am, once again?"

"No," Fen said quickly. "No, that's not why I came out here. I didn't... Ack, I didn't even come to talk about him at all! Can we start over?"

Siofra crossed her arms. She made a soft cooing sound at Aio without turning her attention away from Fen. "Sure."

Fen sagged into a relieved sigh. "I came to apologize to you."

"For what?"

"For what I said to you when I found out you'd married Desemir."

Siofra's laugh was forced. "But that was months ago. And you've been with me every day since the rescue, so why now?"

Fen rapped his knuckles on the bench and lowered his eyes. "I should have apologized sooner." He shook his head. "No, *no*, I shouldn't have said it at all, Si. At all. It was wrong. I was wrong. I was hurt, and I said the one thing I knew would hurt you too. And in hurting you, I broke the only vow I've ever made to myself that mattered."

Siofra pondered his confession. He *had* hurt her, but it had been a necessary hurt, one that had allowed her to grow. She wouldn't have the courage she had now if Fen hadn't turned his back on her. "I forgave you a long time ago, Fen. It did hurt me, to lose my brother, but you're back now, aren't you?" She held out her hands.

Fen seemed unsure in his approach, but when he reached her, he dropped to a crouch and took her hands. "I won't make that mistake again. I have to accept... I *have* accepted that you're your own person, capable of making your choices... deciding what

311

happiness looks like to you, not to me. You're a wife, and..." He gave an astounded chuckle. "And you'll be a *mother* in, what, six months?"

"Longer," Siofra said. "Lotte said Medvedev gestate their young for eighteen months. The physician estimates the growth puts me at the three-month mark if compared to a normal woman, but Lotte was there for Pesha's birth and knows there will be differences. Anyway, I have over a year to go." She tugged him onto the bench beside her. "What's weighed heaviest on my heart during our separation was not knowing *how* you were doing. How you were *really* doing."

Fen flicked his eyes in a circle and laughed. "I've adjusted, you could say."

Siofra laughed. "Adjusted."

"You want me to say I like it here?"

"I know you like it here," Siofra said gently. She watched as Aio and Atio took to the skies together. "Do you think our falcons see each other as siblings or lovers?"

Fen made a choking sound. "What?"

"Or do they mate with other falcons?"

"Why are you thinking about falcons mating, Si?"

"Well," Siofra said. "We mate. With others. Why shouldn't they?"

"*You* have mated," Fen said. His words faded to a grumble. "With two more men than I have."

Siofra turned toward him. "Is that judgment?"

"No," Fen said quickly. He shook his head with a self-reprising squint. "No. It's not. I happen to like Wulf. He's good to you. He's not much for conversation, but... that's not the appeal anyway, is it?"

Siofra burst into laughter. When it died down, she said, "He's not much for anything else either. We haven't..." She rolled her hands in the air, letting her insinuation finish the sentence.

Fen failed to hide his relief. "But I thought... I thought he was..."

"He is."

"Then why haven't you..." Fen gulped. "I don't know why I insist on punishing myself with questions I *really* don't need answers to."

"There's not much to say," Siofra replied. "Desemir gave his approval, and I thought it was what I wanted but..." She inhaled a long breath and tried to smile as she released it. "What I really wanted was to punish *him*, but he's miserable enough without my adding to it. And Wulf, I can see he wants me. I can read it in his eyes whenever he looks at me—"

"We can talk about something else now."

"He's too loyal to my husband," Siofra said. "Whenever we get too close, he becomes Des's loyal soldier once more. I could influence the matter with very little effort on my part, but I prefer he come to me without guilt. I won't beg him to come to my bed."

"No, nor should you," Fen muttered, cringing. "Ah, anyway—"

"If you're so keen to move on," Siofra said with a knowing grin, "then let's talk about you and Pesha. Hmm?"

"Me and Pesha?" Fen's head shook with a poor imitation of incomprehension.

"You seem surprised, but you do realize how much time the two of you spend together."

"I realize," Fen replied, stammering, "that he's my only real friend here, unless you count Lieken, but he seems considerably happier when I forego meaningful conversation and just issue orders he can follow."

"Si? We're being called for supper."

Fen jumped off the bench like he'd been shocked.

Siofra turned toward the sound of Wulf's voice. His gaze was on her bosom, which was lifted by the tight neckline of her pale-yellow gown. *He wants what he can't have. And I won't take what he doesn't offer willingly.*

Wulf snapped his gaze back up. "I hung back as long as I could, but... you know Desi."

"I know Des," Siofra murmured. There was nothing more telling of her husband's view of her being a vessel than the increased demand for her protection. "I wouldn't want him to paddle you for affording me even a few moments of independence."

Fen buried a grin. Wulf shook his head, flustered.

"I'll meet you in the dining hall," Fen said and jogged off before she could respond.

Wulf lifted his brows and flashed a polite smile. "Enjoying your book?"

"For what little time I had to read it," she answered. He offered his arm, but she didn't take it. Talking about her strange relationship with Wulf had only shone a brighter light on her frustrations. Even with Desemir moved to the periphery of her life and thoughts, he still wielded total control over her life and happiness. It wasn't as if she could have either *beyond* the gates of Shadowfen Hall.

"You read a lot," he said, an awkward attempt at conversation, which only raised her suspicions.

"I try to," she answered cordially. "But you already knew that."

"Have I offended you in some way?"

"You offend me by asking."

Wulf reached for her arm and pulled her to stop. "Siofra. I sense—" He cut himself off. He gripped the back of her head in his palm and tugged her into a kiss.

Siofra wanted to punish him for his ongoing rejection of her, but she'd forgotten how *good* it felt to be touched, to be wanted. To submit to a call for affection she understood was vital to her happiness.

She broke away and covered her mouth with one hand while flashing him a detached look. "You sense what?"

Wulf's breathing stilted. He paced, starting in one direction, then reverting to the other. "Tension. I was going to say tension. Perhaps it's my fault."

"It's entirely mine," Siofra remarked dryly. She lifted her skirts and brushed past him before he could see the truth in her expression—the lust. "For presuming there was more to be found than what there is."

"It's not you." Wulf rushed to her side. "It's *not* you."

"I know it's not me. I can see with my own eyes how you look at me."

"At night, when I'm alone..." Wulf suppressed a groan. "I think of you often. More than I should."

"Yes," she said with an impatient sigh, still marching forward. "And therein lies the problem."

"He may have said he'll allow it," Wulf replied. "But he doesn't mean it. When he realizes that, I don't want to be on the other end of his regret."

"Why are we still talking about this?" Siofra demanded when they reached the stairs. "You've made yourself perfectly clear! You desire me, but it isn't the same as *wanting* me, is it? And as all men at Shadowfen Hall serve Desemir, I will find myself running into the same walls over and over, until at last I've lost my mind." She yanked the doors wide. "I won't be joining everyone for supper tonight. In my absence, you can comfortably preen before my husband, regaling him with tales of your great restraint where his poor, neglected wife is concerned. A martyr for the ages!" Siofra stormed off without him.

"What are you going to do?" Pesha asked.

Desemir gripped the balcony so tight, his hands turned as white as his linens. "I let Arranden up here, it's over."

"If he really wanted you imprisoned, Des, you'd be imprisoned. Your guard is impressive, but with law on his side, he could call upon Lord Dereham's forces, and those of the other stewards. He hasn't done that."

"Probably wants to talk to me first," Desemir grumbled. A phantom pain stabbed him in the side. All his *actual* pains were gone now, thanks to Pesha, but his mind didn't seem to realize it. "To bargain. My freedom for my forests."

"And if he does," Pesha said, drawing closer. "There's no question what you'll do. You don't need even an acre of the Darkwood to keep Shadowfen Hall in operation. Your trust fund alone would keep future generations comfortable for a hundred years."

"I'm tired of thinking about it. Speaking about it is even worse." Desemir rolled around and leaned back over the railing. He watched the stars blink in and out. "Siofra wasn't at supper. Again."

"No."

"That's all you have to offer? No?"

"Was there something you expected me to offer?" Pesha asked, in the same flippant tone he used when he was holding something back.

Desemir ground his jaw. "Unless I specifically ask, you haven't shared with me how she's been doing these past weeks."

"The baby is healthy. So is the mother."

"Pesh." Desemir groaned. "She still thinks I'm a monster. You said she would get better and that when she did, we would tell her the truth."

"She has gotten better," Pesha said patiently. "But she now seems doubly determined to move forward and not dwell on the events of that evening. I believe this may be a method of coping with what happened, to keep her and the child safe."

"Not *dwell*..." Desemir emitted a series of gasping starts. "She thinks I left her there to *die*, Pesha!"

Pesha nodded, maddeningly calm. "But she *is* better. She's fully recovered physically, and she's returned to things she loves, like reading. Her bond with Fen is mended, and her relationship with Wulf is... Well, it would be an overstatement to call it anything at all. Thanks to you."

"Thanks to me?" Desemir's face flushed with heat. "I'm forbidden from telling my wife the truth, and I'm a monster if I don't want her fucking her guard, something she only wants to do because of the lies you all fed her to keep her stable."

Pesha took another step and propped his arm against the doorframe. "It's almost as if how she feels about you matters to you."

Desemir shook his head in wild, abrupt strokes. "You've turned putting words into my mouth into an absolute sport over the years, but have I ever asked for it?"

"Then say the words as you want me to hear them, Des. Tell me what's really bothering you."

"Nothing." Des swallowed the lie and turned again toward the forest. He *would* have given every acre to bring Siofra home. His promise to her mattered. It would always matter, even against the thick wall of her hatred. "Nothing is wrong."

Pesha nodded and glanced at the door. "So you're ready for Wulf to start soliciting women for your bed again?"

"Now I know you're being an ass."

"That's a no then."

Desemir's eyes fluttered closed in annoyance. "It's a no. Unless there's something else..."

"There's not," Pesha said, a touch of satisfaction in his voice.

"Have Euric send word to Arranden." Desemir decided the course as the words left him. Whatever the steward had planned for him was preferable to waiting for war to spring from the forest. "An invitation to Shadowfen Hall. He can bring three men, no more. Set it for a fortnight from now."

"Why not sooner?"

"He's left me wondering about his intentions long enough," Desemir answered. "Now it's his turn to toil over mine."

TWENTY-SIX
THE COMFORT OF YOUR LIES

Siofra hung her head over the bowl when the final contents of her stomach left her. Gisela fingered Siofra's hair back from her face, humming soothing words that provided some comfort, despite how horrible she felt.

"Is this normal?" Siofra asked, her voice hoarse and strained. She barely had the words out before she retched again, but nothing came up.

"Very," Gisela said. Snapping linen sounded. She pulled Siofra back into her arms and wrapped the fabric around her neck like a bib. "Breathe, Si. Your belly is disrupted now, and you need to calm it. You have nothing left to give."

"Will it be like this..." Siofra clamped her mouth closed and inhaled hard through her nose. "The whole time?"

"For us, it passes early, usually." Gisela brushed Siofra's matted hair off her sweaty forehead. "What has Lotte said?"

"It was a long time ago, and she remembers very little."

"And Pesha?"

319

"He doesn't know." Siofra's voice cracked. She slapped her hand around, searching for the skin of water, and Gisela moved it toward her. After a long sip, she said, "His mother never told him much. Lotte knew more than he did. And it's not like there were other female Medvedev here for him to ask."

Gisela was silent for a spell. "It is unfortunate."

The privy door swung open. Lotte wore a world-weary look that spoke for her.

"Right." Gisela eased Siofra off of her and jumped up. "I'll go see about the broth."

Siofra pulled herself against the wall. The act required the last of her energy, and despite Lotte's heavy gaze, filled with unspoken demand, Siofra started to doze the moment her head came to rest.

"Siofra. I need you alert."

Siofra moaned and stretched herself higher.

Lotte trod in and knelt in front of her. "Here. Drink this."

Siofra regarded the mug with one eye closed, the other squinting. "What is it?"

"It will restore some of your vigor until we can get proper food in you." When Siofra eyed the mug with more hesitance, Lotte snapped, "Go on, drink."

Lotte rose and crossed her arms. Watched. Waited. Even when Siofra finished the bitter draught, Lotte waited still, counting down against an unseen clock.

But then she did feel stronger. It was enough to push herself up the wall and follow Lotte back into the bedchamber.

"Sit," Lotte ordered. She thrust a hand toward the bed.

"You're more cross than usual," Siofra muttered as she found a spot near the end of her bed. She reached for the thin quilt and wrapped it around herself.

"Cross?" Lotte snorted. "This is not cross, Siofra. This is concern." Lotte stomped to the other side of the room and lifted one of the dressing chairs. She practically threw it in front of Siofra and sat. "The night you came back, I wasn't keen on the way others handled your welfare, but I didn't say anything." She shook her head at an invisible third person. "I didn't say anything because it wasn't my place. If Pesha says you need to believe your own lies, who am I to say he's wrong?"

Siofra tightened the blanket in her fists. "What do you mean, believe my own lies?"

"And I thought to myself, 'Lotte, she'll get better and then they'll tell her.' And I waited, but still, both men—"

"What men?"

"Your brother. Pesha. They insisted you were doing better *because* your little fantasy hadn't been disturbed. That we needed to keep our wits about us when talking to you, be extra careful not to say anything that might come close to the truth. So I said all right. We'll give it a while longer."

Siofra shivered. She looked to see if a window was open, but they were closed. "What are you talking about?"

"But you're suffering, girl. Your husband is suffering. And I seem to recall Siofra Thornheart came to Shadowfen Hall because she was tired of men making choices for her. That she chose to marry Desemir Trevanion of her own volition, not because it was what some fool-headed, though well-meaning, brother told her she should choose."

Siofra sat straighter. "I don't know why we're talking about this now."

"You need to know," Lotte said, meeting her gaze squarely. "The one thing Pesha is right about? That physician will not be returning to Shadowfen Hall—not him, nor others."

"What?" Siofra's nausea returned. "Why?"

"Even if we brought a new one each time..." Lotte answered with an exhausted sigh. "Men talk, don't they? Some men can even do math, Guardians bless them. And if they can do both?"

Siofra hung her head with a grimace. "I'd hoped there was someone Des trusted enough to look past the details. The way he trusts all of you."

"Now don't be thinking you're alone in this. I helped bring Pesha into this world..." Lotte shook her head. "A new generation of Trevanions is a blessing that will light the darkest corners of the Hall."

Lotte's talk of dark corners caused Siofra to shoot a glance at her own. As expected, she spotted Wulf in one of them, slumped in a chair and pretending to not listen.

"You hearing me, girl?"

"I won't have a proper physician," Siofra said. She drew her legs under herself. "It will just be you and Gisela, with Pesha barking orders from the shadows. Is that about the sum of it?"

"And your husband. You'll need him too."

"He'll get his heir. He bought and paid for one, didn't he?" Siofra scoffed and turned her head away. Some days were easier than others when it came to the subject of Desemir, but to hear Lotte speak of dark days ahead brought Siofra's sorrow to the forefront.

"He didn't abandon you in Oakhelm, Siofra."

Wulf stirred to life, planting his boots on the floor with a thud.

"Everyone in the Hall has been upholding this lie for over a month now, including me. But it stops now. It stops because you need each other, more than you need the comfort of your lies." Lotte's round eyes seemed to shake in their intensity.

Siofra shook her head back and forth. "I'm weary, Lotte, of people insisting that the man who wouldn't sell a single acre of his damnable forest to bring me home cares even a *whit* about me."

"That man!" Lotte thundered the words. "That *man* was willing to sell every last acre to Rolfe to get you back, but it was Pesha who talked him out of it!"

Siofra sank back onto the bed. "What did you say?"

"He was ready to give it *all*, Siofra. All of it. He wasn't even going to bargain with the man. He was mad with grief, with worry. I've never seen him like that, not since..." Lotte spun her attention to the corner. "Tell her, Wulfhelm. And if you even *think* of lying, you'll only look the fool, when the truth is already half told."

322

Siofra hated how small her voice sounded when she spoke. "Wulf?"

Wulf dragged his sigh out. His boots shuffled against the floorboards. "It's true."

All the blood in her body seemed to rush straight to her chest. "Why would you keep this from me? Why would anyone think..." She ripped the quilt away and fumbled backward, needing space, distance. "You said half told. The truth is *half* told."

"You want to tell her or leave it to me and my colorful interpretation?" Lotte asked Wulf.

Wulf grunted as he pushed off his chair. He moved toward the bed but didn't sit. "While Fen and I were pulling you out of the barn, Desemir led over a hundred men to the keep. He slew... I don't know how many. Euric lost count in the melee." Wulf looked to Lotte for help, but the old woman's gaze was on Siofra. "Right before they reached Rolfe's bedchamber, Desi took a sword to the gut, through a gap in his armor."

Siofra held her breath.

"But he picked himself up..." Wulf's words slowed in pace. His voice dropped an octave. "Picked himself up, went into the bedchamber of Edmund Rolfe, and slit the man's throat."

"No," Siofra whispered. It was the only word she could find.

"He'd just... made it out of the keep." Wulf struggled to finish, sliding both of his hands down his face. "Right as you... as you... exploded."

"Exploded? Is that what you think—" Siofra's prickly laugh turned into a sob. "Say what you were going to say, Wulf. As I exploded..."

"Desi, he..." Wulf's voice hitched. He swallowed, shooting another pointless look at Lotte. "He caught the force of it."

"I hit him with my red wall?" Siofra's mouth went dry. Her chest pulled the ache from her limbs, drawing it inward into a vise around her heart. "Was he... Was it bad?"

"He nearly died. Pesha was still healing him for weeks," Lotte answered, finishing for Wulf with an impatient glare at the young

323

man. "And that isn't your fault, Siofra. It is *not* your fault. Just as what happened to you in the barn was not Desemir's. But he did right by you. He did right by you, and instead of telling you so, everyone here has led you to simmer on your fears and make them your new truth. Because *everyone here* thinks you're too weak. Are you weak, Siofra?"

"No," Siofra whispered. Every inch of her flesh tingled. Her head felt weightless, as if it might float away, returning her to a recent past where lies were more palatable than truth. "No. I'm not."

"No. You are not. And as the truth bearer, I expect your anger. I will always be the one who disabused you of this fantasy, and you will resent me for it. You should. Perhaps the others just love you more, letting you live mired in falsehoods."

"Lotte..." Wulf turned with a resigned sigh.

"If in your heart your marriage is truly over, then let it be over because of what you *do* know of Desemir. Not what you don't."

Siofra wanted to slip through the bed, the floor... crashing through layers of wood and stone until she plunged deep into the earth.

No, you don't. This is what others think of you. It's why they still regard you as a delicate porcelain vase that couldn't withstand even the lightest drop.

That is not who you are.

"And Desemir, he allowed this? He absorbed my loathing? Why?"

"Only he can answer that question," Lotte said, gently this time. "But it's a question worth asking. Don't you think?"

"I..." Siofra puzzled over her hesitation. Was the life she had now not what she wanted? What she dreamed of, in the part of her heart still vulnerable to the torturous push and pull of love and rejection? Why was it easier to picture Desemir sitting alone at Shadowfen Hall in his indifference than it was to see him running his sword through every man who had aided Rolfe in hurting her?

"I've said what I came to say." Lotte looked from Wulf to Siofra with a decisive nod and knocked the chair back as she stood. "The rest isn't up to me."

Siofra was suspended with inaction. She should say something to Lotte—thank her, some parting words of gratitude, *something*—but the sensation of existing in two realities was stronger than her manners.

She heard Lotte leave. Felt the door half slam behind her. Sensed Wulf trying to sit, then deciding against it.

"No wonder you wouldn't come to my bed," she muttered, her words low and dazed. "It would have been a betrayal not only of Desemir but of me."

"Siofra, I..."

"You're sorry. You didn't want to lie to me. You hated every minute of it," she answered with a bitter scoff. "Do you all truly think so low of me that you believe me incapable of feeling more than one thing?"

"It wasn't up to me," Wulf said, helpless.

"The people who change the world are the ones who decide it *is* up to them," she remarked, though whatever quick anger she'd had for Wulf was gone. It was pointless. He'd been playing the game of men his whole life, and she was still learning. One day she'd become a more worthy opponent.

"What will you do?" he asked.

"What time is it?"

"Ah..." Wulf glanced toward the window. "Closer to midnight than supper."

Siofra frowned. "So Des will be with his women?"

Wulf shook his head. "He hasn't sent for them since before you were taken."

The night was full of surprises. "Will he be sleeping then?"

"Not likely. I'll escort you."

"You will not," she stated.

"I will." Wulf insisted, firm on the matter. "Because he doesn't want you alone in these halls for even a moment. And while you

325

might not think much of my judgment after what you learned tonight, when it comes to keeping the people I love safe, I look to my own wit and wisdom to guide me true." He pulled her robe from the rack. "Can you walk?"

"What kind of a—" Siofra winced when she leaped out of bed too fast. "I could use some help. An arm will do."

But Wulfhelm didn't offer her an arm. Instead, he knelt and scooped an arm behind her knees, sweeping her from her feet and into his arms.

"You're wrong," he said, his voice low and smooth. "I do want you, Siofra. And if you ask me again, after you speak with Desemir, I won't deny you. Because I'll know you want *me* and not just a reprieve from your broken heart."

TWENTY-SEVEN
UNDONE

Thunder tore across the plain, splitting the earth in two. Moments later, lightning painted the sky in illumination and sent a jagged spike deep into the forest. Desemir held his breath, waiting for the telltale sign of orange light that would reveal whether the lightning had touched down—and if the pounding rain was enough to keep it from becoming a problem.

It didn't come.

Desemir swigged the remaining liquor from his mug. He'd never developed the taste for it, like other men of his means had. It sometimes calmed him, like it had for his father, but usually it put his nerves on a finer, sharper edge, where they balanced precariously until his thoughts wore him out or sent him spiraling.

Arranden had sent back confirmation of the meeting in a fortnight. He gave away nothing in his response that might indicate where his mind was on the matter. And why should he? Arranden stood to gain from Desemir's reign of terror on Oakhelm. He held the power coming into the conversation.

Desemir eyed the decanter half-full of amber liquor. The last time Lotte had filled it had been, what... a year ago? Two? He wasn't a very effective lush, but tonight... Tonight, he'd make up for that.

You will never be a man if you cannot shed the spine of a boy.

"Father." Desemir's mouth curled in bitter response. Ludwik hadn't infiltrated his thoughts in months. And Desemir had thought he might finally be rid of the man entirely.

You stand upon the stone I defended. You drink and eat and play in the rooms that still exist because I had the mettle to do what other men would not to fortify my family. And yet you turn your nose up at these very things.

"You were right the first time," Desemir muttered. He rolled the empty mug in his hands, half his attention on the decanter.

You drown in denial, son. Who in the Hall knows the real reason you haven't sent for your whores in over a month? Who, but perhaps Pesha, knows the blood reckoning you laid upon Rolfe and his people has finally granted you the rest that's been eluding you since—

"Des?"

Desemir readied a sound *fuck you* for his father, but the last voice was real. He fumbled the mug, and it went skipping across the stones. He turned to retrieve it, but Siofra was a step ahead, already kneeling to pick it up. She stood and handed it to him.

"What are you doing here?" He found he couldn't look at her. His eyes wouldn't lift from the mug dangling from her fingers.

"I need to ask you something." She flicked her free hand toward the decanter. Her thin robe shifted with the movement, brushing the stones. "Unless you're too far gone for a proper answer."

"I'd like to be, but alas..." Desemir slumped onto the balcony. His fingers dug into the moss under the curled edge. Siofra was in his bedchamber alone, by her own choice, yet he couldn't help from challenging the fact, pushing her away. "Usually you send Gisela if you need something from me."

"Gisela can't ask the question I need to ask you." Siofra stretched sideways and planted the mug on the table. As she returned, her violet eyes swept upward, catching his. His shudder was involuntary.

"Very well." Desemir dug deeper into the moss. He blinked through the languid tug of the liquor and gulped a lungful of air. "Go on."

Siofra took another step, her slippered feet making soft scratches against the stone as she moved. She closed the doors behind her and turned back toward him.

He allowed himself a quick, regretful assessment of her. Her golden hair was swept to the side, curling over one shoulder and to her waist like a rope. Her pale cheeks, flushed from pregnancy but also for reasons yet unclear, set the soft sheen of her eyes into startling relief.

She's the most beautiful creature you've ever beheld, inside and out, and you have crushed her in your cruelty.

Desemir trapped a knot in his throat, forcing it back down.

"I want to know why you lied to me about what happened in Oakhelm."

The question startled him. It reminded him he was alone. With her. Pesha had retired for the evening. Euric's shift was over, and though Cassius was outside in the hall, what defense could he bring against the ire of a Medvedev who believed her husband had deserted her?

But she wasn't angry. Her placid expression was searching, not combative.

"You were unwell." Desemir suddenly wished he had refilled the mug. His throat was clogged with inadequacy, and he was certain she could see it—and that he was woefully unprepared for any kind of conversation.

Siofra scoffed with a hard look to the side. "I didn't come here to be lied to."

"I—"

"And you *just* lied to me." Siofra's chin tilted up with a touch of pride. "You repeated the same useless refrain I've come to expect from my brother and Pesha. That they're *so worried* I'm too delicate to handle the truth."

"You are the opposite of delicate." He didn't know why he said it.

"Yes," Siofra agreed with a hint of a smile. "And you're the only one here, Des, who has never treated me like I'm too fragile for this world. I beg you, don't start now."

Desemir was lost for words. He could only watch the way her arms passed across the lace of her robe when she crossed them, her hair slipping behind them, bouncing with the intrusion.

"I'm not asking you to tell me all your secrets," Siofra said. "I know you have many. I know they're destroying you."

Desemir opened his mouth but closed it again.

No. Just one.

"I'm asking only for *this* truth. Why didn't *you* tell me the truth of what happened in Oakhelm?"

Desemir released the balcony with a rough sigh. She'd told him what she'd accept—what she wouldn't. "Because I wasn't what you needed."

Siofra blanched. "It isn't for you to decide what I need."

"You needed a hero." Desemir's throat bobbed. "I'm just a murderer."

Siofra absorbed his words. She raked her teeth along her bottom lip, eyes to the side in thought. "A murderer, you say." She nodded and returned her eyes forward. "And I say you did the only thing you could when a man came for your wife."

Desemir balked at the word wife. It rang hollow against all that had happened... against everything he'd done to devalue its meaning. "I pushed you. I..." He shook his head. "I pushed you when Rolfe came here, and it's because of *me*—"

"You just didn't want me to hide from myself anymore."

"Maybe. But I'd wanted him dead for years," he said with a flippant shrug.

330

Siofra started forward with a heated stare. "But it was for *me* you actually killed him."

Desemir's pulse hastened with each step she took closer. "Honor demanded it."

"Honor." Siofra rolled the word off her tongue with a snort. "It's not only me you ply with deceptions. You lie to yourself. Do you even know what the truth is anymore? Would you recognize it?"

"I answered your question." Tightness spread across Desemir's chest. "Was there anything else you needed?"

Siofra stopped her approach. Her mouth widened with her eyes. "What if it was you I needed?"

Defensive laughter stung his throat. He trained his glower on the stones. They couldn't pull the truth from his eyes like she would. "How could it be me you need, Siofra? I can't even manage the Hall anymore."

Siofra's hitched breath flowed into a sigh. "Why do you still refuse to let me in? You don't have to do this alone, Des."

Desemir's head shook with more scathing laughter. "Oh, yes, I do. *Yes, I fucking do.* I was born to be alone."

"You say this, but I see so many signs that say different. Like the book you left for me in the library."

"What book?"

"The sonnets."

Desemir was too shocked to lie, surprised she'd made the connection.

"You wanted me to find my way back to you, didn't you?"

"It's just a book," he said, another lie.

Siofra's eyes softened with sadness. She twisted her mouth, choosing her words carefully. "When you first made me your offer... When you told me I could take lovers..." Her tongue passed along her lips. She chuckled to herself. "I thought to myself, what a strange thing to say." She met his gaze. Held it. "For why would I ever want to do that when I have you?"

Desemir's silence replaced his effort to rein in the words evading him.

"I felt like a fool." She dropped her arms to her sides. He directed his gaze to the low cut of her nightgown, the plunge between her breasts. "When I learned I wasn't enough for you. I blamed myself for not having the experience or the wisdom to accept your offer with the grace it demanded."

"I should have..." Desemir swallowed hard. "Explained things better. It's my fault."

"The feeling went away," Siofra said, ignoring his rebuttal, "because you were enough for me. Even with all your faults, your strange desires, your unwillingness to accept real affection. You were enough."

Desemir sank against the balcony. Jealousy clenched in his gut. "What about Wulf?"

"What about Wulf?"

"You made it clear you want him." He tapped his hand on the stone. "Specifically him."

Siofra opened her palms at her sides. "I'm not in love with Wulf, Desemir. He was just a balm for my loneliness."

Her insinuation stole the air from Desemir's chest. He blinked through the pain. "So the two of you..."

Siofra shook her head. "No." With a soft laugh, she said, "Not for my lack of trying. His loyalty came between all my attempts. But then, he knew what I did not. He knew what you had done for me." She had become so close, he could feel her warm breath on his face. "He knew that when I found out, I would come running right back to you, because it's where I belong."

Desemir angled his face away. His eyes closed as he steeled himself with a muted grunt. "Siofra..."

"I'm not in love with Wulf," she stated.

"Are you..." He sucked air through his teeth. "Are you in love with someone else?"

Siofra bit down on the inside corner of her mouth. "Mm. Yes. With someone."

Desemir broke away from the barrier to escape the intoxicating pull of her nearness. He moved to the other side of the balcony. "I'll ruin you," he said finally. The words suffocated him, but they had to be said. For her, they had to be said. "I already have."

"Do I look ruined to you, Desemir?" Siofra sighed. "Though, why am I even asking when you can't even look at me to answer the question?"

"I ruin everything. *Everyone.*" His shoulders swayed with his labored breathing. "I turn everything I touch to rot."

"You think you don't deserve happiness."

Desemir laughed bitterly. "I *know* I don't. But you..."

"What about me? You think you've given me everything, but you've withheld the one thing I want most. The one thing my heart cannot find elsewhere."

Desemir turned his hands to fists at his sides, pumping them. "You deserve a man like Wulf. A man of honor."

Siofra's exhale carried across the space between them like a warm breeze. "And yet here I am, Des. Choosing you."

Desemir's knees buckled. He sank onto the chaise before he could go down. Siofra was on him before he could push her away, winding herself into his lap, her arms around his neck. What started as a groan turned to a whimper from the silky passage of her flesh touching his.

He lifted his head to sound the rebuttals he'd been so certain she needed, but her kiss kept the words buried.

How I've missed you.

How hollow my life has been without you in it.

Desemir lifted her into his arms as he stood. "You're somehow both my greatest strength and weakness, Siofra." He ran his palm across her forehead and rested it on the crown of her head. "My undoing."

"As you are mine," she whispered, craning to affix her mouth to his once more. "I don't need a hero. I need a husband. I need *you*, if you'll have me."

"If I'll..." He was again breathless. With a strangled cry, he pressed her head to his chest. "Oh, Siofra."

Desemir crushed the lingering, stinging doubts screaming for address. He buried them deep as he carried his wife across the balcony—as he swung open the doors and brought her back to his bedchamber, which had felt so cold, so empty without her.

He laid her gently on the bed. Only then did he allow himself a glance at her softly rounded belly. Their child. The future of House Trevanion.

"You can't ruin me," she whispered, her hair splayed around her like a golden halo as she rolled her head against the pillow. "But I invite you to try."

Desemir ran a hand up her thigh, raking her nightgown up and over her waist. He shimmied out of his trousers and climbed onto the bed but stopped, suspended in time as he gazed down at the woman he'd married—the woman he'd insisted he could not love because he knew, *knew* in his heart that he could not be loved.

Siofra snaked a hand forward and clasped it around his cock. Her tongue traveled across her lips as she regarded him with a dreamy, glossy, *hungry* look.

Desemir's eyes rolled back as he entered her, twisting his cries in unison with hers. He moved slowly, memorizing how her velvet flesh felt receiving him... how her hips bucked just enough to draw him in further.

A familiar swell of release surged forth, but he willed it back, to the same place he'd tucked away his doubts and fears. He wanted it to last. To look into his wife's eyes as he made love to her. As he *saw* her, for the first time.

Siofra cupped his cheek with her palm and arced her head back as she came beneath him. Her desire clamped over him, but still he resisted, for her. All of it, for her.

Everything, for her.

TWENTY-EIGHT
SECRETS BETWEEN US

Arranden sat to Desemir's left, Siofra to his right. The first thing Arranden had said when Euric had escorted him into the Hall of Counting was *I'm not sitting at the bloody other end this time, Desemir.*

Desemir bristled at the casual use of his name, even from the steward. But he was at a disadvantage, and calling attention to his discomfort would only deepen it.

Pesha wasn't in the room. Desemir would smooth his brother's hurt feelings later, but Siofra had expressly asked for Pesha *not* to be there, and after what had happened the last time she'd joined him in a meeting, he would deny her nothing.

She wanted a clear mind, unimpeded by Pesha's dampening effect.

Desemir suspected she intended to kill Arranden if things went sideways. He wouldn't let the situation—or her anger—get that far.

"Is she..." Arranden nodded at Siofra.

"Is she what?" Desemir asked, pretending to not understand the insinuation.

"Yes, Steward, I'll be joining you for this meeting today." Siofra wore a dark-blue gown, its neckline stretching up over her neck and blooming into a collar that swept up the sides of her jaw. It had an almost funereal pall to it, and it made her look as formidable on the outside as she was on the inside.

Desemir couldn't stop playing out scenarios in his head of her wearing it, bent into various positions around his bedchamber while he relished the task of discovering which one he most preferred.

He couldn't even look at her without getting hard.

"Your wife? Really?" Arranden shook his head with a brief upturn of his eyes. "You truly are a different man than your father. It's as if you've taken every aspect of him and told yourself you were going to be the precise opposite." He laughed, but it wasn't a friendly sound.

"Compliment accepted," Desemir said evenly. He cleared his throat. "You respected my wishes about bringing only a small guard. I'm surprised."

Arranden's eyes glittered with something Desemir couldn't read. "Because you thought I'd come to take you into custody? Reprimand you? *Kill* you?"

"I didn't know what to expect," Desemir said. He made the admission only because Arranden had made his own concession, coming here practically without defense. A man like the steward was easier to control when he wasn't on the wrong side of equity.

Arranden made a tsking sound. "You haven't bothered to know me at all. Ludwik, for all his dreadful faults, was at least a true man of the Darkwood. He didn't hide away in his keep. When was the last time you even joined us for Torrin's Day?"

"My husband wouldn't need to hide if you had a handle on your men," Siofra said. She'd dropped the sweetness from her voice, replacing it with an iciness that chilled even Desemir. "If they didn't *threaten* to take what is rightfully his."

Arranden laughed with a disbelieving head shake at Desemir. "She speaks for you as well?"

"The baroness is free to speak whatever and whenever she pleases. We don't muzzle our women at Shadowfen Hall."

"A shame, that," Arranden muttered. He angled himself sideways in the chair to face Desemir, effectively blocking Siofra from his view. "I didn't come here to hold you to account, Desemir. Nor even to reprimand you. At least not about what happened in Oakhelm."

Desemir cocked a brow. "You've never been a man to let things go."

"How true," Arranden replied, smiling as if Desemir had praised him. "When I first learned of what happened, I'll be honest. I *was* calling for your head."

Siofra scoffed. Desemir suppressed a grin.

"But..." Arranden rolled his neck into a series of cracks. His jowls quivered when he shook it off. "When I'd calmed and had an opportunity to speak with some of the men who were there that night—Rolfe's men—I came to understand the situation quite differently."

Desemir folded his hands and leaned back. Siofra did the opposite, angling forward, her head slightly cocked.

Arranden coughed and continued. "They presented the night in more favorable terms. Favorable for you anyway. Not for Rolfe." He trapped a laugh. "They said you killed only the men who stood in your way. That you gave everyone—except Rolfe, of course—a chance to run. *Including* his sons."

"I did," Desemir replied. "Not all took it."

"No," Arranden said with a dry laugh. "Though sparing his sons will come back to haunt you one day. But it's what you did for Edmund's widow, Pearl, that resonated most with the citizens of Oakhelm. They join her in comfort that their steward is resting in the Rolfe tomb with his body intact. Most men would have taken his head and sentenced him to an eternity of restless damnation."

337

"I only wanted to end his earthly existence. What he does in the afterlife is of no concern to me."

"Interesting choice," Arranden said, nodding. "One I would not have made."

Desemir's chin twitched. "No?"

"If he'd taken Agnes, I'd have burned the entire village to the ground."

Siofra rolled her eyes. "No, Steward, you would not have. For it would have punished those who served that monster against their will. A punishment twice over, for another's crimes."

Arranden's gaze flicked fleetingly to Siofra. He disregarded her and watched Desemir more intently. "One can hardly blame you for your rage. I admire you for your restraint."

"Restraint would have been submitting Rolfe to you for judgment," Desemir countered.

"Why didn't you?"

Desemir lifted the corner of his mouth. "I think we both know why."

Arranden flushed, but it was the only sign Desemir's accusation had affected him. "You did what you had to do. I would have taken his head, had you brought the matter to me."

Desemir spun his father's ring. He'd always done so in a mindless way, but he'd become disturbingly aware of the peace the act brought him.

"Rolfe was *your* man." Desemir let the insinuation hang upon the light tension between himself and Arranden. "I assumed you were in on it."

"Me?" Arranden brought a hand to his chest in horror. "Desemir, I've made no secret of the contempt I feel for your dogged insistence in continuing your father's misdeeds, but our wives, our *families,* are off-limits. Rolfe stepped too far over this line." He at last looked at Siofra. "I would like to apologize to you, Baroness, for everything you endured at that man's hands."

338

"The apology is not yours to make," Siofra said smoothly. "But his death is enough to sate me."

Arranden's annoyance for her returned. With a light huff, he swung his attention back to Desemir. "It pains me you thought I could have had anything to do with this."

"It pained me to watch Rolfe run off with my wife, and not *one* of the barons raised a finger or their voice in protest."

"We didn't *know!*" Arranden threw his hands outward. "We didn't know *anything* until word of the Oakhelm incident spread over the barony."

"Mm."

"You think me capable of something like this? Truly, Desemir?"

Desemir let the question be answered by silence.

"Unbelievable." Arranden shook his head with a pained look. "Unbelievable. That you could even make such a suggestion knowing what your father did to steal the Darkwood."

"I didn't realize paying over market rate for land was a crime," Desemir replied dryly.

Siofra drummed the fingers of one hand against the back of her other.

Arranden pitched forward. "Even now, you would perpetuate that lie?"

"What lie?" Desemir snorted. "He offered you all *twice* what your land was worth. My father can be blamed for a good many offenses, and I will not defend him against any of them, but it was *your* fault for accepting it. And Weaver's, and Felwood's, and—"

Arranden flopped back in his chair. "Wait. You really believe what you're saying?"

"What does a business transaction have to do with belief?" Desemir aimed an arm at the secretary in the corner. "I have the ledgers. I've read them myself."

Sneering, Arranden looked at Siofra. "You're awfully quiet, Baroness. Have you pulled the truth from my mind?"

Siofra gave Desemir a tiny head shake, but alarm flashed in her eyes. She hadn't read the man's mind, but she had read *something*.

Desemir suddenly regretted excluding Pesha.

With a scoff, Arranden looked again at Desemir. "So Ludwik kept it from you. Maybe he meant to tell you one day but never got the chance because his lover killed him."

"Kept *what?*" Desemir's jaw tensed.

"There would've been no amount of gold worth selling the Darkwood for. Ludwik knew it." Arranden nodded. His chin puckered, eyes narrowed. "He *knew* there had to be something else to sway us. So he had our daughters kidnapped from their beds. *All* of them."

Desemir's blood cooled. Siofra stilled at his side.

"All of them," Arranden said again. "His terms were quite clear. Sell to him at his *most generous* offer, and he'd release the girls untouched. Don't, and he'd sell them into slavery."

"My husband is *not* his father," Siofra said through clenched teeth.

Arranden laughed to himself. "Rolfe was ready to let his girls die. He only relented after the rest of us did. He'd always been a creature of darkness."

Desemir couldn't restrain his words. "Didn't stop you from fucking him."

Arranden's eyes widened. "And you've done us both a great favor, as I was weary of him holding it over my head. Now he cannot." Arranden rapped his bony knuckles on the table. "Nor will you. Because I have spared your life, preserved your freedom, *and* attained the support and satisfaction of Lord Dereham. Oh, and lest you were worried about the wily steward in Newcarrow, I've offered him something he wants even more than vengeance: gold. So, you and I are now allies. Perhaps not friends." He grinned. "But allies."

Desemir couldn't let Arranden see the blow left by his words. He could never know of the sickening rot spreading across Desemir's gut, reaching into his chest like a fingered vise.

My father stole their daughters.

Years later, one of the barons repaid Ludwik's crime by stealing my wife.

"Allies." Desemir practically choked on the word. His mouth was a dry riverbed. He felt Siofra's eyes burning him with concern. "You must want something else."

"You mean my portion of the Darkwood returned to me? Without a single coin changing hands?" Arranden answered. "I believe it goes without saying, no? After I've all but let you get away with murder, and with the blessing of the Lord of the Northerlands?"

Desemir nodded through a series of hard blinks, which did nothing to restore his calm. The revelation that Stanhope was taken care of should have been enough, but even that didn't slow his racing heart. "Consider it yours."

Siofra leaned forward. Her hand fell upon his knee. He couldn't look at her. The loving worry on her face would break him.

"I'll have the paperwork drawn up and sent for your signature," Arranden said, pushing to his feet. "Oh, and that was a nice touch, sending Pearl Rolfe rights to the upcoming season's bark harvest. But I still don't understand why you left their sons alive."

Desemir hardly heard the unasked question. His mind was drawn elsewhere. Flashes of Ludwik's cruelty, memories he'd repressed, flooded into his thoughts like water breaking through a dam.

Siofra kept her eyes on him for another moment before she made a soft, concerned sound and turned toward Arranden. "My husband left the Rolfe heirs alive because he's going to be a father himself. I think a lesson we could all learn from this is that sons should not be held to account for the sins of their fathers."

"Is your husband all right, Baroness?"

"Perhaps the implication that he lacks a conscience has stirred the very thing you've assumed him to not have," Siofra replied. "I'll have Euric escort you out."

"But Desemir—"

"Is *my* concern," Siofra said for him. "Shall we?"

Pesha was stewing in the hall, debating how to address his exclusion from Desemir, when Lieken came to deliver the news Pesha had been waiting for, had been fearing, for years.

"I can't leave. Not until the steward does," Pesha said, his attention pulled between the Hall of Counting and the direction of the west wing. "This has happened before. It turned out to be nothing to fuss about. Is it like that?"

"I..."

"Or is it worse?"

"I don't... I don't know." Lieken's head swung back and forth, then up and down. The poor boy *didn't* know, and how could he? He hadn't been at Shadowfen Hall when they'd been forced to repurpose the west wing for their darkest secret. He'd only been the one assigned to tend it. "But there's—"

Pesha lifted a hand to silence him when the double doors to the Hall of Counting opened. Arranden exited, Euric right behind him.

Pesha nodded at the steward. Arranden, in response, passed a stinging gaze over Pesha and kept walking.

When they were far enough down the hall for Pesha to speak again, he said, "Get Lotte. She'll know what to do."

"I... all right. Will you be coming?"

Pesha glanced into the room and saw Desemir bowled over the table. Siofra gathered him in her arms from behind. "When I can. Now go."

He entered and closed the doors behind him. "What's the matter? What happened?"

Siofra peeled away from Desemir, shaking her head. "Arranden said something upsetting, but I think it's more than that."

Pesha tried not to think about Lieken's panicked words. "What did Arranden say?"

"He implied your father used more than gold to sway the men of the Darkwood to sell their acreage."

"Ahh." He'd heard the rumors but had never asked to confirm what Desemir did and didn't know. "Would you mind giving us a moment, Si? I need to speak with my brother alone."

Siofra looked stricken, but she stood straight and gathered her skirts. It was Desemir who snaked an arm out and grabbed hers.

"Siofra and I have no secrets, Pesh. Not anymore." Desemir's voice was muffled by his sleeved arm, still supporting his face. "You can say what you need to say in front of her."

"I would rather not." Pesha flashed a wary look Siofra's way. "And I think you would rather I not either."

"I don't like the sound of that," Siofra said. "If there's trouble—"

"No trouble," Pesha said quickly. His heart jumped in trepidation; he was a terrible liar. "It has to do with me is all. It's a private matter."

"Since when have you had private matters?" Desemir grumbled. He sat up and glanced at them both. His eyes were shot with red. "Is it about Fen? If so, you already know you have my full blessing."

Siofra offered a bemused grin to both men.

Pesha raked his tongue against the roof of his mouth in agitation, uncomfortably aware of the heated flush splotching his cheeks. "No, it's not about Fen. *Please,* Des. I just need to speak with you alone."

Desemir inhaled through his nose. His arms spread as he exhaled slowly. "Fine." He stood and brought Siofra toward him, his hand on the back of her head. He lingered in the kiss that followed. "Go to our bedchamber, love. I'll be along soon."

Siofra licked her lips and nodded. The look she gave Pesha as she passed left him gutted in the understanding she wouldn't let it go.

But wasn't it time she knew? If Desemir was determined for his marriage to be a proper one, with love and trust, was there any way he could have it without telling Siofra what was in the west wing?

"I meant what I said. She and I have no secrets between us now," Desemir said, spinning in his chair with a distressed glare.

Pesha drew a steadying breath. "Except you do, Des. You do have a secret you've kept from her. And the secret is *waking up*."

TWENTY-NINE
THE LAST FEAST OF WINTERTIDE

Three thousand candles. It was Lotte's best estimate. Whatever the number, it depleted the candle stock of Shadowfen Hall. It had taken them most of the day to pull them from drawers and cabinets to place and light them.

The result was Shadowfen Hall being a tableau of light and warmth for the Last Feast of Wintertide, the final holiday of the dark seasons. The sugary aroma of a glut of baked goods carried on the wind, adding scent to the soft melodies of the ladies singing their hymns, providing the perfect backdrop for the evening Desemir thought might be the best of his life.

Shadowfen Hall had never felt more like home. He had never before *wanted* it to be home, not in the traditional way, conjuring images of love and happiness and familial closeness. That life was for other men. *Love* was for other men.

But at last, it was his, and every moment since he'd realized it had swept him through a range of emotions from gratitude to fear.

He had lived his life like a man who had nothing to lose, and until recently, that had been true.

And with matters in the west wing settling, he could breathe again.

Fen and Pesha huddled near the bonfire, close enough for others to make note of their closeness but too far away for anyone to hear what they said to each other. Wulf and Gisela danced a horrifying quadrille, Cassius and the other guards keeping time to the music with their boots squishing in the mud.

The twin falcons were perched along the balustrade above, occasionally taking to the skies.

Siofra giggled on Desemir's lap as she nibbled on a fritter, laughing at a drunken Euric's war stories—and Lotte calling foul on every last one. Desemir had an arm looped around his wife, his palm resting on the subtle but solid arc of her belly and the child growing within, a son or daughter he'd created with lust but would raise with love.

"Springtide is really around the corner?" Siofra asked skeptically with a hard shiver. Snowflakes dusted the air, but they disappeared when they landed on the damp ground. "Or have you swindled me into a life of eternal winter?"

Desemir laughed into her neck, inhaling her scent as he nuzzled her. "This is the Northerlands, Baroness. We cannot all live in glittering beach towns like Newcarrow."

She wrinkled her nose. "I'll take an entire lifetime of winter over another day there."

"And I'd kill any man who challenged that."

Siofra's eyes twinkled with mischief. "Oh, I *know* you would. I sensed your disappointment when Arranden handled the situation more peacefully." She trailed her lips against his forehead with a soft, content sound. "Wulf is going to break one of his legs if you don't stop him." She pointed at Wulf's frenzied attempt at dancing. "Or Gisela's."

"I once fought for the Warwicks," Euric declared, unprompted. He raised the empty bottle he'd been nursing. Whiskey, he'd said, from the Southerlands. It was the only thing suitable to drink on Last Feast night, when they dined on nothing but sweets.

"Did you now?" Desemir asked playfully. He stroked the back of his hand down Siofra's satin-covered arm.

"I ken I did. *Aye.*" Euric belched.

"No one would ever mistake you for a Southerlander with that accent," Lotte muttered and pulled the empty bottle from his still-raised hand. "Nor a warrior, carrying on as you are."

"I love Euric's stories." Gisela beamed through her flushed cheeks. Her eyes were glossy from the whiskey. "He so rarely tells them."

"He so rarely speaks *at all,* and what a gift it is," Wulf said, laughing to himself as he strutted sideways. He nearly toppled into the bonfire, but Gisela yanked him back with a light reprimand.

"You want a story?" Lotte declared. "I've got one for you. How about the time Des and Wulf chased some poor fox into her den, only for the daddy fox to show up and send the two of them running for their lives, zipping around to and fro like animals themselves." She chortled. "Ah, and I recall Wulf falling in the lake, nearly drowning. Or was it Des?"

Wulf belched. "Drown? Me? I'm an excellent swimmer."

"Wasn't me," Des said, lifting his hands with a laugh.

"It was me," Pesha said from the other side of the fire. He offered Fen an embarrassed look and shook his head. "I was chasing my brother. I didn't even see the fox."

Desemir snorted. "That's right. It bit you, didn't it?"

"On the ass," Pesha admitted.

Fen burst into laughter beside him.

"Have a scar to show for it."

"How about the scar, Pesh?" Wulf hollered. "I know at least one person here who'd like to see your ass."

"I resent the insinuation." Gisela teased him with an upturn of her nose. "Now Desi's ass..."

Everyone laughed.

"Sorry, Si."

"No apology required," Siofra said smoothly with a slow shake of her head. "Every other woman in the Darkwood has seen it."

"Come on now, just most of them," Desemir said, shaking her. He pulled a delighted giggle from her, which sent his heart into his throat.

"I've seen Pesha's ass," Euric said.

Desemir cocked his head. "Eh...?"

Siofra buried a snicker in his hair.

"I think it's about time for the gift exchange!" Pesha declared with a nervous sideways glance at Fen.

Everyone filtered in different directions to retrieve their gifts. Lotte and Gisela gathered the men together. Desemir caught Pesha urging Fen to follow him away from the bonfire.

Desemir took a swig of his mulled wine and lifted Siofra with him as he stood. He gingerly set her on the grass. "I have two gifts for you."

"Two?" Her eyes widened. "I have just one for you, but..." She bit her lip and checked to be sure they were alone before lowering her voice and saying, "Not here."

Desemir pressed his mouth tight with a groan. "You know just what to say to drive me right over the edge."

"That's the idea." She grinned.

"Well," Desemir said, brushing his forehead against hers as she stretched to the tips of her toes to kiss him. "You can show me in *our* bedchamber tonight."

Her lips stilled against his. "What?"

"I don't want..." He grunted through the inadequacy of his words. He was already fumbling. "No. This is about what I *do* want. And that's you, with me, every night. No separate bedchambers. No slipping out in the middle of the night like you don't belong there. No Pesha, huddling in the corner with his suspicions." Desemir wrapped his arms around her upper back. "I never want another woman who isn't my wife warming my bed."

Siofra dropped onto her heels and took a step back. "I'm not asking for that. I know I'm not..." She shook her head, lowering her eyes.

"Enough?" Desemir swallowed the painful lump in his throat, the reminder of how he'd once hurt her terribly with that word. "You *are* enough, Siofra. You were enough then, and you are now. It was me who couldn't see it."

Siofra kept her gaze on the grass. She raised one hand to her eyes. "You don't have to say things you don't mean. I'm not the same girl who came to Shadowfen Hall not knowing a thing about the world. I understand now. I can handle it."

Desemir slid his hand under her chin and lifted it. "I don't *want* anyone else in my bed but you. You're my wife. The mother of my future fifteen children."

Siofra laughed with a sniffle and averted her eyes.

Desemir whispered, "Hey. Look at me."

After a pause, she locked her eyes on his. Her chin quivered.

"You are my *wife*," he said again, firmer so she'd not just hear it but feel it. "Though we have ahead of us our darkest days and nights, as long as we are me and thee, our fire will illuminate the stars in our immortal sky."

"Our vows," she whispered.

"This is what I want. You. I want you. I want you with me *always*. And it leads me to your first gift." Desemir held his breath tight in his chest and dropped to his knees. He felt the others turn from their own gift exchanges to watch. "It's, well..." He reached into his pocket, almost fumbling the thin gold band. "It was unfair to ask you to wear my mother's ring, Siofra. It implies you are just the next in a long line, and you are not..." His voice caught. "You are not that."

Desemir pulled her hand forward. She'd worn his mother's ring at the ball, but otherwise her delicate fingers had been criminally bare. If he dwelt on it long enough, he'd know it as another failure in a long line of them.

But that was an old, tired way of looking at mistakes. It was far more compelling to consider the possibility of redemption.

"It's beautiful." Siofra drew in a sharp inhale. She splayed her fingers to allow him to slide it on. "Me and thee."

"Me and thee."

Gisela let out an excited whoop, and soon, the others joined in.

Siofra pulled Desemir to his feet with an embarrassed laugh. "Come on, get up."

"As for the other gift," he said, leaning down to whisper the words in her ear. "We'll save it for the bedchamber with yours."

"It's cold," Fen complained. "Where the devil are we going, anyway? There's no light out here except the moon, and it's covered by *clouds*. Can you even see, Pesha? Do *you* even know where you're going?" He ran his hands along his arms in dramatic strokes.

It was all Pesha could do to not laugh. Sweet Fen. *Neurotic* Fen.

And who does that sound like?

"It's always cold," Pesha replied, walking a pace ahead so Fen couldn't see the grin he could no longer bother to hide. "And we're almost there."

The walk around the property—down the long stretch of the east wing and back around—was longer than he remembered from the day before, when he'd trekked out to prepare Fen's present. Euric had grudgingly aided him by pulling the cart with his own hands, but Pesha was no longer feeling so grateful to the old guard after the little revelation he'd made in front of everyone.

"You and Euric... really?" Fen asked. His feet made loud tromps in the muddy field as he kept pace.

Was Fen reading his mind?

"Once," Pesha said with emphasis. The end of the word drove a hard swirl of cold air from his mouth. "And a mistake, *clearly*, if all it takes is a few swallows of whiskey to reveal the secret to everyone who knows us."

"Do you prefer older men?" Fen raised his voice to be heard over the escalating snow.

"I have no similar experience to compare it to," Pesha called back. He picked up his pace. "Almost there. Another few paces."

"But compared to your experiences with younger men..." Fen left his words hanging.

Pesha turned his answer into focus. He angled sideways as he pointed, turning back toward Fen. "Just up here."

Fen jogged to his side. "Wait... I... I'd like to go first. If it's okay."

Pesha stopped. He lifted his gaze to the moon and then swept it back to Fen with an anxious sigh. "All right."

Fen screwed his mouth up as he dug into his pocket. He squinted and mouthed, *Give me just a moment.* His eyes widened when his hand emerged. From it dangled a chain with something on the end.

Fen cleared his throat. He held the gift close to himself, and in the dim light, Pesha couldn't see what it was. "I've been thinking a lot. Thinking about how you and Eshe have such an unusual relationship. And, eh, if anyone understands *that,* it's the boy who was locked in a dungeon for most of his life." He chuckled nervously. "But though we adjust to the life we're given, that doesn't mean it isn't hard, does it? It doesn't mean a part of us isn't always fractured. Missing."

Pesha nodded.

"I know there's nothing you can do about the cold and what happens to the lake. But..." Fen thrust his fist outward. From it dangled what appeared to be a small rock, in the form of a misshapen star. It was wrapped in something. "When Si melted the lake, before it froze back over, I went in and... Well, it was *cold.*" He laughed to himself, his eyes cast downward. "But I retrieved a rock from the bottom. Took me a bit to find one I liked, but." Fen flexed his cheeks back and forth. "And Atio, he helped, even though the rocks he found were terrible. But it's why..." Fen dropped the necklace in Pesha's hand. "It's why you see a feather woven around the stone. It's Atio's. He was insistent."

351

Pesha's palm lay open. He couldn't close it. Couldn't bring his hand closer to his face for a better look. He could only stare at the cobbled-together effort born of his friendship with Fen—of Fen's giving heart, which had been dormant since Siofra's marriage.

"I know it's not much..." Fen shifted with a grimace. "I thought it might help you feel closer to Eshe. And now, saying it aloud..." He groaned. "It sounds silly."

"No. No, it's not silly. It's... It's wonderful, Stiofen." Pesha choked. He swallowed. "I mean it. It's perhaps the most thoughtful gift anyone has ever given me." He reached over his head and put the necklace on. The smooth rock, bound in Atio's deepbrown feather, settled just to the right of his heart. "Thank you."

Fen kicked at the ground. "Yours is going to put mine to shame, isn't it?"

"No, actually..." Pesha glanced down the field, at what he'd left for Fen. "I'm wondering if it's me who has miscalculated."

"Are we there?"

Pesha answered by making his way to the small sapling he'd planted the day before. It swayed, without the pull of roots, but that was the point of the gift.

Coming upon the moment where he'd need to explain that, Pesha had second thoughts.

"What is it?" Fen knelt by the thin protrusion of branches. The surrounding earth was a mess of loose soil. Fen brushed only the ends of his fingers along the thin branches. "It's going to be a tree, yes?"

"Do you know where you are?" Pesha asked. Speaking kept his heart rate centered, easy.

"What?"

"Look up."

Fen looked up but shook his head with a confused stare.

"You don't recognize those windows?" Pesha pointed. "Maybe it's because you're usually looking out of them."

Fen took in a breath and held it. "My bedchamber."

"Your bedchamber," Pesha replied. "When it's not so frightfully dark outside, you'll see the tree growing." He pushed through his fear—of heartache, of rejection, of all the things he'd steadfastly avoided for so many years—and said what he'd come to say. "This tree has no roots yet. It won't have them for months, if not years. This tree is *you*, Fen."

Fen's eyes were still on the sapling. "What?"

"You're the rootless tree. You came here for your sister, and now she's happy. She's safe and settled. Is that not what you wanted for her?"

"Yes, but..." Fen's hands dropped away from the tree.

"Now it's your turn." Pesha sucked in a breath and knelt beside him. "You can take this tree and plant it somewhere far from here and make it your home... the place *you* put down roots and find your own happiness."

"You want me to leave?"

"Or..." Pesha closed his eyes for the next words. "Or you can stay, and let this tree grow roots as you put down your own. You can *choose* to stay, not for Siofra but for yourself. So that you might discover your own future and happiness... wherever it might lead you."

Fen wrapped his arms tight. He continued to stare at the sapling, wordless. His face was unreadable, but his coiled tension was even less clear. Was it anger? Confusion? Disgust?

Pesha parceled his breaths, waiting for Fen to say something.

But then Fen launched his entire body at the tree. Pesha started forward but was thrown back by the force of light radiating off Fen.

"Back!" Fen cried. His arms swelled to the sides, his head falling back as he seemed to expand, to grow. The ground beneath them trembled, set to a series of loud cracks and snaps that sounded like boards splintering. Fen lifted off the ground and levitated several feet above it, then rose higher and higher.

Pesha shielded his eyes from the light, but he could see, through his fingers, the sapling rising, growing, *flourishing* into a fully grown tree.

The light died, and Fen went hurling to the ground, but Pesha broke his fall, catching him in his arms. They both rolled to the side, soaking their clothes in the wet field.

"Fen?" Pesha whispered, brushing blades of dry grass from his face. "Stiofen?"

"I used all my vigor." Fen's head flopped against Pesha's chest. "To grow that tree."

Pesha pinched his eyes to clear the tears. He trailed his gaze upward, to what was now a tree as tall as the ones holding court in the Darkwood. "I've never seen anything like that."

"Flourishment," Fen mumbled. His head lolled. "First time I've used it since Newcarrow."

"Does this mean you're staying?" Pesha asked. Tears rolled down his face. Landed on Fen.

"What else could it mean?" Fen asked and passed out in Pesha's arms.

Siofra had just slipped her hand into Desemir's to retire for the evening when Pesha called out. She looked back to see Fen half walking, half dangling from Pesha like a rag doll.

"What's wrong?" she cried and ran toward them. "Pesha, what—"

"He used his gift," Pesha said. He aimed a smile into the distance. "Willingly."

"What?" Siofra bent her knees to get a closer look at Fen. He grinned, buckling. "Why? And for what?"

"I'll let him tell you when he's feeling better," Pesha said. "But instead of resting, as he should be after such a display, your brother insisted he couldn't wait until morning to give you your gift."

"It most certainly *can* wait until morning," Siofra said in slowly growing horror. "He's completely spent. Look at him!"

Pesha handed Siofra a leather bag. She looked inside and saw dozens of papers, of vellum stacked and bowed with the frenzy of ink.

"What's this?" she asked. She flashed a look at Desemir, who was equally confused.

"Our history," Fen muttered. He climbed up Pesha's arm and forced himself to stand. His sway was enough for Pesha to hover close, his hands out and ready for anything.

"Our history?" Siofra asked. "What do you mean?"

"You've always said..." Fen's eyes rolled. Pesha's arms slid around his waist from behind. She noted the shift between the two men, saving it for later. "You've always said your memories of Mother and Father are stained. That you remember only the difficult parts and none of the good ones."

Siofra nodded. She eyed the bag and ran her fingers along the papers. "I... Yes, I suppose that's true."

"But it wasn't all bad, Si." Fen smiled, his eyes closing. "It wasn't. And so I wrote it all down. Every last memory I had of Mother and Father... and of you and of us, before everything changed."

Siofra's breath caught. "This must have taken you weeks. Months."

Fen's head rolled forward in a nod. "Months is right."

"I don't know what to say." Siofra felt Des's palm land on her lower back.

"You're happy." Fen slurred, rolling back against Pesha's chest. "You and this... man." He waved a finger. "Will have a long life and a big family. I'm happy you..." He grimaced and tried again. "I'm happy that you're happy."

"And you?" Siofra asked, still looking at her brother's bag of work. "Are you happy, Fen?"

"I'm content," he answered. "And that's enough."

Siofra tried to catch Pesha's eyes, but he was looking away.

"You deserve more than content," Siofra stated. "You deserve—"

"I didn't just do it for you, Si. I did it for your children. So they know their history. Where they came from."

Pesha dropped down to scoop Fen before he passed out entirely. He hoisted him into his arms with an apologetic brow

355

raise. "He should've given it to you earlier. I didn't know he was going to use his magic like that."

"And you won't tell me what happened," Siofra said.

"Even if I did..." Pesha smiled to himself. "I'm still trying to understand it myself."

"Take him to your bedchamber," Desemir said with a sly grin. "Let him sleep it off there."

"But you two are retiring, aren't you?"

"We are." Desemir lifted Siofra's hand to his mouth with a soft sigh. "But it's time for all of us to move forward. And that means you, brother. I don't need you tonight. And I won't need you any other night. Go on, and be happy."

Pesha's head tilted in skepticism. "But... she..."

"I'm happy," Siofra said. "And Des is happy. And as long as there's happiness between us, there is nothing to fear."

Pesha met Desemir's eyes over the top of her head, but whatever he saw caused him to back away. "If you're certain this is for the best..."

"I'm certain," Desemir replied. "Merry Wintertide, Pesh. Tonight marks a new beginning for us all."

"Merry Wintertide, Des. Si." Pesha tried to smile but turned halfway through the gesture and walked away with Fen in his arms.

THIRTY
MY LOVE

Desemir knotted his fingers through his wife's golden curls as she looked up at him with her wide, violet eyes. Her pretty little lips wrapped perfectly around his cock as she ran her mouth from tip to hilt and back, never lowering her gaze. Her tongue flitted along the underside, her eyes squinting into a satisfied grin with every twitch or moan she prompted from him.

"*Fuck* that's good." Desemir groaned. He pressed his other hand to the bedpost for purchase. "You've made a grave mistake, Siofra. I'll have you on your knees every night now."

Siofra gurgled her response as she kneaded her fingers into his cheeks to drive him deeper.

"Guardians. *Fuck*," he said again, watching the wide O her mouth made to take in the girth of his swollen cock. He was so hard for her. He'd never been so hard for anyone. "If you don't stop, you'll have a mouthful of me soon."

Siofra's mouth twitched into a grin, and she rammed her face all the way to the base. Touching the back of her throat dissolved the remainder of his willpower. He tried to pull away, but her hands were latched on his ass, her eyes tilted upward in anticipation. She swirled her tongue faster on the underside, tightening her mouth.

Desemir sagged as he spasmed, spilling his seed along the back of her tongue and down her throat. She didn't relent at all, locking his groin to her face as if she knew there was more, and there was. His cock jerked another release and then he stumbled away from her.

Siofra, still on her knees, looked up at him with her wide violet eyes and swallowed.

Desemir's cock twitched. When she licked her lips, leaving a glistening trail on the outside, he almost came again.

"Merry Wintertide, Desemir," she purred.

Desemir lifted her to her feet and spun her around to face the bed. He took her wrists in his hands and slid them up the bedpost until her arms were stretched over her head. "You move them even an inch, and I'll punish you."

Siofra turned her head back, dropping her chin on her shoulder. "Have you not realized by now that I enjoy punishment?"

Desemir tilted her hips up and slid his cock inside in one fluid move. She was so wet, there was no resistance, and it made him harder, made him want her all the more, knowing how much *she* wanted *him*. He rocked into her with decisive thrusts, relishing the strangled, scratchy moans she sounded with each impact. "What happened to your smart little mouth? Still want to be punished?"

Siofra stretched her long, lithe body down from the post, arcing her ass even higher—a challenge. "Oh, was *that* the punishment?"

Desemir shoved into her with enough force to dislodge her hands from the post. She re-tightened them, but he came at her again and again, enjoying her struggle.

"You're adorable." Her words were pushed out of her with force. "So sweet."

Desemir grunted and dug his fingers into her small hips, fucking her so hard, he felt his own groin bruise when it crashed against her ass. Her cries faltered, but she showed no sign of wanting him to slow, to stop. His head fell onto her shoulder with the weight of his desire, and he saw that with each forward movement, she brushed herself against the post, adding to her pleasure.

"Harder, harder, *harder*," she whimpered as she came all over him.

He spread Siofra's ass wide with his palms, watching her take him in, her wetness covering everything. "It's like you want me to split you in half." He grunted, granting her wish and taking her with such force, he thought he *might* split her in half, and with it, himself.

"At last, you understand me." She moaned, and Desemir crumbled into her with the weight of his orgasm. He wrapped his arms around her, around the post, his sweaty torso sliding against her back as he dropped to his knees, taking her with him to the floor.

Siofra rolled and straddled him. Her face was splotched with red, mouth parted with the lingering throes of pleasure.

Desemir tucked his hand between her legs and twisted, just as she liked. The spot was so swollen, he feared it would be too sensitive to his touch, but Siofra licked her lips, eyes fluttering back with a long moan as she rode his hand. It didn't take long before she bucked and cried out, coming again. His cock jolted against her ass, wanting more, *so* much more, but what he wanted most before the day turned to the next was to simply hold her.

She fell into his arms, and he pressed her face to his heart.

"You said... There was something else you wanted to give me." She panted her words against his damp flesh. Her knee slid up, brushing the underside of his cock.

"Offer you, more like," Desemir said. His tired hand brushed her nude back, unable to form more than random paths and circles. "I know you were disappointed when Wulf wouldn't come to your bed."

She tensed in his arms.

"My offer, Si, if he's up for it, is for you to have one night with us both." Desemir's heart raced with the words, which sounded

359

so much different aloud than they had in his head. "Both of us together, at the same time. With you."

"I..." Siofra rolled her face atop his chest. "I don't know."

"You don't have to answer now."

"If you're offering because you..." She caught her breath. "Because you think you're not enough for me, then I refuse."

"No," Desemir whispered into her hair. "That's not why I'm offering."

"Then why?" She angled her face up to look at him.

"I want to satisfy you, Siofra." He moved his face down to kiss her. "In every way. In *any* way. You aren't like the other women I've known. You don't fear your desire."

"Why should I?" she asked, defensive.

Desemir laughed. "You shouldn't. They could learn from you, to know what they want and how to ask for it."

"I'll think about it," she said after a careful pause. "Are you happy?"

Desemir was rooted by her question. "I think my heart might explode if I find myself any happier."

"Do you still think you don't deserve this?"

He fell silent. He might have lied to her once, but things were different. "What I think, Siofra, is that I'll keep working to earn this, to earn you."

Desemir peeled away and settled her gently onto the bearskin. He lowered his face to her belly and peppered kisses there. "And you, little one. I work for *you*. I'll be working my hardest to deserve this very honorable job."

Siofra erupted in giggles as he continued his kisses and his silly words, things he'd never have had the courage to say before her, before *this*.

"I love you so much already," Desemir said to his unborn son or daughter.

"Our children will have no grandparents," Siofra said. "Perhaps it's for the best, since neither of us has fond memories of our own parents."

"Mm," Desemir agreed. He pressed his face at the base of her belly arc.

"Perhaps we should though. Learn to speak of them." Siofra wound her fingers through his hair, sighing. "For the sake of our children and their children, we should learn to tell those stories. To feel safe in repeating what has haunted us for so long."

"I'll try," Desemir said. It was the most he could offer.

"Are you afraid our children will turn out like them? Like your father or my parents?"

"I don't know," Desemir said. It felt like a confession, a revealing of a long-buried fear. "I don't know if such things pass in the blood. The evil of Ludwik..."

His words lingered in the air.

"They'll never lack for love, anyway, will they?" Siofra asked with a hopeful sigh. "Fen and Pesha. Lotte, Gisela, Wulf, and the others."

"They'll never lack for anything at all." Desemir closed his eyes and exhaled a warm breath against her flesh. "Happy Wintertide, Siofra." He looked up from her belly and opened his eyes. Locked them on hers. "My love."

Her chest rose and fell in a soft shudder. "My love," she answered.

Desemir rolled to his side and nuzzled his face against her belly. He let one arm fall over her, which she took, lacing into hers, and with a long sigh of contentment, he embraced the soothing end to the best day of his life.

THIRTY-ONE
FAMILIAR

Siofra woke with her face stuck to Desemir's bare chest. Cool air swept into the room, courtesy of the still-open balcony doors. She peeled herself off him and saw the carnage of scattered clothes and the half-drank carafe of the mulled wine Lotte had made for the holiday. Half, because he didn't want to drink her part when she couldn't. The bag containing the Thornheart history hung from the back of a chair pushed back from the table.

Memories from the night before completed the story.

A glance between the gap in the gauzy curtains revealed it was still night. Hopeful to slip easily back into slumber, Siofra groaned and returned to her spot, nuzzling into the crook of Desemir's arm.

Desemir snored softly, unbothered by her nocturnal awakening.

A sharp wail ripped Siofra back up off the bed. She heard it again and then again, and she understood what had pulled her from a perfectly sound sleep.

It was the same sound that had come from the west wing months before. The same one Pesha had so vehemently deterred her from exploring.

She glanced at her husband. He had one hand over his head, the other stretched out for her return. She *should* return to his arms, forget she'd heard anything. Did she care who it was or why? Did it matter when everything else was as it should be *finally*? Some things were not her business in Shadowfen Hall, and she'd made peace with it.

But Siofra's attention was again torn to the sound.

It was distinctly female.

It's not your business, Si.

Leave it.

With a rueful sigh trapped in her chest, Siofra slipped out of bed and fumbled for her robe. She checked Desemir again, but he was as still as stone, his mouth parted in the slow, rhythmic breathing of deep rest.

You're enough. You've always been enough.

Leave it. Leave it and return to him. Nothing good can come from you sneaking around where you don't belong.

You said he could have his secrets.

Leave it.

Leave it.

I hear pain. How many ignored my pain over the years as they passed the Stanhopes' keep?

Who am I, if I do the same?

Siofra jogged on her toes toward the door with one last look back.

Stop me, Des. Stop me from doing this, and I will.

Tell me why I shouldn't help whoever is behind those cries.

Tell me this is wrong.

But Desemir didn't wake. He didn't stop her.

And as she pulled gently on the door, slowing its opening to avoid its telltale creak, she realized if he *had* woken, had tried to stop her, it would have only motivated her more.

Cassius stirred outside the door with a look of shock.

"Siofra." He glanced out the tall windows at the darkness. "Is everything all right? Did you need something?"

"Cassius," she said with a cordial nod. She looked past him, down the hall and toward the sound. "I'm going into the west wing. You're not going to stop me. You're not going to call for Euric or Wulf. You're not going to wake Des, because he's sleeping so deeply, it would be a crime to disturb him even for a moment."

Panic flashed across his face, widening his eyes. "I really don't think it's a good idea, Siofra. The west wing is off-limits."

"You may join me," Siofra said. "Or not. But I'm going, and if you get in my way, you'll discover a side of me few have seen, and even less are still around to speak of."

Cassius swallowed. His cheek twitched with a nervous look. "No one is allowed down there."

Siofra tilted her head. "Do *you* know what's down there? Pardon me, *who* is down there?"

"No," he said quietly, letting the word trail. "But Euric does. Wulf does. And they have been extraordinarily clear with me that no one is to go down there who is not authorized. It's for your own safety, Baroness." He cleared his throat. "Probably rotted floorboards. It happens in houses this old."

Siofra half laughed. "You mean to tell me you didn't hear the crying? The crying that must have been so much louder to someone sitting in this hall than it was for me in the bedchamber?"

Cassius offered a flummoxed look in lieu of a lie.

"Right. Well, I have eyes. If the floorboards are rotted, I'll be sure to step around them."

He flicked his palms outward. "I don't want to get on your bad side, but if I let you walk into danger, Des would have my head on one of the pikes lining the road."

"Very well. Then you're coming. I insist." Siofra marched ahead without waiting for another simpering, weak rebuttal. But Cassius was a man beholden to order, and she'd issued one. He'd follow.

The cries grew louder as she neared the break in the hall that led to the west wing. She was officially as far as she'd ever gone. Once she rounded the corner, there would be no turning back, no way for her to pretend she was following anyone's whims but her own.

"Guardians," Cassius whispered when they turned left and entered the west wing.

They made their way down the hall, an endless row of doors identical to the east wing in almost every way. All but for the sound of a woman crying out for aid without answer.

Near the end of the hall, she stopped. The sound came from her right. She turned back toward Cassius. "Stay out here, or come in, but you don't leave this wing until I do."

Dread tinted Cassius's face as he nodded.

Siofra opened the door. A wail pierced her ears. She clamped both of her hands over them to dull the ringing, but then some-one—Lieken, it was *Lieken*—tried to usher her back out, rambling about danger and Desemir and all manner of things she couldn't make out with the high whine stabbing her head.

"You can't... You don't understand... Des, he didn't mean... It wasn't intentional... Her familiar, she lost her mind... He didn't mean..."

Siofra opened her mouth, and a melody escaped. She lowered her hands in shock. She hadn't meant to sing. There'd been no red wall, no warning, no *tickle*.

Lieken was unhurt physically, but the terror in his eyes indicated another kind of agony.

He flattened himself against the wall and slid away, leaping into the hall. He screamed at Cassius, who flailed his hands, trying to calm him.

Siofra closed the door and shut them both out.

She entered a richly decorated bedchamber—gilt everything, from the decor to the furniture, even the swirling friezes stamped into the ceiling. At the other side was a bed, covered on all four sides by curtains. One of them was half-open, but from where she stood, Siofra could not see what—who—lay beyond.

The wailing stopped. The source of it seemed to lie in wait. Siofra approached the bed, one hand covering her belly, ignoring the warning thrum of her heart as she stepped closer to a truth that could change her life forever.

Des... He didn't mean... It wasn't intentional.

Her familiar.

She lost her mind.

Siofra inhaled a painful, shuddering breath and approached the opening in the curtain.

She stopped breathing.

Her heart seemed to stop as well.

Before her lay another Medvedev. Her green hair was braided back off her face, but half had torn free, and her eyes, the very same color, flashed with wild accusation. Her nightgown was rent down the middle, half on, half stuck to the bed. Feathers were strewn all around, from a discarded pillow on the floor, ripped to shreds.

The female opened her mouth and screamed. Her eyes stayed open, watching. The sound had a practiced feel, like a defense that had always worked.

When Siofra did nothing but gape, the female Medvedev closed her mouth.

She tugged at her disheveled braids.

Her eyes darted around like a frog. She shrieked one wail and then another.

Des.

He didn't mean.

It wasn't intentional.

Her familiar.

She lost her mind.

Siofra's melody broke in her throat. There was no song here to be sung. No chorus adequate for the lamentations of this poor creature—who had been severed from her familiar, it seemed so clear, when nothing else was—whose torment had never ended.

Desemir did this.

He trapped this poor Medvedev here.

He killed her familiar.

He ruined her.

Just like he said he'd ruin you.

Siofra backed up, her feet carrying her farther away from the broken Medvedev lying askew in the bed.

When she hit the wall, the force shoved a scream from her throat.

She sank to her knees and screamed and screamed and screamed until there were no other sounds, no sights, no room, no west wing, and no Desemir.

Familiar

THE WEST WING

372

THIRTY-TWO
FROZEN IN TIME

Desemir slumped on the floor beside his bed with the bottle of whiskey Euric had left for him earlier in the day.

Earlier in the day. The words had a casual ring, as if the day had been like any other. As if Siofra's horrified screams had not rung through the floors and walls and rafters of Shadowfen Hall with the might of an unquenchable fire.

Pesha wore out the same path he'd been pacing for hours, tracking a perfect line. For once, the man with endless opinions had no words, and if Desemir could dredge up even a sliver of humor, he would have happily pointed it out.

But Desemir's voice was gone too. His own screams had taken it, as Pesha and Fen had used their vigor to subdue the wildling that the terrible revelation had turned his wife into—as Cassius and Euric had pinned him on the bed like a conquest so he could not go to her.

And say what?

What words could he add to soften what she'd seen?

Desemir rolled the empty bottle into the corner and tried to stand. Pesha brightened at something to do and rushed over to help him.

"I just need to piss," Desemir grumbled and shooed him off. He stumbled sideways, making a zigzagged path toward the privy in the back of his bedchamber. Pesha maddeningly followed.

"You think I'm going to drown myself in privy water?"

"Can't be certain you won't."

"My pride would prevent such an unseemly exit." Desemir gripped the door to the privy and ambled in. "Hurling myself from the balcony is more in line with my temperament."

"I *told* you she was waking up—"

"And I told you to find Lotte!" Desemir tried three times to extricate his organ, and finally Pesha reached forward with a disgusted scoff and shook his pants loose for him, then stepped back in a huff. Desemir glared over his shoulder.

"The magic has worn off, Desemir."

"Desemir." Desemir made a face. He winced. "You really are cross with me."

"Because you aren't listening!" Pesha smacked the door with his palm. "The magic has *worn off*. Perhaps not entirely but enough that she's *awake* now, Des, do you understand? Lotte's draughts did nothing before, so they won't do anything now. In case you'd forgotten, it's why we hunted down the so-called enchanter and had them spin the spell. Well, it's *gone*, and so is the enchanter, and seeing as no one here knows how to repair or replace the ward, here we are!"

Desemir sagged into the relief when the stream at last started. His hand shook, creating a mess. It seemed fitting. He half expected the stone to crumble off the walls, the friezes to break into jagged, ugly reminders of a once-great manor. "This day was always going to come."

"Then what do you suggest we do about it?" Pesha lowered his voice. "We can't let what happened before happen again. She'll destroy herself. We promised..." His voice choked with emotion. "We promised we wouldn't *ever* let that happen."

Desemir finished at the privy and turned. "I know." His eyes lowered. He collapsed against the doorframe with a defeated cry. "I just..." He met Pesha's eyes with a tight smile. "I thought we had more time, you know?"

Pesha lowered his head with a heavy nod. "I did too."

"And Si... Is she... all right?"

Pesha sucked in a breath with a glance at the doors. "I don't know. Gisela and Fen are with her, and..."

Desemir nodded in sudden understanding. "And Fen isn't speaking to you either, is he?"

Pesha shook his head.

"The tree was a lovely gesture. I'm sorry it was overshadowed by what happened after," Desemir said. He pushed away from the door and almost dropped to his knees, but he was saved by a chair he gripped before he went all the way down. He remembered why he disliked being drunk.

"What, you think..." Pesha followed him. "You think I would allow you to shoulder all the blame for this? I know you have anyway, Des. I *know* what haunts your nightmares, because it haunts mine too. Do you think I sleep any better?"

Desemir glanced back, over his shoulder. "Perhaps we don't deserve sleep. Either of us."

"Why do you insist—" Pesha ran his hands down his face as he shook it. "All these years and you still believe... you still cannot separate yourself from our father. Will you ever?"

Desemir landed half on the bed. He tried to pull himself up onto it but slid back to the ground, where he decided to stay. "We'll find another enchanter."

Pesha sighed. "Maybe it's time, Des."

"Time for *what*?"

"To find another way to relieve her misery."

Desemir didn't miss Pesha's small whimper of pain that followed.

"She's one of us," Desemir stated. "One of us, and she deserves the best we can give her, whatever it is."

"*Years* frozen in time! Years! That was the best we could give her? And now you want to give her even *more*?"

"What else was there?" Desemir howled. "Your mother was gone! Naos, gone! What other Medvedev had the knowledge we needed to save her?"

Pesha spun and wrapped his arms around himself. "Then I'll leave." His shoulders shook. "Tomorrow. I'll try the Easterlands, the border towns. Sometimes men like that can be found in the taverns. I'll see... There has to be someone. We can't ask the Sepulchre..."

"Guardians no," Desemir said with a hard exhale. "I don't know, Pesh. I don't know anymore. I know no more than I did eight years ago. Was it right, what we did?"

"Was it *right*?" Pesha asked, spluttering. "Nothing has *ever* been right since that day, no matter how much we both tried to pretend it was."

Desemir's face contorted as he staved off another obnoxious, unhelpful bout of tears. "Siofra made everything right again. But that was an illusion too, wasn't it? Another poor attempt to assuage an old wound."

Pesha's silence bloated the air. "She's brought out a side of you I thought I'd never see again. She's..." He leaned against the table and rolled his head backward with a sigh. "Do you love her? I used to trust my senses, and I *see* love from you, from her, but right now my senses are damaged. So do you? Love her? Is love what this is, this thing that's changed you, turned you into the brother I used to know?"

Desemir closed his eyes and nodded once. Speaking was impossible.

Pesha dropped to the floor and crawled toward him. "Then you must tell her everything. All of it."

"Tell her?" Desemir asked in horror. "She's carrying our *child*, Pesh. I don't want to cause even more harm to her or the baby."

"Everything," Pesha said again. "You were never going to be able to keep this hidden forever. It was always going to come down to this. But the horrors of our past do not have to lay their stain over the whole of our future."

"They already have."

"What if she can help?"

"How could she help?"

"She's Medvedev," Pesha said.

"Like you, she hardly even knows what that *means.*"

"What if..." Pesha leaned into him, nuzzling against his arm. "What if I could somehow find the Asgill lands?"

Desemir looked down at him with a frown. "We've talked about this. Your mother and Naos were banished from those lands. How can you know they won't hold you in the same regard?"

"There is no way of knowing other than to try. I'm not my mother. I wasn't there when they tried to rise up against their chieftainess. I wasn't *there,* and unless they're a terrible, vengeful people, they have to know there's a difference."

Desemir shook his head.

Pesha sighed against his brother's shoulder. "For now, we'll have Lotte up the draughts. Maybe they do nothing, but they may buy me time to bring someone back who can offer a more powerful relief." He half smiled. "Tell Siofra the truth. She has her own demons, Des. She might be the one woman who will understand and embrace yours."

"*Desemir!*"

Desemir and Pesha both scrambled to their feet, climbing up the side of the bed at the violent intrusion.

Wulf hovered just inside the half-flung door, his cheeks ablaze, one hand on his sword, ready to draw it.

"Wulf?" Pesha scoffed and stepped around Desemir. "What's gotten into you?"

Wulf scowled. His breathing shook his chest and shoulders. "My business isn't with you, Pesha. Step aside."

Pesha recoiled. "Not until you calm down."

377

"You *lied* to her, Desi!" Wulf screamed, raising a fist and wagging it past Pesha. "I thought for sure... I thought for *sure* you'd told her, because how could you marry her with such a secret between you? How could you keep *that* from her?"

Pesha took a step forward. "Wulf—"

"It's all right," Desemir said, though it wasn't all right. He could hardly walk. His head swam with thoughts that came nowhere near his lips. "Wulfie..."

"I have always known who you are, Desi. Always! *And I didn't care.* Because you were my best mate, and you were only hurting yourself," Wulf cried. His voice strained through the words. "But Siofra? She deserves better. She deserves..." His throat flexed. "Guardians damn you, Desi. You couldn't resist breaking her in the same way you've been breaking yourself, all these years."

Desemir flicked his gaze upward, at the elaborate carvings in the ceiling. "She does deserve better. On this we agree."

"You stay away from her." Wulf's chin trembled as he issued the warning. His sword hand rolled around the hilt. "You come anywhere near her, and I'll *run you through.*"

"You threaten my brother again, and you'll take your last breath right here," Pesha hissed. "You *dare* come in here, Wulfhelm, and say such things, to *Desemir*—"

"It's all right," Desemir said again. He lowered his head, and the room spun into violent upheaval. He steadied himself with a hard breath. "I'm glad she has you, Wulfie. Because you're right. She deserves someone who isn't broken. Someone who isn't ruined, as I am. And I won't be going anywhere near Siofra because..." Desemir turned away. "I just won't."

"I'm holding you to it," Wulf promised. "I'll have Euric send you a whole crate of that whiskey you've come to love. It will keep you from doing something foolish. For what it's worth, I don't consider *drowning yourself to death* to be a foolish choice."

"Wulfhelm Kruger, you are relieved of service." Pesha charged forward. "You will lay down your sword and leave Shadowfen Hall immediately."

"No," Desemir said. He wrapped his hand around the nearest bedpost. "No. Siofra likes him. She trusts him. He'll stay, for her."

"Des, he has made himself known he is no longer loyal to you!"

"He is loyal," Desemir replied. "But not to me. And he would be doing me one final, essential service in looking after my wife when I no longer can."

Pesha spun away in fury.

"I'll look after her," Wulf said with a disgusted sneer. "Though I doubt you'll be very grateful for the services *I* provide." His eyes narrowed with a joyless grin. "The services I will no longer refuse her out of some displaced loyalty to a monster unworthy."

"I still can't believe it. You're sure she was Medvedev?" Fen huddled next to Siofra on the bed. She'd said little in hours, not responding to most of his questions. She seemed gone from the room. Away. Though, it was not the same as her escapes into darkness. She was there, with him, but unable to filter through her words and thoughts for something useful.

Or unwilling, he thought, which felt more accurate.

"Yes." Her voice, low and scratchy, surprised him. "Her hair, Fen... It was this brilliant green. I know terrestrial Medvedev have green hair and eyes, but there's nothing in this kingdom that comes close to her color. It's preternatural. Like... like the way our violet is unique, or Pesha's blue."

"And she didn't speak at all?"

"She communicated in screams and wails. I don't think..." Siofra wiped at her tearless eyes. "I don't think she *can* speak, Fen. Something terrible happened to her. Not even Lieken could put it to words. Only that it was Des..." She hung her head and wrapped her arms tight around her chest.

Fen held her. Her pain became his pain, as had often been true throughout their childhood. He *felt* her heartbreak. Her loss of a great love and a life that had made her happy. Her fear for the child growing within her, whom she had to put before all and everyone else.

Though she claimed this had extinguished her love for Desemir, there was stronger evidence to the contrary.

Fen understood two competing things were true.

Siofra and Desemir loved one another deeply.

That same love would keep Desemir from trying to salve the hurt he'd caused, and it would keep Siofra from exposing herself to the potential for further pain.

"There must be some reasonable explanation," Fen said absurdly. Both Desemir and Pesha had been hiding a terrible, terrible secret, and Siofra wasn't the only one wounded in the revelation.

Siofra sniffled. "If there was a reasonable explanation, the west wing would not have been off-limits. We would have been told there was a fractured Medvedev locked away in the disused side of the Hall, which is awful on its own, but why hide it unless the reason was so horrible you had no choice?"

"I'm glad you came to me last night," Fen said. "Instead of letting your red wall... You know..."

Siofra spun around and looked right at him. "There *was* no wall last night, Fen. No tickle. Only this... this raw fear, for my daughter. That if I were to give in to anything I didn't wholly control, I would be putting her at grave risk. My song last night was fleeting and muted."

Fen latched on to the sole piece of joy in her words. "Daughter?"

"I don't know. It's just what I feel." Siofra returned to looking ahead.

"You're saying she... She stilled your red wall?"

She shrugged. "Or destroyed it altogether. I don't know."

"But is this not a good thing?"

She laced her hands in her lap, opening her palms outward. "What does it change, Fen? I killed those men in Newcarrow. I killed Mother and Father—"

"You did *not* kill Mother and Father," Fen replied in a rush. A horrible revelation stole over him. "Si, you've repeated this lie enough for me to realize you actually mean it, don't you? You don't mean in a metaphorical sense?"

Siofra stared at him in horror. "It was *my* red wall. I exposed us, and they took them both away because of me!"

"It was *not*," Fen said roughly. "It was *not*, Si. I was there. I remember things you don't, because of all your mind has kept from you. It was *Mother* who erred. She attempted to heal a woman who'd endured a terrible birthing. The woman died. And then, in his grief and anger, her husband reported Mother and Father to the authorities."

"No." Siofra shook her head. "No, no. That's not how it happened. I was walking down the road, and this man accosted Mother—"

"He was the man who reported her," Fen said. "He was convinced she could raise his wife from the dead. When she said she couldn't..." His chest seized with sorrow. "He had them both arrested for stealing. *Stealing.* He told us..." Fen swallowed, then inhaled sharply. "To run. To run fast and far, or we'd be gathered up and punished with them."

"But we saw... We watched Mother and Father hang."

"Yes," Fen said. He pinched off a rising sob. "Yes, Si. We did watch. We went back. But there was nothing we could do to save them."

"Mother didn't die immediately! We could have healed her."

"Mother's neck snapped." Fen lowered his eyes. "I saw it. I heard it. I still hear it. It was the stewardess who found us and ushered us away."

"But she was alive. I saw her..."

"I don't know what you saw," Fen said, sighing, "but she was dead on impact."

"But then I..." Siofra's head turned, mouth parted in recollection. "Did I not... Did I not kill everyone in the square?"

Fen shook his head. "I don't know why you remember it that way. I wish I could get inside your head and fix it. But you did nothing wrong. *Nothing.*" Fen gathered her tighter. "You might not remember your dark spots, but *I* do. I was there for every last one of them. And the only lives you have ever taken are from that terrible Gawain and his friend, and only because you had no choice."

Siofra shook her head. Her tears streamed freely now. "No, there were others—"

"You were lied to," Fen answered. "*Lied to* by those who could only control you by instilling into you a fear of yourself. I tried to tell you so many times, but you never believed me. I was afraid to push too hard, to drive you even further into your head and make it worse. I just wanted to help you."

"You're the only one who ever helped me for the right reasons," Siofra said through her tears. She nuzzled against his neck. "We should never have come here. I should have listened to you. I should have—"

The door swung open. Wulf stood in the threshold with a wild expression that Fen knew immediately was not for him.

"Can we talk?" Wulf said, his voice strained. "Alone?"

"Si?" Fen asked.

"It's fine," she said distantly. "I'll find you again after."

Fen shifted his glance between his sister and a visibly agitated Wulf. "Are you sure?"

Siofra nodded.

Fen pecked a tentative kiss on her cheek and threw a warning look at Wulf on his way out.

Siofra stood just as Wulf kicked the door closed behind him. His mouth parted, unburdened by words. He unhooked his sword belt and laid it over a chair, never breaking eye contact with her. Piece by piece, he peeled away his outer armor, leaving only his cloth undergarments.

Her heart raced with confusion. It was already so full of emotion, she feared it would burst altogether before the day ended.

Wulf charged forth and gathered her in his arms. His mouth crushed hers in a rage-filled kiss that called to her own wrath.

"I should never have left you feeling abandoned by me." Wulf passed his mouth back and forth against hers with his words. His cock throbbed against her belly. "I was supposed to protect you. I won't ever make that mistake again."

Siofra met his eyes with mired confusion. She *had* wanted him. And a part of her still did, but...

But what?

Her conflict shifted when he hoisted her onto the bed and bunched her dress in his fist as he brushed it upward.

Wulf's hand disappeared under her undergarment. Her head fell back in a swoon. She smothered her resistance in the veil of her pain, which was so consuming, the only escape from it was to give it a name and pretend it was another creature entirely, separate of her.

He climbed over the top of her and stole her moans with more kisses.

Siofra reached for the thin fabric covering his lower half. Her hand encircled the bulge throbbing for release. All she had to do was pull down from the waist and free him. Nothing else separated them from the moment they were in and the one that would change their relationship forever, make it binding and real.

Wulf's crystal-blue eyes swam with desire as his hand stilled, awaiting her move.

Why now?

Why has he suddenly changed his mind about wanting you?

Siofra whimpered at the tease of his touch. Her fingertips rested just inside his waistband, hesitating.

This is important, Siofra. This is your life.

And why should I care about his reasons? Are these men not all the same? Fickle liars, who want only one thing from me?

Desemir loves you.

Desemir is a monster.

A monster who loves you.

Wulf, panting, reached down to do what Siofra had not. He tugged at the band and freed himself.

He's waiting for me to tell him it's okay.

That it's what I want.

All I have to do is smile or reach down to help him, show him I can take my pleasure where I want it. That I no longer belong to anyone but myself.

Ahh, but it would be a lie, wouldn't it?

"Siofra?" Wulfhelm whispered, ragged. "Is everything... Are you all right?"

Siofra pushed gently on his chest and rolled away, breathless. "No. I can't... I can't do this."

I don't want this.

I don't want this with you.

Wulfhelm stumbled back from the bed, fumbling for his clothing. "Guardians. I don't know what came over me. Forgive me, Siofra. I was just so..." He slid into his trousers and stopped, leaning against the wall.

"Angry?" she asked. She tugged her dress back down.

"Angry is an insufficient replacement for the right word," he said. He slumped onto a chair. "Desemir has always been—" He bowed his head. "He shouldn't have brought you here under such deception."

Siofra straightened the rest of the bumps in her dress and sat forward. "But *you* knew, didn't you? About the Medvedev in the west wing?"

Wulf hesitated and then nodded. "It wasn't my place to tell you."

Siofra willed the flush in her cheeks away and pointed at the door. "Leave me."

He looked up in surprise. "What?"

"Leave me!" Siofra cried, leaping from the bed. "You dare speak against Desemir when you kept his secret all this time? You talk of honor and friendship and love, when you *knew* what he was hiding? How are you any better? How is it any less of a lie?"

"Siofra, I thought you knew—"

"Leave me!" she screamed. "Leave me, and tell all the others to leave me, because then at least I can embrace what I should have known all along—that I'm *alone* here. There is no one but Fen who cares a whit about my well-being, or honor, or love, or rage, or deceptions. I don't want any of it! Leave me, Wulfhelm, before..."

"Before you kill me?" he said with a wounded look. "Yes, Si, I know what you can do. I was there that night, remember?"

"How dare you look at me like *I'm* the monster." Siofra charged forward. "Well. Anyone who comes through this door who isn't my brother will get exactly the monster you all believe me to be."

THIRTY-THREE
EVERY LAST DROP OF MY BLOOD

Fen half expected Euric to turn him away from Desemir's bed chamber. But he only grunted and resumed his vigil against impending disaster.

A sudden unwelcome image of him in bed with Pesha smacked Fen. He shook his head to clear it.

"Is he in there?"

"Who?" Euric asked.

Fen might have laughed in another circumstance. "Desemir."

Euric nodded. He stretched his arm backward in an almost unnatural way and knocked three times. His arm retracted, and he returned to pretending Fen wasn't there.

Fen smirked in confusion just as Pesha answered the door.

His face fell.

Pesha's lit up, as though loading words he'd been readying all day.

"No," Fen said and brushed past him, avoiding his eyes. A dull ache rolled across his chest as he felt Pesha's hurt gaze follow him. "I didn't come here for you. I'm here to see your brother."

Pesha's hesitance bloated the space between them. Fen wanted to turn—oh how *badly* he wanted to turn—and demand an explanation from the one person he'd felt truly safe with at Shadowfen Hall.

But he couldn't.

Pesha sighed.

Fen paused but didn't look back. "Don't. Just... don't."

Pesha sighed again. "I'll give you two some privacy. That all right, Des?"

"Why not?" Desemir called from some unseen place.

Fen winced when the door closed with Pesha's departure. He searched for the man he'd come to see.

"Balcony," Desemir said. Fen's eyes caught movement and spotted Desemir's waving arm. The man was slumped forward over the edge. He wore nothing but a shirt, which barely covered his ass.

"You want me to find you a robe?" Fen asked from the room, trying not to look.

"Why?"

"Are you not cold?"

"Cold?" Desemir leaned his head back as if sniffing the air. "Not especially, no."

"I'm coming out," Fen announced.

"I assumed as much," Desemir replied. He swung back off the edge and dropped onto the chaise. Fen saw only the man's feet propped on the arm until he stepped through the doorway.

Desemir had a blanket tugged over his waist. "This better, Stiofen? Not quite so distracting for you?"

"Your naked ass doesn't distract me," Fen answered. "Because I'm not attracted to you."

Desemir seemed surprised. "I'm objectively the better-looking brother."

"Also, objectively, the more damaged one," Fen said back. "Pesha is damaged too, in a different way."

Desemir closed his eyes. "How is she?"

"Siofra? She's..." Fen whistled as he exhaled. "Not well. She's hurt. Afraid. Lost for purpose, for reason. She isn't the only one, but I didn't come here for myself."

Desemir's jaw stretched into a tight line. His chin dimpled.

"You can still make this right," Fen said. He hardly recognized himself. He had a chance to show Siofra she'd made a terrible mistake, to convince her to leave and start over. But convincing *himself*... that leaving was what she needed, what he needed... It was an exhausting battle he was tired of fighting.

"What last night has taught me, Stiofen..." Desemir's words were languid, measured. In between them was the pain he was trying to hide. "Is that there's no fixing this."

"Fixing what?" Fen took a hard step outside. "Whatever it is, it cannot be so bad that the truth is worse than whatever Siofra is imagining."

"What if it could though? Be that bad?"

"Her own truth isn't all light and sunshine either, you know." Fen moved to the balcony, searching instinctively for Atio. The instinct was fresh, like the treasured bond that had strengthened in their months here. One thing Fen knew undeniably: he would never again take the bond for granted. Never again be anywhere he could not be with his familiar. "It's bleak enough that I fear for her if she ever leaves this place and tries to make it on her own."

Desemir shot forward. "She's not thinking of leaving, is she?"

"I don't know," Fen admitted. "She didn't use to keep things from me. Ever since we've come here..." He shook his head and exhaled. "I don't mean for it to sound like an accusation. I'm glad Siofra has discovered her own mind. It's been a joy for me to observe the evolution of her courage, her fierceness. But you asked me if she's thinking of leaving. I honestly don't know. And it's because I don't know that I'm here now, prepared to *beg* you to make this right with her."

"If there were a place..." Desemir settled back down. "A place I could go, where she'd never have to see me again... where I could still keep her safe from my enemies here..."

"You'd run, you mean," Fen accused. "You'd continue to run to avoid facing her."

Lines appeared at the sides of Desemir's mouth. "I promised to *protect* your sister, Stiofen. I have neglected this promise."

"You nearly burned *an entire village* to the ground to save her!"

"I regret that I did not." Desemir strained the words through his teeth. "For I would rather feel the pain of *that* horror than the one afflicting our house right now."

Fen blanched. "Siofra has killed as well. Provoked, perhaps, but slaughter is slaughter." He looked out into the dusk, at the dark outlines of trees and the first hint of a crescent moon. "Siofra realized that though she didn't want to hurt anyone, there was nonetheless—" Fen tried to stop himself. It was a step too far. A betrayal.

"Nonetheless what?"

"I think," Fen said, weighing the risks and deciding them acceptable. *For Siofra.* "I think the reason she created her escape was so she'd have a place to go where she could pretend not to enjoy the power she was given." He swallowed the truth so he could speak it. "There was always a part of Siofra that wanted to kill. Her conscience shut it down and created a place where she could be safe from the terrible reality. But she's not a lamb, and you are not a lion, and if you continue to believe that, to *push* that truth, you will lose her. With her will go your heart. Am I wrong?"

Desemir snorted. "Have I one?"

Fen didn't rise to the diversion. "Do you love her?"

"Do I..." Desemir rolled his head to the side with a scoff. "We were never taught love in this house, Fen. We were taught loyalty."

"Do you *love her*?" Fen asked again. "Do you love my sister? And can you answer this question like a man?"

Desemir's mouth curled upward. When he turned his head, Fen saw the red spindles marking his eyes and the crescents creating a dark cradle beneath. He caught how the man's chest seized with shallow breaths. "I would bleed every last drop of my blood onto these stones to keep her safe. Is that the same?"

Tears pricked Fen's eyes. "If you would die for her, what would you do to keep from losing her?"

"I've already lost her." Desemir's throat bobbed. He clamped his mouth shut. "You can tell her... Tell her she'll be safe in the east wing. I'll never send for her. Never go where I'm not wanted. She and our child will be protected. From the world beyond our forests." He drew a sharp inhale. "From me."

Fen's head shook. "You're missing my point entirely."

"It's your own fault for coming here believing you had one."

Fen slammed his palm against the stone wall. He started to say something else, but any words left would be wasted on a man so intent on drowning in his own pity.

He turned and ran for the door. It opened before he could touch it. Pesha stood on the other side with a drawn look.

"Listening in?" Fen charged, his nostrils flaring.

"Waiting," Pesha replied. "For you to come out. So we could talk."

"Talk? To you?" Fen burst out laughing. "Oh, how hilarious, you thinking we have *anything* to talk about."

Pesha folded his hands and hung his head. "You're hurting. I can see that."

"You are *just* as much at fault as your hopeless brother," Fen spat. He pointed behind himself. "How can he atone for what he cannot even face? And how have you... *allowed* this?" Fen threw his arms wide. "You brought us here, Pesha! You brought us here *knowing* what your brother had done! You let him marry my *sister*. And now he's abandoned her entirely."

"Desemir isn't the monster he thinks he is." Pesha's voice was so low, Fen had to strain to hear. "Will you walk with me?"

"Will I *what*?"

"Walk with me, Fen," Pesha said, "and I'll tell you everything. I'll tell you the whole sordid tale and how it's come to where we are now. As long as you promise not to tell Siofra."

Fen's eyes flashed wide. "Now you want me to keep secrets from my sister? You want me to be complicit in your—"

Pesha snaked a hand out and grabbed Fen's, startling them both. "Just until Desemir finds the courage to tell her himself. He will. I know he will. And soon."

Fen turned back to look at the room. He recovered his hand and wrapped it under his arms, over his chest. "I won't promise you anything. You haven't earned it. So if you want to tell me anyway, you have until the light slips behind the trees to convince me listening wasn't another waste of my time."

THIRTY-FOUR
IN DIRECT LINEAGE FROM KLAUS I

Desemir couldn't recall the last time he'd been down in the Trevanion tombs. It hadn't been when his mother had died. He'd never gone farther than slumping in the front pew of the abbey, listening to the grand minister speak of things that made no sense to a boy who'd lost the only parent who'd loved him. The person who'd been at his left, Arenn Wintersin, was no replacement, with the self-satisfied grin she couldn't drop even for the reading of the rites.

He hadn't come down to watch his father get sealed away either. It was said they'd thrown Arenn's corpse in with him, even though it was no secret she'd killed him. Not with any dagger or sword or mallet, nor even magic. She'd finished him off with wolfsbane, but he hadn't suffered enough, because she'd then sat on his chest and choked the life from him. They found Ludwik with his eyes so bulging, they were practically falling out of his face. His mouth had stretched into a grotesque yawn, a tableau of final, irrevocable horror.

There'd been no reckoning for Arenn. She'd taken the same poison, and they'd found her fallen to the side of Ludwik, her hands still coiled around his neck. Her familiar, Ren, dead beside them.

But then, who could fault her, after what Ludwik had done? Arenn had been a cold and cunning creature but had also been rightfully grieving Ludwik's terrible wrath.

Desemir didn't know if it was true, about them throwing the Medvedev in with his father, but if so, it was one last spiteful push from men who had served Ludwik but had not loved him.

The tombs ran directly under Shadowfen Hall, which was different than the separation most highborn families put between their household and their dead. They were accessed from the back garden, down a hidden stairwell marked only by a modest placard bolted into the stone, reading simply, *Trevanion.*

Though the tombs were rarely visited, it was someone's job to keep the torches lit at all hours. And so they were, a line of beacons guiding anyone who dared a trip to the past to go deeper, farther.

Whoever had built the place hadn't considered how unsettling it would be for their descendants to travel the past on their way to paying respects. They hadn't the foresight to fill the space from the back forward.

Desemir knew most of the names. They were the same men and women he saw every day of his life, their paintings hanging in the Hall of Counting.

The great Klaus the First was the first tomb from the entrance—and the biggest obelisk in the entire crypt. He'd been interred with his wife, Aloisha. Their only son, Friederik, was across from them with his family, and from Friederik an entire dynasty had been birthed.

Desemir walked past Ludwik I and Desemir I, then past Gautier—who'd led one of the wars for the Darkwood and promptly died in it—and his wife Dagnara, who had fought as well, becoming the first woman to run Shadowfen Hall until her son, Klaus II, was old enough to take over. Her painting always garnered a question from visitors, about why the artist had boldly rendered her in the warrior's pose of a man.

They were the names that had become the core of Desemir's curriculum. Highborn boys of the Northerlands were rarely sent to the Council of Universities in the Easterlands, for it was thought to be a pointless immersion in books that had nothing to do with their way of life. The one good thing Desemir's father had done for him was send for a private tutor, who'd defiantly interspersed some traditional learnings into his Trevanion historical studies.

Desemir slowed when he reached the back room—the room where he would one day be entombed. Within were the tenth, eleventh, and twelfth generations of Trevanions. His grandparents, Klaus III and Elaina, and one of his two spinster aunts, Angelika, were in one corner. Ludwik and Lidia, in another... and maybe Arenn and her familiar.

The other side of the room bowed into a semicircle, leaving room for only one more cluster of tombs. His name—*Desemir II, son of Ludwik, in direct lineage from Klaus I*—was already etched there. Below his name was space for his wife and any children who did not reach maturity. Trevanions weren't given names until they were two years old, and so many of the tombs in the mausoleum had small markings for Infant One and Infant Two. Gautier and Dagnara had had seven children who'd never reached naming age.

How many would Desemir have?

How many did he deserve?

His heir would begin a new room. A new generation—the thirteenth. Whether it would be filled with hope or desolation was a future he was incapable of divining.

As Desemir contemplated his fate, he envisioned Siofra's name chiseled into the stone beneath his. *Siofra I, daughter of Rohan, lineage unknown.* He watched the letters form one by one, marking the end of her life.

The dense air thickened, suffocating him. Tears burned his eyes but didn't spill.

He spun away and faced his father's tomb.

Desemir's mouth suspended in indecision. How long had he held his words unsaid? How long had they eaten away at him, rotting him from the inside out, *becoming* him?

Before his better sense returned to stop him, Desemir unbuckled his trousers. He pulled out his cock and sighed with relief when urine streamed in response to the guidance of his hand, tracing his father's name on the stone. He abruptly burst out laughing, and once he started, he found it difficult to rein in his crude art.

Desemir stumbled sideways into the dirt wall and paused to regard his work.

His laughter acquired an edge. It cut into his small burst of empowered joy and sent a whorl of pain straight to his gut. He buckled his trousers in stunned shame. His tears finally broke loose. He stared at his father's name, half of it covered in dust, the other washed clean with his filth.

"All these years..." Desemir brought a fist to his mouth to trap a sob. "Father."

Disconnected memories passed through his mind as he read each letter of his father's name in slow passes.

Lidia, sneaking tarts to eat with Desemir in the Darkwood, laughing heartily at Desemir's newest fantastical tale he'd been so eager to regale her with.

Ludwik, throwing Desemir against a tree for crying over his mother's death.

Arenn, marking him with her cold, catlike eyes as she laid her claim over Ludwik.

Ludwik, wild and crazed with raw fury, taking his dagger to—

"I was trying to help her," Desemir whispered. His words cracked into a high pitch. "I was trying to *help* her, you monster! Why does it matter that I never liked her? I would never have..." Desemir's belly clenched, and a moan escaped his throat. "I was too weak to stop you, wasn't I? And wasn't that always what you said, Father? That I lacked the Trevanion mettle." Desemir snorted, sniffling. He swiped his sleeve across his eyes. "Well, turns out you were right. If I had even an ounce of your infamous apathy, I could have slit her throat and ended her misery *years* ago."

Desemir lowered his eyes to the ground. To the dark swirls he'd created in dust otherwise undisturbed for years. "I have not and will not spare a drop of mourning for you. But I would have endured your cruelty for the rest of my life if it meant none of this had ever happened."

"Desi?"

Desemir dried his eyes in a rush and turned toward Wulf. He'd taken a brazier from one of the sconces and was holding it out to his side.

"What are you doing down here?" Desemir's voice clogged with despair. He cleared his throat to try again, but it was no better the second time.

"I came..." Wulf's eyes were drawn to Ludwik's tomb. They widened, as he seemingly pieced together that it was half-damp. He grimaced and looked up. "To apologize."

Desemir grunted and swept his gaze back to the tomb. "You've held your tongue through too many of my bad decisions. I can't expect you to hold it forever. Nor would I want you to. You're my oldest friend, and..." Desemir finished the thought with a soft exhale.

Wulf slumped against the arched entrance. "Siofra and I..."

Desemir braced himself. "Siofra and you?"

"We stopped it," Wulf said quickly. He winced as if expecting a punch. "*She* stopped it. I... The truth is I might not have. No, not might. I wouldn't have stopped it. I knew my intention when I went to her." He swallowed. "In my anger, I forgot the names of my forefathers, and I acted with the shameful abandon of a man with no house."

Desemir's hands curled into fists. "And how..." He ran his tongue along the back of his teeth. "How far did things go, before she stopped it?"

"Far enough I feel compelled to atone for my lapse in resolve and will accept whatever punishment you deem fit." Wulf straightened as he inhaled. "But not so far I feel I must ask for you to take my sword to your blacksmith and have it melted down."

Desemir grimaced and turned away. He crossed his arms. *She stopped it.* "Is that all?"

Wulfhelm cleared his throat. "I understand why you were afraid to tell her. But did you ever consider she might be able to help? Or Stiofen?"

"I had hoped they might. But they know even less about their magic than Pesha."

"Still." Wulf held his thoughts a moment longer. "She's made of tougher things, Desi. What she endured before she came to us... what she endured in Oakhelm..." He shook his head. "She is not broken by hate. Not like some."

"You don't think I know what my wife is made of?" Desemir turned toward his friend and charged forward a step. "My strong, capable, *courageous* wife? The one I'll never deserve with this darkness I carry?"

"You've spent so damn much of your life in your own head," Wulf said, "that I confess, Desemir, I don't *know* what you think. Not anymore."

"Is this your indictment of me, Wulfhelm?"

"It's my fear of what awaits you if—"

"DESEMIR! WULF! ARE YOU THERE?"

Both scrambled toward the archway at the sound of Lieken's panicked voice. The boy's eyes enlarged with relief at the sight of them. He doubled over to catch his breath.

"Well, what is it?" Wulf demanded.

"It's Siofra." Lieken panted. He bowed over his knees, still gulping for air. "Lotte is with her." He spat into the dirt and wiped his mouth. "Lotte is with her, and it's... It's... the baby... and—"

Desemir didn't wait for Lieken to finish. He pushed past Wulf and leaped over the kneeling Lieken. He tripped upon landing

but kept going, kept running, shattering his promise to stay out of the east wing and out of her life.

Every instinct within Siofra told her to curl her body inward, to return to a place where there was no pain, physical or otherwise. Lotte and Gisela were screaming at her to... to... She didn't even know anymore. Her entire body was soaked with the freezing water from the rags Gisela had mopped all over her. The draught Lotte had forced down her throat had done nothing for the pain.

Is it my daughter? Is it my daughter? Is it my daughter? Is it my daughter—

They answered her with silence, saving their quiet, hushed words for each other instead. She screamed out for Fen, and it seemed like forever, but at last he came, and lay with her in the bed, wrapping her in his healing embrace.

It's the stress, you know.

She needs her husband.

She needs her strength.

She lost the minutes, the hours.

Even through the fog of the women rushing around the room, of Fen whispering his healing words against the back of her hair, Siofra heard *him* outside her door. Desemir. Her husband, screaming her name, his voice straining and breaking with every recitation.

The hints of others' presence were faint against Desemir's hot demands. She received only pieces... Euric and Wulf attempting to calm the wild man beating on the door, begging to be let in.

Siofra blinked Cassius into view. He was explaining something to Lotte with a flustered, drained look. Lotte wouldn't back down from whatever battle they were fighting, and she drove Cassius out—and all the men, except Fen—and soon the screams gradually faded, disappearing down the hall.

Siofra disappeared too. She still didn't know where she went when her mind had been given more than it could bear, but in her heart, she hoped to land somewhere in the recent past—before her world had shattered.

A place where she and Desemir had been happy. Where their flame had been joined to create a unified blaze. Where they had just been me and thee in the immortal sky they'd created by forgetting who they'd been, and becoming who they were.

THIRTY-FIVE

FARREN

Two years.

Two years had passed since Desemir had last found the courage to visit the west wing and sit with Farren.

Little had changed. The path looked the same. It should. The entire wing still received regular cleaning, despite only having one resident.

A familiar mustiness swirled in the dark hall, catching the light beaming through a far window. He sneezed and forced himself to adjust, his gaze fixed on the assortment of paintings lining the walls. Those were the pieces that didn't pass muster, created by artists who had forgotten to include the south wing when painting Shadowfen Hall or had given someone a mustache who never had one. Women with too ample bosoms or not enough. Children with heads bigger than their tiny bodies. They were close enough but not quite, pushed aside but not discarded.

It wasn't Farren's tragedy rendering the wing forgotten. There had always been a reason why each former baron hadn't taken the

401

time to spruce it up. Always an excuse. And so it had remained in its half-forgotten state since the time of Ludwik II.

On his way down the hall, Desemir nudged the painting of the lake that hung askew. He ran a finger along the table beneath and brought back only a thin layer of dust. Small signs confirming no one in Shadowfen Hall spent more time in the west wing than they must.

He didn't need to count the doors. He knew which one was hers.

With his hand hovering close enough to feel the metal handle cool his palm, Desemir gave himself one last chance to turn back.

Everyone he trusted was telling him to make things right with his wife. A wife who was no longer a name on a paper or a vessel carrying his heir but a tenacious, beautiful, and vibrant addition to his life—who had *completed* his life. Desemir's own future had become precariously tied to the fate of Siofra and their child.

But to make things right with Siofra, there was another whose atonement he owed first.

He entered the room. Everything was strewn about, like a storm had blown through. Pesha had prepared him for it; it had been part of Farren's "waking." The magic had subsided, and what remained was a confused, fractured Medvedev who would find no peace in her life.

She wasn't out of bed, but he couldn't see if she was *in* it either. The once-gauzy curtains had been replaced with something heavier since his last visit. He couldn't even make out a shape behind them.

"Farren. It's Des." He didn't recognize his own voice, graveled in timbre and deep in pitch. He approached with his hands up, as though in surrender. He supposed it was a form of surrender.

A low growl emanated from behind the curtains.

He stopped moving.

"Do you..." He blew out a hard breath. "Are you still you? Do you remember me?"

Silence remained, except for the smooth sound of flesh sliding along sheets.

"If you remember me, make a sound."

Farren growled.

Desemir closed his eyes in relief. "So you are still in there."

A piercing wail cut through the room. He clamped both hands over his ears until it ended.

"Message received," he said. He wanted to laugh, to ease the tension. To do *something* other than what he'd come to do. "I didn't come here to upset you, Far. I know my promises mean little to you, but I swear to you, I only want to make this right."

A mangled pillow flew from the opening in the curtains. Feathers floated to the floor.

Desemir swallowed hard. "If you'll allow me to come closer, to come sit with you..." His heart raced so fast, he had to steady himself on a chair. *It was fear that kept you from this room. It is courage bringing you back.* "If that would be all right with you, Farren, then make a sound. Any sound."

He shifted in the silence. How many seconds would he wait for her to change her mind? How long would be too much, too little?

Farren rumbled a low growl.

Desemir exhaled his relief and pressed forward before his fear could return and take over. He pulled back the curtain and took in the sight of her: light green wisps of hair protruding in jagged spikes from her braids of the same color. Scratches lined her face in diagonal swipes, her eyes... Ah, it was her eyes that caused his heart to arrest. Her feral glare ate at his courage. On all fours, she watched him, her shoulders rolled forward like a beast waiting to strike.

Just like her ocelot. Like Nera.

"Can I..." Desemir gestured toward the bed. "Can I sit?"

Farren arched her lower back in a shuddering stretch. When she came back down, she curled into a feline huddle.

Desemir sat and turned his gaze on his palms. He should meet her eyes, no matter how alarming they were, but it was all he could do to not run away screaming.

"There isn't a day that goes by..." A sudden sob choked off his words. He inhaled a breath and released it. "I should have killed him myself. I should have been braver. I should have been stronger. I lived in his shadows because it was the only place he ever allowed me." He shook his head in furious passes. Tears flew off the edge of his jaw. "No. I didn't come here to blame him. I didn't come here to hide from what I did. I have been hiding *every fucking day* of my life since the day we put you here, and I will not..." Emotion trapped his words. "I will not bury my guilt in distractions. I will not look away from what I have done."

Desemir lifted his chin and made himself look at her. He saw once more her disheveled hair, her crazed eyes watching him as she licked the back of her hand.

But then, as a sigh of surprise left him, he saw her as she had once been.

Tall and lithe... her hair the color of spring that curled down her back as she skipped through the halls of Shadowfen like a sprite. Her infectious, devious laugh ringing from pillar to pillar, Nera leaping underfoot.

He saw her sneaking into the woods to the fort he and Wulf had built, asking to play with them. And, when they refused, throwing rocks to bring their poorly built wood platform crashing from the trees.

He watched her carve her initials next to his, Wulf's, and Pesha's in defiance.

He felt her breath on his neck as she dared him to kiss her. Saw the horror in her eyes when he refused.

He remembered hating her—and also loving her, but mostly hating her.

He suffered, for a second time, the rift that followed and would define the rest of what remained of their lives together.

"I'm not asking for your forgiveness," Desemir said, his voice splintered with anguish. "Even if granted, I would never deserve it. I only want you to know that if I could trade places with you, if I could take your suffering and make it mine, I would do it without a second thought. I am *sorry*, Farren. I am so deeply, irrevocably sorry."

Farren rolled her head almost upside down in her strange, catlike pose. A soft purr vibrated the bed.

Desemir's shoulders shook as he stretched his hand across the blanket. He stopped in the center of the bed and waited without expectation. But Farren moved her own hand out from under herself and tapped it across the blanket, fingers arcing like claws as she danced them toward him.

The heat of her palm scorched his. The effect was so electrifying, it was all he could do to not fall backward off the bed and remain there.

Desemir willed his hand to stay beneath hers. He could only stare in numb shock as she kneaded her fingers atop his flesh in the same way Nera used to.

Something broke within Desemir. It was the very thing that had held him together through the years, like a patch on a dam.

Desemir didn't know where it had gone, only that it was never coming back.

He drew his feet up and moved across the bed until his face was inches from hers. Her purring escalated the nearer he drew, and when he lay his chin over her head, the hum became the loudest thing in the room, drowning out even the volatile beating of his patchwork heart.

Siofra refused the escort. Everyone fussed over her choice to leave the bedchamber after her health scare, but Fen had soothed her hurt. Just in time, her brother had come, and the scare was past them.

Another lay ahead.

Wulf lingered several dozen paces behind. He respected her need to go on alone.

She harbored no hesitation in her choice to go see the broken Medvedev. To even think of her thus, without a name, was a stab of ice to Siofra's heart. It was the very fate her mother and father had warned her and Fen about, how if they weren't exceedingly careful, they would become a curiosity, subjugated and treated as an animal.

Or *become* one.

Was Desemir actually capable of such a thing? Her heart told her no, but her eyes...

Siofra didn't know if the Medvedev could communicate with her, but she would try anyway. With Fen, she had always had her additional sense, a way of reading him on a deeper level. Perhaps it wasn't twinsense at all but a trait existent within Medvedev.

She turned down the hall to the west wing and didn't stop until she reached the room. She passed a single glance back at Wulf, holding distance at the other end of the hall. She offered him a nod, and he returned it.

Siofra slipped inside and gently closed the door behind her. A strange sense of peace stole over her that took her only a moment to decipher.

The Medvedev was resting.

Siofra was loath to wake her, but how restful could a severed Medvedev's sleep truly be?

She took one step and then another, until she'd shed the last of her reservations.

When she reached the bed, her heart seized in her chest.

Desemir lay beside the Medvedev, who was curled against him. Like a puppy.

No, like a cat.

"Siofra." Desemir rolled the word from the back of his throat, a hoarse sound full of sorrow. It immediately disoriented her.

"How did you know it was me?" she whispered. She hadn't broken her gaze away from the Medvedev.

"A sense," he answered. He flipped onto his back, gently adjusting the Medvedev as he shifted. She purred in response and coiled tighter around herself.

Siofra stopped breathing.

She was still gaping, stunned, at the feline movements of the Medvedev when Desemir peeled Siofra's hands away from her sides and held them in his.

"Our daughter..." His face crumbled. "Is she..."

"So you did listen when I said she would be a girl," Siofra replied, watching the Medvedev stretch her hind legs in a sharp thrust before snapping them back inward.

"You aren't the first to accuse me of not listening, nor the first to be wrong." There was a tentative edge to his words.

"She's fine. I don't know what came over me earlier, but Fen fixed it. Fen always fixes it." She didn't sound like herself. She heard her voice as if it were a melody carried from afar. That wasn't much different than how she felt, disconnected and light. It wouldn't surprise her to learn later that the day had been a dream.

Desemir released her and pitched forward. He buried his face in his hands. "Thank the Guardians."

"Thank Fen," she stated. Her chest rose with a sigh. "Or the Guardians, if it puts your mind at ease."

He looked back up, stretching his face as he blinked. "I don't know why I said it. I don't even believe in the Guardians."

That surprised her. "You don't?"

Desemir shrugged. He had his eyes trained on one corner of the room. "Maybe they're real. Maybe they're not. I just know they don't bandy us about like puppets. It's only us and our choices. Some just find it easier to blame the Guardians for their misfortune instead of taking control and making better ones."

"And you don't hold them at fault?" She forced herself to at last look away from the Medvedev.

"Siofra," Desemir said with a sigh, swinging his eyes back toward her. They were bleary and bloodshot, full of so much woe, it prompted her to take a step back. "There is no one but me to blame for my misfortune." He pointed his face over his shoulder. "Her name is Farren. Farren Wintersin. And she's Pesha's half sister."

Siofra brought her hands to her face in a soundless gasp. Her head shook in place of words. The implications of his confession tore her thoughts in a dozen directions, sending splinters tearing through every inch of her. She tried to reconcile the horror of Farren's existence with Pesha's privileged lifestyle. To reconcile *any* of what she'd seen and experienced at Shadowfen Hall with *this*.

"No. How—"

"I'll tell you everything," he said. "I should have told you long before now. I can't decide if it was a selfish choice or one born of cowardice." His head shook. "Probably a combination, as I'm possessed of both in equal measure. But if you'll sit with me, I'll put both of those follies aside and give you an honest accounting."

In the midst of such a shocking revelation, Siofra's strongest instinct wasn't to run or scream or cry out but to climb into Desemir's arms, press her face to his chest, and count the beats of his heart. To drift away to its cadence, remembering that every thrum was a sign of life, a reminder to live.

Instead, she nodded.

Desemir waited for Siofra to get comfortable. She settled at the end of Farren's bed, leaning against a thick post, equally distanced from both him and Farren. He noted Siofra's struggle to not stare at Farren.

"I was still a baby when Arenn and Naos Wintersin came to Shadowfen Hall. Arenn was brought on to be my governess. But she had a daughter of her own." Desemir nodded at Farren. "Farren was around two. We were close enough in age that they encouraged us to become playmates, and we were, for a while. But by the time we were old enough to wield our personalities, Farren and I were just too similar. We each had demons in us, Arenn liked to say, and we fought constantly. About everything. There was nothing she and I could agree on. Her familiar, a vicious little ocelot she called Nera, used to stalk me and pin me into corners, sometimes for hours."

Siofra opened her mouth.

Desemir waited for her question, then moved on when there wasn't one. "Arenn would scold Farren for her behavior, but my own mother never said a word to me. She soothed me when Farren played too rough, and blamed Farren for all of it. My mother and Arenn exchanged words on this more than once, but my father already had his roving eyes on Arenn and made no secret of his desire." He shook his head. "And then Naos died, and all the carefully contained chaos was released."

"How did he die?"

Desemir raised a brow with a humorless chuckle. "The general assumption was some combination of Arenn and my father. Naos and Arenn were not in love, nor even really friends. Naos wasn't even Farren's father; he was just someone Arenn got caught up with in the Asgill coup, and they were both thrown out. They stayed together as a matter of necessity, I think. Their fear of the kingdom kept them together. But Arenn no longer needed Naos once she had my father—and a protected life for herself and her daughter at Shadowfen Hall."

Siofra wore an astounded look. "Do you really think they killed him?"

Desemir pursed his mouth and nodded. "I don't think Naos died of anything natural. My father and Arenn didn't even wait a respectable mourning period before jumping into bed together. They flaunted their affair, even in front of my mother, who pretended not to be hurt, but *I* could see her heartbreak. I saw the tears she hid behind her lace veils, heard the pain in her voice when she tried to make a jest of the situation. I remember one time..." He paused to collect himself. "One time walking in on Lotte just holding her while she sobbed. It was the day my dislike for my father turned to hatred." Desemir closed his eyes.

He shook his head. "No. That's a lie. The day I started hating my father was the day my mother died."

Siofra's mouth curled in sympathy. "I know you loved her."

"And he killed her," Desemir said. It was the first time he'd said the words aloud, and he was surprised to realize it didn't hurt any more, or any less, to say them. All he felt was a hollow numbness that followed a truth he could neither change nor forget. "Or Arenn did. It's all the same. But I was almost nine by then, and within months of my mother's death, Pesha was born.

"I wanted to hate him, Siofra. I truly did. But from the start, I felt an intense call to protect him. Arenn abandoned him as soon as she had recovered from the birth. My father even hired a governess for her. A governess for the governess." He shook his head. "Pesha's hair was this shocking blue. Arenn took care to cover her own telltale Medvedev locks but did nothing for her son. When Pesh was around five, I finally swallowed my pride and asked Farren to help him." Desemir lowered his eyes with a nod. "And she did. She taught him how to use his magic. She taught me how to help him. Pesha doesn't remember it this way. He barely remembers Farren at all, other than what happened at the end."

"How does Pesha remember it?" Siofra asked. She'd drawn her knees to her chest and propped her chin atop them. Her bare feet, peeking beneath the hem of her nightgown, curled into the blanket.

"He remembers his mother taking on the role. He was too young to... to know Arenn's selfishness as the rest of us did. To see her cold disregard for everyone but Farren and my father."

"But Pesha was your father's son," Siofra said. "Would that not have been more reason to love him?"

Desemir arched his lip in disgust. "To Arenn, Pesha was only in the way of what she wanted. She complained how her body had changed after his birth. How my father was starting to look elsewhere, as if it would not have happened regardless. As if that were not inevitable from the start."

"This improved Farren's and my relationship some. We didn't *like* each other, but we tolerated one another, for Pesha. We raised him together. By then I was fourteen, and Farren must have been sixteen. Children raising a child." He chuckled to himself. "We had help from Lotte and Euric and even Wulf, who had a crush on Farren and could never tell her no. But then time changed things in another way."

Desemir searched for something to quench the dry patch in his throat. There was nothing. Farren hadn't needed food or drink in years. "As Farren aged, she was... Ah, she was beautiful." He glanced at her, still coiled and resting. "I never took to her myself. She was both my friend and my enemy, but neither of those relationships had a hint of intimacy. I looked forward to the day when she would leave Shadowfen Hall, but that became less and less likely as my father began to take an interest in her."

Siofra's face darkened as though she knew where he was going.

"I found Farren in the garden one day with a split lip and her dress torn. She didn't look wounded though, Farren. She... You see, she was *tough*. She had to be, I suppose. But no, she didn't look wounded. She looked *furious*." Desemir ran his damp palms along his trousers. "I didn't even have to ask. I took one look into her eyes, and I knew. And the first words out of my mouth were not sympathy, nor even a question, but a promise. 'I'll kill him,' I said. And she just laughed."

"Laughed?"

"Because she knew I was a coward! That I'd never do it." Desemir clenched his hands into fists. "And she was right. I did nothing. I watched my father, little by little, break Farren night after night. And I did *nothing*."

"You were a child," Siofra said. "What could you have done? Certainly *killing* your father was not an answer!"

"No," Desemir replied. "I wasn't a child anymore at that point. *Pesha* was a child. I was almost eighteen. And eventually Farren fell apart."

Siofra cast a dazed look at Farren.

411

"She came to me," Desemir said. His words slowed as he neared the end, as he approached saying what he had never before said aloud, not even to Pesha. "She came to me, desperate, begging for my help, to make him stop. I *had* gone to my father, weeks before, and he'd told me that if I couldn't stomach the 'business of men,' then I had no business being one." He grimaced through the pain bisecting the memory. "He had no respect for me and my *distaste* for his appetites. He wasn't going to hear anything I had to say. He..."

Desemir rolled his lips inward to suppress the emotion he'd sworn not to indulge. He would accept no sympathy for his cowardice. He needed Siofra to see him for who he was. To know him for what he'd done.

Siofra leaned forward and cupped his thigh with her palm. He recoiled but she held tight. "Say what you need to say. I'm not going anywhere."

Desemir lowered his eyes. "I should have... I should have done *anything* but what I did... I knew he'd never listen to reason, so I suggested she tell my father she was with child, because it was the only thing I could think of that would turn him off her, however temporary. The suggestion was flawed for *many* reasons. All it would take was the passage of time to show it for the lie it was. And then we would be right back where we started. But even that would have been a mercy compared to what happened."

Siofra squeezed his thigh, reminding him she was listening.

"My father flew into a rage when Farren told him she was with child." He rolled his tongue around in his mouth as the confession pulled him back in time. "I'll never forget the way he roared like a lion, chasing her all over Shadowfen Hall. Euric earned one of his scars trying to stop him. We all tried to stop him, but he was a man possessed."

Desemir's gaze flicked to Farren. Tears clouded his view of her, blending the past with the present. "He got to Nera first. And while Farren watched, he gutted Farren's familiar and bled her dry."

412

Siofra recalled her hand. She'd gone pale. Her eyes darted downward as she absorbed what he'd said.

"Something snapped in Farren when Nera died. She stopped running from my father and instead charged *at* him, flying and clawing her way as we all watched in horror... watched her barreling toward certain death. It was Pesha who climbed upon our father's back and subdued him. Arenn and I carried him back to his bedchamber, and it was the last time I saw him alive." Desemir corrected himself. "It was the last time I saw either my father or Arenn alive."

"I..." Siofra's chin twitched. She braced herself against the mattress.

"You what?"

"Nothing. Go on."

Desemir nodded, exhaling a long, slow breath. "Arenn killed my father and then herself. The physician discovered poison in them both, but they found Arenn with her hands frozen at my father's neck."

"And Farren..." Siofra said the words evenly, as if afraid to turn them into a question he might answer.

"Whatever broke inside Farren," Desemir answered, "just kept on breaking until..." He closed his eyes. "She went wild. First came the hunger strike, then the self-harm. It wasn't long before she forgot how to speak or communicate at all. She started purring and hissing and..." Desemir looked at Farren. "We didn't know what to do. Pesha tried to calm her with his magic, but the relief was temporary. He couldn't be with her at all hours. Euric accompanied me into Darkwood Run, and we passed from tavern to tavern in disguise until we found a cunning man who said he could help."

Siofra mouthed the words "cunning man" in confusion.

"That was what he called himself, but he was a practitioner of magic, an enchanter performing his gifts unsanctioned, beyond the eyes of the Sepulchre. Dark magic, he said, and I suppose it was, for what magic of light could put Farren into a suspended rest, not aging, not changing, needing nothing but air to breathe and warmth for almost eight years?"

"She's been like this *eight years*?" Siofra whispered.

Desemir nodded at his hands, stretched over his lap. "The magic is wearing off, and the cunning man has moved on to other cunning deeds. Without aid, she'll again turn wild, and this time I fear..." He scrunched his face in agony. "I fear there will be nothing we can do for her."

"Is this what happens when a Medvedev is severed from their familiar?" Siofra's question wasn't for him. Her lips moved in wordless answer.

"That's our assumption, but we know so few Medvedev. We know no others who have endured what she has." He laughed bitterly. "We even tried bringing in forest animals, to see... Guardians help us, what fools we were. We knew little then, and we know little now."

"And this is why you cannot sleep..."

"A fitting penance, is it not? While Farren did nothing but sleep for eight years, I was rightfully denied mine." When her expression melted to concern, Desemir raised a hand. "I'm not looking for your sympathy. Nor your understanding. I deserve neither and will accept neither."

Siofra again struggled for words. "Did you bring me to Shadowfen Hall to help her or to assuage your guilt?"

"Both, I guess. I thought I could make up for what had happened with Farren by helping the two of you," Desemir stated before he could replace truth with a lie. "But when I met you and Stiofen, I realized you had been even more sheltered than Pesha."

"Why didn't you send us back?"

"Because I made a promise." Desemir flexed his jaw. "To Pesha. To Farren, even though she could no longer hear me. I'd sworn that if given the chance to help a Medvedev again, I would give everything I could to protect them from what I failed to protect Farren from."

Siofra shook her head in confusion. "It wasn't your job to protect Farren."

"Have you heard anything I've said?"

"I've heard *everything* you said, Desemir." Siofra pitched forward. "*You* did not kill Nera. You did not... You did not drag Farren to *your* bed against her will. You tried to help her, and sometimes... Sometimes it just isn't enough."

"What are you saying? That I should pretend I have no culpability in what made her like this? An innocent man wouldn't have stopped coming to see her! Wouldn't have avoided facing what he'd done!"

She softened. "Do you not think you have atoned enough already?"

"I..." Desemir didn't know how to answer her. How could there ever be an end to his atonement where there was no end to Farren's torment?

"You have been holding this pain in your heart all this time," Siofra said with a slow shake of her head. "You have blamed yourself for your father's cruelty and were then expected to step from the darkness of his shadows to become him, to preserve the mess he made."

"Stop defending me," Desemir said, setting his mouth in a hard line.

"I'm only saying exactly what you said to me when I told you about my parents."

"This is not the same at all. I won't have you see me through clouded eyes. Not anymore."

"You wound me by assuming I cannot see through words to the heart of a man."

"Tack it onto my crimes, for they are legion," Desemir said with a low rumble of laughter.

Siofra regarded him in swollen silence for several excruciating moments. The only sound in the room was the staccato of their harried breaths and the low purr rumbling from Farren.

"What she needs is to be taken home," Siofra said, looking at Farren. "She needs to be with our people if she's to have any chance of healing. I may not know much about what it truly is to be a Medvedev, but I would wager my life that there's nothing in *this* kingdom that can fix what has been broken in her."

"The Wintersins were cast out of Asgill lands, just as the Thornhearts were," Desemir replied. "If Pesha could take her back, he would have already."

"Our *parents* were cast out," Siofra said. "*We* have committed no crime. And we cannot know what they would do to us without going and finding out."

"You sound like Pesha." He almost smiled. "He wanted to go years ago. I forbade him from leaving. It was fear that made me stop him. I couldn't protect him out there like I can here."

"Fear binds us," Siofra replied, her head falling to the side. "It chokes the life out of us, and when we have lost our fight, it kills us. You don't *have* to live like this, Desemir. It is a choice."

"Choice," Desemir said back. He'd come to the end, where he'd need what little remained of his strength to set her free. "I've given this a fair amount of thought, Siofra, and although I gave you a choice when coming into this marriage, it wasn't a fair one. There was no feasible way for you to tell me no. I see this now. And I want to make it right."

Siofra tensed in anticipation. The hurt that flashed on her face came on too suddenly for her to hide.

"I'm going to..." Desemir cleared his throat, but it was no use. There was no pretending the words, a product of his rational mind, were a match for his irrational heart. "My mother has land up near Midwinter Rest. It's not been used in some time, but with the help of Lotte and Gisela and Wulf—"

The flush in her cheeks drained away. Her question came out in a breathless rush. "Are you asking me to leave?"

Courage, Des. Courage for yourself but, more importantly, for your wife. For your child.

416

"You'll be safe there." He pushed his words out with a hard clench in his belly. "You'll have everything you could ever need, everything—"

"Everything I need?" Siofra slid back against the bedpost. "You *are* asking me to leave."

"I'm giving you a choice," Desemir said, forcing an impossible calm over himself. "I'm giving you a *real* choice this time."

"You are not!" Siofra cried. She leaped off the bed and crashed into a table. "You are, now as before, presuming you know what's best for me. Better than I do." She threw a hard glance at Farren. "*And* for her. Of this, Des, yes, you *are* guilty. You are. For not letting others in when you need them, when they could be there for you, when they *want* to be there for you!"

Heart pounding, Desemir reached for her, but she pulled away and backed herself into a corner. "Siofra—"

"You have underestimated me at *every* turn! You would make this choice *for* me, and how is it any different than removing the choice altogether?" She reeled forward, her hands trembling in front of her. "We have a *child* coming, Desemir, and you would rather drown in self-pity than admit you have loved and are loved in return."

Desemir's jaw slackened. His eyes locked on hers, both of them struggling with their breaths, both seemingly daring one another to be the first to address her accusation.

"Siofra." Wulf cleared his throat from the door.

Desemir and Siofra whipped their attention his way in almost perfect unison. The look on Wulf's face was a reflection of how the situation must have looked.

"I'm sorry," he said. "Fen is looking for you."

"Why?"

"He wants to check how the baby is doing after his healing. See if you need more."

Desemir started to tell Siofra they would finish later, but she shoved past him and marched out ahead of Wulf.

Wulf flashed an apologetic wince. "I didn't mean to—"

417

Desemir hunched over the bed and waved a hand back. "Follow her!"

"Desi—"

"Wulf. Go." Desemir slammed his eyes shut and inhaled, letting the breath roll through the tension in his shoulders. "*Please.* She shouldn't be alone."

"And you?"

Desemir's mouth twisted in self-loathing. "I know nothing else."

THIRTY-SIX
PATCHWORK HEARTS

Siofra met Fen halfway to the east wing. His expression crumpled in relief when he spotted her, and he jogged the rest of the way.

"Where have you been?" he asked, wrapping an arm around her. "I woke up and you were just *gone.*"

"You were so tired after the healing," Siofra said distantly. She still belonged to the impassioned exchange with Desemir and regretted leaving. But it had been too much—his confession, the truth about Farren.

You know better. This time, you know better, and if you want to save your marriage, it falls to you to show him how wrong he is.

About himself.

About everything.

"Si?"

"Yes?" She darted her eyes around, remembering herself.

"I asked if you're feeling all right. If the pain is gone." He eyed her with suspicion.

"Yes," she said, throwing a glance over her shoulder. "I went to see Farren, and Des was there."

Fen released her and leaned against the wall. "So you know Farren's story."

Her eyes narrowed. "You already knew?"

"I heard the sordid tale only hours before you," Fen replied, defensive. "Pesha asked me to allow Des to tell you himself."

"And?" Siofra's ears rang. The effect was almost deafening, a scream sounding in her head to get back to her husband, to finish what they'd started.

"And those men have been carrying a terrible burden in their hearts for a long time," Fen said. "I went in to see her... Farren..." He crossed and re-crossed his feet. "She needs to return to our people."

"That's what I said as well."

"You're not yourself," Fen said. He peeled himself off the wall and returned to her with a concerned frown. "Are you sure it's not the baby?"

"No, she's... I feel her." Siofra blinked to rid herself of the languid pull of exhaustion. In her mind, she saw Desemir's tortured face, twisted in the angst of a past he was still wrapped in and a future he couldn't envision. "It's Des."

"Is something wrong?"

"He..."

I've given this a fair amount of thought, Siofra.

There was no feasible way for you to tell me no.

I want to make this right.

My mother has some land up near Midwinter Rest.

"Si?"

"I need to go back to him," Siofra said. She wrapped her arms around her belly and spun toward the way she'd come, toward the west wing. "I've been wrong, Fen. I just don't know what I've been wrong about."

Fen clamped both hands onto her shoulders and met her eyes. "Talk to me, Si. I want to help."

420

Siofra's mouth parted. She sucked in a tight inhale. "Either I'm right and my husband loves me, or I'm wrong, and I've been a great fool."

"Do you want to know what I think?" Fen asked.

"You'll tell me either way." She forced a smile.

"I never imagined I would say this to you." He rolled his palms on her shoulders with a nervous laugh. "I wanted to hate him. I wanted to hate them all. I wanted them to be exactly who I suspected them to be. Like the Stanhopes and every other family who exploited us. But they're not like them at all. I don't know how we got so lucky or if we even deserve it. Pesha is..." He lowered his eyes and shook his head. "And Desemir? He's a mess of regret and bad decisions, but the best one he ever made was marrying you, Siofra."

Siofra lowered her head. Fen pulled her in and held her while she cried.

"What if you're wrong? What if I *am* just another burden he now has to carry?" she asked. "What if all his kindness is just to soften the blow when I land?"

"I'm not wrong," Fen said with a lopsided grin as he pulled back. "In your heart, you already know the truth. And so does he." He kissed her forehead. "You've been surrounded by stubborn men your entire life. You've weathered the storm well thus far."

Lightning cracked at the end of his words. They both turned toward the long front windows and saw rain pelting the earth. A hard rumble of thunder shook the ground.

"I have to get back," she said. Something flashed in the night. It disappeared near the lake. "I have to say what I need to before I lose my nerve."

Fen nodded and released her.

Desemir let the rain wash over him. It soaked his thin shirt and pooled at his feet, spilling over boots that were only half-laced.

The thunder rooted him to the earth, to the land he'd been brought into the world to protect, but the lightning reminded him he'd survived as long as he had not by standing still but by pushing forward, to whatever end.

He avoided the vexing gardens altogether, zagging to the right to cut around the frustrating plot of land. He hadn't decided on a destination, but had he ever? Had he even once had a clear vision of where he was going when he charged forth into the unknown?

I never saw myself living this long, let alone having a future worth fighting for.

Desemir sidestepped down the muddy embankment. The land was still healing from Siofra's red wall, but in the darkness, it was the same land it had always been. The lake was just ahead, and as he watched the moon spreading a halo over the inky surface, he knew why his instincts had aimed him there.

He came to a slippery halt inches from the water's edge. Mud sprayed up, spotting his waterlogged trousers. Peering over the edge, he saw his reflection, fragmented and rippling outward with the rain's unrelenting strikes against the thin layer of ice that had reformed after Siofra had melted it.

Desemir's head fell back. Rain washed over his face, filling his mouth and burning his eyes. He faltered backward, laughing, and imagined himself landing in the mud and rolling—rolling until he became one with the earth. Until he was covered with too much filth to ever wash clean, his exterior matching who he was within.

His laughter died. He brought his hand out, stretching it in front of his face. On it was Ludwik's cursed ring, the grotesque lion the late baron had built his entire reputation on. Desemir wore it not for love but hate, yet somehow those lines had blurred over the years. His hatred had spread to become him, to coat him in the same dark sludge that had become his father.

422

I hate my father because I am my father was the familiar refrain, but the words held less power. They were part of the lie that had pinned him down and kept him from living.

My solitude came hard-earned.

Yes. Siofra's soft voice rang in his ears. *And even with all your gold and land, you are a man destitute, who has stubbornly chosen to live in the poverty of his own lies.*

He wiggled his fingers. Separated them, isolating the one wearing the atrocious sigil of his father.

With a groan that erupted from his belly, Desemir ripped the ring off. He held it up in the moonlight for only a second before he coiled his arm back and hurled it at the lake.

A tremendous weight left him as the ring soared through the air, disappearing. He didn't see it land. The rain obscured all other sounds.

Desemir bowled over. His back arched as he inhaled insatiable gulps of air, rain spraying his tongue and dripping down the back of his throat.

Of this, Des, yes, you are *guilty. You are. For not letting others in when you need them, when they could be there for you, when they want to be there for you.*

And where had that gotten any of them?

Pesha. Farren. Siofra.

Their love for him... their *trust* in him... had been repaid with cravenness.

Desemir rolled upward and stared into the abyss beyond the lake. The forest arced before him in a semicircle, a cocoon keeping the world out, but also him in.

His eyes lowered to his hand. A deep trough remained where the ring had been, a band of raw flesh that would take weeks to heal, months to vanish.

Desemir looked again at the forest. He scanned the dark trees swaying against the night sky, then stilled, absorbing their silent call.

His feet moved ahead of the command. He quickened his pace to a jog, escalating into a sprint.

Desemir ran so fast, both of his feet left the ground in a race against the cloying supremacy of the belief system that had shaped his life and then decimated it.

Desemir wasn't in Farren's room. Siofra started to ask her where he'd gone but scolded herself before the words were out. She whispered an apology and bolted back into the hall.

She rushed up to Wulf. "Where is he?"

"Who? Desi?"

"Yes!"

"I don't know." He shook his head and peeked around her. "I've been following you. He's not in there?"

"I wouldn't be asking if he was." Siofra pressed a hand to her belly. She glanced again at Wulf and made her way back down the hall.

When she reached Desemir's bedchamber in the south wing, she yanked on the doors, stumbling backward from the force. Wulf came up from behind to right her and then charged ahead to survey the room.

"Not here either," he said, but she'd already moved on.

Siofra ran until she reached the central staircase. She paused, calculating. Shadowfen Hall was huge. He could be anywhere.

She spotted Lotte at the base of the steps and ran toward her. "Where is he? Where's Des?"

Confusion colored Lotte's expression. "I haven't seen him in hours, Siofra."

Siofra squeezed the woman's arm and pushed on, toward the Hall of Counting. She asked everyone she passed if they'd seen him, but no one had.

He wasn't in the Hall of Counting either. Exasperated, and with Wulf on her heels, she left the room and ran straight into Euric.

"You're looking for Des," he stated. A flush of exertion pained his face.

Siofra nodded. She bit the inside of her mouth to stave off tears.

"He's outside!" Cassius called from the other end of the hall.

Siofra, Euric, and Wulf all bolted in that direction. Wulf was the first to reach the central hall, but before he could exit into the storm, Siofra leaped forward and laid both of her hands atop his.

"I'm going alone."

Wulf whipped an incredulous gaze from her to the windows on either side of the double doors. "Absolutely not."

Siofra turned toward Euric. "You understand, don't you?"

"I understand," Euric said carefully. "You're after privacy with Des, wherever he's gone. But if you think either of us will let you go out in this storm alone, then you're as mad as he is."

Wulf's eyes briefly widened at Euric's bold implication about Desemir. "He's right. You shouldn't even be going out there at all in your... delicate condition."

"I'm pregnant, Wulf, not leprotic." Her thoughts caught up. She looked at Euric. "Why were you looking for Des?"

"Gisela saw him leave the west wing looking troubled." His mouth pulled inward, as if he'd said too much.

"Farren and I have met," Siofra snapped. "There are no secrets lingering between Des and I. Not anymore." She looked from one to the other. "Desemir *is* troubled. And tonight he stands between two worlds, two choices. You've protected him for years, and this protection has kept him safe—physically. But he isn't safe in his heart and mind. He wasn't as a child, and he's not now. I need him to know he's safe with *me*."

Euric and Wulf exchanged heavy glances.

"We'll keep our distance," Euric said finally. He adjusted his sword belt. "But we won't risk the safety of the three of you."

She realized Euric was referring to her baby. She swaddled her belly in one arm and nodded. "Just don't let him see you."

Siofra broke through the gap in the doors and ran into the night. She was faintly aware of the guards exiting behind her. Desemir could be anywhere, but there was only one destination in her mind, so she took off toward the forest.

The marshy ground gave way under the hard strikes of her boots as she ran. She winced against the rain driving sideways in the wind that ripped across the field. A bolt of lightning startled her, sending her sideways just in time for the thunder to rattle the earth and sky. She threw both of her arms over her face and pushed on.

I've given this a fair amount of thought, Siofra.

No.

My mother has some land up near Midwinter Rest.

No!

This time you're not going to shut me out.

This time, you're going to listen.

The ground hardened some when she entered the forest, but fallen logs and briars slowed her advance. She should have taken a carriage, but there wasn't time to ready one, and she needed to get there, to *be* there, before Desemir slipped so far into the shadows of his mind that even she couldn't pull him back out.

A few minutes in, she stopped to gather her bearings with a defeated groan. All the trees looked the same. There were no clear paths. She'd never taken this route on foot before, so how could she possibly find her way in the dark, in the middle of a powerful storm?

Her eyes were directed upward at the familiar trill of Aio's caw. Aio's wings spread as she dipped into a gap between trees and then returned to the skies.

Waiting.

Siofra's breath caught. She lifted her skirts again and turned in the direction Aio flew. Bracing against exhaustion and the unforgiving chill snaking around her bones, she wound her bedraggled hair into a knot at the nape of her neck, embraced the rain coursing down her face, dripping from her chin, and forced her mind and heart to clear a path.

Siofra neared collapse when she broke into the familiar clearing. She didn't know how much time had passed, but the wobbly ache in her legs and the moisture in her lungs suggested she'd been running for a long time. She looked up in gratitude, but Aio was gone.

Time caught up. She swayed against a tree to gather her breath, gripping her knees. Her vision blurred from the unending rain streaming down her eyes. No amount of blinking offered clarity.

Then when she straightened, she saw him.

Desemir was slumped between roots of the imposing tree, the last bastion of light from his troubled childhood.

Siofra pushed away from her tree and stumbled over a fallen log. She went crashing to the forest floor, grasping for something to hold on to. Her fingers picked through wet leaves and flora of the gloaming. She bit down on a scream and raised her head.

She recognized the shape of him, which she had learned, and loved, for months.

She couldn't tell if his eyes were open.

Siofra drew her elbows back, planted her palms on the ground, and shoved upward. She was already moving forward when she gained her footing, and she didn't stop until she reached him.

Desemir's head swiveled upward at her arrival. A lazy smile spread across his face as he watched her with a dreamy look. He held up his hand, showing her a bottle.

"Where did you..." Siofra shook her head. "I don't care."

"Found it in the tree. Don't remember stashing it there, but I must've had some foresight as a boy. More likely, it was Wulfie." He tapped the bottom edge of the bottle against his head. "Hardly a drop left in it though. Shame."

Siofra knelt before him. She ripped the bottle from his hand and chucked it into the forest.

"You are not drunk," she said. She swiped at his face, clearing it of pine needles and dirt. "I've seen you drunk. I would know."

Desemir sputtered while she cleaned him up. He leaped to his feet and guided her back from him. His gaze swept the length of her, a horrified expression on his face. "You didn't *run* here, did you? You'll catch a chill." He started to shimmy out of his jacket, then seemed to realize it was as soaked as the rest of him. "Siofra."

Siofra lifted her chin. "And what was I to do, leave you out here?"

Desemir wiped the back of his hand across his nose. "Yes!"

"To brood and sulk and drown in the many lies you've come to accept as truths?"

Desemir scoffed. He took a step back and held out his hands. "You cannot understand." He rolled his bottom lip inside his mouth and released it. "You have not done the things I've done. You have not—"

"I'm tired of hearing you rationalize your self-loathing."

His lip curled in a defiant sneer. "You're the one who came out here, who put our daughter's *life* at risk to come tell me things you've already said—"

"I, too, have taken life!" Siofra yelled, thrusting her hands downward. She inhaled a shuddering breath. "I, too, have hurt others. Sometimes by accident and sometimes because I *wanted* to. Because I wanted others to know the pain I felt, and it didn't matter to me whether it was right or wrong." She shook her head. "Are we monsters? Maybe. Maybe, but I don't believe we are, Desemir. I see you and me as imperfect creatures with imperfect pasts, who have somehow, in the middle of all that, made each other *better*."

"Have I?" Desemir laughed and lowered his eyes to the side. "Made you better? Look at you, Siofra. You're... You're soaking wet and madder than an angry boar, hurling insults at me as if they changed a damn thing."

"You're impossible." Siofra shook her head with fury. "You refuse to listen to reason."

428

"Yeah? You're one to talk." He rolled his eyes and threw up his hands.

She sputtered her words. "You speak from both sides of your mouth and expect me to understand."

"I never *asked* you to understand me." Desemir leaned in, beating a fist on his chest. "I never asked you to *care*, and yet here you are, relentlessly stubborn, making yourself *sick*—"

"You are a most vexing man!" She charged forward, but he moved back an equal distance. "You don't know what I want! Even after I've told you, *shown* you, begged you to hear me, you shut me out. You lock the door and discard the key and have the nerve to laugh at me, to *chastise* me, for loving you!"

Desemir's mouth slammed shut. He brought his hand over it, his eyes widening and narrowing as he stumbled backward, to the side. "You need to go back to the Hall."

"No." Siofra planted her boots in the soft ground.

"*Yes.*" He started toward her with a finger raised. "You need to take your misplaced optimism with you to my mother's keep, where you'll be *safe*—"

Siofra threw her head back with laughter.

"See? You're mad," he stated. "You've caught a chill, and it's gone to your head."

"A chill?" Siofra folded her hands over her head. "Oh, Des, you will twist any words, form any explanation, to avoid the most obvious one, won't you? Well, of course you will, for then you'd have to accept that the actual truth doesn't match the one you've stitched together in your head."

"Go *back*, Siofra."

"Or what?" She crossed her soaked arms. "Or *what*? You'll rail at me some more about how little I know, how naive I am?"

"I never said you were naive."

"There are a hundred ways to say something." Her eyes narrowed. "You told me in that room I had a choice."

Desemir held out his hands in a shrug.

429

"You only gave me one option." She took another step toward him. "I want to know what the other one is."

He ground his jaw when she neared. "There isn't one."

"Ah, so it's not a choice."

"You twist *my* words now."

"Oh, no. I understand quite clearly. Much like your proposal, you have presented the illusion of choice without actually providing one at all."

Desemir backed against the tree. His chest rose and fell in violent stops and starts. "What do you *want* me to say, Siofra?" His voice cracked. Tears fell from his reddened eyes, mixing with rain. "That you coming into my life has been a light at the end of a very dark road for me? That even to... even to *look* at you brightens my day? That the very *idea* of sending you more than a few feet away from me is twisting me up inside?" He thrust both of his hands at his belly. "That I am *catastrophically* in love with you, and this truth threatens to eclipse any and all others?"

Somewhere in the middle of his confession, Siofra had started to cry, and by the end, she was shaking.

Desemir trapped a moan in his throat. He reached for her without making contact.

"Yes," she whispered. She turned away, wrapping her arms around herself in a shield from the heartache burning in her chest. "Yes, that's what I want." She clamped down on her lower lip, drawing blood. "But not if you cannot bring yourself to mean the words. Not if... Not if you cannot say them except when pushed to the brink."

His hand landed between her shoulders. His fingers splayed along the back of her neck, then wound into the knot she'd woven in her hair. He loosened it, and her tangled, matted hair spilled down over his forearm.

Desemir twisted it up and pinned it atop her head and came closer. She felt him press against her and then his lips brushed her bare neck, sweeping up over the outside edge of her jaw.

Siofra turned into his arms. His gaze held hers as he at last let her see him in all his vulnerability, his tears coating his pain. She reached a hand up, and he let his cheek fall into her palm, warming her hand with his breath.

"I am catastrophically in love with you, Siofra," he said, drawing out each word. "I'm terrified of this love." His eyes squeezed shut and opened again. "But I don't want to be."

Siofra cupped his face in both of her hands. "I once believed I wasn't worthy of love. That I wasn't built to give or receive such a blessing. Happiness was for those who were not abominations."

Desemir's head shook in wordless passes.

"When in truth," she said, "I had just not yet met the one I was meant to love, and who was meant to love me."

"I don't want to be the man..." Desemir inhaled a sharp breath. "The man who would turn away happiness when it was standing right in front of him. I don't want to be the man who only believes the bad in himself and not... not what could be. The potential for more."

"Then don't be that man." Siofra smiled. "I'm right here. I'm not going anywhere."

"What if the rot inside of me destroys all that is good in you?"

"There is no rot. And you have no such power over me."

"What if you're wrong?" The lines around his eyes deepened. "What if I'm meant to be alone?"

"Desemir. Don't you understand? I am *freeing* you of the burden of this fear. All you require is the courage to accept this freedom." She stretched up to kiss him.

When she ended the kiss, he fastened his hand to the back of her head and crushed his mouth to hers with a desperate groan. "I'll never stop being a vexing man," he said against her lips.

"I didn't think you would," Siofra replied. "And that's the man I fell in love with, so why would I ever want him to change?"

"Say it again," he whispered, resting his forehead against hers. His eyes closed.

"Which part?"

431

"You know which part." He hadn't opened his eyes.

"Ahh, that I love you?" Siofra answered. She slid her hands up his face to make him look at her. "No matter how you twist those words, they all lead to the same place."

"Me and thee," he said, sighing. "I almost let you leave. I was going... I was going to let you leave me."

"There was never any risk of me leaving," Siofra said and kissed him again. "I'm just as stubborn as you. The difference is I'm sharper and get to the truth of a matter much quicker. I don't *brood* as you do."

Desemir's brows shot upward. "You're certain about that?"

She grinned up at him. "I can see you're going to contend this point, aren't you?"

"I can't let you think you've won every argument." He brushed his lips against hers again, tugging her bottom lip with his teeth. "Nor am I convinced you've won this one."

Siofra pulled back. "I can hardly stand the cold in the Darkwood, Des. You wouldn't *really* banish me to the frozen north."

Desemir's eyes took on an impish twinkle. "I thought you enjoyed punishment, Siofra."

"Oh, I do," she said, running her tongue along her bottom lip. "But it's not punishment unless you're the one patiently guiding me through each and every one of my sins."

Desemir hoisted her into his arms. He anchored one hand under her and stretched up to grab a branch with the other before gently backing her into the ebony bark. Siofra hooked one arm around his neck and joined the other to the same branch above them, climbing her fingers toward his until they were laced.

"Sin one," he said through a groan, using his purchase on the tree to raise her skirt, "you're going to make me fuck you out here in the rain, aren't you? When what I *should* be doing is setting you in front of a warm fire?"

Siofra moved her hand from his neck long enough to help him with her dress, and then his pants. A bolt of hot desire shot through her belly and spread downward. She panted through a fractured, fumbled response before throwing her head back against the tree.

Desemir ground his jaw as he struggled to maneuver around their soaked clothing. "Can't answer me?" He pressed against her, spreading her legs even wider, hitching her dress at the waist. "Or won't?"

Siofra reached lower and circled his cock with her hand. She waited for the expected widening of his eyes, teeth raking over his bottom lip, before guiding him into place with a whimper.

"You already know my answer," she purred as he drove into her, erasing the last of her pain with every thrust. "It hasn't changed."

"Is that a challenge, Siofra?" Desemir said, breath burning her neck as his pace quickened. She knew every throb by heart; felt him draw near to an end that was only the beginning.

"A choice," she whispered as her own pleasure crested. "I choose joy."

434

EPILOGUE

Desemir fiddled with the trunks on the carriage rack. He checked the tightness on the straps a few more times and shook the load to test for give. Pesha's soft chuckle only made Desemir more determined to ensure his brother's belongings were secure for the long trip.

"Thanks to you, this will be a most safe journey." Pesha sputtered a failed attempt to restrain laughter.

"You jest, Pesh, but when your trunks do *not* go rolling into a ravine, you'll be thanking me in earnest."

Pesha's laughter faded. He shook his head and squinted up at the trunks warming under the springtide sun. "I don't even know if they'll allow trunks or belongings or *things*." He screwed his mouth into a pensive frown. "Or Asgill outcasts."

"Arenn and Naos were cast out of Asgill. Not you."

"They tried to overthrow and murder the chieftainess," Pesha said. "I may be a generation removed from that crime, but Farren was born there."

"Farren was an infant when her mother joined a coup," Desemir said.

"And Fen..." Pesha's thoughts trailed off. He kicked at the dirt, his eyes still on the carriage. "I should have told him no. I can *still* tell him no. We're not beyond the point of no return."

Desemir planted his hand on a trunk and looked at Pesha. "You didn't ask him to join you. He offered."

"From politeness." Pesha scoffed and lowered his eyes to the side.

Pesha wasn't ready for the deeper truth of Fen's eagerness to join the voyage, so Desemir offered another truth instead. "Why not look at this as an opportunity for fresh beginnings for yourself as well?"

"What do you mean?"

"From the time our father died, you've been determined to save me from my mistakes." Desemir chuckled. "And I am eternally grateful for your sacrifice, Pesh. I couldn't have asked for a truer brother than you. Whether I deserved it is a matter beyond my deciding."

Pesha flushed. "But?"

"But," Desemir said carefully, "can you honestly say *you* have lived? Mistakes are a part of living, brother. They guide us toward the paths we inevitably take. Is it not time for you to turn your attentions to your own needs?"

"Eh..." Pesha scrunched his face and angled it toward the field and the lake beyond. On their way out, he would stop and retrieve Eshe, placing her in the cistern Lieken had crafted for her journey. That, too, was a danger, but Pesha needed encouragement, not a reminder of everything that could go amiss.

"If nothing else," Desemir said, "accept that Fen has *chosen* to go, a decision only he could have made."

"Not entirely true," Pesha replied with a tight scowl. "I all but forced him into the carriage in Newcarrow."

Desemir rolled his eyes. "I forgot you have an answer for everything. I'll miss it terribly."

Pesha seemed to disappear into his thoughts. "It has to be done though. For months, we've tried. And we really have tried everything here, haven't we?"

"We have." Desemir ignored the pit of dread spreading across his belly.

"I can only calm her for so long... Lotte's draughts are effective for *hours,* if that... Do you think the Sepulchre is responsible for the taverns being dry of magi these days?"

"Perhaps." Desemir pressed his toes to his boots. Pesha couldn't see his fear. He must believe what Desemir was still convincing himself of: the trip to Asgill lands in the Hinterlands, to find an answer for Farren's condition, was the right thing to do.

It was the *only* thing to do. Nothing else had worked.

"She's my sister," Pesha said. He nodded to himself and swept his gaze in the direction of the lake. "She's my sister, and if there's even a small chance..."

"Of course there is. Why wouldn't they aid one of their own? An innocent." Desemir sighed. "You'll help her, then you'll come back..." He didn't finish. *Would* Pesha come back? And *should* he? What could Desemir offer him that would be greater than what his own people could?

Pesha threw himself at Desemir and crushed him into a hug. "I love you, Des. You're my brother, and the only man who ever tried to be a father to me. You say I haven't lived, and I cannot deny that. But only death could keep me from returning home to you."

"I love you too, Pesh." Desemir squeezed his mouth and eyes shut to quell the rise of emotion. He clapped his hands on Pesha's back and stepped away. "Don't make the promise on my account though. I've taken your love and devotion for granted, and there are others more worthy."

"Or just as worthy," Pesha said with a light smile. "Do you really think Siofra can control her power now? She won't have me or Fen..." Tension crept back into his expression.

"She knows what to do if it happens again. Twice now she's redirected her magic to avoid disaster. We have to trust her at some point, don't we?"

Pesha's brows lifted and fell. "Still. Another reason for me to return, I guess. I did promise to train her, and I failed astoundingly."

"Her red wall was uncontained because she never learned to understand it in the cages men built for her," Desemir said. He glanced toward the steps and the Hall, where his wife and Fen would be saying their own good-byes. Overhead, their falcons swooped in strange loops, doing the same. It would be the first time both the twins and their familiars were separated. "She knows she's safe here. She knows she can leave at any time."

"She won't." Pesha offered him a reassuring nod. "I was wrong about the two of you." He started to smile. "Perhaps the *only* time I was wrong in my entire tenure at Shadowfen Hall, but—"

Desemir reached forward and cupped his brother's face with a playful tug. "Do you suppose Fen will tolerate this brash arrogance for long?"

"I've learned from the very best."

Desemir grinned. "I've kept you for too long. Should I let Fen know it's time?"

Pesha approached the carriage and peered through the window, where Farren was stretched across one of the benches, resting. "If you don't mind. I prefer to use my magic to keep her calm and not Lotte's draughts as much as I can."

Desemir nodded and started toward the steps. "Be safe, Pesh. If you smell even a whiff of trouble..."

"I know. And Des... You did the right thing with the stolen Darkwood parcels. Selling them back would have just put them into the hands of lesser men. But donating the profits to the citizens of Darkwood Run is a move that would have Ludwik spinning in his grave."

"Yeah? I'm counting on it." Desemir reached for his finger to spin the phantom ring. "Find me again at the first snow."

He felt Pesha's broad smile. "And the last."

"You're *sure* it's all right? It could be months. Pesha says time passes differently in our homeland, so maybe years? I don't know. I don't know, Si. Maybe this is a terrible idea. Ugh."

Fen hadn't stopped his neurotic fussing. He plucked stray hairs off her gown and pushed more from her face. He'd brushed his fingertips atop her shoulders no less than a dozen times, as if it accomplished anything at all besides giving his hands something to do.

"Staying would be a terrible idea," Siofra said. She tried to smile, though what she wanted to do was cry. What if it was the last time she saw her brother? What if it *was* a terrible idea, and she was urging him on toward his doom? What if the Medvedev held the children of the accused to the same account as the accused themselves?

This is killing me, Desemir had said the night before, whispering the words against her hair. Neither of them had slept at all. *But it's the right thing. It's the only thing, isn't it? Farren deserves a second chance, and Pesha is the only one capable of taking her to the place where she might get it.*

And Fen, she'd said, curling against his hard chest, *belongs at his side now. Not mine.*

I belong at your side.

As I belong at yours.

We must be strong for them tomorrow, Siofra. It's what they'll need from us. When they're gone, we can adequately distract ourselves anyway, can't we? Bury our sorrows in our unslakable lust?

I suppose that is something to look forward to.

Siofra completed her smile, for Fen. "No, you must go. Farren needs Pesha, and Pesha needs you."

Fen snorted, contorting his face. "Pesha doesn't need me. It just seemed wrong to let him go alone."

"Sure." Siofra suppressed a laugh. "Nonetheless."

"Nonetheless," Fen said with a long sigh.

"If you..." Siofra steeled herself to say the words. "If you get there and decide that life suits you better, all I ask—"

"You think I wouldn't come back to you?" Fen asked in horror.

"All I ask," Siofra said, "is you find a way to send me a raven, so I know you're all right. So I know not to worry about you."

Fen shook his head in agitation. "You're mad if you think I would ever leave you for longer than I had to. You're a part of me, Si. The better half."

"Debatable," she replied, grinning. "Just the same, Fen. I know I'm where I'm meant to be. You have yet to determine where that place is for you."

"And the baby... What if I'm not back in time? What if something goes wrong? No one else can heal you like I can. I was too hasty, making this decision, too—"

Siofra cut him off with a hug. "Go, brother. Go with my blessing. Go with my love. And go with peace in your heart, for you have done everything you can for me, and now it's time for you to find *your* way."

An hour later, Siofra stood in the center of the west wing hall, watching the workers move from room to room in a bustle of liveliness. Every window had been opened and every floor swept, and the airing and dusting could begin.

Desemir slid his arms around her from behind. She tilted her head back and was rewarded with a kiss.

He trailed his lips backward from her mouth to her forehead and then nudged her to the side. Together, they stumbled into the nearest room. Desemir kicked the door closed and lifted her into his arms with a deeper kiss.

"Lotte wouldn't approve," she murmured. She thrust a playful hand down his pants.

Desemir cocked his head. "You're the one taking this to the next level." He leaned in to nip her mouth with his teeth. "I just wanted to kiss my wife in private."

"Oh? My mistake." Siofra untangled herself from his arms and stepped back with a grin.

"Get back here." Desemir tugged her back with a snap and hoisted her onto a nearby desk. "You wanted to open the west wing. Well, this comes with a certain responsibility, Siofra."

She twisted her hands around and up his back. "And what sort of responsibility would that be?"

"These rooms deserve a proper opening." Desemir widened his eyes knowingly. "And as the master and mistress of Shadowfen Hall, it falls to us to ensure they are *all* given equal attention."

"I require more clarity," Siofra replied with a teasing wink.

Desemir trailed his hand up the inside of her leg and slipped his fingers inside the band of her undergarment. He found what he was after and thrusted upward, driving a gasp from her. "How's this for clarity?"

Several hard thuds on the door startled them. His hand whipped away in a flash. Siofra leaped off the desk and straightened her dress.

"Judging from the indecent looks on both your faces, I'm most grateful for knocking first," Lotte said with an exasperated head shake. "I need to know whether we're keeping the curtains or replacing them. If we're replacing them, we'll need to place an order with the clothier right away." She put her hands on her hips. "Which will take *months*, so better to do it now, before autumnwhile hits and everyone starts hunkering down for the long winter seasons."

"You could've made that decision yourself," Desemir said. He tried to smile through his flustered arousal.

"And deny the two of you the joy of discussing draperies?" Lotte scoffed. "I think not."

"Anything not made of wood or stone should be replaced with something new. Fresh," Siofra said. "Don't you think, Des?"

"Mm. Yes. Whatever Siofra wants."

Lotte narrowed her eyes, passing a suspicious look from one to the other. "You'll say anything to get rid of me, won't you?"

"Yes," Desemir said at the same time Siofra said, "No."

Siofra shook her head. "My mother told me anything made of cloth or leather hold remnants of the past. I should think this is an opportunity for us to make a new future. In fact, we have a certain... responsibility, right, darling?"

Desemir's eyes fluttered wide. He recovered with a hard swallow. "Yes. Yes, we do."

Lotte grimaced and made for the door. "I don't want to know what secret *code* the two of you are speaking in, so we'll leave it at that."

When she was gone, Siofra buried her face in Desemir's shirt, and they both dissolved into laughter.

"I think she's on to us," Desemir said.

"Mm," Siofra agreed, still laughing.

"We'll have to be quiet. I realize how *hard* it is for you—"

Siofra gathered his bulge in her hand. "What were you saying? Something is *hard?*"

Desemir gulped with a low groan. "You're in for it now."

"I can be quiet," Siofra stated.

Desemir quirked his brow in skepticism.

"*Sometimes* I can be quiet. Like when I want you to make love to me." She smiled whimsically. "But then sometimes, Des, I really just want you to fuck me."

"*Fuhhhck,*" Desemir hissed.

"Probably not just now," Siofra said, "with Lotte listening and all."

He sucked in through his teeth. "You don't play fair at all."

"You would never *want* me to play fair."

Desemir exhaled into a soft grin. "I love you exactly as you are. Never doubt it. Never change a thing." He reached for her hair and wound a section around his hand. "I think it's time you let your hair be natural, Si."

"What? Really?"

He nodded. "You can always cover it if you want to, but with me, you don't have to hide who you are." He made a sweeping gesture with his free hand. "With anyone here."

Siofra's desire melted into something warmer, something she loved even more than their frenzied passion for one another. She reached up and gripped his collar with both hands. "We're going to do good things here, Des. The west wing is only the beginning."

He lowered his eyes to the side. "I know."

"Do you?" She tilted her face under his to look at him. "It was *your* idea to help the people of Darkwood Run. You could have so easily kept that land or even sold it back to those terrible men."

"It was once rightfully theirs."

"No, it was *legally* theirs. It's not the same. Your father's methods may have been uncouth, but it doesn't excuse how the other barons starved their people to pad their profits."

Desemir shook his head with a humorless laugh. "My father would have been all too happy to starve his people if the Barony of Shadowfen had a village like the others."

"I thought we agreed you're not him."

"You're right." Desemir wrapped her in his arms and kissed the top of her head. "Forgive me."

"There's nothing to forgive." Siofra pulled back enough to crane her neck upward, meeting his eyes. "Because I love *you* exactly as you are. Never doubt it. Never change a thing."

"Except the curtains," Desemir replied.

Siofra lifted onto her toes to kiss him, happy and safe in the knowledge there would be many more kisses to come. "Except the curtains."

The Book of All Things continues with a new story in
The Claw and the Crowned.

For more information, and exciting bonus material,
visit www.sarahmcradit.com

ABOUT SARAH

Sarah is the *USA Today* and International Bestselling Author of over forty contemporary and epic fantasy stories, and the creator of the Kingdom of the White Sea and Saga of Crimson & Clover universes.

Born a geek, Sarah spends her time crafting rich and multilayered worlds, obsessing over history, playing her retribution paladin (and sometimes destruction warlock), and settling provocative Tolkien debates, such as why the Great Eagles are not Gandalf's personal taxi service. Passionate about travel, she's been to over twenty countries collecting sparks of inspiration, and is always planning her next adventure.

Sarah and her husband live in a beautiful corner of SE Pennsylvania with their three tiny benevolent pug dictators.

www.sarahmcradit.com

SARAH M CRADIT

WEAVER *of* WORLDS